TOEFL
iBT SPEAKING

不是權威不出書！練托福，
當然就讓最專業的托福總監帶你練！

捷徑文化
Royal Road Publishing Group

托福總監說在前頭

▶托福總監告訴你！
百分百真正的托福考點攻略在這裡！

在閱讀本書時，你可能會發現許多特別的語言學習方式，這些都是托福總監秦蘇珊老師精心研發的「有機英語學習法」！透過此學習法讓大家能在時間內有效學習托福必考的考點全攻略。

考點攻略 1. 透過「詞彙語塊」的形式記憶，自然形成大腦資料庫。

什麼是「語塊」？語塊是指經常在一起使用的一組詞，類似片語或搭配詞。語塊既有可能是習慣搭配，如：sedimentary rock（沉積岩），也有可能是片語動詞，如follow up on an issue（追蹤一個問題）。

語言學家和神經學家發現，比起孤立地記單字，人們對語塊的記憶會更加準確牢固。且當學習者從其大腦的「資料庫」裡「調出」語塊時，因為不是用母語詞對詞地做翻譯，所以語言使用者的犯錯機率減少，反應速度也同時提高了。因此，本書在屬於學術類的第四部分中，將題目材料中的學術類實用語塊摘錄出來，並提供說明。

> **例** 在答中世紀文學相關的題目時，本書會教你 heroic deeds（英雄事蹟）、Knights of the Round Table（圓桌武士）、embark on an adventure（開始冒險）等語塊。

考點攻略 2. 不只要會做題目，更要練習說話時的文法。

很多華人考生寫文法選擇題時沒有什麼困難，但在說話或寫作中情況就大不相同了。 ETS 的評分準則指出：「對文法的有效運用」是得到滿分的要求之一。由於在各種各樣的情境中練習口語常用文法對於獲得高分極其重要，所以本書在很多章節會專門針對不同題目講解增強文法的策略。書中也設計了「托福總監帶你練」小專欄，提供了很多例句，便於考生掌握這些文法知識。

> **例** 要在第四題和第六題中表現卓越，你應該熟練掌握一些「使役動詞」。回答新托福考試口語題目時最常用的使役動詞有：cause, make, allow, enable, have, help, require, motivate, get, convince, assist, encourage, permit 等等

考點攻略 **3.** 不只說出好內容，也要能有好發音。

英文口語說得好不好，與發音的很多方面有關，包括單個音節的發音、重音位置、語調、停頓等等，説英語時的韻律和節奏也能幫助他人明白話語所傳達的意思。因此，本書提供的學習材料首要目標就是讓考生的表達清晰易懂。為了達到這一點，書中所有例題和練習題，搭配的回答範例中都用粗體標出了應重讀的音節。

> **例** 複合名詞的重音通常在第一部分的母音上（background, laptop, handbook）

考點攻略 **4.** 無論聽說讀寫，都要會換句話說。

換句話説的能力是通往考高分最重要的技能！原因有：

❶ **因為 100% 會考！**沒錯，新托福考試的閱讀部分會直接考你會不會換句話説，而聽力、口語和寫作部分也會間接考查這一能力。閱讀和聽力題中很多選擇題的選項都是對原文語句的改述；而在閱讀部分，有一類難度較高的題型：句子簡化題，其實就是在考你怎麼換句話説。

❷ **因為在訓練換句話說的能力時，考生將被迫用英語思考**，這會使考生在考試中更加有自信，並提高做題速度。

❸ 考托福的你，想必是想出國唸書的，要是什麼句子都只會一種説法，在國外會很辛苦，所以除了為了考試做練習，更要**為了你的未來生活做練習**，換句話説的能力是不可或缺的！

把學術性語言換句話説，對於詞彙量不足或對相關主題缺少暸解的考生會非常難，因此本書從第 1 章開始，就會引導考生熟悉各種類型的情境，幫助考生擴大詞彙量，提高閱讀速度、聽力能力和用英語思考的能力。

考點攻略 5. 訓練用關鍵字記筆記。

　　有些考試是不允許記筆記的，因此在準備時，大家常會忽略這一項。但**托福可以記筆記，所以考生應儘早開始訓練，嘗試用各種不同方式記筆記。**本書會提供大量有針對性的記筆記策略，例如：

> **例** （p.213）要記好第四題的筆記，只需簡單的三步：
>
> 1. 記下關鍵術語，通常都是標題，並記下足夠的單字以幫助自己定義這個術語。
> 2. 用縮寫從小文章和小講座中摘取一些描述性片語。在闡述教授的例子時會用到這些片語。
> 3. 使用圓圈、箭頭、底線、數位等畫出筆記結構並做些註解，這些能幫助你答題。

考點攻略 6. 培養預測下文的能力。

　　預測下文的能力對於任何希望取得新托福考試高分的考生都非常重要。在聽學術類講座時，**如果能預知下文將要呈現的資訊，那作答速度就會快上許多。而且還能更快地抓住要點、更準確地記下關鍵資訊。**在聽講座或對話時，考生如果能預測到教授接下來很可能會講什麼，那麼即使沒聽出一兩個單字，也不必過於擔心。

> **例** 通過不表達觀點的學生所說的隻字片語，可以預測另一個學生將要說什麼。例如，不表達觀點的男生會說：What do you mean? 從這句話可知，表達觀點的女生將會在輪到她說話時將自己之前說的話換句話說。再舉個例子，不表達觀點的學生也許會說：Do you really think so? 同樣，從這句話可預測表達觀點的學生接下來會說：Yes, I do, because...

考點攻略 7. 掌握篇章中的大特點（如：開頭語、主題擴展、例證、結論等）。

　　篇章中的「大」特點有很多，例如文章的組織結構，或例如作者開始談論某個歷史事件的方式。另外，理解教授在講座中提供範例的能力也是一種重要的技巧。**當考生抓住了篇章的整體，就能進行更細的資訊處理。這樣即使不認識文章裡的某些單字，也能基本理解文章的主要意思**！這種技巧對於獲得口語高分極為關鍵！所以，本書很多章節都提供了掌握篇章大特點的策略。

解釋原因的最佳方式是什麼？有兩個要素是必不可少的：

1. 舉出一些具體細節或事實，用於闡釋主題並使其融入上下文。

2. 使用表明即將說出原因、以及用於串聯觀點的詞語。

一些適用於在日常話題中表述原因的句型：

表述原因的句型	
The reason I...	Due to my interest in...
This is because...	...for the reason that...
Because I...	My motivation for...

考點攻略8. ── 掌握篇章中的小特點（如：詞性、單字、修辭等）。

　　這種技能一般是指對一篇閱讀文章或聽力文本的語言特徵的掌握能力。**這些特徵既包括單字的發音方式，也包括在學術類閱讀文章、講座和對話中使用的字彙、片語。** 考生一定都希望記住經常出現在新托福考試中的單字和片語，因此本書列出了大量這類單字和片語。

 第三題要求考生告訴評分人聽力對話中表達觀點的學生是否支持學校的某項計畫或政策，因此，考生應該要會用多種表示支援或反對的動詞片語。

可以使用以下幾種基本的結構：

1. 主詞 + 簡單動詞 + 受詞，例如：He supports the plan.

2. 主詞 + 片語動詞 + 受詞，例如：He agrees with the plan.

3. 主詞 + be 動詞 + 受詞，例如：He is for the plan.

4. 主詞 + 表達觀點的動詞 + that 補語（子句），例如：He thinks (that) the plan is reasonable

考點攻略 9. ▸ 瞭解如何銜接與連貫。

　　銜接（Cohesion）是語言的一個特性，指的是單字和片語從文法上被連接起來的方式。很多考生知道怎樣學習詞彙和文法，但不知道如何提高自己串聯詞句的能力。實際上，**有很多方法能夠加強口語語言的前後銜接，如利用介系詞、連接詞、冠詞和指示詞。**本書有四章內容都提到加強銜接性的策略。

　　而連貫性（Coherence）指的就是怎樣串聯觀點。很多考生知道如何有邏輯地聯繫各段觀點，使作文更加連貫，卻不知道怎樣達到口語回答的連貫性。而連貫性反映了清晰闡述觀點的能力，是口語評分準則中的重要一項！考生可通過多種方法來加強口語回答的連貫性，包括重複關鍵字、運用某些敘述技巧以及理清邏輯關係等。

考點攻略 10. ▸ 搭配題材記憶、聚焦學習記得牢。

　　本書的分類方式以「題材」為依據，而非將同個題型中各種可能碰到的情境與話題都混合在一起考。將一個一個題材區分開來，這種學習是最為科學的。**研究人類記憶的專家發現，人們在記憶事實或學習技能時，若能將其呈現在一個具體的「情境」或「題材」中，人們就會記得更深、學得更好。**因此這本書為考生們在記單字和掌握詞彙、片語的過程中，搭配題材學習能使考生記得更牢、更好。

▶托福總監告訴你！這本書的結構與重點

★本書內容

・新托福題目類型及常考重點的分析
・各題型的解題策略
・重要的口語技能訓練
・實用的答題模板範本與詞語表
・大量模擬試題
・大量高品質的回答範例（以粗體標出重音音節！）

★本書結構

　　本書是根據「題目的情境與題材」劃分章節。這是因為這種章節劃分的方式可使考生更快地學習（並記憶）與某一常考主題相關的基礎知識，也便於考生更扎實地掌握這些情境中最常用的答題範本和詞彙、片語。在情境中學習，絕對比脫離情境學習更為有效！

本書第一部分	本書第二部分		本書第三部分		本書第四部分	
整體介紹	托福口試第一題	托福口試第二題	托福口試第三題	托福口試第五題	托福口試第四題	托福口試第六題

　　本書的**第一部分**對新托福考試做了整體介紹，並詳細闡述了口語部分的考試結構、每道口語題目要考的重點。

　　第二部分全面介紹新托福口語考試的第一題和第二題。各個章節分別介紹最典型的情境和要考的內容。每個章節的情境都經過精心挑選，反映出真實考試中出現頻率最高的話題和詞彙。每章都會側重培養不同的語言能力，例如：對過去事件的描述、對現狀的描述等等。每章提供四道模擬試題，每題均有回答範例。每章還有「托福總監幫你預測可能會出現的題目」小單元，幫你瞭解與本章主題相關的常見考題，並鞏固本章所學的技能和詞彙。

　　對學生和教師都大有裨益的是，本書安排的情境和考試內容的難度是遞增的。這種安排不僅讓準備考試過程的壓力減輕了，對技巧、能力的強化更加有效，也能夠大幅提升複習效率。

　　第三部分主要介紹新托福口語考試第三題和第五題。為什麼跳過第四題呢？這是因為第四題和第六題一樣，是屬於「學術類」的題目，而第三題和第五題則是「校園會話」類。為了學習上有統一性，所以本書特別做了「將第三題與第五題擺在一起學、將第四題和第六題擺在一起學」的設計。

　　每一章都有三道模擬題，並配有完整的回答範例，範例的錄音原文可在本書特別收錄 2 查到。另有大量基礎技能訓練，如一些情境化的發音練習，可以幫助考生提高第三題和第五題的分數。每章重點討論的情境和重點訓練的技能都經過精心挑選，可以更有針對性、也更全面地練習，效率也相對更高。

　　第四部分講解的是學術類題目，即新托福口語考試的第四題和第六題。第四題要求整合文章和講座資訊，第六題要求概述講座內容。對每道題目，本書都分為四個學術領域（物理科學、人文藝術、生命科學和社會科學）進行講解。也就是説，考生可以反覆練習與四個學術領域相關的學術類題目。本部分每個章節也有三道模擬題，配有回答範例，聽力錄音原文可在附錄 2 查到。每章依然精心設計了基礎技能訓練，旨在幫助考生在第四題和第六題上提高分數。

下面的表格就為身為考生的你列出托福考官最愛出的題型、情境，並指出各種題型與情境中需要用的技巧、策略、及所需的基礎能力。想知道自己有哪些能力需要加強？想要挑戰看看以哪些情境為主題的題目？快速地看過這個命題筆記一覽表，就能完整瞭解這本書的使用方式囉！

章節	題型 & 題材情境	策略	得分考技
1	Task 1 Personal preference 第一題：個人喜好 Familiar topics：A favorite person 日常話題：最喜歡的人	如何組織第一題的答題思路	重讀關鍵詞，讓聽者更易理解
2	Task 1 Personal preference 第一題：個人喜好 Familiar topics：A memorable past experience 日常話題：難忘的經歷	解釋原因的最佳方式	談論過去經歷需要掌握的動詞時態
3	Task 1 Personal preference 第一題：個人喜好 Familiar topics：A favorite activity in the present 日常話題：最喜愛的活動	第一題記筆記的訣竅	如何用動名詞使你的表現更出色
4	Task 1 Personal preference 第一題：個人喜好 Familiar topics：Something you want in the future 日常話題：將來要做的某件事	如何用人稱代名詞巧妙銜接上下文	怎麼連音使回答更自然
5	Task 1 Personal preference 第一題：個人喜好 Familiar topics：Something special in your culture 日常話題：本國文化的特色	不留痕跡套用答題範本	我發的詞尾 s 音，你絕對不會誤解
6	Task 1 Personal preference 第一題：個人喜好 Familiar topics：A thing that has profoundly affected you 日常話題：對你影響深遠的某物	描述「物」的三招	形式主詞大妙用

章節	題型 & 題材情境	策略	得分考技
7	Task 2 Paired choice 第二題：二選一 Familiar topics：Communication and the media 日常話題：交流與媒體	第二題的答題思路	得心應手用縮寫
8	Task 2 Paired choice 第二題：二選一 Familiar topics：Food, travel and the arts 日常話題：餐飲、旅行和藝術	第二題記筆記的訣竅	「比較句先行」的文法
9	Task 2 Paired choice 第二題：二選一 Familiar topics：Work and money 日常話題：職業與金錢	巧妙借用題幹	真情流露靠語調
10	Task 2 Paired choice 第二題：二選一 Familiar topics：Education—Primary and secondary 日常話題：教育——初等和中等教育	表明立場	掌握好句型，暢談事物的必要性
11	Task 2 Paired choice 第二題：二選一 Familiar topics：Education—University 日常話題：教育——大學教育	連接詞的強大功能	發好位於單字中間的 /l/ 音
12	Task 2 Paired choice 第二題：二選一 Familiar topics：Life choices and life lessons 日常話題：生活中的抉擇和經驗教訓	重複關鍵字	用 would 表達喜好與意願
13	Task 3 Summarizing an opinion 第三題：概述觀點 Campus life：University investments and expenditures 校園生活：大學的投資與支出	第三題的答題思路	用飽滿的雙母音和長母音打動考官的耳朵

章節	題型 & 題材情境	策略	得分考技
14	Task 3 Summarizing an opinion 第三題：概述觀點 Campus life：University services—Health center, cafeteria and library 校園生活：大學服務——健康中心、餐廳和圖書館	第三題記筆記的訣竅	間接引語用處多
15	Task 3 Summarizing an opinion 第三題：概述觀點 Campus life：University services—Housing, transportation and facilities management 校園生活：大學服務——住宿、交通和設施管理	預測話題——眼觀四面，耳聽八方	發音該停頓還是滔滔不絕？
16	Task 3 Summarizing an opinion 第三題：概述觀點 Campus life：University course offerings 校園生活：大學課程設置	能輕鬆地自我糾正，就是老道的口語王	美國人用哪些動詞片語來表示支持與反對
17	Task 3 Summarizing an opinion 第三題：概述觀點 Campus life：Student affairs 校園生活：學生活動	找到能流利表達自己想法的方法	複合詞的重音就是華人考生最怕的地方！
18	Task 3 Summarizing an opinion 第三題：概述觀點 Campus life：Student employment and internships 校園生活：打工與實習	小冠詞，大作用	標準英語口語中常用片語動詞的用法
19	Task 5 Communicating a solution 第五題：討論解決方法 Campus life：School deadlines 校園生活：學校活動的期限	第五題的答題思路	發好位於音節末尾的 /l/ 音
20	Task 5 Communicating a solution 第五題：討論解決方法 Campus life：Scheduling conflicts 校園生活：時間衝突	第五題記筆記的訣竅	用 could 和 should 表達可能性與建議

章節	題型 & 題材情境	策略	得分考技
21	Task 5 Communicating a solution 第五題：討論解決方法 Campus life：Problems with transportation and buildings 校園生活：交通及房屋問題	表明個人立場的三個步驟	不容小覷的常見發音錯誤（can、can't、have、have to）
22	Task 5 Communicating a solution 第五題：討論解決方法 Campus life：Mistakes and accidents 校園生活：犯錯與意外	怎麼發揮四個指示詞的作用	口語中的萬能句型，what 名詞子句作主詞
23	Task 5 Communicating a solution 第五題：討論解決方法 Campus life：Financial and other resource shortages 校園生活：資金與其他資源的短缺	掌握描述假設情形的句型	/ɛ/ 和 /æ/ 發錯音，意思差很大！
24	Task 5 Communicating a solution 第五題：討論解決方法 Campus life：People problems 校園生活：人際關係問題	像講故事一樣回答第五題	介系詞片語置於句首——闡釋細節的第一法寶
25	Task 4 Synthesizing a text and a lecture 第四題：整合文章及講座資訊 Academic subjects：Physical sciences 學術問題：物理科學	第四題的答題思路	簡單但容易發錯的 ed 結尾音
26	Task 4 Synthesizing a text and a lecture 第四題：整合文章及講座資訊 Academic subjects：Humanities and the arts 學術問題：人文藝術	第四題記筆記的訣竅	動詞片語——闡釋細節的第二法寶
27	Task 4 Synthesizing a text and a lecture 第四題：整合文章及講座資訊 Academic subjects：Life sciences 學術問題：生命科學	怎麼猜測讓人抓狂的專業術語	準確讀出專業術語

章節	題型 & 題材情境	策略	得分考技
28	Task 4 Synthesizing a text and a lecture 第四題：整合文章及講座資訊 Academic subjects：Social sciences 學術問題：社會科學	超恐怖的專業術語怎麼定義	美國人最常用於舉例的動詞片語
29	Task 6 Summarizing a lecture 第六題：概括講座內容 Academic subjects：Physical sciences 學術問題：物理科學	第六題的答題思路	説得快 ≠ 清晰流利，小虛詞幫你解決大問題
30	Task 6 Summarizing a lecture 第六題：概括講座內容 Academic subjects：Humanities and the arts 學術問題：人文藝術	第六題記筆記的訣竅	引出要點：最不易失手的動詞片語和句型
31	Task 6 Summarizing a lecture 第六題：概括講座內容 Academic subjects：Life sciences 學術問題：生命科學	語言要正式還是隨意？	美國人怎麼用重音突出對立概念，強調重點
32	Task 6 Summarizing a lecture 第六題：概括講座內容 Academic subjects：Social sciences 學術問題：社會科學	輕鬆給出邏輯清晰的回答	回答學術類題目的用詞武器

▶托福總監告訴你！這本書適合誰用？該怎麼用？

★本書適用對象

本書專為準備參加新托福考試並希望提高口語技能的考生編寫。本書利用「有機英語學習法」，幫助考生進行有重點的系統學習，從而在短時間內全面提高英語口語技能。自學考生以及新托福考試的輔導教師均可從本書中獲益。

★自學的我，該怎麼運用這本書？

使用本書重點 1. ─ 針對弱點加強

先制定一個學習計畫，列出時間和學習安排。如果自學者認為自己的文法相對薄弱，就應該在文法和句型方面適當增加學習時間。如果學術類詞彙方面比較薄弱，就應增加記憶專業術語的時間。如果最大的問題在聽力理解方面，就應多做聽力練習。建議：所有的考生都應該花些時間在發音上，尤其是與說話節奏和重音位置相關的練習，因為回答是否清晰易懂，和這兩方面關係最大。本書中的回答範例和「托福總監帶你練」欄目中的句子練習都非常實用，應該盡可能多加練習。

使用本書重點 2. ─ 記錄語塊與換句話說的方式

無論是在課堂上學習還是自學，學習者每天都應該記錄下本書中的語塊以及換句話說的方式。這很重要，因為新托福考試經常會考到常用單字和片語的換句話說。例如，自學者可以把 theoretical perspective 當作一個語塊來記，並且記得這個語塊換句話說就是 theoretical point of view。或者也可以把 give a recap of something 與意近的 run through something again 一起記。自學者一定要把重要的語塊都背下來，因為它們經常會出現在新托福考試中！

使用本書重點 3. ─ 練習思考更有個性與創意的答案

此外，也可以多練習思考個性化、有創意的答案，反映出個人的經歷和立場，在答題時就能獲得評分者的青睞。但有一點需要提醒：如果評分人認為你給出的回答有創意到離題的地步、或和內容講的背道而馳，他們就可能會給 0 分。本書第 5 章提供了將回答變得更有個性與創意的具體策略。

最後，也建議考生可以找朋友一起複習。書後可以找到所有練習的回答範例，透過兩人以上的對話，不但可以更好地練習口說能力，也能互相激勵。

★我是老師，該怎麼運用這本書？

建議使用本書的教師可以在課堂上使用「有機英語學習方法」。例如，教師可以幫助學生理解什麼是題材、語塊。要想瞭解可以利用的資源和更多關於「有機英語學習方法」的建議，可以登錄 http://blog.sina.com.cn/susanchyn，留言給我。你的任何問題我都會悉心回答喔！

Preface 作者序

從很久以前開始，我的朋友和學生們就都常跑來求我寫一套新托福考試的備考輔導書。這都是因為我曾在美國教育考試服務中心（ETS）工作過很多年，在那裡取得了終身職位，所以對托福的考試方式、出題方式都非常熟悉。我曾在 ETS 的多個崗位任職過，從最初的單個項目作者，一直到負責多種英語考試研發工作的主管，其中也包括了托福和多益考試的研發工作。因此，我對研發考試方式和英語考試標準化的專業方法都十分熟悉。

在 ETS 時，我很幸運有機會向專家們學習，而且隨著職位的上升，還有幸參與制定並調整新的考試評估體系。大家現在所看到的托福 iBT，就是我與團隊成員努力的成果！

在本系列書中，我依自己從 ETS 獲得的多年經驗，制定出一套全新的準備考試大綱，以期幫助考生順利通過新托福考試，並為他們以後的語言學習奠定基礎。本系列圖書是專門為以中文為母語的你們量身編寫的。與很多其他西方教育者不同，我因為個人生活和工作的緣故，對華人文化和你們的學習方式都比較瞭解，非常清楚你們在學習英語過程中的優勢和劣勢。所以在本系列圖書的編寫過程中，我結合你們的優勢，幫助你們在最短的時間內取得最顯著的進步；同時也指出你們常見的不足之處，以便於你們有重點地去彌補和提高學習效率。我把這種學習方法稱為「有機英語學習方法」，也就是把大家熟悉的學習方式（如背誦和模擬考）與科學的學習策略（如語言學）結合在一起，可以說是中西合璧的一種學習方法吧！

對於考生來說，時間很緊迫，而且壓力很大，高分似乎永遠遙不可及。不過現在你們可以放下心來，因為在本系列圖書中，我所選取的學習材料和提供的學習策略都能確保你快速提升學習能力，並在新托福考試中考取高分。如果認真讀完了本系列圖書，我保證你們的時間不會白費。當你們坐在考場中時，就會知道自己已經做了最充足的準備！

祝大家好運！

托福考試命題總監

Susan Chyn 秦蘇珊

Contents 目錄

第1部分

An Overview of the TOEFL ® iBT
命題總監告訴你：托福到底在考些什麼？

第2部分

Familiar Topics: Tasks 1 and 2
第一題&第二題：
命題總監教你，日常話題沒問題！

Task 1: Personal Preference 第一題：個人喜好

Task 2: Paired Choice 第二題：二選一

第3部分

Campus Life: Tasks 3 and 5
第三題&第五題：
命題總監教你，校園生活一把罩！

Task 3: Summarizing an Opinion 第三題：概述觀點

Task 5: Communicating a Solution 第五題：討論解決方法

第4部分) Academic Subjects: Tasks 4 and 6
第四題&第六題：
命題總監教你，學術問題小意思！

特別收錄

Section ❶

An Overview of the TOEFL ® iBT

第❶部分

命題總監告訴你：
托福到底在考些什麼？

What the TOEFL ® iBT Measures
新托福考試考什麼？

　　進考場前，多少要知道一下新托福考試的實際情況。新托福考試的時間長度大約為四小時，分為四個部分。閱讀與聽力部分在前面，之後有一次短暫的休息，才進入之後的口語與寫作部分。

新托福考試測驗題目與時間表
（上色的字為不計分的實驗性題目）

	題目類別	題數	時間長度
閱讀	3 篇閱讀文章 +2 篇實驗性閱讀文章	每篇 12 ～ 14 道題目	60 分 + 40 分鐘
聽力	2 段對話、4 段講座 或 +1 段考前講座和 1 段考前對話	對話：每篇 5 道題目 講座：每篇 6 道題目	60 分鐘 + 30 分鐘
中間休息			10 分鐘
口語	2 小段閱讀文章、 2 小段對話、 2 小段講座	6 道題目	20 分鐘
寫作	1 小段閱讀文章、 1 小段講座	2 道題目	50 分鐘

★口語和寫作部分沒有不計分的實驗性試題。

★新托福考試的四類考題都允許考生記筆記。考試結束後，所有筆記會被統一收集起來並銷毀。

A Comprehensive Look at the Speaking Section
新托福考試怎麼命題：口語命題全解

　　口語是新托福考試中公認的最具挑戰性的考試之一。一方面，六道口語題目中有四道包含聽力材料；另一方面，口語部分的題目會涉及豐富的學科和情境。因此，為了應對這樣的考試，考生不僅必須具備一定的語言技能，以抓住學術話題中的關鍵資訊，還必須能概括和綜合所獲得的資訊，快速將這些資訊轉化為自己的回答。

▶口語考試怎麼進行？

　　考生考完閱讀和聽力，休息 10 分鐘之後便是口語考試。此時感到有些疲憊是正常現象。好在口語部分非常短暫，只有 20 分鐘，而且這一部分沒有實驗性的題目。

　　考生須面對電腦進行口語答題，之後由評分人進行人工評分。進入考場，考生須戴上耳機確認電腦是否運作正常。電腦將指示考生測試麥克風，為了以防萬一，考場上也會有監考員幫助考生解決問題。然後，電腦裡會有聲音開始解釋口語題目的考試流程和要求，這表示考試正式開始。這些說明不會顯示在電腦螢幕上，但是題目會出現在螢幕上，電腦會同時念出每道題的內容。例如，做第一題時，考生可能會在螢幕上看到並聽到這樣一道題目：

Describe a park that you have visited and explain why that park is memorable to you. Include details and examples in your explanation.

　　和閱讀、聽力以及寫作部分一樣，在整個口語考試中，考生能在電腦螢幕的一角看到時鐘。但是，口語考試中的這個時鐘尤為重要，因為考生的準備時間非常有限（根據題目的不同，可能是 15 秒、20 秒或 30 秒），答題時間也很有限（根據題目的不同，可能是 45 秒或 60 秒）。時間到後，電腦螢幕上會出現一條訊息，表示考生的答題時間已經結束。

　　有兩道「綜合型」口語題目，即第三題和第四題，含有短篇文章，這些短篇文章也會出現在電腦螢幕上。

　　在整個口語考試中，考生可以記筆記，並利用這些筆記作答。考試結束後，這些筆記會被監考員收走並銷毀。考生的回答會被錄音，並以電子資料的形式發送到 ETS 的評分網路系統。

下面是新托福考試口語部分的結構簡介：

新托福考試閱讀部分：模擬案例

題目	題型	情境	搭配材料	每題作答時間
第一題	個人喜好	日常話題	無	45 秒
第二題	二選一	日常話題	無	45 秒
第三題	概述觀點	校園生活	閱讀：短篇文章 聽力：短篇對話	60 秒
第四題	整合文章及講座資訊	學術問題（四大學術領域中的一種）	閱讀：短篇文章 聽力：短篇講座	60 秒
第五題	討論解決方法	校園生活	聽力：短篇對話	60 秒
第六題	概括講座內容	學術問題（四大學術領域中的另一種）	聽力：短篇講座	60 秒

▶命題人到底想看到什麼？

　　新托福考試口語部分的六道題目可分為兩大基本類型：（1）「獨立型」題目；（2）「綜合型」題目。「獨立型」題目要求考生簡要地回答問題，「綜合型」題目則複雜一些，要求考生聽一段短篇講座（或短篇對話）後作答，或者先讀一段短篇文章，再聽一段短篇講座（或短篇對話），然後作答。總體來說，口語部分不僅僅考查口語能力，還考查考生的閱讀和聽力能力、對學術詞彙的掌握、分析能力和組織觀點的能力。評分準則會綜合考慮所有這些能力，因此新托福考試的評分人會整體關注三大類能力：表達（包括發音和流利程度）、語言運用（包括詞彙和語法）和主題展開（包括內容的組織和「綜合型」題目中回答的完整程度）。「獨立型」題目和「綜合型」題目各有一套評分準則。針對每道口語題目，每位評分人能給出的最高分為 4 分，最低分通常為 1 分。當考生沒有回答問題、完全離題或背誦範本而未使用自己的語言時，評分人會給出 0 分。

▶六道題目命題特徵的比較

　　六道口語題重點考查的技能各不相同，但有一些題目具有某些相同特徵。例如：第一題和第二題都要求考生談論「日常話題」。這兩道題相對比較容易回答，這樣就能幫助考生進行熱身。正如前文所述，ETS 將日常話題類題目稱為「獨立型」口語題，因為考生不需要讀文章或聽錄音材料就可以回答問題。其餘的四道題是「綜合型」題目，意味著需要先聽再作答，或者先讀再聽，最後再作答。第三題和第五題的情境是校園生活，第四題和第六題的情境是學術問題。

　　由於這六道題之間有諸多相似之處，要拿到高分，就必須清楚地理解這六道題各自的考查目的、特點和評分標準。

個人喜好：第一題命題揭秘

　　口語第一題經常要求考生回憶一個特殊的人或者一次獨特的經歷，考生必須簡要解釋為什麼這個人或這次經歷如此重要。

66 命題範圍 99

　　第一題是「日常話題」類題目，考官可能會問考生對教育、工作、家庭、愛好、旅行和假期等方面的看法。這道題目沒有標準答案，因為命題人希望考生基於個人學識或經歷作答。但是，不管考生的個人喜好是什麼，都要在規定的答題時間內，對其進行詳細的描述或者解釋。

　　考生有 15 秒的準備時間，之後有 45 秒時間對著麥克風回答問題。要想在第一題上拿到高分，考生的回答必須能讓評分人理解，表達流利（偶爾有不恰當的停頓也沒關係）且邏輯連貫。一些微小的錯誤不會影響得分。

二選一：第二題命題揭秘

　　口語第二題會給出兩類人對某一問題的不同觀點，讓考生選擇其一，並說出自己支持該觀點的理由。本質上說，第二題和第一題非常相似，唯一的不同之處在於第二題要求考生從出題人預先列好的「單子」中選擇一個傾向，而第一題則是考生自己來陳述一種喜好。和第一題一樣，第二題的話題也屬於日常話題，可能會涉及考生個人生活的某個方面，也可能涉及社會的某些大的方面，因此，可以基於自己的經驗回答問題。

66 命題範圍 99

　　第二題可能會出現的題目有：你比較傾向於騎車還是開車，生活在農村還是大城市，和高中的老同學住在大學宿舍還是和一個不認識的人同住等等。更常見的問題還包括：手機對人們生活的影響是正面的還是負面的，允許寵物進入公園是好是壞，等等。毋庸置疑的是，在這道題中，總會出現一個選擇，考生必須清楚地陳述自己的觀點並支持這一選擇。

　　和第一題一樣，第二題有 15 秒的準備時間，考生可以利用這個時間整理答題思路並做些筆記。然後，有 45 秒的作答時間。要想在第二題上拿到高分，考生的回答必須能讓評分人理解，表達流利（偶爾有不恰當的停頓沒關係）且邏輯連貫，一些微小的錯誤不會影響得分。

概述觀點：第三題命題揭秘

　　口語第三題是「綜合型」題目。這道題要求考生先閱讀一篇文章，然後聽一段關於校園生活的內容。這裡的閱讀材料一般是一篇關於大學政策的小短文，長度在 75~100 個詞之間。根據閱讀材料的長短，會給你 40 秒或 45 秒的閱讀時間。大學政策的內容可能涉及學生如何獲得經濟補助、誰能被大學錄取等。

聽力內容是一段小對話，時長 60~80 秒，長度為 150~180 個詞，通常是兩個學生的對話，他們會討論閱讀材料中提及的政策。其中一位學生的觀點會非常鮮明，而他（她）就是考生需要重點關注的人。在四道「綜合型」題目中，考生應就聽到的內容仔細記筆記。而對於第三題，最重要的是記下觀點相對強烈的那個人的想法。對話結束後，題目會要求考生用自己的話簡要闡述男生或女生（實際上就是觀點比較鮮明的那個人）的觀點，並解釋為什麼他（她）會持有這樣的觀點。因此，第三題被稱為「提煉並解釋」式的題目。

考生有 30 秒的時間來查看筆記並做準備，作答時間為 60 秒。要想在第三題拿到高分，考生的回答必須「完整」。也就是說，概括講話者的觀點時，不能漏掉任何一個要點。同時，考生的回答還必須能讓評分人理解，表達流利（偶爾有或沒有不恰當的停頓）且邏輯連貫。一些微小的錯誤不會影響得分。

整合文章及講座資訊：第四題命題揭秘

口語第四題是和學術話題相關的「綜合型」題目。ETS 會從以下四大學術領域中選取話題：物理科學、人文藝術、生命科學和社會科學。考生首先要讀一段長度為 75~100 詞的閱讀材料，然後聽一段涉及閱讀材料話題某一方面的短篇講座。短篇講座的時間長度通常為 60~90 秒。和第三題一樣，閱讀材料的目的是提供範圍比較廣的背景資訊，為之後更為具體、針對性更強的聽力材料做鋪陳。因此，第四題被稱為「概括與具體」式的題目。

聽短篇講座時，考生應記筆記，尤其要注意記下主要觀點。題目會要求解釋短篇講座所討論概念的一到兩個方面。例如：解釋講座中提到的例子怎樣說明了某條原理。

這一題的準備時間是 30 秒，作答時間為 60 秒。

要想在第四題拿到高分，考生的回答依然必須「完整」，也就是說必須能向從未讀過或聽過相關材料的人清晰描述總體話題，而對具體觀點的陳述也必須在規定時間內完成。同時，考生的回答還必須能讓評分人理解、表達流利（偶爾有或沒有不恰當的停頓）且邏輯連貫。一些微小的錯誤不會影響得分。

討論解決方法：第五題命題揭秘

第五題的情境依然是校園生活，會要求考生聽一段討論某一問題的短篇對話。對話長度一般為 60 ～ 90 秒，包含一個和學生相關的問題和兩個可行的解決方法。例如：某個大學生錯過了期末考，需要想辦法補救。或者：一名研究生面臨一個艱難的職業抉擇。考生應就問題的本質和兩種解決方法記下詳細的筆記。

對話結束後，題目會要求考生：1）簡要描述或概括問題所在；2）列出兩個解決方法；3）說說這兩個解決方法中，你認為哪種更好；4）解釋你的選擇為何是合理的。

考生有 20 秒準備時間和 60 秒作答時間。

記住：這道題目要求考生給出自己的觀點及合理解釋。許多考生把第五題和另外一道校園生活類題目（即第三題）混為一談，但第三題只要求概述說話者的觀點（不用說出自己的觀點）。

　　第五題沒有閱讀材料。要想在第五題拿到高分，考生的回答依然必須「完整」。也就是說，在快速描述問題、列出兩個可行對策、表明自己的選擇並解釋其合理性時，不能漏掉任何一個要點。而且作答時間還只有一分鐘！同時，考生的回答還必須能讓評分人理解，表達流利（偶爾有不恰當的停頓也沒關係）且邏輯連貫。一些微小的錯誤不會影響得分。

概括講座內容：第六題命題揭秘

　　第六題要求考生先聽一段學術類小講座。和第四題一樣，第六題涉及的具體學科出自物理科學、人文藝術、生命科學和社會科學四大領域，但同一場考試中這兩道題涉及的學術領域通常會不一樣。也就是說，如果第四題涉及的學科是生物學，那麼第六題涉及的可能是社會科學領域中的人類學。小講座中，教授會解釋一個概念或介紹一個歷史事件，然後舉出兩個具體的例子。小講座時間長度為 90 ～ 120 秒，但也可能更長。

　　講座結束後，考生要：1）概括講座的主要觀點；2）用教授的例子解釋主要觀點。考生有 20 秒的準備時間和 60 秒的作答時間。應在筆記中記下小講座的主要觀點、關鍵例子或有一定邏輯關係的觀點，以及任何重要的專業術語。

　　第六題沒有閱讀材料。

　　要想在第六題拿到高分，考生的回答依然必須「完整」。即必須簡要描述核心概念或話題，然後運用教授引用的例子解釋核心概念，而作答時間只有一分鐘！同時，考生的回答還必須能讓評分人理解，表達流利（偶爾有或沒有不恰當的停頓）且邏輯連貫。一些微小的錯誤不會影響得分。

▶口語測驗的搶分策略

考試之前……

1. 確保自己理解每道題目的要求：概述材料內容還是給出自己的觀點？準備回答和正式作答的時間有多長？
2. 瞭解每道題的評分標準。
3. 練習把握回答每道題目的時間。
4. 練習在口語中把片語和整個句子換句話說。

考場上……

1. 不要害怕麥克風！那只是一台機器，不會咬你。說話時，假裝在和你最喜歡的英語老師交談，最好是一位很嚴格但你真心喜歡的老師。
2. 遇到有閱讀材料的題目時，快速閱讀以瞭解其大致觀點。不必太執著於細節，因為稍後在聽力材料中會提及相關細節。
3. 想一想聽力材料開場白和首句提到的主題。
4. 有小對話或小講座時，認真聽錄音並用有效的方法記筆記，筆記要有條理。注意記下關鍵字和例子。
5. 注意合理分配時間。一定要好好利用時間，完成題目中要求的所有任務。

6. 使用有效的連接詞連接觀點。

7. 不要嘗試使用自己不常用的難字。

8. 不要「一字不差」地套用範本。要在內容和表達上把範本轉化成自己的語言。

9. 不要嘗試將論點的正反兩個方面都進行論證。只選擇一個立場或「最喜歡的」，然後進行論述就好。

10. 說話語速不要太快以致難以分辨。語速放慢，注意重音放在正確的音節和單字上，而且要有合理的停頓。

11. 結束回答時，不要使用：That's it! / That's all! / OK, I'm finished.

12. 即使覺得某道題目自己答得很糟糕，也不要慌！回答下一道題時還是要保持專注和樂觀。

Section ❷

Familiar Topics: Tasks 1 and 2

第❷部分
第一題 & 第二題：
命題總監教你，日常話題沒問題！

Task 1 ▸ Personal Preference

第一題 個人喜好

▶提問形式

第一題是口語考試六道題目中最容易的一題。第一題的話題籠統、易懂，而且考生可以決定從哪一個方面對此話題做出回答。例如，考官可能會問：What subject in school do you like best? Please give your reasons.

▶回答時要注意什麼？

由於第一題的情境為「日常」環境，你不用思考很久再開口回答。不必使用難詞，也不用去分析問題。而且，你很可能以前就曾經用英語討論過這些話題。例如，你的英文老師或者母語為英語的朋友就可能問過你：What's your favorite food? 你頭腦中很有可能已經儲存了所需要的全部基本詞彙。

在回答第一題和第二題中關於食物的問題時，沒有必要使用像 haute cuisine（高級料理）和 sautéed flounder（嫩煎鮃魚）這種生僻華麗的「GRE 式」詞彙。只要口頭回答得清晰、連貫、切題，就可以得到高分。所以，你所需要做的，就是練習將所掌握的詞彙和自己的觀點串聯起來使之達意。

▶什麼是日常話題？

你也許會問，準備第一題時到底要複習哪些話題呢？什麼樣的話題算是「日常話題」呢？我們可以透過下頁這個圖表理解這個話題的範圍。通常，最裡面的兩個圓圈：「自己」以及「你的家庭和朋友」，代表了考試中的「日常話題」。

當然，人們最熟悉的話題一定和個人處境以及最親近的人相關。另外，從圖表中可以看出，最裡面的兩個圓圈並不是很大。與討論抽象問題和學術話題時使用的語言相比，這兩個圓所包含的詞彙量較少（文法結構也相對比較簡單）。在談論自己的時候，當然不需要使用很多生僻詞彙啦！當我們和家人或朋友相處交流時，會討論共同感興趣的話題。比如，你可能會問父母他們喜歡什麼音樂，或者向同學推薦一個電視節目。這就是回答第一題和第二題時使用的語言。

然而，隨著交際面擴大，人們使用的語言會逐漸複雜起來。一旦人們開始談論專業的話題（在學校裡或在工作中）的時候，所用語言的範圍會擴大，複雜性也會增加。當我們和老師、教授交流時，所用的語言就會和第三題、第五題「校園生活」類話題所考查的語言水準一致。

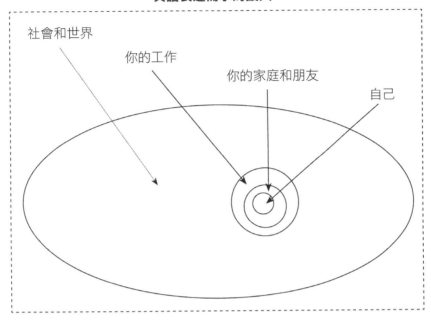

英語表達需求的擴大

社會和世界

你的工作

你的家庭和朋友

自己

註 這個語言能力模型通過擴大的同心圓展示了各社會領域對於語言需求的影響。這一模型最先由設計出跨部門語言圓桌量表（Interagency Language Roundtable Scale）的美國研究員提出。

　　當人們必須以自己並不熟悉的學術領域為話題進行交流時，對語言的要求就更高了。從最外面的兩個圓可以看出，學術和專業領域的語言範圍很廣。這類語言就是口語考試第四題和第六題所要考查的內容。要回答這兩道題，就需要更多的詞彙、更複雜的文法形式和更加抽象的觀點。本書會基於不同題目的特點提供明確的備考策略，對症下藥，各個擊破，以助你取得理想成績。

▶第一題的四個主要情境

　　既然已經知道，要掌握「日常話題」並不需要海量的材料，就可以鬆口氣了。但好消息可不僅如此，第一題和第二題所運用的情境十分類似，有時甚至是完全相同的。這一點很有利，因為你在準備這兩道題目的情境時，就等於可以同時學習兩道題的常用片語和實用答題範本。

　　第一題中最常見的情境可分為四類：
1. 人物　2. 活動和經歷　3. 社會現象和文化現象　4. 物件和個人物品

　　也就是說，涉及個人喜好的問題會要求考生談談一個特別的人、社會文化事件、物品或一次特別的經歷，然後解釋為什麼。有些題目可能會要求考生對特定的問題發表一下個人見解，可能會要求針對某學生報評論版面上所提到的社會問題談談自己的看法，例如：學生是否應該兼職。還有一些題目會要求考生談談個人生活的某個方面，例如：你的學校、家庭、工作、興趣愛好、一本你喜歡讀的書、你對旅行的偏好以及你想怎樣安排假期。

1 Describing a Favorite Person
描述一個你最喜歡的人

在本章，你將學到……

★ 如何組織第一題的答題思路
★ 詞彙和音節的重音

解讀常考題

　　第一題中很常見的一類題目就是要求考生描述一個自己喜歡或崇拜的人。在這一情境中，可能要求考生講講自己最喜歡的老師、最好的朋友、最喜愛的名人、最崇敬的音樂家或者對自己有特殊意義的某個人。要想取得高分，就需要有效地描述出這個人的性格特點、優點、成就甚至外貌特徵。

　　考生還應能夠說明為什麼對這個人有著強烈的感情。使用恰當的描述性詞彙和片語，有助於為觀點提供實在的論據。

　　接下來，我們來看一道描述自己喜歡的人的例子。

▶舉例試題

Describe the author whom you most admire. Include details and examples to support your choice.

Preparation Time: 15 Seconds
Response Time: 45 Seconds

托福總監告訴你怎麼答！

　　在描述這個作家時，考生應著重注意評分人的三個評分標準：**表達**，包括發音；**語言運用**，包括對片語和實用答題範本的合理使用；還有**主題的展開**，要保證所有的句子語言銜接緊密，邏輯連貫流暢。

策略：如何組織第一題的答題思路

　　上題的構思只需三個步驟：
1. 選擇一位作家；
2. 描述這位作家的背景、作品等；
3. 舉例並給出理由，說明為什麼喜歡這位作家，至少舉出一部作品，並至少說出一條理由。

　　首先，應迅速選出一位自己比較熟悉，至少有話可說的作家。這位作家不一定就是你最崇拜的，只要自己覺得容易描述就行。例如：如果你可以輕鬆地用英語談論《哈利·波特》系列中的一部，那就說說它的作者J.K. 羅琳。或者，如果你喜歡《三國演義》這部中文小說，就可以說自己最崇拜的作家是羅貫中。不要花太多的時間去思考，要學會快速而明智地做出決定。

高分回答

注意看，仔細聽，這裡面標上**粗體套色**的地方都要發重音才道地喔！ *Track 001*

There are **many wonderful authors**, but if I **had** to **choose** a favorite, **I'd pick John Steinbeck**.（←明確而突出的主題句）

John Steinbeck is an American author who **wrote a lot of books** about **poor people** in California.（←馬上提供背景資訊）

For **example**, he wrote about migrant farm workers during the Great Depression.（←舉例）

One reason I ad**mire Steinbeck** is that his **writing** is **very simple**. Another reason is that his **characters are so realistic**.（←給出兩點理由）

In **Steinbeck's famous novel** *Of Mice* and *Men*, I was **moved** by the **characters George** and Lennie. They **each** have **weaknesses**, but **Steinbeck** shows the **depth** of their **friendship**.

托福總監為什麼覺得這是高分回答？

　　一旦選定了要描述的人事物，立即把它在一張紙上寫下來，儘量寫英語。考試時只有 15 秒鐘構思和做筆記的時間，所以要抓緊時間。然後再用縮寫形式寫下三到四個其他單字。

　　以上面的 John Steinbeck 為例，可以寫下 cal 表示 California，用 mig work 表示 migrant workers, 用 real 表示 realistic，還可以將作品名 *Of Mice and Men*（《人鼠之間》）簡寫為 Mice。

　　第一題的答題時間最多只有 45 秒，這就意味著無法詳盡地闡述話題。那麼，想取得高分，首先要有一個明確而突出的主題句，然後給出相對準確、連貫和清晰易懂的論據，幾句話就夠了。若說出的語句令人費解、囉唆重複或邏輯混亂，便不會得到理想的分數。

　　在上面的回答範例中，主題句是：There are many wonderful authors, but if I had to choose a favorite, I'd pick John Steinbeck. 第二句話的作用是為不熟悉這位作家的評分人提供一些背景資訊：John Steinbeck is an American author who... 介紹完畢後，如果時間允許，可以多舉例，如：For example, he wrote about migrant farm workers during the Great Depression. 然而如前所述，所有支援主題句的細節和事例應銜接自然，且不能重複。在整個答題過程中，應該儘量做到發音清晰，語速平穩，句與句之間過渡流暢。

要答好第一題中有關人物的問題，可運用以下策略：

1. 談到一個人的成就時，多用關係子句和多種動詞時態。例如，談到一位令人欽佩的老師，可以說：When Mr. Li taught me, he spared no effort in explaining the most difficult part of Calculus proofs.

2. 講講這個人怎樣給你的生活帶來影響。此時，你可能需要使用一些使役動詞（如：made me learn）、一些表達情感的動詞（如：I was proud to know him），並綜合運用多種時態。例如，談到一位著名的影星，可以說：The celebrity Nicole Kidman has inspired me to work as a volunteer for social causes.

3. 描述這個人的個性，應該多用形容詞。例如：...has a warm, outgoing personality. /...is patient and dedicated.

4. 如果可能的話，勾勒一下人物的外貌特徵，使用常見的形容詞，如：tall, rugged man / kind, wrinkled face。其他能夠獲得高分的描述性片語包括修飾性片語，如：with a bald spot on the top of his head / a face that radiated kindness。

5. 如果描述的是一位外國人，一定要掌握這個人的名字在英語中的正確發音。也就是說，如果想說自己崇拜的人是貝多芬（Beethoven）或者赫丘利（Hercules），不要按照自己母語習慣念他們的名字，否則評分人可能聽不懂。

6. 在關係子句中，可以使用 who，而不是文法上正確的 whom，這是符合日常口語習慣的說法。如可以說 the person who I respect most，而不必說 the person whom I respect most。

7. 可省去關係子句中的關係代名詞，這也是符合日常口語習慣的表達。如可以說 the person I most admire，而不必說 the person who(m) I most admire。當然，兩種說法都可以，評分人不會因為這些文法問題扣你的分，因為母語是英語的人通常都是這樣說話的。

8. 若描述的人依然健在，須使用現在時態。如：My mother is definitely the person I most admire. 或 The person I most admire is a little-known animal rights activist working with lions in Africa. 若想描述這個人之前的行為，應轉而使用可以表達某種過去行為的動詞。如：My mother pushed me to succeed, and when I was small I thought she was unreasonable.（一般過去式）或 Ever since I was a child, my mother has encouraged me to aim high.（現在完成式）然後可以再回到現在時態或者現在完成時態：Now I am grateful for her support. 或 That is why my mother has been such a good role model for me.

　　除了使用以上這些策略，也應積累本書提供的實用答題範本，這樣才能漸漸掌握一整套的應試工具。具備了這些技能，你就能從容應對考試了！

▶模擬試題①

　　請回答下題。回答時，可嘗試使用下面列出的實用答題範本。

> **Describe the celebrity you most admire. Include details and examples to support your choice.**
>
> Preparation Time: 15 Seconds
> Response Time: 45 Seconds

實用答題範本 🎧 **Track 002** 聽聽看！別人的高分回答！（高分回答原文請見 P.277）

The celebrity I most admire is...
Although he was..., he was able to VERB...

得分考技：重讀關鍵詞，讓聽者更易理解

　　新托福口語考試是基於整體考量進行評分的，也就是說評分人在聽考生回答時，會同時衡量多個方面，包括詞彙、文法、觀點的組織及發音，然後給出一個最終分數。以上任何一方面的小錯誤都不會影響評分人給考生打出最高分。然而，如果考生的回答令人費解，便不會得到高分，評分人特別在意這一方面。

　　怎麼讓評分人知道你在說什麼？一方面，考生的發音要準確，不影響別人的理解。例如：walks 一詞要把結尾的「ks」音清晰地發出來，bright 一詞的雙母音要發正確。另一方面，說話時要有一定的韻律。在語言中，韻律即說話的節奏、重音和語調。韻律受到很多因素的影響，包括音節的長度、響度、音高，一個詞中音高的起伏、母音的長度，以及何時停頓。要想在新托福口語考試中給出清晰易懂的回答，就必須注意控制這兩個方面。

　　人們傳達思想的一個重要手段，就是讓聽者注意到關鍵字。有很多方法可以達到這一點，包括重音的運用。包含了資訊的詞語就是關鍵詞。母語為英語的人會用重音讀關鍵詞來強調意思。因此，要重讀的詞就包括了名詞、形容詞、副詞和主要的動詞。有些關鍵詞被強調的頻率高於其他關鍵詞，這要取決於情境。

　　實際上，一個單字中通常會有一個主要的重音。這個重音聽起來更加重要，因為它的發音更長、更響且音高更高。一個音節重讀，其他的就會相對較輕。如果將重音放錯音節了，甚至忽略了重音，說出來的單字就會令人費解。

托福總監帶你練

下面是練習重音的句子，注意句子中的**粗體套色**部分。反覆聽錄音，然後跟讀。 🎧 **Track 003**

1. Of **all** the **people** I **know**, I **most respect** my **father**.
2. I **look up** to my **grand**mother a **lot**.
3. The **scientist** Albert **Einstein** is the individual I **most** respect.
4. When I'm **asked** to **say** who I **most** admire, I **always think** of **one person**.
5. **All** of these **factors** are **reasons why** I admire my **mother**.

▶模擬試題②

　　請回答下題。回答時，可嘗試使用下面列出的實用答題範本。

Who is the person you most respect? Include details and examples to support your choice.

Preparation Time: 15 Seconds
Response Time: 45 Seconds

以下是一個回答範例，應重讀的部分已用**粗體套色**標出。 *Track 004*

> The person I most respect is, without a doubt, my high school math teacher, Mr. Miller. Mr. Miller is probably the best teacher I've ever had, but he's also an unusual person in his own right. To look at him, he's just a short, unexceptional man who's basically very introverted. However, when he's teaching in our classroom, Mr. Miller has a special talent for making complex mathematical concepts clear to his students. In other words, he's quiet, but very clear and very effective. His ability to teach well is the reason why I admire him so much.

　　換你試試看了！也回答看看你最崇拜的人是誰吧！可以參考下面的答題範本來組織答案喔！

> **實用答題範本**
>
> ...is probably the best...I've ever had.
> ...has a special talent for...

• 單字重音正確發音策略

1. 將最重要的詞的發音發清楚，不要著急。
2. 重讀關鍵詞，而不是功能詞。
3. 重讀的音節要比別的音節發得更長、更響亮、音高更高。

▶ 模擬試題③

　　請回答下題。回答時，可嘗試使用下面列出的實用答題範本。

> **What characteristics do you think make a person a good leader? Explain why these characteristics are important.**
>
> Preparation Time: 15 Seconds
> Response Time: 45 Seconds

> **實用答題範本**　　🎧*Track 005* 聽聽看！別人的高分回答！（高分回答原文請見 P.277）
>
> In my mind, one of the most important characteristics of a good leader is...
> Good...can VERB...

托福總監幫你預測可能會出現的題目！

1. What is one of the most important characteristics a teacher should have?
2. Who is the person who has had the most influence in your life?
3. What are the characteristics of a good friend?
4. What characteristics make a good parent?
5. In your family, who is the person you most enjoy spending time with?

• 最後再練習一下「描述喜歡的人」最實用的答題模板！

1. There are many wonderful..., but if I had to choose a favorite, I'd pick...

例 • There are many wonderful authors, but if I had to choose a favorite, I'd pick John Steinbeck.

• There are many excellent athletes, but if I had to choose a favorite, I'd pick Bolt.

2. One reason (that) I admire...is that...

例 • One reason I admire Steinbeck is that his writing is very simple.

3. The...I most admire is...

例 • The celebrity I most admire is Jackie Chan.

• The author I most admire is J.K. Rowling.

4. Of all the teachers I have had, Mr. Jones…

例 • Of all the teachers I have had, Mr. Jones is the kindest.

5. Of all my friends, John is...

例 • Of all my friends, John is the nicest.

6. My...is the one who I most admire.

例 • My high school chemistry teacher is the one who I most admire.

• My grandfather is the one who I most admire.

7. My...is the person I trust the most.

例 • My mother is the person I trust the most.

• My classmate is the person I trust the most.

8. Although he was..., he was able to VERB...

例 • Although he was born poor, he was able to become skilled at martial arts.

• Although he was strict, he was able to teach difficult concepts.

• Although he was shy, he was able to make me laugh.

9. ...is probably the best...I've ever had.

例 • Mr. Miller is probably the best teacher I've ever had.

• She's probably the best friend I've ever had.

10. I particularly enjoyed...

例 • I particularly enjoyed the character Hermione.

• I particularly enjoyed taking his advanced physics class.

• I particularly enjoyed watching her in *Gone with the Wind*.

11. ...has a special talent for...

例 • Mr. Miller has a special talent for making complex mathematical concepts clear to his students.

• My friend has a special talent for singing.

12. In my mind, one of the most important characteristics of a good leader is...

例 • In my mind, one of the most important characteristics of a good leader is the ability to inspire others.

13. Good...can VERB...

例 • Good leaders can motivate their people.

• Good teachers can inspire people.

2 Describing a Memorable Past Experience
描述一次難忘的經歷

在本章，你將學到……

★如何談論過去的經歷、正確掌握動詞時態
★如何在答題時闡述理由

解讀常考題

　　新托福口語考試第一題，有時會要求考生描述過去的某個活動或經歷。

　　在回答有關經歷的題目時，實際上是在講一個小故事。評分人已經聽過成千上萬的回答，所以他們非常希望聽到一些考生能夠講出有趣的個人回憶。在45秒內，把你個人的「故事」講得越是精彩，得分就會越高。

　　以下是描述一段難忘的經歷的例題。

▶舉例試題

Talk about an unforgettable meal that you had with family or friends. Include details and examples to support your choice.

Preparation Time: 15 Seconds
Response Time: 45 Seconds

托福總監告訴你怎麼答！

　　在談論一件生活往事時，要注意聽眾是誰、怎麼跟他們講這個故事。在考試中，聽眾就是那些並不認識你的評分人。這表示首先要說出一個明確的主題句，這樣評分人在聽回答時，才能對你要講什麼有個大致的瞭解。如上面的例題，要講一次 unforgettable meal，例如你可以說：I enjoy eating good food and have eaten many wonderful meals. But the most unforgettable meal I've ever had was when I was at a small restaurant in New York. 之後，就可以添加一些細節，如什麼場合、餐廳怎樣、食物怎樣等等來完成故事。如果回答易於理解，展現了扎實的語言運用能力，邏輯銜接緊密、連貫流暢，就能得到高分。

得分考技：談論過去經歷需要掌握的動詞時態

　　談論過去經歷的一個困難之處就是必須掌握不同的動詞時態。實際上，在說的過程中，需要不斷變換多種過去時態。有時要用一般過去式陳述事件，有時又要用到過去完成式，或者某個助動詞如 would 或 used to。而在描述你當時的感受時，可能又要使用一般過去式……。

高分回答

注意看，仔細聽，這裡面標上**粗體套色**的地方都要發重音才道地喔！

I be**lie**ve my most unforgettable **meal** was a celebration **dinner** I attended in **high** school.（←明確而突出的主題句）
I was on our **high** school's **math** team, and our **team** had won **first prize** in a **math** contest in Boston.（←馬上提供背景資訊，用兩種時態來轉換）
In **all**, there were **four** members on my team. **That** night our **math coach** told us that he would **treat** us to a **meal** at **any** restaurant in Boston in **view** of the **fact** that we had **worked** so **hard**. We de**ci**ded that we **wanted** to **eat** lobster, and so our **coach took** us to a **famous** seafood restaurant. The **lobster tasted** es**pe**cially **good** because we were **so** happy and **proud**.

托福總監為什麼覺得這是高分回答？

　　第一句是明確的主題句，讓評分人知道這頓難忘的飯是一次慶祝晚宴。第二句為評分人提供了事情的背景，解釋自己當時參加了數學小組。注意第二句話中該考生解釋事件背景時所使用的時態：I was on our high school's math team, and our team had won first prize in a math contest in Boston.

　　本句的第一個分句使用了一般過去式，第二個分句則使用了過去完成式來表述慶功宴之前所發生的事情。第三句使用一般過去式為評分人描述了數學小組的情況。第四句的動詞時態就稍複雜一些了：That night our math coach told us that he would treat us to a meal at any restaurant in Boston in view of the fact that we had worked so hard. 前半包含了一個間接引語，使用了 would，表示教練將要請數學小組的四個成員吃飯。後半句是一個子句，說明了教練請他們吃大餐的原因。第五句也包含了兩個分句，每個分句都使用了一般過去式：We decided that we wanted to eat lobster, and so our coach took us to a famous seafood restaurant. 最後一句仍然包含兩個分句，且都使用了一般過去式：The lobster tasted especially good because we were so happy and proud. 注意這句話如何對整個故事做了生動的總結：因為遇到這麼一件令人自豪的事，所以龍蝦吃起來別有一番滋味。

　　更多描述過去行為的例句：
Because I had quit my job, I was there for the whole summer.
I have fantastic memories of Rome.
The scenery was amazing.

> I had a great time climbing the mountain.
> All the dishes were really spicy.
> I would go back again if I got a chance.

要答好第一題中有關過往經歷的問題，可運用以下策略 ：

1. 從「講一個故事」的角度進行思考。
2. 回答時，要給出強有力且明確的主題句，並提供一點事件背景。
3. 使用多種時態，包括一般過去式、過去完成式以及不同的助動詞，如 would 和 used to。
4. 講述事件細節，說明其難忘原因時要靈活運用不同的動詞時態。
5. 儘管時間有限，還是應盡可能給故事加個結尾，如：Being together with my family made that meal very special.

▶模擬試題①

請回答下題。回答時，可嘗試使用下面列出的實用答題範本。

Describe a memorable celebration you once had. Include details and examples to support your choice.

Preparation Time: 15 Seconds
Response Time: 45 Seconds

實用答題範本　　🎧 *Track 007* 聽聽看！別人的高分回答！（高分回答原文請見 P.277）

...was the best celebration I've ever attended.
Friends and family came in from...

策略：解釋原因的最佳方式

　　兩個日常話題題目都要求考生「給出原因」。在第一題中，可能需要給出具體細節和例子來解釋為什麼自己認為某個地方或事件很特別。在第二題中，則需要陳述自己贊同哪一觀點，然後給出具體細節來說明原因。顯然，在口語考試中，清楚地闡釋個人喜好是十分重要的。

　　那麼對於考生來講，解釋原因的最佳方式是什麼？有兩個要素是必不可少的：
1. 舉出一些具體細節或事實，用於闡釋主題並使其融入上下文。
2. 使用表明即將說出原因、以及用於串聯觀點的詞語。

▶模擬試題②

再來看一道關於講述經歷的例題。

Talk about an academic class that influenced your life and explain why that class was important. Include details and examples to support your explanation.

Preparation Time: 15 Seconds
Response Time: 45 Seconds

以下是一個回答範例，請注意這位考生是如何帶出「原因」的。　　*Track 008*

Most classes I've taken have been rather boring, mainly because the teachers just went through the motions. That's why it's easy to remember one class that really influenced me—an English class where my teacher pushed me to achieve.（←給出原因）

This was a tenth-grade English class and we had a lot of writing assignments. I thought my essays were good, and my teacher was also enthusiastic. Still, she kept asking me to rewrite my papers, to make them better. In her class, I learned how to edit my own writing. More importantly, I learned never to be satisfied with mediocrity.

托福總監評析

　　本回答的第一句通過對比表述了該考生的喜好：大部分課程都沒有給自己帶來過積極的影響。這種反襯使第二句話（即主題句）格外突出。注意，句型「That's why it's...」起了使前後文銜接緊密的作用。這個片語不僅將兩句話聯結在一起，而且提醒評分人把注意力放在後文。

　　另外，也可以看到考生如何通過子句 an English class where my teacher pushed me to achieve 來「給出原因」。聽了這句話，評分人立刻就會明白這位英語老師的獨特之處在於積極鼓勵學生不斷進取，而不是像有些老師那樣 go through the motions。隨後幾句話詳細描述了課堂內容，同時也說明了這些行為的目的和效果（to make them better）。結尾句點明了這位教師的課對該考生影響深遠的最重要原因，也使得整個回答前後連貫，一氣呵成。可以看出，有意義的細節能夠支撐所闡述的主題。如果能夠有條理地組織這些細節並使用合適的句型闡述原因，就能讓評分人聽得更懂。

一些適用於在日常話題中表述原因的句型：

表述原因的句型	
The reason I...	Due to my interest in...
This is because...	...for the reason that...
Because I...	My motivation for...

It was...because...	It was only because...
There are...reasons why...	If...had not..., I would never have...
That's why I...	As a result, I...
The reason this experience was so meaningful to me is that...	Without the influence of..., I would never have...
For one thing, ...	...made me realize...
Another factor was...	...caused me to do...
My love for...was due to...	...led me to do...

▶練習看看！

聽下列表述原因的句子。反覆聽錄音，然後跟讀。試試看用這些句子描述人生中對你影響最大的一堂課。

🎧 *Track 009*

1. The **reason** I **liked** this class is because...
2. The **reason** **history** was my **favorite** **class** was my **teacher**.
3. **Because** I had to **push** myself, I learned **discipline**.
4. **That's** why it was **so** important.
5. It was **special** because I was **motivated**.

要在日常話題題目中更有效地表述原因，可運用以下策略：

1. 要明白：評分人不知道你要說什麼。他們只能一步一步跟著你說的內容走。這表示你的陳述要有條理，觀點之間的邏輯關係要清晰，才有助於他們的理解。
2. 陳述主題句後，選擇兩三個有意義的細節來解釋為什麼你有這種感受。細節就是原因！不必每次都用 because 來引出原因，可以通過講故事或描述某個場景來闡釋原因。
3. 運用適合在口語中使用的句型來表述原因。在日常話題題目中，應避免使用像 accordingly 和 in consideration of 這樣過於正式、華麗的詞。
4. 儘量在最後一句表述最重要的原因，這樣就能總結之前所表述過的所有觀點。

　　不同類型的句型能夠幫助評分人預測接下來的內容。清晰的結構，能讓評分人知道你接下來要說什麼，這就有可能讓你得到更高的分數！

▶模擬試題③

　　請回答下頁的題目。解釋原因時，注意內容要銜接緊密、邏輯連貫。回答時，可嘗試使用下頁列出的實用答題範本。

Describe an experience when you were feeling sad and a friend made you happy. Include details and examples to support your explanation.

Preparation Time: 15 Seconds
Response Time: 45 Seconds

實用答題範本 🎧 *Track 010* 聽聽看！別人的高分回答！（高分回答原文請見 P.277）

Fortunately, my best friend was there to VERB...
Although the memory of...is..., ...

托福總監幫你預測可能會出現的題目！

1. Describe a special trip you took. Explain why it was special for you.
2. Describe a situation in the past when you needed help from someone. Who helped you and what was the result?
3. Talk about a project that was difficult for you to accomplish. How was it difficult?
4. Talk about a recent experience you had that was special. Why did you think it was so special?
5. What was your favorite place to go as a child? Describe it and explain why you liked going there.

• 最後再練習一下「描述經歷」最實用的答題模板！

1. One of my most unforgettable...was...
例 • One of my most unforgettable experiences was...
   • One of my most unforgettable days was...

2. An activity I participated in when I was young was…
例 • An activity I participated in when I was young was dancing.

3. a(n)...I had in high school
例 • a difficult test I had in high school
   • an experience I had in high school

4. That night...told us/me he/she would VERB...
例 • That night our math coach told us that he would treat us to a meal at any restaurant in Boston in view of the fact that we had worked so hard.
例 • That night my classmate told us she would study harder.
   • That night my cousin told me he would help me.

5. We decided that we wanted to VERB...
例 • We decided that we wanted to eat lobster.

- We decided that we wanted to fly to Bangkok.
- We decided that we wanted to do volunteer work.

6. ...tasted especially good.
例
- The lobster tasted especially good.
- The fresh fish tasted especially good.
- My mother's soup tasted especially good.

7. ...meant a lot to me.
例
- The experience meant a lot to me.
- Her advice meant a lot to me.

8. I will never forget the time/day I...
例
- I will never forget the time I went to Paris.
- I will never forget the day I took the college entrance exam.

9. The...was very special/unusual because...
例
- The cafe was very special because...
  The food was very unusual because...

10. We had an incredible...
例
- We had an incredible day.

11. We all got together for a(n)...
例
- We all got together for a family gathering.
- We all got together for a class reunion.

12. The experience made me realize that...
例
- The experience made me realize that I should study harder.
- The experience made me appreciate how much I loved working with people.

13. ...was the best celebration I've ever attended.
例
- My grandfather's seventieth birthday party was the best celebration I've ever attended.

14. Friends and family came in from...
例
- Friends and family came in from all over the country.

15. Fortunately, my best friend was there to VERB...
例
- Fortunately, my best friend was there to console me.
- Fortunately, my best friend was there to help me.

16. Although the memory of...is..., ...
例
- Although the memory of that election is still painful, the memory of my friend's kindness is strong.

③ Describing a Favorite Activity in the Present
描述最喜愛的活動

❝ 在本章，你將學到…… ❞

★第一題如何記筆記
★如何靈活運用動名詞，使你的表現更出色

解讀常考題

第一題經常會問到「愛好或習慣性的活動」。要回答此類問題，通常需要依靠多種形式的現在式（如：I travel to Europe every few months.），也要使用不定詞（如：I like to go fishing.）以及未來式（如：Sometimes I will go to movies on weekends.）。還有，在描述娛樂活動時，最常用的結構就是動名詞。

現在，看一道關於最喜愛的活動的例題。

▶舉例試題

What is your favorite way to relax? Include details to support your choice.

Preparation Time: 15 Seconds
Response Time: 45 Seconds

托福總監告訴你怎麼答！

每當回答關於愛好或習慣性活動的問題時，最好先陳述一下你喜歡做的事是什麼，如：

To relax, I like to go jogging. 隨後再提供具體事例，說明活動的內容及方式，如：什麼時間慢跑、和誰一起慢跑、在什麼地方慢跑等。換言之，你要告訴評分人你的愛好是什麼，平時都做什麼活動，給出的事例和細節越連貫切題，得分就會越高。但是要記住，回答一定要自然，表達出個人經歷和感受，而非一概而論。

更多可用來描述喜愛的娛樂休閒活動的例句：

To me, Barcelona is one of the nicest places in the world.
Whenever I have a spare weekend, Qingdao is the place I like to visit.
Playing chess is the activity I most enjoy doing.
I think cooking is probably the most enjoyable activity I know.

策略：第一題記筆記的訣竅

在第一題中記筆記不像在第三到第六題中那麼重要。然而，它仍是一件有助於組織觀點的戰略武器，可幫你保持鎮靜、從容地給出高分回答。

由於只有 15 秒的準備時間，動作一定要快。你需要非常迅速地決定要說的話題。然後，需要用縮略形式寫下一些詞彙，幫助你集中觀點並讓通順的英語「脫口而出」。每個人記筆記的方式都有所不同，你需要經過一段時間的練習，找出適合自己的方法。

在做第一題的筆記時，有以下幾個要點：

1. 寫下一個單字或縮寫，表示決定談論的話題。

2. 寫下幾個單字或縮寫，提示將用到哪些例子來論證觀點。

3. 若時間允許，寫下一些句型或連接詞，將上面所說的內容連在一起，如：可寫下「even th」來代表 even though。

高分回答

注意看，仔細聽，這裡面標上粗體的地方都要發重音才道地喔！ *Track 011*

My favorite **way** to **relax** is to **watch television**. **Even though most** of the **time** the **TV programs** I **watch** are not particularly **good**, they're **still** relaxing **to watch**. On the **weekends**, I **like** to **watch old movies**, especially **action films** and **dramas**. Casablanca is an **example** of a **film** I **really love**. During the **week**, I'm usually **busy**, but **sometimes I'll download movies** onto my computer so I can **watch** them later. **By** watching foreign **films**, I learn a **lot** about other **countries**. I **can't** always understand everything in the **dialog**, but **that** doesn't make them **less fun** to **watch**.

托福總監為什麼覺得這是高分回答？

通過分析這個回答，就能看到怎樣通過記筆記來獲得一個較為完整的回答。第一句是一個主題句，讓評分人得知該考生最喜愛的放鬆方式是 watching television。第二句提供了個人資訊，說明為何選擇看電視來放鬆：因為是一種消遣。第三和第四句講述了該考生週末愛看的節目，並舉了一個例子。第五句說明了在工作日看什麼：沒時間看節目，下載電影留著稍後看。最後兩句進一步解釋了喜歡看電視的原因，並提供了其他細節。

在 15 秒內，你也許能記下這樣的筆記：

TV
old movies — CB
download
learn

有些人也許還能寫下更多東西，但即使是這樣簡短的筆記也能在整個回答中起到提示和引導的作用。CB 是 *Casablanca*（電影《卡薩布蘭卡》）的簡寫。將這些詞語列出，形成一個「框架」，並寫上像 download 這樣的關鍵字，就能迅速串聯思路，合理運用時間，在規定的 45 秒內給出例子和細節。看看所列出的詞彙，回顧一下上面的回答，看看這樣的筆記怎樣起到組織回答框架的作用吧！

要做好第一題的筆記，可運用以下策略：

1. 盡可能使用英文單字或縮寫而非中文。的確，這會有點慢，但是等到開口回答的時候你就會覺得萬幸了，因為不必再翻譯一遍。
2. 追求廣度，莫追求深度。換句話說，這不是寫小說，用一個詞代表一句話都算多了。
3. 將筆記上的單字和片語作為記憶提示器。這些詞就像路標，給你信心，告訴你下一步朝哪兒走。
4. 儘量寫下表示兩個例子或理由的單字。準備時間不一定充足，但在開口回答時，最好有這些筆記在眼前（尤其是在緊張的情況下）。
5. 若沒時間寫下兩個例子或理由，就寫下第一個例子。如：想坐火車去一個地方的名字。

▶模擬試題①

請回答下題。回答時，可嘗試使用下面列出的實用答題範本。

Describe a public park that you visit frequently. Include examples and details to explain why you visit it.

Preparation Time: 15 Seconds
Response Time: 45 Seconds

實用答題範本　　🎧*Track 012* 聽聽看！別人的高分回答！（高分回答原文請見 P.278）

In this park is a(n)...with...
Every visit is...

得分考技：如何用動名詞使你的表現更出色

大多數問及愛好或習慣性活動的題目（尤其是用現在式提問的題目）都要求考生能夠靈活使用動名詞。對動名詞不同用法的掌握越是熟練，回答問題時的表現就會越出色。

來看看下面的例句，注意其中的動名詞。

1. I enjoy **eating** seafood.
2. I like **going** to the zoo.
3. I have fun **traveling** to new places.
4. My family frequently goes **camping**.
5. I enjoy **spending** time **reading**.（這句話用了兩個動名詞！）

像 like 這樣的動詞後面還可以接不定詞，如：

1. I like **to eat** spicy foods.
2. I like **to be** outdoors.

考生們，注意了！要牢牢記住上面的動名詞句型，以便在回答第一題時能信手拈來！

▶模擬試題②

現在來看看下面這道關於穿著的例題。

What kind of clothes do you most like to wear? Explain why these clothes are your favorites.

Preparation Time: 15 Seconds
Response Time: 45 Seconds

下面是一個回答範例，動名詞已用**粗體**標出。 *Track 013*

At **school** and in other relatively casual settings, I **love wearing jeans** and a **cotton t-shirt. Then,** if it's summer, I'll wear **sandals;** if it's winter, I'll wear tennis shoes. If I **could,** I'd **wear jeans** every **single day** because they're **so comfortable.** I **like** the **fact** that I **don't have** to **think** very much about **what** I'm **going** to **wear**—I can **just pop** them **on.** And **another good thing** about **wearing t-shirts** and **jeans** is that many **people wear** this **style** of clothing, so I **don't** stand **out** too **much.** I **like blending** in with the **crowd.**

回答這題前，我們來看看幾個包含動名詞的句子。反覆聽錄音，然後跟讀。 *Track 014*

1. I **enjoy** wearing **casual clothes.**
2. I **love** being **outdoors** in the **springtime.**
3. **Jogging** is **one** of my **favorite** activities.
4. **Whenever** I have **free time,** I go **swimming.**
5. I'm **good** at **playing video games.**

現在，自己練一練這道題目，描述你最喜愛穿的衣服，要練習使用動名詞喔！

要在日常話題題目中正確使用動名詞，可運用以下策略：

1. 所有的動名詞都以「動詞 + ing」結構組成。
2. 描述你喜愛的一項活動時，可以使用 like、love、enjoy 這樣的動詞，並在其後面加動名詞，如：I like hiking in the woods.

記住：動名詞也可當作主詞！如：Mountain climbing is my favorite activity. / Playing chess is something I love to do. 回答第一題時，用動名詞形式作主詞就能輕鬆使句子結構多樣起來！

▶模擬試題③

請回答下題。回答時，可嘗試使用下面列出的實用答題範本。

What form of transportation do you find most enjoyable to take; for example, bicycles, cars and trains? Give reasons and examples to support your choice.

Preparation Time: 15 Seconds
Response Time: 45 Seconds

實用答題範本　　　🎧 *Track 015* 聽聽看！別人的高分回答！（高分回答原文請見 P.278）

I have to say that I find...the most civilized way to travel.
Once you're on board, you can relax because you...

托福總監幫你預測可能會出現的題目！

1. What do you like to do in your spare time?
2. Describe your favorite place to visit.
3. What do you miss most when you are away from home?
4. What time of year do you like most?
5. What is your favorite subject to read about?

• 最後再練習一下「描述喜愛的活動」最實用的答題模板！

1. **Even though most of the time...are not particularly good, they're still relaxing to watch.**

   例 • Even though most of the time the TV programs I watch are not particularly good, they're still relaxing to watch.
   • Even though most of the time the sports competitions I watch are not particularly good, they're still relaxing to watch.

2. **...is an example of a film I really love.**

   例 • *Casablanca* is an example of a film I really love.
   • *Forrest Gump* is an example of a film I really love.

3. **By watching..., I learn a lot about...**

   例 • By watching foreign films, I learn a lot about other countries.

4. **One of the...I go to a lot is a(n)...in my hometown.**

   例 • One of the parks I go to a lot is a city park in my hometown.
   • One of the museums I go to a lot is an art museum in my hometown.

5. **In this park is a(n)...with...**

   例 • In this park is a large lake with footpaths that wind around it.
   • In this park is an outdoor concert arena with chairs for people to sit on.

6. Most of the time, however, we just sit on the benches, VERBing...

例 • Most of the time, however, we just sit on the benches, talking as we watch people go by.

• Most of the time, however, we just sit on the benches, enjoying the scenery.

7. Every visit is...

例 • Every visit is a little different.

• Every visit is special.

8. Then, if it's summer, I'll wear...; if it's winter, I'll wear...

例 • Then, if it's summer, I'll wear sandals; if it's winter, I'll wear tennis shoes.

• Then, if it's summer, I'll wear a skirt; if it's winter, I'll wear pants.

9. If I could, I'd wear...every single day because they're so comfortable.

例 • If I could, I'd wear jeans every single day because they're so comfortable.

• If I could, I'd wear tennis shoes every single day because they're so comfortable.

10. And another good thing about wearing...is that many people wear this style of clothing, so I don't stand out too much.

例 • And another good thing about wearing tee shirts and jeans is that many people wear this style of clothing, so I don't stand out too much.

• And another good thing about wearing a sweatshirt is that many people wear this style of clothing, so I don't stand out too much.

11. I have to say that I find...the most civilized way to travel.

例 • I have to say that I find trains the most civilized way to travel.

• I have to say that I find airplanes the most civilized way to travel.

12. Once you're on board, you can relax because you...

例 • Once you're on board, you can relax because you don't have to worry about traffic.

• Once you're on board, you can relax because you have already gone through all the security checks.

13. Trains can be very romantic if you are VERBing..., and if...

例 • Trains can be very romantic if you are crossing through interesting scenery, and if you have a good companion—or even a good book to read.

• Trains can be very romantic if you are traveling through beautiful mountains, and if the weather is good.

14. No matter what you do, you can VERB...

例 • No matter what you do, you can look outside at the scenery rushing by.

• No matter what you do, you can feel the cool air on your face.

4 Describing Something You Want in the Future
描述要做的某件事

66 在本章，你將學到…… 99

★如何利用人稱代名詞來加強語言的前後銜接
★如何運用連音使回答更自然

解讀常考題

新托福考試口語部分的命題人試圖將不同類型的問題平均分配到每套考題中。顯然，每套考題的形式都會有些許差別，所以考生需要準備應對多樣的考題類型，掌握多種動詞時態。

在第一題中，這就表示題目會問到過去、現在和將來的行為，所以就要做好準備應對這些所有情境。本章之前，已分析過的第一題例題涉及的是當前和過去的活動，本章則會開始講解如何應對第一題另一個常考情境：未來的活動。

針對未來的問題可能會是：

What will you do (on a certain date)?
What do you want to do (after something happens)?
What would you do (if something happens)?

以上最後一個問題用了虛擬語氣，在回答中也要用到虛擬語氣。但是，在大多數涉及未來的問題中，主要運用「I will + 動詞」和「I am going to + 動詞」這兩種結構來回答。

現在，看一道關於未來的例題。

▶舉例試題

What project will you begin in the near future? Include details and examples to support your choice.

Preparation Time: 15 Seconds
Response Time: 45 Seconds

托福總監告訴你怎麼答！

這道題要求談一項立即準備著手實行的計畫。這個計畫中的活動規模可能並不大，但這無關緊要。你可以講講學校佈置的某個任務（如一份報告），或者是一項家庭計畫（如幫父母修理什麼東西）。記住使用表示時間的片語，指明準備實行這一計畫的時間。你需要在整個回答中使用「I will + 動詞」和「I am going to + 動詞」的結構，或者其縮略形式「I'll+ 動詞」及「I'm going to + 動詞」。

策略：如何用人稱代名詞巧妙銜接上下文

除了熟練掌握動詞時態，考生還應能夠將詞彙和句子緊密地組織在一起，這一點很重要。從很多方面來講，銜接相當於黏合詞語的「膠水」。如果話語內容銜接緊密，聽者就能很容易地理解説話者想表達的意思。因此，如果在新托福考試的回答中注意語言的銜接，評分人就會注意到這一點並為此加分。而且，良好的銜接通常會使文章前後邏輯更加連貫，觀點更加統一。

有很多方法可以使口語回答的內容銜接更加緊密，這裡重點講解代名詞在提高句子銜接方面的作用。最常用的代名詞就是人稱代名詞，而其中最常用的是人稱代名詞的主格、受格和形容詞性物主代名詞。

高分回答

注意看，仔細聽，這裡面標上粗體的地方都要發重音才道地喔！ *Track 016*

Recently I decided to **start** writing a **blog**. Although I'm **not** yet **sure** exactly what I'll **write** in it, **most** likely I'll **talk** about interesting **things** that happen to **me** during the **day**. For example, I **might write** about my volunteer **job**, where I **tutor little children**. **They** always **ask** me surprising **questions** and make me **laugh**. **They** help me **see** the **world** through their **eyes**.
I **plan** to **post** one **entry** every **day** or so. Because I **enjoy** photography, I will **post pictures** that **go** with my **text**. Hopefully, I will **have many** visitors to my **blog**, as I **want** to **read** their **comments** and **write back** to them.

托福總監為什麼覺得這是高分回答？

看一下以上回答使用的人稱代名詞。it 指代前文提到的 blog。they 指代前文中的 little children，me 指代的是 I。their 和 them 指代的都是前文提到的 visitors。

人稱代名詞這種文法結構並不難，然而在快速組織語言進行回答時，可能常常會忘記要用。但可以看到，像以上回答使用人稱代名詞，講話內容之間的聯繫就會更加緊密，也使評分人更易理解，回答的得分將更有可能提高一個等級。

要正確運用人稱代名詞使語句的銜接更加緊密，可運用以下策略：

1. 複習不同的代名詞形式，並反覆出聲朗讀這些代名詞。
2. 在練習回答口語試題時，盡可能多地使用人稱代名詞的指代功能。如果一開始時覺得有困難，可先把答案寫下來。
3. 在閱讀本書的過程中，參考回答範例，注意範例中如何使用人稱代名詞。聽錄音，注意它們的發音。試著記下這些句子，大聲朗讀出來。

▶模擬試題①

請回答下題。回答時，可嘗試使用下面列出的實用答題範本。

> **Some people think that the world will be extremely different ten years from now. What do you think? Give detailed examples in your answer.**
>
> Preparation Time: 15 Seconds
> Response Time: 45 Seconds

實用答題範本  *Track 017* 聽聽看！別人的高分回答！（高分回答原文請見 P.278）

I believe that the world will be...ten years from now.
With global warming, I think that we'll begin to see...

得分考技：怎麼連音使回答更自然

根據口語考試評分準則（詳見 P.274 特別收錄 1），要得到 3 到 4 分，須達到的一個標準是「表達流利」。表達流利的一個方面就是能夠較為流暢自如地說出自己想說的話，不會出現猶豫、停頓。

而表達流利的另一個方面則表現在連音的能力上。英語句子要講得自然，單字會出現連讀，詞與詞間的界線不會那麼明顯。英語單字的讀法並不是完全遵循其拼法，單字中間也常常會出現停頓，而當以輔音結尾的單字後連著一個以母音開頭的單字時，兩詞間的停頓則會完全消失。母語人士不會分開讀這兩個詞，這兩個音被連在了一起，即在發音時會從一個詞滑到另一個詞，如：That's an example 會讀成 that﹏s﹏an﹏egzampl。

這種現象被稱為連讀或者連音。在上面的例子中，that's 中的 s 與 an 中的 a 連在了一起，而 an 中的 n 滑向了 example 中的 /lg/。這些在單字發音中的變化是連音的一些重要特徵。

▶模擬試題②

來看一道針對未來提問的練習，回答中要注意運用連音技巧。

> **If you could have any job you wanted, which would you choose and why? Provide specific details to support your answer.**
>
> Preparation Time: 15 Seconds
> Response Time: 45 Seconds

下面是一個回答範例。 *Track 018*

I would **have** to **say** my **dream job** is being a biologist. In **fact**, I'm **working** to**ward** that **goal now**. I enjoy traveling, visiting the **natural habitats** and studying animal **species** that intrigue me. **Fieldwork** has **taken** me to **many different places** in **China already**. In **Sichuan**, I have ob**served pandas** in **nature reserves**. And I **plan** to **visit more exotic places** in the **world** during my **graduate studies** and **after** I **receive** my advanced degree. As I become older, I see myself becoming a professor. This will allow me to continue with my research while interacting with young, inquisitive minds, which is my other passion in life.

換你試試看了！回答問題前，先練習發音中的連音技巧。底線表示應該連音的音節。反覆聽錄音，然後跟著讀。　　🎧 *Track 019*

1. I've_always wanted to be an_accountant.
2. My dream job is to serve_as_an anchor on_a major news network.
3. The career I hope to pursue is_in_advertising, as_a salesperson.
4. The job of my choice would be to work_as_an_engineer.
5. Ideally, I'd like to be a real_estate broker.

現在，自己練一練這道題，描述你會選擇的職業吧！

正確運用連音技巧的策略：

1. 在輔音和母音間通常會有連音，這是很自然的現象，如：an_apple。
2. 不要將兩個母音連讀，例如：在 very eager 中，連讀的話就成了 very /j/ eager, 這裡應確保兩個詞各自的發音都很清晰。
3. 連讀兩個相同的輔音時，將這兩個輔音讀成一個很長的輔音，例如：good_destination 中，將兩個 d 讀成一個發音較長的 /d/。
4. 認真聽本書為各例題或練習題的參考回答所配的錄音，將其看做連音範例。在書上做標記，標出有語音連接現象的地方，努力模仿錄音中的發音。

▶ 模擬試題③

請回答下題。回答時，可嘗試使用下面列出的實用答題範本。

If you were to buy a gift, who would you give it to? Give reasons and examples to support your choice.

Preparation Time: 15 Seconds
Response Time: 45 Seconds

實用答題範本　　🎧 *Track 020* 聽聽看！別人的高分回答！（高分回答原文請見 P.278）

If I were to buy a gift, I would give it to...
If I could afford it, I would buy him... to show him how much I love him.

托福總監幫你預測可能會出現的題目！

1. What city that you have never visited would you like to visit most?
2. Describe one of your goals and explain why it is important to you.
3. What career do you want?
4. If you wanted to improve your hometown, what would you do?
5. If a foreigner came to visit you at your home, how would you entertain him or her?

• 最後再練習一下「描述要做的某件事」最實用的答題模板！

1. Recently I decided to start VERBing...

例 • Recently I decided to start writing a blog.
  • Recently I decided to start making a birdhouse.

2. For example, I might VERB...

例 • For example, I might write about my volunteer job, where I tutor little children.
  • For example, I might help carry out a recycling campaign.

3. I plan to VERB...every day or so.

例 • I plan to post one entry every day or so.
  • I plan to practice yoga every day or so.

4. Because I enjoy..., I will VERB...

例 • Because I enjoy photography, I will post pictures that go with my text.
  • Because I enjoy sports, I will start a basketball club in my school.

5. I believe that the world will be...ten years from now.

例 • I believe that the world will be vastly different ten years from now.
  • I believe that the world will be a better place ten years from now.

6. With global warming, I think that we'll begin to see...

例 • With global warming, I think that we'll begin to see the sea level gradually rise.
  • With global warming, I think that we'll begin to see more flooding.

7. At the same time, I believe that we're VERBing...

例 • At the same time, I believe that we're advancing in technology and medicine.
  • At the same time, I believe that we're working hard to fight pollution.

8. I would not be surprised if, in ten years, we'll have found a(n)...

例 • I would not be surprised if, in ten years, we'll have found a new mode of transportation or a cure for cancer.
  • I would not be surprised if, in ten years, we'll have found a way to provide food to the world's population.

9. I would have to say my dream job is being a(n)...

例 • I would have to say my dream job is being a biologist.

• I would have to say my dream job is being an architect.

10. I enjoy VERBing..., VERBing...and VERBing...

例 • I enjoy traveling, visiting the natural habitats and studying animal species that intrigue me.

• I enjoy sketching, creating models of buildings and designing for interior spaces.

11. And I plan to visit more...in the world during my graduate studies and after I receive my advanced degree.

例 • And I plan to visit more exotic places in the world during my graduate studies and after I receive my advanced degree.

• And I plan to visit more metropolitan areas in the world during my graduate studies and after I receive my advanced degree.

12. This will allow me to continue with my research while VERBing..., which is my other passion in life.

例 • This will allow me to continue with my research while interacting with young, inquisitive minds, which is my other passion in life.

• This will allow me to continue with my research while exploring mountain terrains, which is my other passion in life.

13. If I were to buy a gift, I would give it to...

例 • If I were to buy a gift, I would give it to my boyfriend.

• If I were to buy a gift, I would give it to my grandmother.

14. That's because he's been with me through...—the most difficult period in my life.

例 • That's because he's been with me through thick and thin for the last three years—the most difficult period in my life.

• That's because he's been with me through my high school years—the most difficult period in my life.

15. I can't imagine how I could have VERBed...without him.

例 • I can't imagine how I could have pulled through without him.

• I can't imagine how I could have succeeded without him.

16. If I could afford it, I would buy him...to show him how much I love him.

例 • If I could afford it, I would buy him something special to show him how much I love him.

• If I could afford it, I would buy him a nice watch to show him how much I love him.

5 Describing Something Special in Your Culture
描述本國文化的特色

66 在本章，你將學到…… 99

★如何巧妙利用答題範本，給出個性化的回答
★ s 位於詞尾時的發音

解讀常考題

　　雖然文化並非第一題中的常考情境，但還是會不時地出現，所以要做好準備。考生想必一定非常熟悉自己國家的文化和生活方式，但用英語表達出一些細節還是有難度的。考生要有能力談論本地文化中獨有的飲食習慣、慶祝的節日和國定假日。如果有些事物在英文中已經有了現成的譯法，那麼只要瞭解這些譯法並去使用即可。然而，有些事物，如某些食品和文化習俗等，也許在英文中並不存在完全對應的說法，或者你並不知道這樣的說法。在這些情況下，就可以描述這個物品或這種習俗是怎樣的。如果必要，也可以先用中文說出這個單字，然後立刻用英語對其進行定義。

　　評分人也許對一些特殊的習俗或事物不瞭解，那麼對這些事物要解釋到什麼程度呢？在談論本國文化的某個特別方面時，要使答案相對簡練，不要試圖在 45 秒內解釋清楚太多細碎的概念。說出一個恰當、具體的主題句，緊接著舉出有趣的、容易理解且容易描述的例子就可以了。評分人喜歡聽有關不同國家生活方式的有趣故事。

　　現在，看一道關於文化特色的例題。

▶舉例試題

> **If visitors from another country planned to visit your country, where would you recommend they go? Explain your choice in detail.**
>
> Preparation Time: 15 Seconds
> Response Time: 45 Seconds

托福總監告訴你怎麼答！

　　回答這道題時，先要想出一個能讓外國人感興趣的地方。可以選擇一個著名的旅遊景點，或是一個不那麼著名但是你很喜歡的地方，前提條件是你能夠描述且說清楚那裡為什麼有趣。主要目的是要讓回答有說服力，而且融入自己個人的看法。

策略：不留痕跡套用答題範本

之所以建議你讓回答聽起來盡可能獨具「個性」，原因有很多。評分人已聽過數以百計的回答，對常用的補習班句型早已瞭若指掌。如果他們懷疑某位考生的回答是背誦的，並不能反映考生的真實能力，就很可能會給出低分。實際上，如果情節嚴重，評分人甚至會打出 0 分！相反地，要是聽到十分有趣的回答，涉及的地方或事實稍有與眾不同之處，或者反映了考生的親身感受，評分人就會很開心，因為這樣的回答會給他們無聊的工作增加樂趣。另外，當他們聽到這些個人感受時，會更加確信考生是在描述真實情況，而不是用背的。

當然，很多考生喜歡去背誦一些回答範例或範本，這在一定程度上能讓考生準備得更充分。但即使是套用範本的內容，也應說出「個性化」的回答，讓評分人覺得有趣、真實、值得給高分。

要說出「個性化」的答案，可運用以下策略：

1. 瀏覽練習題目，用英語列出一張單子，包含自己喜愛的人物、場所、事物和想法。如：最喜愛的食品是蝦子、最喜歡遊覽的地方是首爾、最喜歡的電影是《星際大戰》。這是個腦力激盪練習，目的是找出所有自己喜歡的、包含了個人感情和經歷的、又能用英語好好說清楚的事物。
2. 在準備開始練習某個具體題目時，有很多方法可以讓你充分利用實用答題範本。你可以選取幾個範本，套入個性化的內容，創造出屬於自己的新句子，或者參考別人回答範例中的句子，在其中套入自己獨特的內容。當然，你也可以運用本書所推薦的基本原則和策略，完全重新構思自己的回答！
3. 不管用什麼方法，建議你在練習時，用英文將你「個性化」的回答寫下來，然後出聲讀出這些句子，隨時加強記憶。

高分回答

注意看，仔細聽，這裡面標上粗體的地方都要發重音才道地喔！ *Track 021*

If I were **asked** to **give** suggestions about **cities** to **foreign** visitors, **I** would recommend New York City—it is **truly** a **city** that **never** sleeps. **There** are endless things to **do** and **see** all **year** long. **No** matter **what** you're in the **mood** for, **New York has** it. Some **great** restaurants, **hotels** and **shops** are located in this **city**. **I'd** suggest the visitors **start** the day off by **walking** around in **beautiful Central Park, then** have **lunch** downtown in The **Village** and **go** shopping in **Soho**. In the **evening**, they could **go see** a **Broadway** show. **Then**, the **next** day, the visitors could **visit** the **Statue** of Liberty, **walk** around Times **Square** and **maybe** even **see** a **New York Yankees** baseball game. **And**, if they **didn't want** to **spend** a lot of **money**, **New York** is the **perfect city** for **people-watching**.

托福總監為什麼覺得這是高分回答？

　　第一句陳述了這個地方的名字並給它加了個「標籤」，即 it is truly a city that never sleeps。這個標籤為下文打下了基礎，即舉例說明這裡每天從早到晚都有很多事情可以做。隨後的每句話都列舉了訪客們可以進行的活動，使回答顯得非常充實。

　　如果你想依據上面的高分回答來組織自己個性化的回答，例如選擇大連作為推薦城市，可參考下文。進行了個性化加工的部分已用括號 [ ] 括起。

高分回答之個性化改造

If I were asked to give suggestions about cities to foreign visitors, I would recommend [the city of Dalian]—it is truly a city that [is very romantic]. There are endless things to do and see all year long. No matter what you're in the mood for, [Dalian] has it. Some great restaurants, hotels and shops are located in this city. I'd suggest the visitors start the day off by walking around in beautiful [Xinghai Square], then have [a seafood] lunch [nearby] and go shopping in [Zhongshan Square]. In the evening, they could go see [the Dalian Sightseeing Tower]. Then, the next day, the visitors could visit [Binhai Road], walk around [Tiger Beach] and maybe even see a [Dongbei singing and dancing performance]. And, if they didn't want to spend a lot of money, [Dalian] is the perfect city for people-watching.

▶模擬試題①

　　請回答下題。回答時，可嘗試使用下面列出的實用答題範本。

What is the most efficient type of transportation in your country? Include specific examples and details in your explanation.

Preparation Time: 15 Seconds
Response Time: 45 Seconds

實用答題範本　　🎧 *Track 022* 聽聽看！別人的高分回答！（高分回答原文請見 P.278）

...is by far the most efficient transportation in my country.
I can easily get to the suburbs and even small towns outside...

得分考技：我發的詞尾 s 音，你絕對不會誤解！

　　對很多學習英語的人來說，要發好詞尾 s 的發音是有難度的，因為詞尾 s 在不同的情況下發音不同。如果發錯了複數形式中詞尾 s 的音，如 many festivals，評分人會認為你不知道單複數變化的規則；若省略或發錯了動詞的第三人稱單數形式下詞尾的 s，例如將 he talks 説成了 he talk，評分人就會認為你不知道動詞變化的基本規則。因此，正確發出詞尾 s 的發音是非常重要的。

　　位於詞尾的 s、es 以及縮寫形式 's 的發音會因為其跟在不同的音後面而有所變化。以下是三條發音規則：

1. 在以 /t/、/p/、/k/、/f/、/θ/ 等清輔音結尾的詞後，s 發音為 /s/。如：type 變成 types。
2. 在以 /d/、/b/、/g/、/m/、/n/、/w/、/v/、/l/ 等濁輔音結尾的詞後，s 發音為 /z/。如：land 變成 lands。
3. 以 sh、ch、s、z 結尾的詞，變複數或變第三人稱單數形式時詞尾加 es（ge/dge 結尾的詞，詞尾加 s），發音為 /ɪz/。如：resource 變成 resources；teach 變成 teaches。

▶模擬試題②

　　接下來就來練習看看 s 位於詞尾時的發音！我們一起來看看另一道有關本國文化特色的例題。

What custom from your home country do you like the best? Describe the custom and explain why you like it.

Preparation Time: 15 Seconds
Response Time: 45 Seconds

　　下面是一個回答範例，應重讀的部分已用**粗體**標出。注意其中詞尾 s 的發音！

🎧*Track 023*

Many people call **Thailand** the "**land** of **smiles.**" And, as a **Thai,** I **do** think smiling is characteristic of **Thai** people. I **like** this **custom** because I **believe** it **helps make** our society more **peaceful** and **civilized. Generally** speaking, **Thais** are **friendly.** But, in **fact,** a **smile** in **Thailand** can mean **many different things. Smiling** can be **used** to **say** hello or to **thank** someone. But we **also smile** to apologize or to **smooth over** an **awkward** situation. It is **true** that on the **outside** the **Thai** personality is **cheerful,** but **do not** make the **mistake** of **thinking** a **smile always means** that **person** is **happy. If** you **spend time** in Thailand, you will **learn** the **meaning** of **different smiles.**

　　換你試試看了！下面進一步練習詞尾 s 的發音。注意用底線標出的詞，反覆聽錄音，然後跟讀。

🎧*Track 024*

1. If I had **friends** coming from overseas, I'd **suggest** they visit <u>Los Angeles</u>.
2. **My** recommendation to foreign <u>guests</u> would be that they **go** to **several small** <u>towns</u>.
3. In Italy, I think that <u>visitors</u> should definitely **see** the <u>canals</u> of Venice.
4. The **reason** I **believe** visiting Berlin would be **good** <u>is</u> that the **young people there** are **very interesting.**
5. <u>Visitors</u> should **go** to Sydney, **where** there are **great** <u>cafes</u> and amazing <u>beaches</u>.

現在，試試用這一道題目描述你最喜愛的本國習俗吧！

詞尾 s 的正確發音策略

1. 確保掌握三條基本規則，判斷詞尾的 s 發音是 /s/, /z/ 還是 /ɪz/。
2. 聽本書所配的回答範例錄音，注意結尾為 s 的詞，並試著模仿。
3. 詞尾 s 的發音不僅是語音問題，還表示單字的複數形式和第三人稱單數的動詞變化。

不要偷懶！多練習這些發音，直到牢牢掌握為止。你的努力一定會換來考試成績的提升！

▶模擬試題③

請回答下題。回答時，注意詞尾 s 的發音，可嘗試使用下面列出的實用答題範本。

What do you miss most about your home when you are away? Use specific details in your explanation.

Preparation Time: 15 Seconds
Response Time: 45 Seconds

實用答題範本　　🎧 *Track 025* 聽聽看！別人的高分回答！（高分回答原文請見 P.279）

I am from...and what I miss the most is the...

...in...is hard to describe, but if you ever visit, you'll understand.

托福總監幫你預測可能會出現的題目！

1. Describe an important national holiday in your home country.
2. Talk about a popular game or sport that is played in your country.
3. If a foreigner visited your country, how would you entertain him or her?
4. Describe your country's national flag and talk about where it is flown.
5. Describe an important lesson that you learned from your culture.

• **最後再練習一下「描述本國文化特色」最實用的答題模板！**

1. **If I were asked to give suggestions about cities to foreign visitors, I would recommend...—it is truly a city that...**

   例　• If I were asked to give suggestions about cities to foreign visitors, I would recommend New York City—it is truly a city that never sleeps.

   • If I were asked to give suggestions about cities to foreign visitors, I would recommend Paris—it is truly a city that likes to enjoy itself.

2. There are...things to do and see all year long.

例 • There are endless things to do and see all year long.

• There are countless things to do and see all year long.

3. Some great X, Y and Z are located in this city.

例 • Some great restaurants, hotels and shops are located in this city.

• Some great cafes, theaters and museums are located in this city.

4. I'd suggest the visitors start the day off by walking around..., then have lunch in...and go shopping in/on...

例 • I'd suggest the visitors start the day off by walking around in beautiful Central Park, then have lunch downtown in The Village and go shopping in Soho.

• I'd suggest the visitors start the day off by walking around the Bund, then have lunch in a nearby restaurant and go shopping on Nanjing Road.

5. And, if they didn't want to spend a lot of money, ...is the perfect city for people-watching.

例 • And, if they didn't want to spend a lot of money, New York is the perfect city for people-watching.

• And, if they didn't want to spend a lot of money, Seoul is the perfect city for people-watching.

6. ...is by far the most efficient transportation in my country.

例 • The bus is by far the most efficient transportation in my country.

• The subway is by far the most efficient transportation in my country.

7. Most cities have...covering extensive webs of routes.

例 • Most cities have large fleets of city buses covering extensive webs of routes.

• Most cities have beltways covering extensive webs of routes.

8. In the city of..., where I live, you can go literally anywhere by...

例 • In the city of Chengdu, where I live, you can go literally anywhere by bus.

• In the city of Tokyo, where I live, you can go literally anywhere by subway.

9. X can travel...during the rush hour, so at peak traffic times it is actually faster to VERB X than to VERB Y.

例 • Buses can travel in dedicated bus lanes during the rush hour, so at peak traffic times it is actually faster to take a bus than to drive a car.

• Bicycles can travel in dedicated bicycle lanes during the rush hour, so at peak traffic times it is actually faster to ride a bicycle than to drive a car.

10. I can easily get to the suburbs and even small towns outside...

例 • I can easily get to the suburbs and even small towns outside Chengdu.

• I can easily get to the suburbs and even small towns outside London.

11. Many people call...the "land of..."

例 • Many people call Thailand the "land of smiles."

• Many people call Malaysia the "land of festivals."

12. And, as a..., I do think...is characteristic of...people.

例 • And, as a Thai, I do think smiling is characteristic of Thai people.

• And, as a Korean, I do think respect for elders is characteristic of Korean people.

13. Generally speaking, ...are...

例 • Generally speaking, Thais are friendly.

• Generally speaking, French are formal in style.

14. It is true that on the outside...is/are..., but do not make the mistake of thinking...always means...

例 • It is true that on the outside the Thai personality is cheerful, but do not make the mistake of thinking a smile always means that person is happy.

• It is true that on the outside the Japanese are always bowing, but do not make the mistake of thinking bowing always means the same thing.

15. If you spend time in..., you will learn the meaning of...

例 • If you spend time in Thailand, you will learn the meaning of different smiles.

• If you spend time in Sweden, you will learn the meaning of "lagom," or "everything in moderation."

16. I am from...and what I miss the most is the...

例 • I am from Italy and what I miss the most is the little cafes.

• I am from Hong Kong and what I miss the most is the dim sum.

17. ...in...is hard to describe, but if you ever visit, you'll understand.

例 • Cafe culture in Italy is hard to describe, but if you ever visit, you'll understand.

• Walking down the street in Hanoi is hard to describe, but if you ever visit, you'll understand.

18. The...is always very friendly.

例 • The waiter behind the counter is always very friendly.

• The taxi driver is always very friendly.

• The street merchant is always very friendly.

19. Although there are...in many countries, they can't compare with X's...

例 • Although there are coffee shops in many countries, they can't compare with Italy's cafes.

• Although there are noodle shops in many countries, they can't compare with Japan's udon.

6 Describing a Thing That Has Profoundly Affected You
描述對你影響深遠的某物

66 在本章，你將學到…… 99

★如何描述不同的物品
★如何熟練使用形式主詞，給考官留下深刻的印象

解讀常考題

第一題有時會讓考生描述某件物品，這類常見話題看似容易，實際上卻相當有難度。當題目要求描述對你有特殊意義的某物時，你需要做三件事：
1. 簡要描述這件物品
2. 描述對這件物品的感受
3. 給出理由或例子來説明為什麼會有這樣的感受

即使是用母語，描述自己的感受也並非易事。描述如手錶、自行車這類的實體事物，或電影、圖書一類的藝術作品的特質，也需要技巧。要回答這類問題，最好的方法是生動勾勒出這件物品的形象，讓評分人能夠想像出來，如：The quilt had very bright colors and was full of memories. 然後，解釋為什麼這條被子對你來說很重要。如：I treasure that quilt because I inherited it from my grandmother.

現在，看一道關於描述有重要意義的物品的例題。

▶舉例試題

Describe the object that is the most important to you and explain how you received it. Using details and examples, explain why it is important.

Preparation Time: 15 Seconds
Response Time: 45 Seconds

托福總監告訴你怎麼答！

這道題不僅要求考生描述一件物體並說明它的意義，還要求說明是怎樣得到這件物品的。所以，考生在回答時就需要使用多種動詞時態，包括：現在式、一般過去式和過去完成式等。

策略：描述「物」的三招

　　你選擇描述的物件可能是一件實物，如一輛競賽用自行車；也可能是一件作品，如一本書或者一件雕塑。根據物件不同，需在描述中用到特定的語言結構及詞彙。描述一件實物時，要用描述有形物體的形容詞。具體來説，有兩種方式，即簡要列舉其組成部分，或描述其功能，如：

描述組成部分的説法
1. My bicycle has low handlebars, a racing seat and narrow tires.
2. My bicycle consists of low handlebars, a racing seat and narrow tires.
3. My bicycle includes low handlebars, a racing seat and narrow tires.

描述功能的説法：
1. My bicycle is able to go 45 miles per hour.
2. My bicycle can go 45 miles per hour.
3. My bicycle is used for going 45 miles per hour.

　　描述文藝作品等物時，則要使用不同的描述語言，包括很多抽象的形容詞和副詞，如：

書籍	音樂	藝術品	玩具
is moving	is very dramatic	has simple elegance	is fun to play with
is poignant	has a good beat	is very unique	brings back memories
is thought-provoking	has a beautiful melody	has flowing lines	is very cute
has a good plot	has rich harmonies	has bold colors	is an antique
has convincing characters	is rhythmically complex	has an interesting texture	was made by my father

高分回答

 Track 026

As far as **prized** possessions go, **old** family **photos** are **probably** the **most** important **things** I **have. These** photos **go back** several generations, as **far** as my **great** grandparents. **Some** of the **photos** are **framed** and **hang** on the **wall.**（←描寫照片形態）
These include wedding photos and family **portraits.** Other **photos,** the **smaller ones,** are **contained** in photo **albums.**（←描寫照片大小和形態）
Some of the **pictures** in the **albums show** my **grand**parents when they were **little children.** It's **amazing** to **see** the **clothes** they **wore,** especially the **women's styles,** with the **big hats** and **long dresses. These** photos have been **passed down** to **each** generation, and if **something** happened to them, they **couldn't be** replaced. At **some** point, I **need** to **digitize** these **photos** to **protect** them.

托福總監為什麼覺得這是高分回答？

　　該考生第一句立刻說出自己擁有的最重要的東西：old family photos，由此可推斷該考生可能從家人那裡獲得了這些照片，這一點隨後也得到了證實。注意對照片形態的描述如何運用到現在時態和被動語態：...are framed 和 ...are contained in photo albums。對有些細節還做出了非常詳細的描述，如：especially the women's styles, with the big hats and long dresses。還要注意最後兩句怎樣表現出濃重的個人色彩。這樣的句子不僅有助於將回答個性化，也可作為一個很好的收尾。

要描述好對你有深遠影響的某物，可運用以下策略：

1. 要以一個突出且意思清晰的主題句開頭，說明這件物品是什麼。
2. 根據描述物件的不同（有時是有形物體，有時是帶有精神文化價值的作品），使用的修飾語應不同。
3. 描述有形物體時，常用具體的語言來描述其構成和功能；描述文藝作品時，則常會用抽象的修飾語。
4. 由於描述物品具有難度，上策就是提供很多關於這件物品和你個人感受的細節，但使用的文法結構要簡練。如：The shiny seat of my racing bike makes me very happy.

▶ 模擬試題①

　　請回答下題。回答時，可嘗試使用下面列出的實用答題範本。

Describe the characteristics that you think a house or apartment should have. Include specific examples and details in your explanation.

Preparation Time: 15 Seconds
Response Time: 45 Seconds

實用答題範本　　🎧 *Track 027* 聽聽看！別人的高分回答！（高分回答原文請見 P.279）

Two things are important to me when it comes to...
The second important thing is that...needs to be...

得分考技：形式主詞大妙用

　　多數學生在學習英語的過程中都學習過形式主詞。帶有形式主詞的句型並不難掌握，它們可以與不定詞或子句連用。兩種基本結構如下頁表格所示：

結構	It + be 動詞	There + be 動詞
例句	It is hard to describe my favorite thing.	There are many reasons why I love my laptop computer.
	It is true that *Gone with the Wind* is popular all over the world.	There seems to be something special about that cafe.
	It is said that The Beatles practiced a lot together before they were famous.	There is no doubt that Cao Xueqin was a great writer.

奇怪的是，不知道為什麼，大多數考生在回答中都不使用形式主詞。這就表示，如果你是新托福口語考試中為數不多的能熟練使用這些結構的考生，就會給評分人留下一個深刻且正面的印象。

很多老師都警告考生寫作中不要頻繁地使用形式主詞結構。但在口語中，這一結構卻有很多優點。

優點 1：形式主詞結構很適合用來講故事，如：It was two years ago that I received the diary from my mother. 這句話可以很順地接到下一句，就是形式主詞的功勞。

優點 2：形式主詞結構在口語中能夠強調特定的事物，如：It is Beethoven's *Fifth Symphony* that has most influenced me.

優點 3：形式主詞結構能總結他人觀點和想法的有效方式，如：It is clear that the man does not like the new plan. 這種用法在回答口語考試第三題時尤其好用。

▶模擬試題②

接下來就來練習使用形式主詞！先看一道關於對你影響深遠的事物的例題。

Describe a painting or piece of music that has profoundly influenced you. Explain why the work is important to you.

Preparation Time: 15 Seconds
Response Time: 45 Seconds

下面是一個回答範例，應重讀的部分已用**粗體標出**。注意畫線句子如何恰到好處地使用了形式主詞。

🎧 *Track 028*

The **musical** **work** that has **left** the **strongest** im**pression** on me is **Mozart's** **opera**, *The Marriage of Figaro*. I **love** this **opera** because the **music** is **very** di**verse**, **ranging** from **fast** to **slow**, and **comical** to **dramatic**. The **plot** in**volves** a **Count** who is pursuing a **maid** in his **house**, to his **wife's** dis**may**. It is a**mazing** how the **melody** in **each solo** aria re**flects** **each** cha**racter's** personality. And I am **always** **moved** by the **harmonies** in the en**semble** **pieces**, be**cause** they're **timed** at dramatic **moments** in the **story**. I **listen** to *the Marriage of Figaro* **again** and a**gain** be**cause** of this and be**cause** it **has** a **happy** **ending**. It has **caused me** to be**come** more **interested** in **Mozart** and in **other** **operas**.

聽聽看下列句子，練習形式主詞結構。反覆聽錄音，然後跟著讀。 *Track 029*

1. It's **obvious** that **sports** magazines are **popular** among **men**.
2. **There** are **several** features that I **like** about the **sculpture**.
3. It's **too bad I'm so busy**; otherwise I'd **play chess all day long**.
4. **There's no doubt** that I'm **somewhat** addicted to **video games**.
5. It is **said** that the **best** restaurants are the **ones located** in hotels.

現在，自己練習回答這道題吧！注意有效使用形式主詞。

掌握形式主詞結構，可運用以下策略：

1. 複習形式主詞的文法結構，包括與不定詞或子句連接的結構。
2. 記住幾個最常見的形式主詞句型，例如上頁列出的幾個。加入和自己親身經歷有關的詞彙，讓這些句子變得個性化。反覆朗讀這些屬於你自己的句子，直到可以脫口而出為止。
3. 每次做口語練習題時，使用一個形式主詞的句子。問問自己：這句話是否自然？如果不自然，看看本書提供的例句和回答範例，尋找好的示範，然後修改原先寫的句子。

▶ 模擬試題③

請回答下題。回答時，注意使用形式主詞句型，可嘗試使用下面列出的實用答題範本。

What resource has helped you to do something better than before? Use specific details in your explanation.

Preparation Time: 15 Seconds
Response Time: 45 Seconds

實用答題範本　　*Track 030*　聽聽看！別人的高分回答！（高分回答原文請見 P.279）

...is the resource that has helped me the most.
I also rely heavily on...to VERB...

托福總監幫你預測可能會出現的題目！

1. What kind of film do you like most?
2. Describe the features of a cafe or restaurant that you like.
3. Which kind of magazine do you like the most?
4. Describe your favorite toy or game.
5. Talk about a book that is important to you.

•最後再練習一下「描述對你影響深遠的某物」最實用的答題模板！

1. As far as prized possessions go, ...are probably the most important things I have.

例 • As far as prized possessions go, old family photos are probably the most important things I have.

• As far as prized possessions go, old letters that my parents wrote to each other are probably the most important things I have.

2. Some of the...are framed and hang on the wall.

例 • Some of the photos are framed and hang on the wall.

• Some of the paintings are framed and hang on the wall.

3. These...have been passed down to each generation, and if something happened to them, they couldn't be replaced.

例 • These photos have been passed down to each generation, and if something happened to them, they couldn't be replaced.

• These heirlooms have been passed down to each generation, and if something happened to them, they couldn't be replaced.

4. Two things are important to me when it comes to...

例 • Two things are important to me when it comes to my place of residence.

• Two things are important to me when it comes to movies.

5. First is the...

例 • First is the view.

• First is the author's use of language.

6. If it's...we're talking about, preferably it should have..., so when I VERB...I can VERB..., or maybe even VERB...

例 • If it's a house we're talking about, preferably it should have a nice yard, so when I look out the window I can enjoy the view of trees and flowers, or maybe even watch birds flying around.

• If it's a short story we're talking about, preferably it should have a good plot, so when I read it I can immerse myself in the story, or maybe even imagine myself as the main character.

7. The second important thing is that...needs to be...

例 • The second important thing is that the neighborhood needs to be quiet.

• The second important thing is that the tune needs to be catchy.

8. The musical work that has left the strongest impression on me is...

例 • The musical work that has left the strongest impression on me is Mozart's opera, *The Marriage of Figaro*.

• The musical work that has left the strongest impression on me is *Yesterday* by the Beatles.

8. I love this...because the...is very diverse, ranging from...to..., and...to...

例 • I love this opera because the music is very diverse, ranging from fast to slow, and comical to dramatic.

• I love this watercolor because the color is very diverse, ranging from blues to reds, and grays to blacks.

10. And I am always moved by the...in..., because they're...

例 • And I am always moved by the harmonies in the ensemble pieces, because they're timed at dramatic moments in the story.

• And I am always moved by the words in the music, because they're so simple and true.

11. It has caused me to become more interested in...and in other...

例 • It has caused me to become more interested in Mozart and in other operas.

• It has caused me to become more interested in Picasso and in other oil paintings.

12. ...is the resource that has helped me the most.

例 • The Internet is the resource that has helped me the most.

• The online dictionary is the resource that has helped me the most.

13. I used to spend a great deal of time at..., VERBing...

例 • I used to spend a great deal of time at the school library, poring over the few reference books in the school's collection.

• I used to spend a great deal of time at my friend's house, borrowing his exercise equipment.

14. Now I wonder how I ever lived without...

例 • Now I wonder how I ever lived without the Internet.

• Now I wonder how I ever lived without a washing machine.

15. I also rely heavily on...to VERB...

例 • I also rely heavily on chat software to stay in touch with friends and family.

• I also rely heavily on my cellphone to check on the weather.

Task 2 ▸ Paired Choice

第二題 二選一

　　口語考試的第二題會給考生兩個選擇，要求從中選擇其一。考生必須通過論述理由和舉例來解釋為什麼選這一項。從語言上講，第二題涉及的文法和邏輯比第一題要略微複雜，故難度也略有增加。

▶提問形式

　　第二題會以幾種不同形式提問，下面根據在新托福考試中出現頻率由高到低依次列舉：

1. Some people like to A. Other people like to B. Which of these do you prefer? Why?
2. Do you agree or disagree with the following statement? People should A. Why do you feel this way?
3. Many people A. Why do you think they A?
4. Do A work better than B? Why?

　　實際上，第二題的問題多以上面第一種或第二種形式出現。

　　考生在陳述自己的選擇時，只要說明所選項的優點即可，但是有時需要將兩項做一個對比，並闡釋你為什麼更偏愛其中的一項。你的回答可以簡單地以 yes 或 no 來開頭，然後再解釋你同意與否的理由。但不管具體問題是什麼，在回答第二題時，你都需要說明你的選擇並給出理由。在說明理由時，你可以使用說明「狀態」或「想法」的句子，如：I think that A is good because... 或者 ...and that is why I agree that... 在某些情況下，你可能還要用到虛擬語氣，如：If I had the choice to A or B, I would choose to A. 或者 A would be better if...

▶考官會怎麼評分？

　　第二題和第一題一樣，都是以日常話題為內容的「獨立型」題目，但第二題的問題相對較短。考生有 15 秒鐘的準備時間來構思，也許能寫下一兩個單字。同樣，回答問題的時間也是 45 秒鐘。像第一題的回答一樣，第二題的回答也會根據三個標準來給分：1）是否易使人理解；2）語言運用的品質；3）觀點表達的連貫程度。

▶第二題的六個主要情境

　　第二題的話題通常較為容易，不需要考生使用難度很大的詞彙。如：兒童是否應該參與體育運動？你比較喜歡聽收音機還是看電視？如果你的回答明白易懂、有條理，就可以得到最高分。然而，要想流利地談論第二題的話題，理解會出現的情境是非常重要的。

　　第二題中最常見的情境可分為六類：

1. 交流與媒體
2. 餐飲、旅行和藝術
3. 職業與金錢
4. 教育（初等和中等教育）
5. 教育（大學）
6. 生活中的抉擇和經驗教訓

　　接下來的章節會分別講解以上每一種情境，並提供多道題目、回答範例和相關的實用答題範本。通過在情境中練習這些題目，你可以更容易地記住考試中會用到的詞語。

Communication and the Media 交流與媒體

在本章，你將學到……

★ 如何組織第二題的答題思路
★ 如何使用縮寫形式讓口語表達更自然

解讀常考題

第二題中非常典型的話題就是交流和媒體。在這一情境中，你可能會被問到關於該不該聽家人的話？比較喜歡打電話還是面對面聊天？等等的問題。也可能必須回應某個說法，如：電視對兒童的影響、使用手機的合適時間等。第二題中關於交流與媒體的主題其實都很類似，可能只是在提問形式上稍稍有不點同而已。

現在，看一道關於交流的例題。

▶ 舉例試題

When far away from each other, some people prefer to communicate with family and friends by letters and e-mail. Others prefer the telephone. Which do you think is better?
Include details and examples in your explanation.

Preparation Time: 15 Seconds
Response Time: 45 Seconds

托福總監告訴你怎麼答！

這道題是第二題中最常見的形式，考生必須決定自己支持哪一種觀點。記住，想在第二題中獲得高分，需要做好以下方面：表達能力（包括發音）、詞語運用（包括對語塊和實用答題範本的自然運用）、話題的展開（句子的銜接必須流暢自然）。本書提供的策略以及練習題一定會幫助你在這三個方面增強能力！

策略：第二題的答題思路

這題的構思需要三個簡單的步驟：
1. 迅速確定你偏好的交流方式：寫信或電子郵件，還是打電話。
2. 思考你要說什麼，理由是什麼。快速寫下一兩個單字。

3. 給出一個強有力的主題句表明立場，通過舉例和論述原因來論證。

在第一步，你應該迅速做出選擇：寫信或電子郵件，還是打電話？明智的做法是給出一個簡單的答案。不要回答說：這兩種交流方式你都會用到，因為你喜歡電話帶來的貼近感，同時也喜歡信或電子郵件，因為能反覆閱讀上面的文字。

為什麼不要這樣做呢？至少有三個理由。首先，你只有 45 秒的答題時間，其間要給出堅實的主題句然後通過論證支持自己的觀點。如果試圖論證兩方的優點，就可能面臨問題：兩方面都說得很籠統，而且時間不夠用。其次，對於一個母語非英語的人來說，要在短時間內很有說服力地闡明兩方的相對優點，是非常有難度的，你這是在給自己出難題。這樣一來，你出現文法錯誤或前後不連貫的機率就會增加。還有，評分人不會因為你從兩方面進行論證就給出比較高的分數。因此，選擇更容易闡述的一方更有益。你在做出選擇時，不一定非得實話實說。這是在考英文，不是在測謊！所以說謊也沒關係，選擇你能夠流利、清晰並連貫闡述的觀點就對了。

接下來要準備作答內容了。15 秒的準備時間並不長，你也許只能寫下一兩個單字或者一個語塊。如：可以寫下 phone、very busy 和 voice 作為答題思路。即使不做任何筆記，在短暫的準備時間裡你也必須思考支持觀點的理由和要舉的例子有哪些。至少要想好怎樣開頭、想好第一條理由是什麼。

高分回答
 Track 031

As **much** as I **love** to **hear** a **friendly voice** over the **phone**, I **truly** believe that the **best** way to communicate with **my family** and **friends** is through **e**-mail and **mes**saging.（←迅速表明立場）
I **love** using **e**-mail to **stay** in **touch** for a **lot** of **rea**sons. **E**-mail is convenient because **people** can **read** it whenever they have **time**. And it's **great** to be able to **send** along **photos** and other **attach**ments.（←說明理由，支持立場）
Last week, for **exam**ple, **I** sent my **class**mates a **fun picture** of me at the **zoo**, standing in **front** of a **giraffe**.（←舉例，論證理由）
Of **course**, I **enjoy phone** calls **too**, but **e**-mail is definitely my **preference**.

托福總監為什麼覺得這是高分回答？

　　注意該考生怎樣在第一句話中迅速且清晰地表達了立場。考生還這樣歸納了問題中的選擇：As much as I love to hear a friendly voice over the phone... 在第二句開始，考生給出了兩個理由：方便，且可以發送照片。在動物園拍照的例子用來說明第二個理由。在最後一句話中，考生重申了要點：發電子郵件是他最喜歡的交流方式。通過 Of course, I enjoy phone calls too... 這句話，考生總結了整個回答，順便很簡練地提及了問題所給的選擇（e-mail/letter 還是 telephone），但沒有真正去論證電話的優點。

要答好第二題中有關人際交流的問題，可運用以下策略：

1. 迅速判斷第二題提問的形式（上題是第一種，也是最典型的形式：Some people...）。然後快速決定你比較喜歡的交流方式：by letter and e-mail, or by telephone。
2. 利用這 15 秒去思考第一句話怎麼說、支持觀點的理由有哪些。如果必要，可以快速寫下一兩個單字。
3. 在回答時，說出一個強有力的主題句，這個主題句要能清楚表明你的立場，同時又能提及問題中的選項。例如：Given a choice between writing letters and talking on the phone, I prefer to write letters.
4. 不要試圖兩種選擇都論證。
5. 至少用兩個理由支持你的選擇。在說到交流溝通的話題時，理由可以是：convenience, maintaining a close relationship with someone, being able to express your feelings 等。
6. 試著舉出至少一個相關例子，如有可能，從你的個人經歷中舉例。例如：Last week, for example, I sent my classmates a fun picture of me at the zoo.
7. 說說交流活動或交流方式對你有怎樣的影響。可以解釋一下打電話會讓你產生怎樣的感受，例如：happy、at ease；或寫電子郵件怎樣改變了你的生活方式，例如：I can stay connected with people all over the world.

▶ 模擬試題①

請回答下題。回答時，可嘗試使用下面列出的實用答題範本。

Some people believe that a person should not give advice to friends because the friendship will be harmed. Do you agree with this view? Include details and examples in your answer.

Preparation Time: 15 Seconds
Response Time: 45 Seconds

實用答題範本　　🎧 *Track 032* 聽聽看！別人的高分回答！（高分回答原文請見 P.279）

In general, I don't think it's a good idea to VERB...
No matter how close the friend is, ...

得分考技：得心應手用縮寫

　　在新托福考試中，考生會在聽、說、讀、寫四個部分遇到不同類型的英語。總括來說，考生在考試中聽到的口語會相對非正式些，比較像是交談（雖然一些講座或者小型講座可能會包含一些較為學術的語言）。在回答口語題時，你也可以使用非正式的會話式口語。要想說得自然，其中一個要點就是能得心應手地運用詞語的縮寫形式。

　　在口語考試的第一題和第二題中，當我們在談論日常話題時，使用如 wouldn't 這樣的縮寫形式是完全合適的，例如：I wouldn't want to give advice to a good friend. 又如 she's：She's my closest friend, so I give her advice. 使用縮寫形式也很合適；再例如

there's：There's a chance she might get angry. 和 should've：My friend should've... 另外常用的縮寫形式還有 That's 及 It's 等。

　　然而，不要使用俚語或者其他例如 gonna 這樣的口語體表達。同樣，要記住：不要在學術或其他正式體裁的寫作中使用俚語和縮寫形式，包括新托福考試的寫作部分。

　　下面是一些可以在托福口語考試中使用的縮寫形式：

I will → I'll	You will → You'll	He will → He'll	She will → She'll	They will → They'll	We will → We'll
I have → I've	You have → You've	He has → He's	She has → She's	They have → They've	We have → We've
I had → I'd	You had → You'd	He had → He'd	She had → She'd	They had → They'd	We had → We'd
I am → I'm	You are → You're	He is → He's	She is → She's	They are → They're	We are → We're

could have → could've	would have → would've	should have → should've	might have → might've

There is → There's	That is → That's	It is → It's

托福總監帶你練

聽聽看下列例句，練習判斷哪些是縮寫形式。反覆聽錄音，然後跟讀。 *Track 033*

1. If I **hadn't watched** so much **TV** as a **child**, I **would**'ve been **much healthier**.
2. Be**cause** there are **so** many **cable** channels **now**adays, it's **good** to **watch TV** for **learning**.
3. If I'd **given** my **friend** ad**vice** about his **girl**friend, **he'd** have been of**fended**.
4. **It's difficult** to **say which** is **more** important—the **ra**dio or the **tel**evision. They're **both** important, **but** the **im**pact of **tel**evision seems to be **growing**.
5. **Talking loudly** on a **cellphone** is an annoying **habit**. **That's why** I think **people** should **not** be allowed to use **cellphones** in **certain public places**.

▶模擬試題②

> **Some people believe that television has benefited society. Others believe it has harmed society. Which view do you agree with and why? Use details and examples to explain your opinion.**
>
> Preparation Time: 15 Seconds
> Response Time: 45 Seconds

下面是一個回答範例，應重讀的部分已用**粗體**標出。注意畫線部分如何自然運用了縮寫。

 Track 034

> 　　In **my** o**pin**ion, **tel**evision does more **harm** to society than **good**. To be **sure**, we're **often** enter**tained** and **educated** by **some TV** programs; but in **gen**eral, the

effect is **damaging**. For **one** thing, **w**atching **television** keeps us from doing **many** other things that are **more** worth**while**, whether it's **doing physical exercise** or **reading good books**. Another way that we're **harmed** by **TV** is through the **negative influence** of **violent programs** and **advertising**. **Young** people are **particularly susceptible** to **advertising**. For **all** of these **reasons**, I believe that, overall, **television** has **had** a **negative influence** on society.

現在，自己練一練這道題目，說說你對電視的看法。試著使用縮寫形式。

• 想在口語考試中正確使用縮寫形式，可運用以下策略：

1. 說話時放輕鬆。
2. 大聲朗讀上頁表格中列出的縮寫形式，這樣會讓你更加確信自己的講話清晰易懂。
3. 使用合適的縮寫形式（即上表中列出的那些），而不要使用 gonna 或 wanna 這樣的俚語形式。評分人會認為在考試中使用俚語既不符合標準也不合適。
4. 注意，縮寫形式很少會是重音，而緊隨其後的動詞或形容詞通常才是重音。例如：**Another way that we're harmed by TV...** 這就表示需要將詞語分組，以「組」為單位進行練習，例如：將 **we're harmed** 作為一個單位，以此來確保重音的位置是對的。
5. 不必為了獲得高分就非要使用縮寫形式不可。但如果你可以在回答中自然而清楚地使用幾個這樣的形式，評分人很可能會給出較正面的評價：這是因為他們習慣於在日常生活中聽到這樣的講話方式。

▶模擬試題③

請回答下題。回答時，可嘗試使用下面列出的實用答題範本，並練習使用恰當的縮寫形式。

Do you agree or disagree with the following statement? Students should not be allowed to take mobile phones into the classroom. Explain your reasons by using specific details.

Preparation Time: 15 Seconds
Response Time: 45 Seconds

實用答題範本　　　🎧 *Track 035* 聽聽看！別人的高分回答！（高分回答原文請見 P.279）

I disagree with the statement that...
My reasons are as follows: First, students need to VERB...

托福總監幫你預測可能會出現的題目！

1. Some people think that children should be permitted to watch whatever television programs they want to. Others think parents should control the television programs their children watch. Which view do you agree with? Explain why.
2. Do you agree or disagree that people should always tell the truth? Please give detailed reasons.
3. Some people say that advertisements make us buy things we don't need. Others say that advertisements improve our lives by telling us about new products. Which view do you agree with? Use specific reasons and examples to support your answer.
4. Do you agree or disagree with the following statement? Television has reduced friends and family communication. Use specific reasons and examples to support your opinion.
5. When famous people such as actors, athletes and singers give their opinions, many people listen. Do you think their opinions are important? Give specific reasons and examples.

• 最後再練習一下「描述交流」最實用的答題模板！

1. I like to express myself...

例　• I like to express myself in writing.

　　• I like to express myself on the phone.

2. I have trouble expressing myself…

例　• I have trouble expressing myself on the phone.

3. As much as I love to VERB..., I prefer to VERB...

例　• As much as I love to talk on the phone, I prefer to send text messages.

4. The best way to communicate with...is through...

例　• The best way to communicate with my family and friends is through e-mail and messaging.

　　• The best way to communicate with my family is through the telephone.

5. Of course, I enjoy...too, but...is definitely my preference.

例　• Of course, I enjoy phone calls too, but e-mail is definitely my preference.

6. That's why I VERB...

例　• That's why I send e-mails.

7. In general, I don't think it's a good idea to VERB...

例 • In general, I don't think it's a good idea to give advice to friends, even if we have good intentions.

• In general, I don't think it's a good idea to write e-mails.

8. No matter how close the friend is, ...

例 • No matter how close the friend is, there's a chance that he or she will take our advice the wrong way.

• No matter how close the friend is, I don't want to interfere.

9. I only give advice to...when...

例 • I only give advice to my best friend when she asks for it.

10. To be sure, we're often VERBed by...

例 • To be sure, we're often entertained and educated by some TV programs.

11. For one thing, ...keeps us from VERBing...

例 • For one thing, watching television keeps us from doing many other things that are more worthwhile.

• For one thing, watching television keeps us from exercising.

12. Another way that we're harmed by TV is through...

例 • Another way that we're harmed by TV is through the negative influence of violent programs and advertising.

• Another way that we're harmed by TV is through violent programs.

13. I believe that, overall, television has had a...influence on society.

例 • I believe that, overall, television has had a negative influence on society.

• I believe that, overall, television has had a beneficial influence on society.

14. I disagree with the statement that...

例 • I disagree with the statement that students shouldn't be allowed to use phones in class.

• I disagree with the statement that the Internet has a negative impact.

15. My reasons are as follows: First, students need to VERB...

例 • My reasons are as follows: First, students need to check their messages between classes.

• My reasons are as follows: First, students need to communicate frequently.

8 Food, Travel and the Arts
餐飲、旅行和藝術

在本章，你將學到……

★第二題如何記筆記
★「二選一」時用哪些文法結構會得高分

解讀常考題

　　餐飲、旅行和藝術是第二道題目的常考情境。這世上人人都要吃飯，基本上每個人也都很享受用餐時間。所以，餐飲和餐館成為第二題中如此常見的情境也不足為奇了。

　　另一個廣受歡迎的活動就是旅行。閒暇時人們都喜歡旅行，即使有時受到日程或預算的制約，不能去很遙遠的地方。因為人們總夢想著去這裡或那裡旅行，所以第二題經常會問考生喜歡的旅遊目的地，甚至是旅行的方式。

　　藝術囊括了各種各樣的音樂、戲劇、電影和繪畫，也是第二題中較為典型的情境。這類題目可能會問考生比較喜歡古典音樂還是流行音樂，也可能會問考生比較喜歡獨自去聽一場演唱會還是和朋友結伴同行。

　　這三個常考情境答起來通常不難，因為這些都是大眾喜愛的活動。儘管如此，要想在這些問題上獲得高分，就要能夠準確回答題目所問的特定問題。另外還需要多加練習，掌握的相關詞彙和知識越多，在考試中的發揮就會越好。

　　現在，看一道關於餐飲的例題。

▶舉例試題

In modern times, food has become easier to prepare. Has this change made our lives better? Use specific reasons and examples in your explanation.

Preparation Time: 15 Seconds
Response Time: 45 Seconds

托福總監告訴你怎麼答！

　　這道例題的重點是食物的烹飪。具體來講，就是要問丟入微波爐或開水中就能做好的冷凍食品和微波食品，對我們的健康有好處嗎？考生需要列舉一兩個冷凍（或微波）食品的例子，然後論證它們有沒有改善人們的生活。如果只選擇一種食物作為例子，則可能需要說出更多的理由，說明其為什麼改善了或沒有改善人們的生活。

策略：第二題記筆記的訣竅

　　和第一題相比，第二題記筆記比較重要一些，考生可以利用自己記的筆記來組織思路，保持鎮靜，回答得是否出色有時就取決於筆記內容！

　　和第一題一樣，第二題也只有 15 秒準備作答時間。這幾秒鐘稍縱即逝，所以需要迅速抉擇，從兩種觀點中選出一種。選擇的應該是最好回答的觀點或說法，不一定要代表你真正的想法。在做筆記時，可寫單字也可縮寫，以幫助自己集中思路，說出正確的英文。如果時間允許，可用縮寫記下不選另外一種觀點或說法的理由。就像之前曾說過的，每個考生都有不同的筆記風格，你需要不斷練習，找到最適合自己的方法。

　　在為第二題做筆記時，注意下面幾點：

　　1. 寫下一個單字或者縮寫表明話題。

　　2. 寫下幾個單字或縮寫，表示要舉哪些例子來支持觀點。

　　3. 若時間允許，寫下一個句型或連接詞將上面某些內容聯繫起來，例如：To be sure, good food...

高分回答

注意看，仔細聽，這裡面標上**粗體**的地方都要發重音才道地喔！　　*Track 036*

Certainly, we **benefit** from **food** that is **easier** for us to pre**pare**. We can **save** a **lot** of **time**, which can be **spent** on **many** other interesting activities that **modern life affords** us. **One** good example is instant **noodles**. We **simply pour** some **hot** water into a **cup** or a **bowl** of instant **noodles** and, in a **matter** of minutes, we can enjoy a **meal** of **steamy** and **tasty** noodles. **This** is **perfect** when we **don't** have **time** to **cook** at **home** or when we **can't find** a **kitchen** while traveling. To be **sure, good food still** has to be **prepared** the **old-fashioned** way. But **how many** of us **need** to have a **banquet** every **day**? In **my** opinion, **saving time** is a **lot more** important in our **quick-paced modern life**.

托福總監為什麼覺得這是高分回答？

　　分析一下以上回答，看看怎樣的筆記能組織出這樣嚴密的回答。第一句簡明回答了題目所問的 Has this change made our lives better? 接著第二句解釋了冷凍、微波食品怎樣讓我們獲益：save a lot of time。第三句舉了一個例子：instant noodles（泡麵），接下來則解釋了泡麵的烹調過程及所需時間。這是一個非常有說服力的論據，尤其他還將麵條描述得非常美味！接下來的一句起到了很好的銜接作用：This is perfect when... 將泡麵與前述觀點（微波、冷凍食品的好處是省時）聯繫起來。然後，又從反面論證，先承認微波、冷凍食品的品質確實比不上傳統方式烹調的食物，但又用反問質疑，難道要每天舉行宴會嗎？最後一句用不同的措辭重申了開始的主題句。

15 秒內，可以記下下列單字及縮寫：

benefit
inst noodles
save time
≠ banquet

這些筆記非常簡短，但你自己看得懂就好。≠ 意為「不等於」，表示後面這個詞是個反證。換言之，instant noodles 不等於 banquets。據此符號，考生就知道接下來該説：微波、冷凍食品雖品質欠佳，但做起來省時省力。通過筆記搭出「框架」，並記下 benefit、instant noodles 等關鍵字，你就可以更專注地回答，也能掌握好答題時間。

想在答第二題時做好筆記，可運用以下策略：

1. 儘量使用英文單字或縮寫。這樣在作答時，就不必再進行翻譯了。
2. 追求廣度，莫追求深度。用一個詞代表一句話都算多了。
3. 將筆記上的單字和片語作為記憶提示詞。這些詞能夠給你提示，告訴你下一步朝哪裡走。
4. 儘量寫下表示兩個例子或理由的單字。如果時間有限，至少寫下一個。
5. 如果要從反面論證（不一定要），就可以使用反證符號。例如：≠（不一定要用這個符號，也可以使用其他符號，自己知道是「反證」的意思就好）。「≠ banquet」表示 Instant noodles are, of course, not the same as a banquet.

▶ 模擬試題①

請回答下題。回答時，可嘗試使用下面列出的實用答題範本。

When taking a vacation, some people prefer to travel directly to the end destination; other people like to stop at places along the way. Which do you prefer? Include details and examples in your explanation.

Preparation Time: 15 Seconds
Response Time: 45 Seconds

實用答題範本　🎧 *Track 037* 聽聽看！別人的高分回答！（高分回答原文請見 P.280）

That is why my favorite trip was when I VERBed...
We took our time, VERBing through...scenic landscapes, exploring...

得分考技：「比較句先行」的文法

想在第二題中表現出色，學會用英文作比較是很重要的。這種「你比較支持哪種説法或觀點」的問題本質上就是比較選項：你比較傾向哪種？哪種比較好？為什麼？因此，會比較的考生可以説出非常精彩的觀點和論證，但如果沒有掌握作比較時需用的文法結構，就會非常難拿高分。

比較兩種說法或觀點時，應遵循一些重要規則：

1. 單音節形容詞和副詞的比較級形式是詞尾加 -er。如：

The café on the corner is large. My favorite café, across town, is larger.

2. 以 y 結尾的雙音節形容詞和副詞的比較級形式是變 y 為 i，後面再加 er。如：

The food I make at home is healthy. But the food my mother makes is healthier.

3. 一般來說，多音節的形容詞和副詞的比較級形式不是在詞尾加 -er（除上面第二條規則所述情況外），而是在基本形式之前加 more 或 less，之後加 than 構成比較級。如：

Traveling around in my native country is exciting. Of course, traveling abroad is more exciting. Touring my own city is, for me, less exciting.

托福總監帶你練

聽下列例句，練習使用比較句。反覆聽錄音，然後跟著讀。 Track 038

1. I feel that nutritious eating is more important than convenience.
2. Taking a vacation in a city is more attractive to me.
3. Comedy shows on TV are less engaging than dramas.
4. I prefer flying to driving because it's much quicker.
5. In general, I like large restaurants better than small ones.

▶模擬試題②

Some movies, like dramas, are thought-provoking. Other movies are designed primarily to entertain. Which type of movie do you prefer? Use specific reasons and examples to support your answer.

Preparation Time: 15 Seconds
Response Time: 45 Seconds

下面是一個回答範例，應重讀的部分已用粗體標出。注意畫線句子如何清晰明確地表明瞭考生立場。 Track 039

In general, I like entertaining movies better than dramas.（←用比較表明立場）My life is hectic and filled with pressure. I have too many papers to write and too many exams to prepare for. Almost every minute of my waking hours, my mind is either occupied with the materials I have to learn or the things I have to do. So, occasionally, when I need a reprieve from this madness, I want to enjoy something that does not tax my mind.

Thought-provoking movies often cause me to think, taking up precious time or making my already tired mind even more tired. Entertaining movies, on the other hand, make me relax. For example, *E.T.*, the fun film about children who take home a little extraterrestrial creature. After watching a movie like this, I am reinvigorated and ready to tackle the next job on hand.

現在，自己練一下這道題目，說說你對電影的看法。試著用比較級形式看看吧！

• 想在口語考試中正確使用比較級，可運用以下策略：

1. 第二題的多數題目會給出兩種選擇，然後問 Which do you prefer? 當你解釋自己為何選其中一種時，經常會用到比較級，如：I prefer mysteries because they are more suspenseful.

2. 如果用了比較級結構，要確保文法正確。要熟悉比較級的文法規則，包括 good、better、best 這樣的不規則變化及其用法，如：I like spicy food better than plain food.

3. 比較級是表達偏好的一大利器。然而，回答第二題的問題並不是非要用到比較級結構不可。回答時，可以只描述自己的喜好，如：I love dramas because they pull you into a different world. 換句話說，不必一定要明確地說出：I love dramas better than comedies because they pull you into a different world.

▶ 模擬試題③

請回答下題。回答時，可嘗試使用下面列出的實用答題範本，並練習使用比較級形式。

Some people enjoy reading novels or other works of fiction. Others enjoy non-fiction. Which do you prefer? Include details and examples in your answer.

Preparation Time: 15 Seconds
Response Time: 45 Seconds

實用答題範本　　🎧 *Track 040* 聽聽看！別人的高分回答！（高分回答原文請見 P.280）

Given a choice between fiction and non-fiction, I prefer to read..., especially... (and...) Visiting other worlds by reading...can be incredibly...

托福總監幫你預測可能會出現的題目！

1. Some people have a few foods that they eat most of the time. Other people frequently try new dishes. Which approach to eating do you have? Include reasons and examples in your explanation.

2. Do you agree or disagree with this statement? Meals prepared at home are tastier than meals in restaurants. Use specific reasons and examples to support your answer.

3. Do you agree or disagree with the following statement? The best way to travel abroad is with a tour guide. Include reasons and examples to support your answer.

4. Some people like to go to places they have never visited before. Other people like to travel to familiar places again and again. Which do you prefer? Use specific reasons and examples to support your answer.

5. Do you agree or disagree with this statement? Artists and musicians are important to society. Include specific reasons and examples to support your answer.

• 最後再練習一下「回答餐飲、旅行和藝術話題」最實用的答題模板！

1. Certainly, we benefit from...

例 • Certainly, we benefit from food that is easier for us to prepare.

• Certainly, we benefit from tasting many new foods.

2. We can save a lot of time, which can be spent on...

例 • We can save a lot of time, which can be spent on many other interesting activities that modern life affords us.

• We can save a lot of time, which can be spent on visiting famous sites.

3. To be sure, ...still has to be prepared the old-fashioned way.

例 • To be sure, good food still has to be prepared the old-fashioned way.

• To be sure, gourmet cuisine still has to be prepared the old-fashioned way.

4. In my opinion, ...is a lot more important in our quick-paced modern life.

例 • In my opinion, saving time is a lot more important in our quick-paced modern life.

• In my opinion, air travel is a lot more important in our quick-paced modern life.

5. When I'm on a vacation I like to stop along the way and VERB...

例 • When I'm on a vacation I like to stop along the way and visit many places of interest.

• When I'm on a vacation I like to stop along the way and enjoy things on the spur of the moment.

6. That is why my favorite trip was when I VERBed...

例 • That is why my favorite trip was when I drove across the country with my best friend.

• That is why my favorite trip was when I backpacked across Europe.

7. We took our time, VERBing through...scenic landscapes, exploring...

例 • We took our time, driving through gorgeous scenic landscapes, exploring many small towns.

• We took our time, crossing through splendid scenic landscapes, exploring shops and restaurants.

8. By choosing to stop at little, out-of-the-way places on our way, we had the chance to experience so much more than if we'd VERBed directly to...

例 • By choosing to stop at little, out-of-the-way places on our way, we had the chance to experience so much more than if we'd flown directly to Los Angeles.

• By choosing to stop at little, out-of-the-way places on our way, we had the chance to experience so much more than if we'd gone directly to Copenhagen.

9. In general, I like...movies better than...

例 • In general, I like entertaining movies better than dramas.

• In general, I like serious movies better than comedies.

10. So, occasionally, when I need a(n)..., I want to enjoy something that does not tax my mind.

例 • So, occasionally, when I need a reprieve from this madness, I want to enjoy something that does not tax my mind.

• So, occasionally, when I need a break, I want to enjoy something that does not tax my mind.

11. ...movies, on the other hand, make me relax.

例 • Entertaining movies, on the other hand, make me relax.

• Animated movies, on the other hand, make me relax.

12. After VERBing..., I am reinvigorated and ready to tackle the next job on hand.

例 • After watching a movie like this, I am reinvigorated and ready to tackle the next job on hand.

• After traveling to some place faraway, I am reinvigorated and ready to tackle the next job onhand.

13. Given a choice between fiction and non-fiction, I prefer to read..., especially... (and...)

例 • Given a choice between fiction and non-fiction, I prefer to read novels, especially science-fiction and fantasy.

• Given a choice between fiction and non-fiction, I prefer to read non-fiction, especially biographies.

14. I find that when I read works of..., they VERB...

例 • I find that when I read works of fiction, they take me to another world and my imagination can run free.

• I find that when I read works of non-fiction, they make me appreciate the world around me.

15. Visiting other worlds by reading...can be incredibly...

例 • Visiting other worlds by reading novels can be incredibly entertaining.

• Visiting other worlds by reading history books can be incredibly educational.

16. What's more, I'm able to VERB...

例 • What's more, I'm able to leave all my troubles behind.

• What's more, I'm able to understand more about previous societies.

Work and Money
職業與金錢

❝❝ 在本章，你將學到…… ❞❞

★回答時怎樣巧妙地借用題幹
★如何用語調來強調語意

解讀常考題

有關職業和金錢的話題也是第二題經常涉及的話題。世界上有很多與金錢、職業相關的諺語，如：Hard work never did anyone any harm.（努力工作對任何人都絕無害處。）、Money makes the world go around.（有錢能使鬼推磨。）所以第二題有很多題目會涉及這個話題也不足為奇。

這些題目常會要求考生談論金錢和個人滿足感，哪個對他們來講更重要。有些問題會探究考生的興趣和價值觀，例如問對金錢的慾望會怎樣影響職業選擇。另一些問題則會問到：高薪是否是你在生活中最關注的東西，還是有其他更重要的東西？

現在，看一道關於職業的例題。

▶舉例試題

When you choose a career, which factor is more important to you, money or your personal satisfaction? Include details and examples in your explanation.

Preparation Time: 15 Seconds
Response Time: 45 Seconds

托福總監告訴你怎麼答！

本題問考生，在選擇職業時，高薪和個人價值的實現哪個更重要？有些考生可能會對題幹中的這個分句產生不解：which factor is more important to you 的意思是要我從後面提到的兩個 factor 中選一個嗎？通常，人們會根據多種因素選擇職業：薪水多少、自己是否感興趣、從這份職業中能學到多少、甚至工作地點離家的遠近。新托福考試的命題人則在這道題中明確將考慮因素限定為兩個，供考生選擇其一。

策略：巧妙借用題幹

新托福考試口語部分的評分原則上明確指出，考生如果「借用」太多題幹詞句，得分

就可能會偏低。具體來説，原則上指出，得 1 分的考生「可能過多依賴於重複題幹」。那麼，有什麼好方法來避免有意或無意地重複題幹呢？

一種策略就是改變題幹措辭，換句話説。例如，在上題中，題幹措辭是：which factor is more important to you, money or personal satisfaction? 這樣的話，就不能回答：The factor that is more important to me is money. 而應該這樣回答：I would rather have a job that gives me money.

下表列出了一些可供參考的換句話説方法：

題幹措辭	換句話說的回答方式
Which of these do you prefer?	I would like to have... I would like to VERB...
Which option would you prefer?	I think that VERBing...is the better approach.
Do you agree or disagree with the following statement?	I believe the statement is reasonable. In other words, I think...
Which factor is more important to you?	I would rather have...
Which way of life do you think is better?	I prefer to VERB...
Which opinion do you think is better?	I tend to support the opinion that...is...
Which approach do you think is better for students?	My opinion is that students should VERB...

高分回答

注意看，仔細聽，這裡面標上粗體的地方都要發重音才道地喔！   *Track 041*

In **college**, when I **first** be**gan** stud**ying** finance, my **only thought** was **how** I could **earn** a **large amount** of **money**. Finance is **all about** making **money**. However, **after a year** of **work**ing for an **investment bank**, I **realized** that my **salary** was **not worth** the emotional and **physical toll** the **job** was **taking** on me. During that **year**, I **learned** that my **well**-be**ing** and **personal** satis**fact**ion were **just** as im**port**ant as **monetary wealth**— and in **many ways**, **more** important. Without **health** and **peace** of **mind**, it is **hard** to enjoy life. **Now**, the **most** important **issue**（題幹的改述）for **me** when I **look** for a **job** is **whether** it will **challenge** me and **allow** me to **grow**. **Personal growth** is **more** important than a **top salary**.（題幹的又一種改述）

托福總監為什麼覺得這是高分回答？

注意第一句怎樣迅速而明確地表達了該考生上大學時對這個問題的看法。接下來通過自己一年的職場體會，總結自己當時對這個問題的認識。最後兩句話則表明自己現在對該問題的看法：Now, the most important issue for me when I look for a job is... 該回答將題幹提到的 more important factor 改述為 the most important issue，這樣一來，該考生給出的顯然是原創回答，而非對題幹的簡單重複。

> **要對題幹進行恰當的複述，可運用以下策略：**

1. 考試前，熟悉典型的題幹措辭，這樣就能夠做好應對每一個題幹的準備。
2. 考試中，迅速瀏覽題幹措辭，回答時就知道如何進行變換。
3. 不必在第一句中就對題幹進行複述。如上面這道例題的回答範例所示，可以很有效地將對題幹的複述用在結論中。

▶ 模擬試題①

請回答下題。回答時，可嘗試使用下面列出的實用答題範本。

> **Do you agree or disagree with this statement? A successful person has money and power. Support your opinion with details and examples.**
>
> Preparation Time: 15 Seconds
> Response Time: 45 Seconds

> **實用答題範本**　　🎧 **Track 042** 聽聽看！別人的高分回答！（高分回答原文請見 P.280）
>
> True success encompasses much more than X and Y.
> And a successful person takes time to VERB...and VERB...

> **得分考技：真情流露靠語調**

　　語調掌握不好是口語得分低的一個常見原因！這很可惜，因為語調不僅是語言中最好把握的一項技能，也是能最快掌握的。語調是對音調高低的把握，在英語中的用途十分廣泛。提問時會提升語調，而降低語調（例如在句尾）則表示某個觀點的表達結束了。説話的人也可以通過提高或降低語調來區分、突出某些詞語。音調高低可告知聽者一句話中哪個詞最重要，以及有多重要。

　　語調變化也是表達情感和製造反差的標誌，對於傳達語意極其重要。由於在片語或分句中可能會有很多重音，所以當聽到一個相對較高的音調突然下降，就可推測這個單字比其他單字更重要。

　　下面是一個例子（底線「＿」表示音調平緩，斜線「＼」表示音調突然由高轉低）：

In my opinion, ...

　　音調在 my 這個詞升高，然後迅速降低。這個高音調表示説話者正在強調這是他或她個人的觀點，也表明説話者對這個問題非常有熱情，使其説出的話更加值得注意。

正確運用語調，應遵循下列一些重要規則：

1. 説到最重要的詞時，音調應上揚且與其他詞的音調高低有所區別，表示這是你想強調的。
2. 通過改變音調強調某詞時，聲音大小和發音長度也要與其他詞有較大區別。
3. 用相對較高的音調來説某個單字時，常常表示這個詞傳達了一個新資訊。用更高的音調則表示這個資訊非常重要。

托福總監帶你練

聽聽看下列例句，練習正確運用語調。反覆聽錄音，然後跟著讀。 *Track 043*

1. Given a **choice**, I **prefer** to **work** in a **team**.

2. **Working** in **groups** is **just not** efficient since a **lot of time** is **spent talking** and **arguing**.

3. I'd **like** a **stimulating** job, but I **don't** want to **starve**.

4. For **me**, a **high salary** is an im**port**ant criterion.

5. Ful**fill**ment, **not money**, is the **key** to a **stable** and **happy life**.

▶模擬試題②

> **In your future career, would you prefer to work independently or would you rather work in a group with others? Include details and examples in your answer.**
>
> Preparation Time: 15 Seconds
> Response Time: 45 Seconds

下面是一個回答範例，注意錄音中說話者對語調的運用。 *Track 044*

> I would **rather work** in a **group** environment in the future. I am an **extrovert**. I **enjoy** being with **people**, **either** at **work** or at **play**. The **presence** of **other people** energizes me, which is the **magic** of my personality, I guess. **Naturally**, through the **years**, I have **learned** to **work** very well with other **people**. And the **interesting thing** is that **people** also en**joy work**ing with **me**. In my **future** career, I believe my personality and **teamwork skills** will be**come** my professional **strengths**. I **think** I will contribute **greatly** to the productivity of any **work team** I am on. I can **just see** myself making everyone **open up** and **willingly** contribute their **ideas** to **solve** any **problem**. **Naturally**, I would **take** advantage of **these strengths** and look for **jobs** that would **allow** me to **thrive** in a **group** setting.

現在，自己練習這道題目看看，試著用恰當的語調來強調重要的詞語。

• 想在口語考試中正確把握語調，可運用以下策略：

1. 在考試中，想強調重要的詞時，利用語調作為一種交流手段。
2. 在強調語意時，要綜合運用單字音節的音調、聲音大小和發音長度的變化。

3. 準備考試時，試著模仿自然的英語口語，可以參考本書大量例題和練習的回答範例，尤其是其中用粗體標出的重音。

4. 在口語表達中，學習利用提高音調來突出某個重音，表示你想特別強調的語意。

▶模擬試題③

請回答下題。回答時，可嘗試使用下面列出的實用答題範本，並練習使用合適的語調。

> **Some people like to work at home. Others like to work in the office. Which place do you prefer to work? Give specific details and examples to support your answer.**
>
> Preparation Time: 15 Seconds
> Response Time: 45 Seconds

實用答題範本　　　🎧 *Track 045* 聽聽看！別人的高分回答！（高分回答原文請見 P.280）

The nature of my work is such that I need to VERB...
That's why working at/in...is much better.

托福總監幫你預測可能會出現的題目！

1. Do you agree or disagree with this statement? Meals prepared at home are tastier than meals in restaurants. Use specific reasons and examples to support your answer.

2. Some students like to have part-time jobs in the evening. Other students prefer to find part-time jobs during the day. Which time do you think is better for students to work part-time? Include specific reasons and examples to support your choice.

3. Some people prefer to work for themselves or start a business. Others prefer to work for an employer. Would you rather work for yourself or work for someone else? Give specific reasons to explain your choice.

4. Do you agree or disagree with the following statement? Borrowing money from a friend can damage the friendship. Use reasons and specific examples to explain your answer.

5. Some people like to spend the pocket change that they have left every day. Other people like to save it. Which approach do you prefer? Use specific reasons to support your answer.

• 最後再練習一下「描述職業與金錢問題」最實用的答題模板！

1. **In college, when I first began studying..., my only thought was how I could earn a large amount of money.**

   例　• In college, when I first began studying finance, my only thought was how I could earn a large amount of money.

- In college, when I first began studying computer engineering, my only thought was how I could earn a large amount of money.

2. However, after a year of working for a(n)..., I realized that my salary was not worth the emotional and physical toll the job was taking on me.

例 • However, after a year of working for an investment bank, I realized that my salary was not worth the emotional and physical toll the job was taking on me.

• However, after a year of working for an advertising agency, I realized that my salary was not worth the emotional and physical toll the job was taking on me.

3. Without..., it is hard to enjoy life.

例 • Without health and peace of mind, it is hard to enjoy life.

• Without a good income, it is hard to enjoy life.

4. ...is more important than a top salary.

例 • Personal growth is more important than a top salary.

• A balanced life is more important than a top salary.

5. People aren't...when they have money and power.

例 • People aren't necessarily successful when they have money and power.

• People aren't always happy when they have money and power.

6. True success encompasses much more than X and Y.

例 • True success encompasses much more than wealth and status.

• True success encompasses much more than a fancy house and a corner office.

7. One example of success is VERBing..., because you are up for the challenge.

例 • One example of success is sticking through a tough math class until the end of the year, because you are up for the challenge.

• One example of success is taking your company public, because you are up for the challenge.

8. And a successful person takes time to VERB...and VERB...

例 • And a successful person takes time to teach his or her children and help others.

• And a successful person takes time to reflect and give back to the community.

9. I would rather work in a(n)...in the future.

例 • I would rather work in a group environment in the future.

• I would rather work in an independent setting in the future.

10. I enjoy VERBing..., either at work or at play.

例 • I enjoy being with people, either at work or at play.

• I enjoy solving problems, either at work or at play.

11. Naturally, through the years, I have learned to VERB...

例 • Naturally, through the years, I have learned to work very well with other people.

• Naturally, through the years, I have learned to work independently.

12. I think I will contribute greatly to the...of any work team I am on.

例 • I think I will contribute greatly to the productivity of any work team I am on.

• I think I will contribute greatly to the creative energy of any work team I am on.

13. I prefer to work in...

例 • I prefer to work in the office.

• I prefer to work in my apartment.

14. The nature of my work is such that I need to VERB...

例 • The nature of my work is such that I need to interact with my colleagues frequently.

• The nature of my work is such that I need to have a quiet place where I can think.

15. If all the members of our team..., we can easily communicate with each other and quickly resolve any issues that might have VERBed...

例 • If all the members of our team are there on site, we can easily communicate with each other and quickly resolve any issues that might have cropped up.

• If all the members of our team have smart phones, we can easily communicate with each other and quickly resolve any issues that might have come up.

16. Working at/in...is not very convenient for me because...

例 • Working at home is not very convenient for me because I still live with my parents in a small apartment.

• Working in the office is not very convenient for me because there is so much traffic.

17. That's why working at/in...is much better.

例 • That's why working in the office is much better.

• That's why working at home is much better.

⑩ Education—Primary and Secondary
教育──初等與中等教育

❝ 在本章，你將學到…… ❞

★口語考試中如何表明立場
★如何談論事物的必要性

解讀常考題

因為有很多考生是學生，所以第二題的很多題目都和教育有關。本章情境涉及的話題包括了從幼稚園到高中三年級的孩子所學的科目、學校政策以及家長的教育理念。

所謂的「Primary Education」，通常包含了從幼稚園到小學六年級這一階段。這一階段給孩子們提供了社交和學習基礎學術技能的機會。「Secondary Education」包括國中和高中，任務是幫助年輕人準備好繼續接受高等教育、高級職業培訓或投入到工作中。所以，和初、中等教育相關的題目就會涉及學生生活各方面，包括學校的要求和課外活動等。有些題目還會問到家長是否應讓孩子學習樂器或外語；另一些問題會問到體育課和學校組織的其他體育活動對於年輕人的價值。

現在，看一道關於中等教育的例題。

▶舉例試題

Some high schools require students to wear uniforms. Others do not. Which policy do you think is better? Include details and examples in your explanation.

Preparation Time: 15 Seconds
Response Time: 45 Seconds

托福總監告訴你怎麼答！

這道例題的題目針對「要求」提問，讓考生陳述高中生是否應該穿制服。考生需要給出支持或者反對穿制服的有力理由。

策略：表明立場

在口語考試中，儘快表明自己的立場通常是明智之舉，尤其是在答第一題和第二題時，因為這兩題都只有 45 秒作答時間。有很多方法可以用來明確表態，可用 I think...（或 I don't think...）開頭，然後陳述自己的觀點，例如回答上題時可以說：I think that young people should wear uniforms in school.

考生不必第一句話就用一個 because 子句。在上面的例子中，第一句話也可變成：I think that young people should wear uniforms in school because it fosters strict discipline. 但這樣聽起來就會偏長，所以也可等到第二句、甚至是第三句話再給出理由。

下表列舉了一些明確表示立場的方法：

表示支持	表示反對
I believe (that)...	I don't believe (that)...
I think (that)...	I don't think (that)...
I feel that...	I do not feel that...
In my opinion, students should be permitted to...	In my opinion, students should not be permitted to...
I agree with the statement that...	I disagree with the statement that...
I like the idea of VERBing...because...	I don't like the idea of VERBing...because...
It is my belief that students should be allowed to...	It is my belief that students should not be allowed to...
It is my view that students should be required to...	It is my view that students should not be required to...

高分回答

注意看，仔細聽，這裡面標上**粗體**的地方都要發重音才道地喔！ **Track 046**

I bel**ieve** that **high schools** should **not** re**quire** their **students** to **wear** uniforms because uniforms **stifle self**-ex**pression**.（←直接表明立場）
Uniforms **strip** people of their individu**ality**. Experimen**tation** and **self**-expression are im**por**tant **parts** of **child** development.
All young people **will**, in **one** way or an**other**, ex**press** their individuality. **Thus high** school students who are **forced** to **wear** uniforms will find **other**, less ap**propri**ate, **ways** to ex**press** them**selves**. For ex**ample**, they'll **wear make**-up and **jewel**ry. **Instead** of **worry**ing about whether **high** school students **look** the **same**, the **school** administrators should **find a way** to al**low** students to **celebrate diversity**. When **students** are al**lowed** to **wear** different **clothes**, they can **active**ly ex**plore who** they **are**. **That** way, they can **gain confidence** and **self**-esteem.

托福總監為什麼覺得這是高分回答？

在第一句中，該考生直截了當地表明瞭立場，並用了一個簡短的 because 子句：...because uniforms stifle self-expression. 第二句本質上是用另外的詞語重申這個 because 子句的意思。隨後幾句解釋了為什麼個性的表達對年輕人很重要。之後，在倒數第二句中，該考生用不同的措辭再次強調了主要觀點：When students are allowed to wear different clothes, they can actively explore who they are. 最後一句則是對這句話在邏輯上進行延伸，進一步說明不穿制服的好處。

更多針對高中生穿制服問題表態的例句：

Wearing a uniform every day makes life easier because students don't have to worry about what to wear every day.

High school students often hate their school uniforms because they are uncomfortable; for example, having to wear ties.

I really don't think that high school students should be allowed to wear their own clothes.

要好好表明立場，可運用以下策略：

1. 記住，不必選擇與自己真實想法一致的觀點。就算你說謊考官也不會知道。

2. 選擇某一種觀點時，不要猶豫不決，也不要論證兩方都有優點。當然，可以簡要地承認另一方的優點，但是應該要利用這點間接帶出於自己的立場才是正確的。如：Though uniforms are efficient for school administrators, there are too many reasons why students shouldn't have to wear them.

3. 評分人感興趣的是你怎樣通過論證說明自己的立場，而不是陳述立場時的辭藻有多華麗。換句話說，清晰明確的陳述是最重要的。

4. 不必頻繁地使用像 personally, I think... / generally speaking, I believe... 這樣的片語。偶爾使用一次沒問題，但是過度使用就會惹人不快。因為，聽了你的表態之後，評分人更關心的是具體、連貫、銜接緊密的論證。

▶ 模擬試題①

請回答下題。回答時，可嘗試使用下面列出的實用答題範本。

> **Do you agree or disagree with this statement? Parents should determine the careers for their children. Give specific details and examples to explain your answer.**
>
> Preparation Time: 15 Seconds
> Response Time: 45 Seconds

實用答題範本	🎧 *Track 047* 聽聽看！別人的高分回答！（高分回答原文請見 P.280）
Many of my friends have complained to me how... She says she VERBed...only to please her parents.

得分考技：掌握好句型，暢談事物的必要性

第二題的題目常會問到是否「有必要」去做某事。如：Some people say high schools should teach music. Other people say that music classes are not necessary. What is your opinion?

有很多種方法可以用來表述某事必要與否。例如：可使用 need 作為動詞或名詞；可使用名詞 necessity；還可使用與 need 同義的說法。下頁的表格中列舉了一些句型，可用在回答中：

句型	例句
...should VERB...	Parents should motivate their children.
...is required.	Familiarity with technology is required.
...should be required.	A gap year should be required.
...needs...	A student needs good discipline.
...needs to VERB...	The high school needs to provide club activities.
There's no need to VERB...	There's no need to wear uniforms.
There's no need for...to VERB...	There's no need for parents to choose their child's career.
The need for...is...	The need for cultural literacy is clear.
...is in need of...	A child is in need of supervision.
I VERBed...out of necessity.	I learned English out of necessity.
It is a matter of necessity to VERB...	It is a matter of necessity to exercise every day.
...is a needless...	Worry is a needless activity.
It is essential that...	It is essential that students are exposed to the arts.
It is vitally important that...	It is vitally important that people use cellphones during school hours.
It is critical that...	It is critical that primary school teachers have good communication skills.
It is crucial that...	It is crucial that students focus on a particular field of study.
It is unnecessary for...to VERB...	It is unnecessary for children to do household tasks.

托福總監帶你練

聽下列句子，練習談論必要性。反覆聽錄音，然後跟著讀。 *Track 048*

1. **Traveling abroad** is unnecessary for **children**.
2. It's **crucial** for **students** to re**view** their **assignments** every **morning**.
3. The **need** for **teachers** to re**ceive** a **decent salary** is **great**.
4. There's **no need** to **teach** foreign **languages** to **small children**.
5. It is a **matter** of ne**cessity** that **young children get** enough exercise.

▶模擬試題②

> **Some students choose to take a year off and travel or work, before they go on to college. Other students go directly from high school to college. Which do you think is better? Include details and examples in your explanation.**
>
> Preparation Time: 15 Seconds
> Response Time: 45 Seconds

下面是一個回答範例，應重讀的部分已用**粗體**標出。注意回答中是怎樣談論必要性的。

 Track 049

> I **don't** think that **graduating high school students** should **take** a **year off** before they **attend** college. **Taking** a year off is unnecessary because **many** universities have **study abroad** programs that **let students take classes** in other **countries**. For **example**, a **classmate** of mine went to **London** to **study. He received college credit** for the **courses** he **took** there. And he **took** advantage of the **six-week** winter **break** to **backpack** through**out** Europe. **Then**, when he **returned home**, he signed up *for* a university-s**ponsored internship program, which allowed** him to **receive college credit** for **working** at a **bank**. In **this** way, he was able to both **travel and work** while getting a **college** education.

現在，自己練一練這道題目看看吧！説説你對高中畢業生是否應該在上大學前休一年的假期這個問題的看法。試著使用恰當的句型來表達必要性。

• 想掌握表達事物必要性的方法，可運用以下策略：

1. 練習上面表格中列出的句型，直到可以熟練運用每一個句型。確保重音和語調的正確。例如，在句子 That policy is not necessary 中，讀 not 一詞的聲音要更大聲，並提高音調。
2. 特別留心題幹中問到的「要求」以及是否人們「應該」做某事。這些題目通常需要使用表達必要性的句式。
3. 區分清楚表示「需要」的名詞（例：necessity）和動詞（例：need to + 動詞）的用法。運用時要使用正確的搭配。
4. 在使用 need 動詞片語時，要注意介系詞的正確用法。如：There's no need for...to VERB...。介系詞的正確使用能夠幫助你在流利程度和總分上提分。

▶模擬試題③

請回答下題。回答時，可嘗試使用下面列出的實用答題範本，並練習表達事物必要性。

> **Some people think that students should study during weekends. Others think that students should relax and spend time with their families. Which approach to studying do you think is better for students and why?**
>
> Preparation Time: 15 Seconds
> Response Time: 45 Seconds

實用答題範本 🎧 *Track 050* 聽聽看！別人的高分回答！（高分回答原文請見 P.281）

I think students should VERB...during weekends.

To succeed, we have to VERB...

托福總監幫你預測可能會出現的題目！

1. Do you agree or disagree with the following statement? Children should be required to learn a foreign language in primary school. Use details and examples to explain your answer.

2. Some students like to do their homework early in the morning. Others like to do it late at night. Which time do you think is better for students to do homework? Include specific reasons and examples to support your choice.

3. Do you agree or disagree with the following statement? Participating in team sports helps develop children's sense of cooperation. Give specific reasons to explain your choice.

4. Do you agree or disagree with the following statement? High schools should charge money so they can offer quality education. Use reasons and specific examples to explain your answer.

5. Some people think teachers should be paid based on their experience. Other people say teachers should be paid according to how much their students learn. Which viewpoint do you support? Give specific reasons and examples.

• 最後再練習一下「有關初等和中等教育話題」最實用的答題模板！

1. I believe that high schools should not require their students to wear uniforms because uniforms...

例 • I believe that high schools should not require their students to wear uniforms because uniforms stifle self-expression.

• I believe that high schools should not require their students to wear uniforms because uniforms are boring.

2. Uniforms strip people of their...

例 • Uniforms strip people of their individuality.

• Uniforms strip people of their creativity.

3. All young people will, in one way or another, VERB...

例 • All young people will, in one way or another, express their individuality.

• All young people will, in one way or another, find ways to be cool.

4. When students are allowed to wear different clothes, they can VERB...

例 • When students are allowed to wear different clothes, they can actively explore who they are.

• When students are allowed to wear different clothes, they can feel relaxed at school.

5. I VERB （表達觀點的動詞） it's a good idea for parents to dictate what career their children should pursue.

例 • I don't think it's a good idea for parents to dictate what career their children should pursue.

• I believe it's a good idea for parents to dictate what career their children should pursue.

6. Many of my friends have complained to me how...

例 • Many of my friends have complained to me how unhappy they are with their jobs.

• Many of my friends have complained to me how they wish they had listened to their parents.

7. For example, one friend says she VERB...

例 • For example, one friend says she dreads going to work every morning.

• For example, one friend says she can't find a job with her degree in Literature.

8. She says she VERBed...only to please her parents.

例 • She says she took the job only to please her parents.

• She says she studied Pharmacy only to please her parents.

9. They allow me to VERB...and they never give me any...

例 • They allow me to explore my own interests and they never give me any pressure.

• They allow me to find my own way and they never give me any criticism.

10. I don't think that graduating high school students should VERB...before they attend college.

例 • I don't think that graduating high school students should take a year off before they attend college.

• I don't think that graduating high school students should get a job before they attend college.

11. Taking a year off is unnecessary because...

例 • Taking a year off is unnecessary because many universities have study abroad programs that let students take classes in other countries.

- Taking a year off is unnecessary because students will be able to travel during summers if they want.

12. In this way, ...was able to VERB...while getting a college education.

例 • In this way, he was able to both travel and work while getting a college education.

- In this way, she was able to have an understanding of the world while getting a college education.

13. I think students should VERB...during weekends.

例 • I think students should study during weekends.

- I think students should take it easy during weekends.

14. Nowadays, there is too much...

例 • Nowadays, there is too much competition.

- Nowadays, there is too much work to do.

15. To succeed, we have to VERB...

例 • To succeed, we have to study a lot.

- To succeed, we have to invest a lot of hours.

16. X often take up evening hours on weekdays, eating into our time for Y.

例 • Extracurricular activities often take up evening hours on weekdays, eating into our time for homework and pre-class preparation.

- Group review sessions often take up evening hours on weekdays, eating into our time for individual study.

17. Quite frankly, there's no way for me to finish...by Friday night.

例 • Quite frankly, there's no way for me to finish all my homework by Friday night.

- Quite frankly, there's no way for me to finish the reading assignments by Friday night.

 Education—University
教育——大學教育

⟪ 在本章，你將學到…… ⟫

★如何利用連接詞來加強銜接性
★如何發好位於單字中間的 /l/ 音

解讀常考題

　　口語第二題通常會問到大學生的生活和學校的政策。可能會要求考生談論大學、或職業學校學習的各個方面。一些題目會問到：與人文學科相比，理工科的課程要求有何不同？另一些題目會問到哪種唸書習慣最好，還有一些會問到科技對教育的影響，例如：Should students do research on the Internet or in the traditional library? 或問到最佳的學習方法：Are study groups an efficient way to learn? / Is writing a term paper a good way to master a subject?

　　現在，看一道關於大學教育的例題。

▶舉例試題

> **Nowadays, some people like to take courses online. Do you prefer distance courses or traditional classroom instruction? Include details and examples in your explanation.**
>
> Preparation Time: 15 Seconds
> Response Time: 45 Seconds

托福總監告訴你怎麼答！

　　這道題要求考生思考哪種學習模式更有吸引力：通過網路進行的「遠端課程」，還是在實體教室中進行的課程。要使回答站得住腳，應談論在家用網路學習的效率、和其他同學交流的機會、或利用其中一種學習模式的效果。不管支援哪種學習模式，想得高分，必須靈巧地將觀點緊密、連貫地串聯起來。

策略：連接詞的強大功能

　　連接詞在文法上是非常實用的連接工具，可使內容銜接得更緊密。連接詞的功能非常強大，既可以連接片語和子句，也可以連接兩個獨立句子。

連接詞的種類很多，下表列出了一些口語中常用的連接詞：

並列連接詞	從屬連接詞	連接副詞
and	although	as a result
but	because	consequently
for	even though	however
nor	if	moreover
so	until	rather
yet	when	yet
or	unless	nevertheless

用連接詞組織出一個前後銜接緊密的回答，只需簡單的四個步驟：

1. 複習具體的文法規則，確定不同的連接詞在句中可使用的位置。下面的例句，展示了連接詞在不同位置的用法：

   例1 Humorous professors attract many students; on the other hand, they may not be the best teachers.

   例2 Although humorous professors attract many students, they may not be the best teachers.

   例3 It's true that humorous professors attract many students. They may not be the best teachers, however.

2. 除文法之外，選擇連接詞時還要考慮句子的邏輯關係。例如：moreover 表示為最初的觀點添加資訊；however 表示將與之前的觀點產生矛盾或進行對比。

   例1 University tuition is high. Moreover, the rates keep increasing each year.

   例2 University tuition is high. However, there are ways to get financial aid.

3. 不要在句子的開頭反覆用 and。and 在句首時表達的意思很模糊，會讓評分人覺得考生的能力較弱。

4. 不要只靠連接詞來組織結構。即不要認為僅僅列舉出想說的點（如只用 first, second, third）就能組成一個內容銜接緊密的回答。

高分回答

注意看，仔細聽，這裡面標上粗體的地方都要發重音才道地喔！　Track 051

I prefer traditional classroom instruction to online classes because I believe that, when I'm surrounded by people in a room, I can learn more. The energy is good. It's also comforting to know I can ask my teachers questions as I think of them. I don't have to send an e-mail or wait in a queue for a response. The teacher is able to see what I see. So, for example, if the class is going over an assignment we didn't understand, our teacher can answer specific questions right then and there. And in the classroom setting, I'm able to meet students who become my friends or study partners. Plus, I can focus on learning, instead of being distracted by urges to surf the web, chat with friends or do other random things in my dorm.

托福總監為什麼覺得這是高分回答？

在上面的回答中，該考生運用的連接詞非常恰當，如下面列出的幾句話，請注意觀察和學習。連接詞已用底線標出。

1. I prefer traditional classroom instruction to online classes <u>because</u> I believe that, when I'm surrounded by people in a room, I can learn more.
2. <u>So</u>, for example, if the class is going over an assignment we didn't understand, our teacher can answer specific questions right then and there.
3. <u>Plus</u>, I can focus on learning, instead of being distracted by urges to surf the web, chat with friends or do other random things in my dorm.

想透過連接詞加強句子之間的銜接性，可運用以下策略：

1. 瞭解基本的連接詞種類、作用和用法，考前應多加練習。這一技能對加強句子間的銜接性非常關鍵，會有利於提高分數！
2. 使用最常用、簡單、非正式的連接詞（相對於在寫作中使用的較為正式的連接詞來講）。如：用 I majored in physics, even though it was not my first choice. 而不要用 I majored in physics, notwithstanding the fact that it was not my first choice.
3. 不要忘了邏輯性！銜接緊密的句子通常在邏輯上也很連貫。要考慮觀點的條理性和邏輯性。
4. 在考試中，不要把連接詞作為組織語言的唯一方法。銜接和連貫要依靠多種語言手法，除了連接詞，還包括對代名詞、限定詞、重複單字及改述技巧的使用。

▶模擬試題①

請回答下題。回答時，可嘗試使用下面列出的實用答題範本。

> **Do you agree or disagree with this statement? It is beneficial to go to a university that is far away from your hometown. Include details and examples to support your opinion.**
>
> Preparation Time: 15 Seconds
> Response Time: 45 Seconds

實用答題範本　　　　🎧 *Track 052* 聽聽看！別人的高分回答！（高分回答原文請見 P.281）

I agree that students who go to faraway universities can VERB...
Nevertheless, as a result of living far away, students become...

得分考技：發好位於單字中間的 /l/ 音

/l/ 這個音位於一個詞的中間位置時，其發音並不好掌握。因為單字結構不同時，我們的舌頭也需要以不同的方法移動。很多亞洲考生因為發不好這個音，影響了評分人的理解。

其中有兩種單字結構尤其值得注意：

1. /l/ 位於兩個母音之間，如：

feeling　　**belong**　　**falling**

要發出這種情況下的 /l/ 音，需要將舌尖放在門牙後面，抵在齒齦處，在發出 /l/ 音後接母音的同時放下舌頭。很重要的一點是，/l/ 音要很快地連上第二個音節，這樣 feeling 這個詞聽起來就像 fee-ling。同時，重音要落在正確的音節上。

2. /l/ 後接輔音，如：

cold　　**yield**　　**world**

要發出位於母音後、輔音前的 /l/ 音，也要將舌頭抵在門牙後面的齒齦上。在念這種結構的單字時，發 /l/ 音時要使舌頭保持在此位置，並將母音和 /l/ 音都發得略長一些。發 /l/ 音時要將聲帶振動的位置移至喉嚨的後部，而且在發完 /d/ 音之前不要讓舌尖離開齒齦位置。

托福總監帶你練

聽下列句子，練習位於單字中間的 /l/ 的發音。注意用底線標出的單字。反覆聽錄音，然後跟著讀。

Track 053

1. Our **campus** is very <u>old</u> and has **one** of the **best** university <u>libraries</u> in the <u>world</u>.
2. **Students** who **don't review** their **notes** every **day** risk <u>failing</u> their <u>classes</u>.
3. I'm **supposed** to **have** my **transcript** <u>mailed</u> **out** in a <u>sealed</u> envelope; can **this** office **help** me with **that**?
4. **Many** institutions <u>hold</u> nighttime <u>classes</u> for **students** who **work** during the **day**.
5. I'm <u>feeling</u> pressured about <u>selecting</u> a <u>college</u> advisor.

▶模擬試題②

Some people think that attending a university is necessary. Others think that a university education is not important. What is your opinion? Include details and examples in your explanation.

Preparation Time: 15 Seconds
Response Time: 45 Seconds

下面是一個回答範例，應重讀的部分已用**粗體標出**。注意 /l/ 的發音。 **Track 054**

It's **good** for **certain people** to **get** a university education, but I **don't think** it's **necessary** for everyone. It's **true** we **need** to have **people** who are **versed** in **law** or **medicine**. We **also need** to have **people** who **work** to **advance** our **knowledge** in **science**. **These** professions **do require** a **college** education and **even beyond**. But we **also need** to have **people** who do **other** jobs—**jobs** that are **just** as important—if we're **going** to **have** a functioning **economy**.

For ex**a**mple, if you enj**oy** f**i**xing **things**, you can be**come** an electrician or a **plumber**. If you enj**oy** m**a**king **people** l**oo**k **good**, you can be**come** a beautician or a **hair styl**ist. For **these** professions, you can go to vocational **schools** to **learn** the necessary **skills**. **As** you can **see**, it's **not** necessary for **every person** to att**end** university.

現在，自己練一練這道題目，説説你對接受大學教育的看法。儘量留意位於單字中間位置的 /l/ 的發音！

• 要正確把握位於單字中間的 /l/ 音，可運用以下策略：

1. 注意這個 /l/ 音是在兩個母音之間，還是在母音後、輔音前。練習舌頭的移動。
2. 在練習時，將 /l/ 音誇大，比正常情況下念得時間更長一些，直到熟練掌握舌頭的移動並能自然發出這個音。
3. 有時位於詞中的 /l/ 音是在複合詞中，如 railroad。這種情況下，應將 rail 基本看做一個單獨的詞，這樣在 rail 中的 /l/ 音就是一個詞尾的 /l/ 音。然而，如果是 railing 這樣的詞，就應該將它發成 rai-ling，遵循上面講過的發音原則。

▶模擬試題③

Do you agree or disagree with this statement? It is more difficult to be a professor than a student. Include details and examples to support your opinion.

Preparation Time: 15 Seconds
Response Time: 45 Seconds

實用答題範本　　　　　🎧*Track 055* 聽聽看！別人的高分回答！（高分回答原文請見 P.281）

Being a professor may be hard in the sense that...
That's why I think it's much more difficult to be a(n)...

托福總監幫你預測可能會出現的題目！

1. Do you agree or disagree with this statement? Physical exercise should be required for first-year university students. Use specific reasons and details to support your answer.
2. Some students like to review their class notes every day. Other students prefer to wait till before the exam and go through their notes then. When do you prefer to review your notes? Use details and examples to explain your answer.
3. Do you agree or disagree with this statement? Science and engineering majors should be required to take a writing course. Give specific reasons and details to support your answer.

4. When preparing for a final exam, some students prefer to have a group study session. Others prefer to prepare alone. Which method do you prefer? Use specific reasons and examples to support your response.

5. Some university students like to live in a single room. Others prefer to live with roommates. Which living arrangement do you prefer? Use specific reasons and examples to support your answer.

• 最後再練習一下「有關高等教育話題」最實用的答題模板！

1. I prefer X instruction to Y classes because I believe that, when I'm..., I can VERB...

例 • I prefer traditional classroom instruction to online classes because I believe that, when I'm surrounded by people in a room, I can learn more.

• I prefer online instruction to traditional classes because I believe that, when I'm at home, I can save money.

2. It's also comforting to know I can VERB...

例 • It's also comforting to know I can ask my teachers questions as I think of them.

• It's also comforting to know I can take courses which are usually overcrowded.

3. So, for example, if the class is VERBing..., our teacher can VERB...

例 • So, for example, if the class is going over an assignment we didn't understand, our teacher can answer specific questions right then and there.

• So, for example, if the class is doing an experiment in the lab, our teacher can advise us how to use correct lab methods.

4. Plus, I can focus on..., instead of being distracted by...

例 • Plus, I can focus on learning, instead of being distracted by urges to surf the web, chat with friends or do other random things in my dorm.

• Plus, I can focus on my studies, instead of being distracted by the shops downtown.

5. I agree that students who go to faraway universities can VERB...

例 • I agree that students who go to faraway universities can benefit from the experience.

• I agree that students who go to faraway universities can learn more.

6. Although it's not easy to leave behind friends and family, at a distant university you can learn about... (and...)

例 • Although it's not easy to leave behind friends and family, at a distant university you can learn about the geography and culture of the new place.

• Although it's not easy to leave behind friends and family, at a distant university you can learn about the history of a different place.

7. Unlike students who live nearby, they don't VERB...

例 • Unlike students who live nearby, they don't get to go home on weekends.

• Unlike students who live nearby, they don't know their way around.

8. Nevertheless, as a result of living far away, students become...

例 • Nevertheless, as a result of living far away, students become stronger and tougher.

• Nevertheless, as a result of living far away, students become more independent.

9. It's good for certain people to VERB..., but I don't think it's necessary for everyone.

例 • It's good for certain people to get a university education, but I don't think it's necessary for everyone.

• It's good for certain people to study advanced mathematics, but I don't think it's necessary for everyone.

10. But we also need to have people who do other jobs—jobs that are just as important—if we're going to VERB...

例 • But we also need to have people who do other jobs—jobs that are just as important—if we're going to have a functioning economy.

• But we also need to have people who do other jobs—jobs that are just as important—if we're going to have a complete range of services.

11. For example, if you enjoy fixing things, you can become a(n) X or a(n) Y.

例 • For example, if you enjoy fixing things, you can become an electrician or a plumber.

• For example, if you enjoy fixing things, you can become a repairman or a tailor.

12. For these professions, you can VERB...to learn the necessary skills.

例 • For these professions, you can go to vocational schools to learn the necessary skills.

• For these professions, you can become an apprentice to learn the necessary skills.

13. As you can see, it's not necessary for every person to VERB...

例 • As you can see, it's not necessary for every person to attend university.

• As you can see, it's not necessary for every person to have a white-collar job.

14. Well, I'm afraid I disagree with...

例 • Well, I'm afraid I disagree with the statement.

• Well, I'm afraid I disagree with that point of view.

15. Being a professor may be hard in the sense that...

例 • Being a professor may be hard in the sense that one needs to have certain qualifications.

• Being a professor may be hard in the sense that it takes a long time to get a PhD.

16. But once a person becomes a professor, ...

例 • But once a person becomes a professor, the hardest part is over.

• But once a person becomes a professor, there's not that much work to do.

17. So we push ourselves really hard, to the point where...

例 • So we push ourselves really hard, to the point where it seems that life is only work and no fun.

• So we push ourselves really hard, to the point where all we do is work, work, work.

17. That's why I think it's much more difficult to be a(n)...

例 • That's why I think it's much more difficult to be a student.

• That's why I think it's much more difficult to be a teacher.

Life Choices and Life Lessons
生活中的抉擇和經驗教訓

❝ 在本章，你將學到…… ❞

★如何通過重複關鍵字來加強回答的邏輯連貫性
★如何用情態動詞 would 表達喜好與意願

解讀常考題

　　第二題還會涉及人生抉擇和經驗教訓。關於生活抉擇的題目如：When should people get married? / Should people live in the city or in the suburbs? 關於生活經驗教訓的題目會問考生從生活中學到了什麼、是怎樣學到的，如：Do people learn from their mistakes? / Do they learn from their parents? / How should children be raised? 這些問題所涉及的語言不會特別難，但探討的話題相對較深。回答這類問題時，典型的模式是：From this encounter, I learned that... / Although the decision to study in a boarding school was a difficult one, I think I benefited from the experience.

　　現在，看一道關於人生抉擇的例題。

▶舉例試題

Do you agree or disagree with this statement? Children should help do household tasks when they reach a certain age. Include details and examples to support your opinion.

Preparation Time: 15 Seconds
Response Time: 45 Seconds

托福總監告訴你怎麼答！

　　這道題要求考生回答孩子是不是應該做家事。考生應先表明自己的立場，然後進一步說明原因。回答過程中，應儘量重複關鍵字，使前後有連貫性。這樣做的目的是使觀點明確，有理有據。

策略：重複關鍵字

　　內容的銜接性和連貫性是高分作文和口語共有的特點。上一章已經講到，前後銜接指的是詞語、分句和句子在文法上連接起來的方式。而連貫性則指觀點的流暢展開，是「意

思上的聯繫」。很多考生或許已經聽說過一些方法，通過在段落中有邏輯地將觀點串聯，使寫出的作文更加連貫，但很多考生並不知道怎樣讓口頭回答變得連貫流暢。如果口語回答缺乏連貫性，評分人的思路就很難跟上考生觀點的展開，因此會給出較低的分數。

在回答中達到連貫性的一種方式是重複關鍵字。但是，這並不等於對整個片語或分句進行機械的、不假思索的重複。重複是要講究技巧的。通過重複關鍵字來組織連貫的回答，只需簡單的三個步驟：

1. 說話時，首先要考慮話語的意思和內容。
2. 根據句子所表達的意思，找出前一句話（或再之前的句子）中最重要的話題或觀點，然後選定關鍵字（或片語）。
3. 站在聽者（即評分人）的角度考慮問題，試著「架構」一節一節的「橋樑」，用關鍵字將前一句話和後一句話連接起來。

高分回答

注意看，仔細聽，這裡面標上粗體的地方都要發重音才道地喔！　 Track 056

I **strongly agree** that **children** should **help** their **family** with **house**work. The **first benefit** for **children** is **teamwork training**. **Sharing house**work is a **perfect** opportunity for **young children** to **learn how** to **work** within a **group**, albeit a **group made up** of **his** or **her kin**. **This** experience will **surely** be **very helpful** when the **child** goes **out** in the **world** and begins to **work** with other **groups**. Another **benefit** that **comes** with **work** at a **young age** is the development of a **good work** ethic. Unsurprisingly, **good citizens** of a **society tend** to be individuals with a **sense** of **duty** and a **love** for **honest** work. Since **teamwork** and a **work e**thic are important to a **prosperous society**, **I** think we should encourage **parents** to involve **children** in **house**hold **tasks**.

托福總監為什麼覺得這是高分回答？

在這個回答中，首句為主題句，直接表明了態度。你可以看到這個回答從第二句開始慢慢構建連貫性，重複了首句的關鍵字 children，而第三句重複了前兩句的兩個關鍵字：housework 和 children，第四句又重複了兩個關鍵字：child（children 的變化）和 group，都是前一句中出現過的詞。第五句提到了 benefit（是對第二句觀點的重複）和前一句話中出現的 work。第六句又提到 work，陳述做家事對兒童的另一個益處。最後一句則重複了很多之前說過的詞：teamwork、work ethic、society 和 household tasks（household tasks 是從題幹摘取的關鍵字）。最後一句非常巧妙，不僅使回答更加連貫，也總結了考生的觀點。

要透過重複關鍵字加強回答的連貫性，可運用以下策略：

1. 在回答問題時，腦中要明白知道你提出的觀點到底要傳達什麼意思。
2. 從自己前面說過的句子中選出一兩個關鍵字。選關鍵字時要有技巧，不要盲目重複詞語。

3. 為評分人著想，儘量讓他們輕鬆地理解你的觀點，將每句話都看做連接上下句的「橋樑」。
4. 在重複詞語的時候使用同義詞或進行同義改述。
5. 結尾句可再次加強連貫效果，以使結論更加有力。

▶模擬試題①

請回答下題。回答時，可嘗試使用下面列出的實用答題範本。

> **Do you agree or disagree with this statement? We can learn more about ourselves by making mistakes. Include details and examples to support your opinion.**
>
> Preparation Time: 15 Seconds
> Response Time: 45 Seconds

實用答題範本 🎧 *Track 057* 聽聽看！別人的高分回答！（高分回答原文請見 P.281）
I VERB （表達觀點的動詞） that people can learn from their mistakes.
For example, VERBing...

得分考技：用 would 表達喜好與意願

新托福口語考試的很多題目都會問到在某些情況下你會怎樣做（what you would do），所以掌握情態動詞 would 是極其重要的。例如：第二題和第五題都要求考生從兩種觀點中選出一種並說明選擇的原因。甚至在第一題中，即使你可以隨意選擇所「偏愛」的事物或活動，也應牢固掌握情態動詞 would 的用法，例如要會使用類似下面的句子：If I could go anywhere in the world on vacation, I would travel to the South Pole.

在英語中，情態動詞 would 有很多用法，但是在考試時，主要應該注意下列兩種用法：
1. 表達對某事物的偏好；
2. 表達想去做某事的意願。

這兩種情況都涉及非實際及想像的情況，主要會用到兩種文法結構：

結構	would + 動詞原形	would + 動詞原形 + 動詞不定式
例句	Given a choice, ... 1. I would study French. 2. I would rather stay at home than travel.	Given a choice, ... 1. I would choose to study French. 2. I would love to travel. 3. I would prefer to stay at home.

托福總監帶你練

聽下列句子，練習情態動詞 would 的用法。反覆聽錄音，然後跟著讀。 *Track 058*

1. **I would like to learn more about French culture** through **first-hand** experience in **France**.
2. **Given a choice** between **working** and doing **nothing**, **I would choose to work**.

3. If I saw a **child** on the **street** who was **having** an emergency, **I'd do** what I **could** to **help** him.
4. I'd **love** to **live** in a **big old house** in the **countryside**.
5. If I was in **trouble**, **I'd** probably **try** to **solve** the **problem** by my**self**.

▶模擬試題②

Some people say that childhood is the best time in life. Others say that old age (the "golden years") is the best time. Which time do you think is best? Include details and examples in your explanation.

Preparation Time: 15 Seconds
Response Time: 45 Seconds

下面是一個回答範例，應重讀的部分已用**粗體標出**。注意回答中 would 的用法。

Track 059

Although I'm **still young**, **I'd say** that **old age** is the **best time**. **Childhood** is a **time** when we **busy** ourselves with **learning**, and **middle age** is the **time** when we **strive** to **apply** what we have **learned**—to ad**vance** whatever **cause** we have undertaken. However, in **old age**, we can **sit back** and **relish** our accom**plishments**. Of **course**, it's impossible for us to di**vide** our **lives neatly** into **three distinct stages**. I'm **sure** there are **happy times** in **each stage**. But **on** balance, I be**lieve** we'll **have** the **most time** to **enjoy** our **lives** in our **golden years**. At **least** I **hope** so. I would **like** to re**lax** and en**joy** my **old age**, surrounded by **friends** and **loved ones**.

現在，自己練一練這道題目，說說你對人生黃金階段的觀點。試著在回答中使用情態動詞 would。

• 想掌握情態動詞 would 的用法，可運用以下策略：

1. 複習情態動詞 would 用於表達意願和喜好時的基本文法結構。為了記住文法規則，可在心裡默念：Given a choice, I would...。如：Given a choice, I would relax all the time. / Given a choice, I prefer to relax. 學會用這些結構會給你的回答加分，尤其是在第二題和第五題中。
2. 讀題時，注意題幹中是否出現了 would 一詞，如：Would you like to travel somewhere you have never been before? 這暗示你也許需要在回答時使用情態動詞。
3. 記住，在口語中，I would... 通常被簡化為 I'd...，應在回答中熟練運用這兩種形式。

▶模擬試題③

Some people like to live in large cities. Other people like to live outside of cities, in the suburbs. Which living environment suits you? Include details and examples to support your opinion.

Preparation Time: 15 Seconds
Response Time: 45 Seconds

實用答題範本　　　　　🎧*Track 060* 聽聽看！別人的高分回答！（高分回答原文請見 P.282）

That's why I would definitely choose to live in...

In..., there are also lots of places where people can VERB... (and VERB...)

托福總監幫你預測可能會出現的題目！

1. Do you agree or disagree with this statement? Having children makes people's lives more difficult. Use specific reasons and details to support your answer.

2. Some people like to learn about many different cultures. Other people prefer to focus on their own culture. Which approach to culture is your preference? Use details and examples to explain your answer.

3. Do you agree or disagree with this statement? If we see people in an emergency situation, we should immediately help them. Use specific reasons and details to support your answer.

4. Some people like to carefully plan what they are going to do in their free time. Others like to decide what they will do at the last minute. Which attitude do you prefer? Use specific details and examples to support your response.

5. Do you agree or disagree with this statement? A person can learn more from personal experience than from the advice of family and friends. Use specific reasons and details to support your answer.

• 最後再練習一下「表達抉擇和陳述經驗教訓」最實用的答題模板！

1. I strongly agree that children should help their family...

　例　• I strongly agree that children should help their family with housework.

　　　• I strongly agree that children should help their family do chores.

2. The first benefit for children is...

　例　• The first benefit for children is teamwork training.

　　　• The first benefit for children is learning life skills.

3. **This experience will surely be very helpful when the child goes out in the world and...**

   例 • This experience will surely be very helpful when the child goes out in the world and begins to work with other groups.

   • This experience will surely be very helpful when the child goes out in the world and has to manage a home.

4. **Another benefit that comes with work at a young age is the development of...**

   例 • Another benefit that comes with work at a young age is the development of a good work ethic.

   • Another benefit that comes with work at a young age is the development of self confidence.

5. **I VERB（表達觀點的動詞） that people can learn from their mistakes.**

   例 • I agree that people can learn from their mistakes.

   • I don't think that people can learn from their mistakes.

6. **Basically, we VERB...what it is that we don't know, or what we can't do.**

   例 • Basically, we learn what it is that we don't know, or what we can't do.

   • Basically, we are confronted with what it is that we don't know, or what we can't do.

7. **For example, VERBing...**

   例 • For example, learning how to cook a stew.

   • For example, giving a public presentation.

8. **This mistake taught me that I actually didn't know...**

   例 • This mistake taught me that I actually didn't know as much as I thought I did.

   • This mistake taught me that I actually didn't know the proper method.

9. **If we VERB..., we have learned more about ourselves.**

   例 • If we identify the problem, we have learned more about ourselves.

   • If we understand the reason for our errors, we have learned more about ourselves.

10. **Although I'm still young, I'd say that...is the best time.**

    例 • Although I'm still young, I'd say that old age is the best time.

    • Although I'm still young, I'd say that early childhood is the best time.

11. **Childhood is a time when we VERB..., and middle age is the time when we VERB...**

    例 • Childhood is a time when we busy ourselves with learning, and middle age is the time when we strive to apply what we have learned—to advance whatever cause we have undertaken.

- Childhood is a time when we are innocent, and middle age is the time when we feel all the pressures of life.

12. However, in old age, we can VERB...and VERB...

例 • However, in old age, we can sit back and relish our accomplishments.

- However, in old age, we can slow down and take it easy.

13. I'm sure there are...in each stage.

例 • I'm sure there are happy times in each stage.

- I'm sure there are special moments in each stage.

14. I would like to VERB..., surrounded by friends and loved ones.

例 • I would like to relax and enjoy my old age, surrounded by friends and loved ones.

- I would like to retire from my job, surrounded by friends and loved ones.

15. I am a young person, and so I like to live where...

例 • I am a young person, and so I like to live where the action is.

- I am a young person, and so I like to live where other young people are.

16. That's why I would definitely choose to live in...

例 • That's why I would definitely choose to live in a big city.

- That's why I would definitely choose to live in the suburbs.

17. Cities are often X and Y, but I love the energy.

例 • Cities are often noisy and dirty, but I love the energy.

- Cities are often crowded and stressful, but I love the energy.

18. In..., there are also lots of places where people can VERB... (and VERB...)

例 • In cities, there are also lots of places where people can find good food and good entertainment.

- In the suburbs, there are also lots of places where people can relax and enjoy the clean air.

19. Although young people don't have a lot of money, they can always VERB...

例 • Although young people don't have a lot of money, they can always find places to get together, grab a bite to eat and listen to good music.

- Although young people don't have a lot of money, they can always have a good time in cities.

Section ❸

Campus Life: Tasks 3 and 5

第❸部分
第三題 & 第五題：
命題總監教你，校園生活一把罩！

Task 3 Summarizing an Opinion
第三題 概述觀點

第三題題目形式：先要求考生閱讀一篇討論校園某項新政策的小文章。然後，考生會聽到一段對話：兩位學生討論閱讀材料中所討論的政策。對話結束之後，題目會要求考生總結強烈贊同或不贊同該政策的那個學生的觀點。想獲得高分，需要在回答中盡可能多地抓住這位學生給出的理由。

▶小文章

小文章篇幅在 75 ～ 100 個單字之間，考生會有 40 ～ 45 秒的閱讀時間，閱讀時間取決於小文章的長度。有些文章是刊登在大學校刊上給編輯的信，還有一些是簡短的公告。無論體裁如何，小文章都會討論一項政策、計畫或提案。一般會出現支持新政策的兩種理由。同樣，給校刊的來信通常也包含支持作者的兩種理由。記住，要在閱讀中找到這些理由，這樣才能夠與之後播放的錄音中「觀點鮮明強烈」的學生的觀點進行對比。

▶對話

在小文章之後，會有一段長度為 60 ～ 80 秒的學生對話。一般都是一個男生和一個女生。對話中，一位學生會先談論小文章中提到的計畫，隨後兩位學生展開討論。有時，其中一位學生只說一兩個字，所以談話似乎是一個人在滔滔不絕，但其實兩人的語速並不快。判斷學生的觀點並不難，因為其中一人對政策問題始終持有強烈的意見，這位學生通常比另一位說得多，並且會對問題做較為詳細的闡述。相反，另一位學生相對被動，主要是「襯托」那位觀點突出的學生，通常很少反對或辯駁，只說類似 Oh, yeah, I see what you mean 這樣的話。所以考生可以忽略這位被動的學生，而將注意力放在那位積極抒發自己見解的學生上，第三題最後問的就是這位學生的觀點。題目不會考查小文章中的細節，這些只是作為背景資訊。在第三題中，準確記下相對而言觀點更為鮮明、堅定的人的想法是非常關鍵的。

有時候，聽力材料中可能只有一位說話人回應新計畫或政策。這一獨白也會包含兩個理由或解釋，說明為什麼說話人喜歡或不喜歡該政策。

▶提問形式

對話結束後，考生會聽到並在電腦螢幕上看到題目。考生有 30 秒鐘的準備時間，在這期間可以進行思考、查看筆記並標示關鍵字。在「嗶」的一聲之後，有 60 秒的回答時間。

第三題的題目措辭都非常相似，最常見的形式如下：

1. The man expresses his opinion about the university's plan. State his opinion and explain the reasons he gives.

2. Briefly summarize the proposal in the student's letter. Then state the woman's opinion about the proposal and explain her reasons.

3. The painting class is considering a change in schedule. Explain the man's opinion of the proposed change and his reasons.

大多數第三題的問題都會以第一種形式出現。

▶評分人如何對第三題評分？

根據評分準則，綜合型題目的評分標準基本上與第一題和第二題一致，只有一處不同：回答必須充分傳達「題目要求的相關資訊」。這表示回答時必須抓住意見強烈鮮明者的觀點和邏輯。如果答案不完整，即使講得流利、文法正確，還是會被扣分，所以考生回答第三題時必須緊扣話題。

大多數第三題的話題都是很好理解的，涉及的都是非常典型的大學校園問題，只要熟悉大學建築、政策之類問題的文化背景，理解主題就不成什麼問題。首先，小文章很短，且易於理解。其次，學生所用的語言一般不會有艱深詞彙。只要準確理解對話，語言表達清晰易懂且有條理，並對學生觀點進行了完整的概括，就能得到高分。

但是，有時候即使能聽懂對話，可能還是難以跟上該學生論證的邏輯。邏輯非常關鍵！要想完整地掌握對話中的推理，進行流利的討論，理解情境非常重要。

▶第三題的六個主要情境

第三題中最常見的情境可分為六類：

1. 大學的投資與支出
2. 大學服務──健康中心、餐廳和圖書館
3. 大學服務──住宿、交通和設施管理
4. 大學課程設置
5. 學生活動
6. 打工與實習

接下來的章節會分別講解以上每一種情境，並給出多道題目、回答範例和實用答題範本。透過在情境中練習這些題目，你可以更容易地記住考試中會用到的字彙。

13 University Investments and Expenditures
大學的投資與支出

在本章，你將學到……

★如何組織第三題的答題思路
★如何發雙母音和長母音

解讀常考題

第三題常涉及大學管理人員做出的財政方面決定。例如：大學怎樣決定修建一座新圖書館或體育館。其他常見的公告有：為幫助學校節省開支，而提出的削減成本提案等。學生們必須支付學雜費，而且要使用大學提供的設施和服務，所以他們肯定會對大學怎樣花錢有自己的看法。

現在，看一道關於大學開支的例題。

▶舉例試題

Narrator: You will now read a short passage on a campus situation and then listen to a talk on that same subject. Then you will be asked to answer a question from both the reading and the talk. After the question you will have 30 seconds to prepare and 60 seconds to respond.

Narrator: State University is planning to expand its library. Read the article from the university newspaper about the plan. You will have 45 seconds to read the article. Begin reading now.

Reading Time: 45 Seconds

Library Expansion Will Enable Growth

The State University Library recently announced a $40 million expansion, to include new shelf space for books and an area with study cubicles. At present the library's shelves are almost completely full, which has caused problems with crowding. Best practices for libraries say that shelving should be occupied at 86 percent. The library staff already manages a collection that includes thousands of books, subscriptions and journals. The new space will not only accommodate library collection growth, it will also provide new services for students such as multimedia production, writing centers and group study areas.

Narrator: Now listen to two students discussing the article.

🎧 *Track 061* （播放錄音檔 061，錄音原文見特別收錄 2 的 P.292）

The woman expresses her opinion about the university's plan for library expansion. State her opinion and explain the reasons she gives for that opinion.

Preparation Time: 30 Seconds
Response Time: 60 Seconds

Narrator: You have 30 seconds to prepare.
Narrator: Begin speaking after the beep.

策略：第三題的答題思路

對於四道綜合型口語題，評分人會評判考生是否「完成」題目的具體要求。要完成第三題的要求，成功回答，只需三個簡單的步驟：

1. 閱讀小文章、聽錄音時做筆記。小文章會給出實施計畫的兩條主要理由。
2. 回答時，首先說明這個學生是支持還是反對這項計畫。提供的細節足夠讓聽者理解計畫涉及的內容即可。
3. 然後，說明學生對每條理由的看法。在時間允許範圍內儘量多給出有關其看法的細節。

因時間有限，你應只提供用來「完成」題目的資訊。如有下列情況，會被扣分：

1. 語言表意模糊，概括不清晰。
2. 未包括學生反對或支持該計畫的兩個原因之一，或兩個都沒包括。
3. 誤解並錯誤地陳述材料中的事實。
4. 未能在闡述中表現出緊密的銜接和連貫性。
5. 缺乏對基本文法和詞彙的掌握。
6. 發音和重音不正確，讓人難以理解你的表述。

出現個別小錯誤、使用極淺顯的詞彙回答問題都是可以的，對拿高分並無太大影響。

高分回答

注意看，仔細聽，這裡面標上粗體的地方都要發重音才道地喔！ *Track 062*

The **woman** does **not** like the **library** ex**pan**sion **plan**, which will **add more space** and **more books** to the **library** col**lec**tion.（←提出一位學生的觀點）
She thinks it's un**nec**essary to build a **new wing** if the **library** acquires electronic **books** and **journals** instead of **hard**-cover **re**sources. **E**-books do **not take up** **phys**ical **shelf space** and are **also eas**ily **up**dated. She **also** thinks it's a **bad idea** to provide ad**di**tional **study** space in the **library**. It would make **more** sense for the university to **use** the **money** to **build** an ad**di**tion to the **cafe**teria, where **students** could go to **study**. There's **not** enough **study** space in **that** part of **campus**. More**over**, **this** would be convenient for **students** because they could get **snacks** during **study** breaks.（←說明學生持該觀點的理由）

托福總監為什麼覺得這是高分回答？

該考生開門見山地答出對話中女生的觀點和兩個理由，答題思路非常清晰。

要答好第三題，可運用以下策略：

1. 找到文章重點，即校方提出的新專案的內容，以及兩條理由。
2. 聽對話時，快速判斷出哪位學生「觀點鮮明強烈」，是支持還是反對該政策。
3. 注意該學生的論證。盡可能多地針對其提出的兩個要點做筆記。
4. 開門見山地回答題幹的要求。在上面的回答範例中，首句立刻闡明了女生的觀點。
5. 概括這個學生的觀點時，應簡要說明這項政策是什麼，添加的細節足以讓不瞭解情況的聽者明白事情的背景即可。
6. 如果該學生不同意提案，要描述其駁斥小文章所給出的兩條理由的兩個論證。
7. 如果該學生同意提案，要描述其支持提案的兩條理由。這些理由可能與小文章所給出的有所不同。
8. 不要花時間概括小文章提到的所有細節。你的時間會不夠用的！
9. 不要加上你個人的觀點。

　　在回答第三題時要當心：有些考生會給出自己對政策或計畫的看法，這種回答會被扣分！記住：第三題要求考生概括的是觀點鮮明強烈的那位學生的看法。

▶模擬試題①

　　請回答下題。回答時，可嘗試使用下面列出的實用答題範本。

Narrator: City University's radio station recently expanded its broadcasting area. Read the article about this project. You will have 45 seconds to read the article.

Reading Time: 45 Seconds

University Radio Station Expands Reach

Today City University officials announced it would invest $10 million in the University's radio station, WXY-2. The station will expand its broadcast area and programming content as part of the project. After years of broadcasting to a university audience, the radio station will now be able to rebroadcast the WXY-2 signal, through the recent addition of new powerful transmitters.

The station will now be able to reach the three adjoining counties in our state, thereby expanding our listening community. WXY-2, already a regionally recognized leader in radio programming, will also enhance its innovative rock and roll programming by adding jazz and folk music.

Narrator: Now listen to two students discussing the article.

🎧 *Track 063*（播放錄音檔 063，錄音原文見特別收錄 2 的 P.292）

The man expresses his opinion about the radio station's plans for expansion. State his opinion and explain the reasons he gives for holding that opinion.

Preparation Time: 30 Seconds
Response Time: 60 Seconds

實用答題範本 🎧 *Track 064* 聽聽看！別人的高分回答！（高分回答原文請見 P.282）

The man is happy about the news that...
University students will have more opportunities to VERB...

得分考技：用飽滿的雙母音和長母音打動考官的耳朵

　　對於評分人來說，「容易理解」是一個非常重要的評分標準，而評分人對考生的回答產生理解困難的原因之一就是考生雙母音的發音不準確。

　　雙母音是在單一音節中的母音組合，發音時從一個母音滑到另一個母音。雖然發出的是兩個音，聽者聽到時卻會將其作為一個單位。如果考生不能將雙母音發得夠清楚，評分人可能會聽成不同的母音而誤解詞義。英語中大概 10% 的單音節單字包含雙母音，所以練習雙母音對考生來說非常重要。另外，還有更多單字包含的母音是長母音，將這些音發清楚也很重要。

　　常見的重要雙母音和長母音如下表所示：

類型	發音	範例
雙母音	/e/	day
	/aɪ/	eye
	/aʊ/	now
	/ɔɪ/	boy
	/o/	low
長母音	/i/	seen
	/u/	true

托福總監帶你練

　　聽對話，練習母音的發音方式。注意用底線標出的含雙母音或長母音的音節。反覆聽錄音，然後跟著讀。 🎧 *Track 065*

1. **Woman:** Have you <u>seen</u> the <u>plan</u> about the <u>new</u> student <u>hou</u>sing?
   Man: Yeah, they're <u>say</u>ing all the dorm <u>rooms</u> will be sunny and have <u>good</u> <u>light</u>.
2. **Man:** Did you <u>read</u> the a<u>nnounce</u>ment in the paper? They're <u>going</u> to <u>tear</u> <u>down</u> <u>Sloan</u> Laboratory?
   Woman: <u>Sloan</u>? That building has been <u>on</u> campus for a hundred <u>years</u>!

3. **Woman:** I <u>found</u> <u>Jay's</u> letter to the editor ri<u>di</u>culous, the **one** <u>say</u>ing <u>smo</u>king should be <u>allow</u>ed in **class**.

   Man: I a<u>gree</u>. The **last thing** we <u>need</u> is to be su<u>rroun</u>ded by cigarette <u>smoke</u> all <u>day</u> long.

• **想發好雙母音和長母音，使回答更易理解，可運用以下策略：**

1. 先通過聽錄音或有發音功能的線上字典學習這些發音，然後重複誦讀。錄下自己的發音，聽聽是否將每個母音都念得夠長。
2. 在發長母音或雙母音時，確保每個母音都發得夠長。不要將音發到一半就停住。
3. 考試中不要著急！從容地將每個母音組合的發音發清楚、發完整。

▶ 模擬試題②

請回答下面關於大學投資的問題。回答時，可嘗試使用下面列出的實用答題範本。

Narrator: Read a student letter in the university newspaper. You will have 45 seconds to read the letter. Begin reading now.

Reading Time: 45 Seconds

Shortage of Dormitory Rooms

The University is experiencing a housing shortage due to an unforeseen number of first-year students. To address this problem, we should do what many other universities are doing—convert lounges and study areas in main campus dormitories into open rooms for "triples," rooms with 3 students. This investment in converted open rooms would allow us to house the unexpected first-year students. The converted spaces would provide the same amenities as other dorm rooms, including desks and bookshelves. Furthermore, because these spaces are usually very large—16 by 17 feet in size—the rooms would be very spacious and comfortable.

Sincerely,

Ken Moore

Narrator: Now listen to two students discussing the letter.

🎧 *Track 066* （播放錄音檔 066，錄音原文見特別收錄 2 的 P.292）

Briefly summarize the proposal in the student's letter. Then state the woman's opinion about the proposal and explain the reasons she gives for holding that opinion.

Preparation Time: 30 Seconds
Response Time: 60 Seconds

實用答題範本　　🎧 *Track 067* 聽聽看！別人的高分回答！（高分回答原文請見 P.282）

What the student recommends is...

That's why she's against...

• 最後再練習一下「有關大學的投資與支出的說法」最實用的答題模板！

1. The woman does not like the...
例 • The woman does not like the library expansion plan.
  • The woman does not like the idea of a new stadium.

2. She thinks it's unnecessary to build...
例 • She thinks it's unnecessary to build a new wing.
  • She thinks it's unnecessary to build additional dorms.

3. She also thinks it's a bad idea to VERB...
例 • She also thinks it's a bad idea to provide additional study space in the library.
  • She also thinks it's a bad idea to construct new dorms.

4. It would make more sense for the university to VERB...
例 • It would make more sense for the university to use the money to build an addition to the cafeteria.
  • It would make more sense for the university to tear down the old dorms.

5. This would be convenient for students because they could VERB...
例 • This would be convenient for students because they could get snacks during study breaks.
  • This would be convenient for students because they could study there.

6. The man is happy about the news that...
例 • The man is happy about the news that the university radio station is going to expand.
  • The man is happy about the news that a new chemistry lab is being built.

7. University students will have more opportunities to VERB...
例 • University students will have more opportunities to work in the radio business.
  • University students will have more opportunities to learn about being a DJ.

8. What the student recommends is...
例 • What the student recommends is taking the lounges and study areas in the main dorms and converting these spaces into dorm rooms.
  • What the student recommends is building dorms closer to campus.

9. The other point the woman makes is that...
例 • The other point the woman makes is that freshmen need to socialize.
  • The other point the woman makes is that students need a new cafeteria.

10. That's why she's against...
例 • That's why she's against converting those rooms into big dorm rooms.
  • That's why she's against investing in a new library.
  • That's why she's against the proposal.

University Services—Health Center, Cafeteria and Library
大學服務—健康中心、餐廳和圖書館

在本章，你將學到……

★第三題如何記筆記
★如何利用間接引語幫你提高分數

解讀常考題

　　新托福口語考試第三題還會針對校園服務的話題提問，這樣的服務涉及學校的健康中心、餐廳和圖書館。各學校的保健服務各有不同，但是通常都提供一系列的醫療保健服務，包括常規的醫療服務和急診。以此情境為背景的題目中，閱讀材料可能會是一條公告，例如：公告學校經營的醫療設施要關閉，所以今後學生就必須得去看私人醫生。

　　和學校自助餐店或餐廳相關的話題可能涉及食物的品質、設備或服務，例如：一個學生向校刊投訴自助餐的價格。

　　圖書館的政策也是第三題常見的話題。學生們總希望學校圖書館的開放時間能夠延長。學校管理人員和圖書管理員常常會考慮到預算問題、自習區域的噪音情況和擴大筆電使用權問題，例如：報紙上的一篇關於圖書館計畫在夏季縮短開放時間的文章。在所有這些情境中，對話中的學生會針對閱讀材料中的觀點或計畫提出支持或反對意見。

　　現在，看一道關於大學醫療保健服務的例題。

▶舉例試題

Narrator: The university health center is planning to change its sports medicine services. Read the article in the university newspaper about the change. You will have 45 seconds to read the article. Begin reading now.
Reading Time: 45 Seconds

> ### Sports Medicine Services
> Beginning next fall, the Sports Medicine Clinic, which is affiliated with the University Health Center, will offer sports medicine services only to members of varsity teams. Student athletes seeking to use the Sports Medicine Clinic can continue to make appointments through their team trainer or contact the Clinic directly. Sports medicine services for athletes include physical therapy, sports nutrition, sports psychology and consultations with surgeons. Non-athlete students who seek medical care for a sports injury will now need to make appointments with the regular doctors at the University Health Center.

Narrator: Now listen to two students discussing the article.

🎧 *Track 068* （播放錄音檔 068，錄音原文見特別收錄 2 的 P.293）

The man expresses his opinion about the university's plan to change sports medicine services. State his opinion and explain the reasons he gives for that opinion.

Preparation Time: 30 Seconds
Response Time: 60 Seconds

Narrator: You have 30 seconds to prepare.
Narrator: Begin speaking after the beep.

策略：第三題記筆記的訣竅

　　前面已經講過答第一題和第二題時如何做筆記。而綜合型題目要根據聽到的錄音和讀到的小文章做筆記，這兩類題目的筆記策略是不同的。

　　第三題的答題準備時間有 30 秒，準備時間比第一題和第二題要長一些。

　　做第三題的筆記時，需要遵循以下幾個步驟：

1. 讀小文章時，找到大學的新政策，寫下來。
2. 聽對話時，注意聽學生的觀點，記下這個人的性別，弄清楚他（她）是支持還是反對小文章提到的新政策。
3. 重點聽學生的觀點，抓住他（她）支持或反對新政策的兩個理由，用簡寫形式記下來。

高分回答

注意看，仔細聽，這裡面標上粗體的地方都要發重音才道地喔！ *Track 069*

The university has announced that it will allow only university team athletes to use the Sports Medicine Clinic. Students who aren't team athletes will now have to go see regular Health Center doctors. The man says that he supports the university's decision. His reasons are as follows: First, he believes that having successful athletic teams is a priority for the university. If the university wants to attract excellent high school athletes, it needs to have excellent facilities, including sports medicine facilities. Second, the man says that working out and other forms of exercise are very popular among students. As a result, he says there have been large numbers of students who weren't university team athletes at the Sports Medicine Clinic. The Clinic wasn't able to deal with those numbers, and so it wanted to limit the services to just team athletes.

托福總監為什麼覺得這是高分回答？

　　分析一下就知道怎樣做筆記可以幫你組織出如此嚴密的回答。第一句和第二句明確陳述了這項新政策是什麼：以後學校只為學校的運動員提供醫療服務，普通學生只能去常規的保健中心就診。第三句表明了該男生的意見：他支持這項政策。剩下的句子說明他支持該政策的兩個理由。第一個理由：體育運動對於該學校很重要，必須要招募到優秀的運動員，因此優質的醫療服務也很重要。第二個原因：現在參與體育活動的普通學生太多了，因此體育醫療診所的空間已經不夠了。

做這道題目的筆記時，可記下如下的單字及縮寫：

```
sports medicine
M pro
athletics important
elite
too many reg stud
```

如果你能夠記下更多該男生的觀點，那當然更好，但上面這些已經夠你講出一個出色的回答了。sports medicine 是描述學校新政策時所要用到的片語。M 是 man 的縮寫（如果陳述觀點的是女生，就寫 W）。pro 是「支持」的意思（如果表示反對，可用 con）。athletics important 是對男生給出的第一個理由的速記：athletics are important to this university。elite 是談論第一個理由時可以用到的低頻形容詞，描述學校想要招募哪種類型的運動員。too many reg stud 是 too many regular students 的簡寫，是該男生覺得新政策合理的第二個理由。準備好了這個框架，你就可以組織出一段出色的回答。現在，回顧一下上面的回答，想想你在組織框架時會怎樣記筆記吧！

想做好第三題的筆記，可運用以下策略：

1. 題目不會直接考查小文章中的內容，這些內容只提供一些背景資訊。只需記下小文章中的關鍵字（通常都是小文章的題目）。

2. 一般情況下，主要說話者只有一個人，其觀點鮮明。在記筆記時，只需要集中注意力聽此人的觀點，因為最後的問題會提問該人的觀點。快速判斷這個人是男性還是女性，記下 W 或 M。

3. 對話中，沒有表達觀點的學生通常只說些沒有實質內容的話，如 Really? 和 Yeah, that's right，不需留意這個學生所說的內容。

4. 注意對話中表達鮮明觀點的學生所說的內容，弄清他（她）支持或反對這一觀點的兩個理由。

5. 及時用簡寫形式記下這兩個理由。

6. 根據這些筆記，組織出一段前後銜接緊密且連貫的回答。

▶模擬試題①

請回答下題。回答時，可嘗試使用下面列出的實用答題範本。

Narrator: Read a student letter about food services in Central College newspaper. You will have 45 seconds to read the letter. Begin reading now.

Reading Time: 45 Seconds

New Dining Services

The new food court that has replaced the dormitory dining hall has made students very happy. We no longer have to eat overcooked food that has been sitting on steam tables for hours. Instead, we can have things like pizza right out of the oven, tasty hamburgers

---

and freshly made French fries. Everyone can see how popular the food court is from the large number of students going in and out every day. Outsourcing food services to private contractors was a great idea.

It's a win-win prospect for the administration and students alike!

Sincerely,

Mark Oliver

Narrator: Now listen to two students discussing the letter.

🎧 *Track 070* （播放錄音檔 070，錄音原文見特別收錄 2 的 P.293）

Briefly summarize the views expressed in the student's letter. Then state the woman's opinion about the letter and explain the reasons she gives for holding that opinion.

Preparation Time: 30 Seconds
Response Time: 60 Seconds

實用答題範本　　　　　🎧 *Track 071* 聽聽看！別人的高分回答！（高分回答原文請見 P.282）

A student named...has written a letter to the college newspaper, praising...

She believes that the college should hire...

得分考技：間接引語用處多

　　第三題到第六題的回答很可能要用到間接引語。間接引語是什麼呢？舉例來看，回答第三題時，一開始可能會這麼說：The man says that... / The woman said that... 在回答第四題和第六題時，一開始可能會這麼說：The professor describes how... / The professor talked about how...

　　這些「間接引用別人的話用的句型」，就是間接引語。現在可以看出間接引語有多麼重要了吧！六道題目中的三道題目都需要用到！很明顯，掌握間接引語能夠幫助你提高分數，也會加強你傳遞資訊的清晰程度、文法的準確性。

　　口語中到底什麼才是間接引語呢？報刊上的文章和小說裡，如果引用一個人的話，會使用「直接引語」，用引號標出、一字不漏地列下那個人講的話。但在口語對話中，我們通常不在乎一個人具體的措辭，只要傳達出這個人大致的意見和觀點就足夠了。在這些情況下，可利用間接引語，也被稱為「轉述性引語」。

　　使用間接引語要遵循幾條特定的規則：

　　1. that 是從屬連接詞，通常放在間接引語之前。

　　2. 在所組成的新句子中，引語的核心動詞，即子句的動詞，通常要向過去推一個時態；例如一般現在式要變成一般過去式。

　　3. 指代時間和地點的詞通常要和新的「視角」及新的時態保持一致。

　　4. 例外：如果間接引語涉及真理或事實，時態不用向過去推。

在新托福口語考試中，第四點規則很重要，特別是在第三題中，因為第三題會涉及對人們的觀點和事實的討論。仔細研究上面例題的對話，可看到第四點在實際中的應用：

(man) Student: Hey, athletics are important to this university. They want players to be successful.

因為體育運動在學校中居於首要地位，是一個眾所周知的事實，所以當用間接引語轉述該男生的話時，可以使用現在式，不用往後推成過去式。這樣，間接引語句就會變為：

The man said that athletics are important to the university and that the university wants athletes to be successful.

為了有更全面的認識，再看一下談論運動醫療診所的這道題給出的回答範例，逐句和特別收錄 2（p.293）的對話原文進行對比，注意間接引語中的動詞是怎樣變化的。你會發生，考生在絕大部分的轉述中保留了一般現在式，但是在回答的倒數第二句，使用了現在完成式來描述學校「正在進行並對現在造成了影響」的活動。在使用間接引語時，做出這樣的判斷是很重要的。

間接引語中還有一個重要的內容，那就是情態動詞的時態變化。考試中，你要能將 will 和 can 這樣的情態動詞轉化為正確的過去式。下面是一些最典型的形式：

直接引用	間接引語	表達意義
can	could	Ability（能，可以）
may	might	Possibility（也許，有可能）
may	could	Permission（表示准許或請求許可）
will	would	Future（將；將會）
must	had to	Obligation（必須；應該）

托福總監帶你練

聽下列句子，注意間接引語的使用。引出間接引語的動詞和引語中的動詞已經用底線標出。反覆聽錄音，然後跟著讀。

🎧 *Track 072*

1. The woman <u>says that</u> the food vending carts on campus often <u>sell</u> healthy foods, such as fresh fruit and juice.
2. The man <u>says that</u> there <u>are</u> lots of ways to get books; for example, through the interlibrary loan system.
3. The professor <u>said that</u> the man <u>could turn in</u> his term paper the following day.
4. The woman <u>explains that</u> she never <u>goes to</u> the university health center because it is too crowded.
5. The professor <u>said that</u> the woman <u>had to register for</u> her chemistry lab section before the end of the week.

• 要在口語考試中用好間接引語，可運用以下策略：

1. 間接引語的主要規則是：引語的動詞，即子句的動詞，通常要向過去推一個時態。

2. 在很多新托福考試口語部分的題目中都有這樣的例子，即你總結某個人的觀點時涉及的是某個「事實」，此時間接引語中通常保持一般現在時態。

3. 回答問題時要在間接引語中保持動詞時態的一致。換句話說，如果以一般現在時態開始：The woman says that...，就按照這個路線繼續。不要反覆地在一般現在時態和過去時態中變來變去。

4. 間接引語中的情態動詞需要有變化，正如左頁表格所列。記住這些變換的形式，正確使用。

▶模擬試題②

　　請回答下面關於大學圖書館服務的問題。回答時，可嘗試使用下面列出的實用答題範本。

Narrator: The university has decided to shorten the time that undergraduate students are allowed to keep books. Read the announcement about this new policy. You will have 45 seconds to read the announcement.

Reading Time: 45 Seconds

Library Lending Policy

Administrators at the university library announced today that the circulation period for undergraduates will be shortened from two months to one month. The borrowing period for graduate students and faculty will remain unchanged, at six months. Library director Joan Mills told reporters, "Because of the large numbers of students at the undergraduate level, we are acquiring many electronic books to allow greater access to materials. However, for hard cover books, there are limited numbers." Mills went on to say that the new policy will enable more undergraduate students to take advantage of the many fine books in the university collections.

Narrator: Now listen to two students discussing the announcement.

🎧*Track 073* （播放錄音檔 073，錄音原文見特別收錄 2 的 P.294）

The woman expresses her opinion about the library's new policy. State her opinion and explain the reasons she gives.

Preparation Time: 30 Seconds
Response Time: 60 Seconds

實用答題範本　　　　🎧*Track 074* 聽聽看！別人的高分回答！（高分回答原文請見 P.283）

The woman is not at all happy with...
She believes that...is unwise.

• 最後再練習一下「有關大學服務的說明」最實用的答題模板！

1. The man says that he supports the university's decision. His reasons are as follows: ...

2. A student named...has written a letter to the college newspaper, praising...

> 例 • A student named Mark has written a letter to the college newspaper, praising the food in the new food court.
> • A student named Karen has written a letter to the college newspaper, praising the doctors at the health center.

3. From the conversation, we know that the woman doesn't share X's point of view.

> 例 • From the conversation, we know that the woman doesn't share Mark's point of view.
> • From the conversation, we know that the woman doesn't share the man's point of view.

4. She believes that the college should hire...

> 例 • She believes that the college should hire a nutrition expert.
> • She believes that the college should hire more librarians.

5. The woman is not at all happy with...

> 例 • The woman is not at all happy with the new library policy.
> • The woman is not at all happy with the dining hall menu.

6. She believes that...is unwise.

> 例 • She believes that reducing the borrowing period to one month is unwise.

7. In her opinion, if the problem is..., that problem won't be solved by...

> 例 • In her opinion, if the problem is there aren't enough books for all the undergraduate students, that problem won't be solved by buying multiple copies of books for the core subjects.

8. Her reasoning is that...

> 例 • Her reasoning is that there are just too many branches of academic knowledge.
> • Her reasoning is that the cafeteria management cares only about money.

9. The woman's other point is that...

> 例 • The woman's other point is that the new borrowing period is not practical.
> • The woman's other point is that greasy foods are bad for students.

10. When students start VERBing..., it will become difficult for everyone to VERB...

> 例 • When students start ignoring the due date, it will become difficult for everyone to keep track of the books.
> • When students start eating junk food, it will become difficult for everyone to stay healthy.

University Services—Housing, Transportation and Facilities Management
大學服務──住宿、交通和設施管理

❝ 在本章，你將學到…… ❞

★如何預測對話中說話人接下來要說什麼
★表達過程中如何恰到好處地進行停頓

解讀常考題

在新托福考試中，與大學住宿、交通和設施管理相關的情境在第三題中出現的頻率很高。住宿的情境大多與校內住宿相關，較少涉及校外住宿。校內住宿可能會涉及使用宿舍廚房或自習室的規定、住宿費以及怎樣才符合入住學生宿舍的條件等。

和交通相關的情境可能涉及學生是否可以開車或校內的停車規定、校園公車的時間或費用，也可能涉及與腳踏車相關的規定。

設施管理的內容非常寬泛，包括了各種服務，例如：垃圾處理和資源回收、教室和宿舍寢室的清潔、空調系統的維護、校園內的戶外照明、以及怎樣達到「綠色校園」等等。例如，一位學生可能給寫信向學校提議冬季校園建築物內採用環保能源提供暖氣。

現在，看一道和學校住宿相關的例題。

▶舉例試題

Narrator: The housing department is holding a lottery to determine who may stay in university dorms next year. Read the announcement in the university newspaper about the lottery. You will have 45 seconds to read the announcement. Begin reading now.

Reading Time: 45 Seconds

Housing Lottery Deadline

Any returning student who hopes to stay in university housing next year must fill out a form to be eligible for the lottery. The first 1000 students whose names are drawn may pick the dorm they want. The next 100 names will be placed on a waiting list in case some students choose to give up their bed spaces. The lottery is being held because over half the university's available dorm spaces have been reserved for incoming freshmen. University policy requires students age 19 and under to reside on campus. Students who are not granted bed spaces must find housing off campus.

Narrator: Now listen to two students discussing the announcement.

🎧 **Track 075** （播放錄音檔 075，錄音原文見特別收錄 2 的 P.294）

> The woman expresses her opinion about the university's plan to hold a housing lottery. State her opinion and explain the reasons she gives for that opinion.
>
> Preparation Time: 30 Seconds
> Response Time: 60 Seconds

Narrator: You have 30 seconds to prepare.
Narrator: Begin speaking after the beep.

策略：預測話題──眼觀四面，耳聽八方

　　回答綜合型題目時，讓考生頗為頭痛的一點就是要跟上對話的內容。母語不是英語的人會覺得對話者的語速很快。然而，如果能夠通過訓練，預測出下文的內容，理解要點就會變得容易得多。

高分回答

注意看，仔細聽，這裡面標上**粗體**的地方都要發重音才道地喔！　　🎧*Track 076*

The university is **making some dorm rooms** available to **returning students** but **because** there **aren't** enough **bed spaces**, they **have** to **take part** in a lottery. **Some returning students** will get **spaces**; **some** will be **put on** a **waiting** list. The **woman** thinks the **housing lottery** is a **bad idea**. Although she **supports** the idea of **saving dorm room spaces** for **incoming freshmen**, she **thinks** the **lottery** is **unhelpful** for **returning students**. That's **because** they **need** to **plan ahead**. For **example**, the **woman wants** to **room again** with her **current roommate**, but it is **difficult** under the **lottery** system to **know whether both women** will get a **space** and be able to **pick** the **same dorm**. The **other thing** that the **woman dislikes** about the **lottery** system is the **waiting** list. **If** she gets **put on** the **waiting** list and **finds out too late**—for **example**, in the **summer**—that she **doesn't** have a **bed space**, then **all** the **good**, **cheap apartments** will be **gone**.

托福總監為什麼覺得這是高分回答？

　　大多數對話都有一個可預測下文的結構，其中的互動形式也有可以預測的模式。語言考試中，這一特點尤其突出，為了科學地測量一個人的語言能力，這類考試的題目必須有一定的模式。考生可以利用這種「可預測性」來預測（甚至猜測）後文要說到的內容，即使聽漏了一兩個單字也無關緊要。

　　第三題（和第五題）對話的互動者大部分都是兩個學生。在他們的互動中，說話人會輪流提問，然後回答對方。仔細聽，就能知道要將注意力集中在哪位說話人身上，以及這個人可能會說什麼。

第三題的互動

在第三題的對話中，會有一個觀點十分鮮明的學生。題幹中問的正是這位學生的意見：What is the man/woman's opinion of...? 第三題的對話通常從不表達觀點的學生的提問開始：So, what do you think of...? 然後，表達觀點的學生開始說話，基本上都是：It's good 或 It's bad 一類的話。從此處開始，考生就需要跟上這個表達觀點的學生的思考邏輯了。

表達觀點的學生一般會在自己發言的時候多說一些，觀點也會更多，這樣也就更難跟上。然而，通過不表達觀點的學生所說的隻字片語，可以預測另一個學生將要說什麼。

例如，不表達觀點的男生會說：What do you mean? 從這句話可知，表達觀點的女生將會在輪到她說話時做解釋。也許她會將自己之前說的話換句話說。再舉個例子，不表達觀點的學生也許會說：Do you really think so? 同樣，從這句話可預測表達觀點的學生接下來會說：Yes, I do, because...

那麼，每當聽到 What did you think of...? 和 Do you really think so? 這樣的短句時，你就應該準備好，注意聽兩個方面的內容：1）這個學生是支持還是反對；2）他（她）給出的詳細理由。

在前面例題中的這段對話裡，一開始男生說：Hi, Tiffany. How's everything? 正如推斷的那樣，女生接著便開始表達意見：Not great. Did you read that announcement about the housing lottery? 這就是利用對話預測下文的方法。

第五題的互動

在第五題的對話中，預測下文內容的技巧和第三題非常相似。主要的不同之處在於，這裡需要注意的是某位「有問題」的學生。

第五題的對話通常以「非問題學生」的提問開始，如：How's going, Jane?。之後，「問題學生」通常會說 Not good 這樣的話。從此時開始，考生就需要跟上「問題學生」的解釋，瞭解是哪裡出了問題，然後預測此人下面要說的話。

第五題的對話有兩種模式。第一種，也是最典型的一種，是由「非問題學生」來問所有的問題，例如：So, what are you going to do? 然後「問題學生」接著說：Well, I could...，之後再說 Or, I could...。 第二種，「非問題學生」比較主動，會給「問題學生」提一些建議：You could try doing... 或 Have you thought of doing...?（對於第五題的情境、問題和技巧的詳細分析可參考第 19 章至第 24 章）。

想成功預測第三題和第五題對話內容，可運用以下策略：

1. 認真注意每段對話中的關鍵人物。第三題的關鍵人物是表達觀點的學生，而第五題的關鍵人物是「問題學生」。
2. 熟悉對話中的互動模式：會問哪種類型的問題（So you probably don't like the... policy?）以及通常會接什麼樣的回答（No, I really am against it）。
3. 不表達觀點的學生和「非問題學生」通常發言很少。但是，可以利用他們簡短的問題（Do you think so?）和評論（That's too bad）來預測接下來另一個人要說的內容。
4. 如果聽漏了一兩個單字，不要驚慌。因為你已經瞭解了互動的總體模式，偶爾漏掉一兩個詞也無關緊要。

▶模擬試題①

請回答下題。回答時，可嘗試使用下面列出的實用答題範本。

Narrator: Read a student letter in the newspaper about parking lot fees. You will have 45 seconds to read the letter. Begin reading now.

Reading Time: 45 Seconds

Parking for Students

It is well-known that the university B-Lot, located a mile away from classroom buildings, usually sits empty. Yet the main lot in the middle of campus, A-Lot, is always full. What is particularly puzzling is why the monthly parking fee for students is currently the same for both places: $120!

This makes no sense. The university should charge more for the convenience of parking right next to classrooms: $160 a month for the privilege of being nearby in the parking garage and $60 for parking in faraway B-Lot. This would help even up the number of cars in each location.

Sincerely,

June Walker

Narrator: Now listen to two students discussing the letter.

 Track 077 （播放錄音檔 077，錄音原文見特別收錄 2 的 P.295）

Briefly summarize the views expressed in the student's letter. Then state the man's opinion about the letter and explain the reasons he gives for holding that opinion.

Preparation Time: 30 Seconds
Response Time: 60 Seconds

實用答題範本　　　 *Track 078* 聽聽看！別人的高分回答！（高分回答原文請見 P.283）

A student has written a letter in order to address...
She questions the logic of VERBing...

得分考技：發音該停頓還是滔滔不絕？

很多考生都會擔心自己在回答問題過程中停頓。他們會問：我最多能停頓幾次才不影響分數呢？實際上，新托福考試中的口語回答不僅允許幾次停頓，而且這些停頓還是絕對必要的！母語是英語的人說話過程中都會有簡短、自然的停頓，所以沒有必要擔心停頓的次數。唯一會使考生丟分的停頓被評分人稱為「不恰當的停頓」，即時間相對長，顯然是由於考生不知道下面要說什麼，不得不停下來的停頓。

也就是說，考生應該擔心的是停頓得不夠。評分人經常遇到的情況是考生說個不停，說出的話像機關槍掃射一般。這常常是因為這位考生背下了好多範本，急著要說完。有些

考生回答時說得很快，則是因為他們錯誤地認為說得越多，得分就越高。但是，說得越快，肯定就越考慮不到重音和語調，結果反而會更糟！ETS 的評分人不會去數你說了多少個單字。實際上，他們可能連一半的內容都沒有聽懂，因為你沒有把話講清楚。評分人比較想聽到你使用重音、語調和停頓來將句子的每個部分分清楚，這樣他們更容易聽懂你的意思。

　　想達到簡短、自然的停頓，你需要掌握下面三個要點：
　　1. 要區別簡短、自然的停頓和長時間不恰當的停頓。不要害怕簡短的、利於表達意思的停頓。
　　2. 要知道句子中大概幾個字停一次算是自然停頓（下面會帶著你練習）。
　　3. 結合語調和重音來停頓。例如，在說完一句話、進行停頓前，聲調應先降下來。

托福總監帶你練 *Track 079*

　　在這裡聽聽看什麼叫做「自然停頓」。聽下列句子的錄音，注意停頓的位置。畫底線的字各為一個單位，底線斷掉之處就是適合你停頓或換氣的地方。如果在底線連在一起的部分停頓，則會顯得不自然。反覆聽錄音，然後跟著讀。

1. The woman thinks it's good that the university plans to confiscate all bicycles that have been abandoned.
2. A student has written a letter to the editor recommending that kitchen facilities be added to all dormitories.
3. The man doesn't like the idea of having to move into off-campus housing.
4. Most of the time, when students throw out garbage, they don't separate out the paper and the metal for recycling.
5. The university announced a new van service that will be available for students who call before two a.m.

• 想在口語考試中做到停頓自然，可運用以下策略：

1. 有兩個因素決定停頓的位置：表意單位和文法單位（這兩種單位常有重疊）。例如，前面 P.134 的「高分回答」中，動詞片語 need to plan ahead 和名詞片語 the waiting list 就是這種單位，在每一個單位的前後都應有一個很簡短的停頓。
2. 應形成簡短停頓的文法單位有名詞片語、動詞片語以及子句，句子結束之後可進行較長的停頓。
3. 如果在每個單位中添加重音和語調，然後再簡短地停頓，評分人就能夠很容易聽懂你的回答。有些無重音的音節，包括母音 /ə/，聽起來也會像在停頓；例如 a new van service 中的 a。
4. 口語很自然，但儘量少用。不要頻繁地說 you know、uh、like、I mean 這樣的話。如果在說的過程中一時很難找到合適的詞，做個深呼吸，然後用更簡單的詞再解釋一下你想表達的觀點。這會讓你的回答自然而流暢，比說一串沒有實際意義的口語更有可能獲得高分。
5. 簡短的陳述中不需要任何停頓。

▶模擬試題②

請回答下面關於設施管理服務的問題。回答時，可嘗試使用下面列出的實用答題範本。

Narrator: The university is facing a problem with aging infrastructure and has announced plans for building maintenance. Read the article about these plans. You will have 45 seconds to read the article. Begin reading now.
Reading Time: 45 Seconds

Maintenance Work Planned

An eight-year phased plan to deal with the university's aging buildings and crumbling infrastructure was announced this morning. Administrators did not reveal the precise budget for the plan, but acknowledged it would likely be "hundreds of millions of dollars." Rusted pipes, rainwater leaking into building foundations and flooding in lecture hall basements are only a few of the problems cited. More than 20 buildings need repairs. Officials said that the Physics Building and the university gymnasium have been targeted for new cooling, energy and drainage systems next spring. Maintenance workers will try to avoid disrupting regular campus activities.

Narrator: Now listen to two students discussing the article.

 Track 080 （播放錄音檔 080，錄音原文見特別收錄 2 的 P.295）

The woman expresses her opinion of the maintenance plans that have been announced. State her opinion and explain her reasons for holding that opinion.

Preparation Time: 30 Seconds
Response Time: 60 Seconds

實用答題範本  *Track 081* 聽聽看！別人的高分回答！（高分回答原文請見 P.283）

The woman is critical of...
And one downside of VERBing...is that...

• **最後再練習一下「談論大學中的服務」最實用的答題模板！**

1. **Although she supports the idea of saving dorm room spaces for incoming freshmen, she thinks...**

    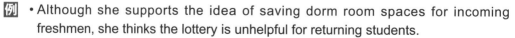 • Although she supports the idea of saving dorm room spaces for incoming freshmen, she thinks the lottery is unhelpful for returning students.

    • Although she supports the idea of saving dorm room spaces for incoming freshmen, she thinks the university should also provide housing for returning students.

2. That's because they need to VERB...

例 • That's because they need to plan ahead.

• That's because they need to find low-cost housing.

3. The other thing that the woman dislikes about...is...

例 • The other thing that the woman dislikes about the lottery system is the waiting list.

• The other thing that the woman dislikes about the lottery system is not being able to coordinate with her roommate.

4. A student has written a letter in order to address...

例 • A student has written a letter in order to address the parking problem on campus.

• A student has written a letter in order to address the lack of parking space.

5. She questions the logic of VERBing...

例 • She questions the logic of charging the same monthly fee for both parking lots.

• She questions the logic of allowing resident students to pay the same fee.

6. The man adds that he thinks resident students should VERB...

例 • The man adds that he thinks resident students should have to pay a little more for parking than commuter students, no matter what lot.

• The man adds that he thinks resident students should not be allowed to park on campus.

7. The woman is critical of...

例 • The woman is critical of the university's plan for building maintenance.

• The woman is critical of the proposed recycling plan.

8. Her biggest concern is that...

例 • Her biggest concern is that an eight-year plan is too long a plan.

• Her biggest concern is that garbage bins are not being used by students.

9. And one downside of VERBing...is that...

例 • And one downside of waiting so long to fix all the old buildings is that emergency repairs will have to be done.

• And one downside of taking the shuttle bus is that the bus is often late.

University Course Offerings
大學課程設置

在本章，你將學到……

★回答中如何做到輕鬆地自我糾正
★表示支持與反對的動詞片語有哪些

解讀常考題

　　第三題很多題目都涉及大學課程怎樣設置的問題，如課程表中課程的設置、因為資金原因而突然取消的某些課程、以及教特定課程的大學老師。很多還與各院系內課程的要求和政策相關，如文科和理工科的課程要求。其他問題關係到大學生和研究生的具體選課要求，例如：主修人類學的學生必須要修多少門數學課。此外，很多問題涉及選修課的政策，例如：化學系的學生要選多少門選修課。還有一些問題與開設課程的人數下限或旁聽課程的規定有關。

　　現在，看一道關於大學課程設置的例題。

▶舉例試題

Narrator: City University has begun offering online courses to students. Read a student letter in the newspaper about taking classes online. You will have 45 seconds to read the letter. Begin reading now.
Reading Time: 45 Seconds

Online Classes

City University's new practice of offering a large number of classes online is a welcome new development for all students. This semester 18% of all students living on campus are taking their credit hours online, and that number is expected to grow. Dozens of crowded, popular courses in psychology, economics, Spanish and many other subjects are given online now. By using laptops in our dorm rooms, we're able to watch lectures streamed live over the campus network. These courses help the university offer more courses to more resident students and keep tuition fees down.
Sincerely,
Jill Hammer

Narrator: Now listen to two students discussing the letter.

 Track 082 （播放錄音檔 082，錄音原文見特別收錄 2 的 P.295）

A letter has been written to the newspaper about the university's online classes. State the man's opinion of the letter and explain the reasons he gives for that opinion.

Preparation Time: 30 Seconds
Response Time: 60 Seconds

Narrator: You have 30 seconds to prepare.
Narrator: Begin speaking after the beep.

策略：能輕鬆地自我糾正，就是老道的口語王！

在口語中，即使說母語的人也會講錯話、犯文法錯誤，所以做些補充說明、改變說法、糾正發音和用詞錯誤，這些都很自然的事。對於母語不是英語的人來說，在講話過程中思考用詞、講錯話或糾正剛說過的話當然就更正常了！因此，對於任何想在考試中保持鎮靜和表現出色的考生，知道「何時糾正」和「怎樣糾正」是一種很重要的技巧。考生自我糾正的頻率應該多高呢？答案是，只有當你覺得自己在選詞或是在文法方面出現了非常明顯的錯誤，而且你知道怎樣糾正時，才去糾正。

高分回答

注意看，仔細聽，這裡面標上粗體的地方都要發重音才道地喔！ *Track 083*

The **man** is **not** in **favor** of the university's **new practice** of **giving classes** online. He **disagrees** with the **letter** writer and **says** that **serious students won't like learning** this **way**. The **man** says that **having large numbers** of **students sit** in their **dorm rooms listening** to **lectures** on their **laptops** is **bad** for **two reasons**. **First** of all, he **thinks** that **personal interaction** between **students** and **teachers** and between **students** and **other classmates** is important. The **exchanges help inspire learning**. His **other point** is that **certain classes** are **especially unsuited** for **online lectures**. He **cites language classes** as an **example** and com**pares** his economics class to a **Spanish** class. He can **learn** economics from his **textbook**, but he **wonders** how **students** can **learn** to actually **speak Spanish** if they're **not** able to **practice talking** in a **classroom**.

托福總監為什麼覺得這是高分回答？

在上面的回答中，如果你在談論男生觀點時說成了：She disagrees...，那麼就有必要進行糾正，可以說：I mean, **he** disagrees...，來證明自己其實知道正確的說法，只是一不小心講錯。你給評分人展示了自己真正的能力，同時也使表達更流利。

還有其他的糾正方法。例如，重複某個之前說錯的詞或片語，並改成糾正後的說法，不管是語音、用詞還是文法都可以糾正。同樣，你還可以把前面講過的話換句話說。例如：First of all, he thinks that personal communication with students, with teachers—that personal interaction between students and teachers...

還有一種自我糾正的方法是利用口頭語，例如：I mean, ... / That is to say, ... / What I'm trying to say is... 甚至用一個口頭語 um（不過不應該過多地使用 um 和 uh）。最重要的是你能夠往下說，繼續講，接著組織出意思清晰且精準的句子，傳達你獨特的觀點。

想有技巧地自我糾正，可以運用以下策略：

1. 準備考試時，先列出自己比較弱的方面，然後專攻這些方面。這種「熱身」能讓你減少任何「因生疏造成的錯誤」，增強你的自信心。
2. 在考試時，儘量少犯錯誤，盡最大努力構思好答題思路。然後，深呼吸，說話時語速要平穩，這樣可以做到邊說邊思考，更好地控制語言。
3. 不要糾正自己犯的所有小錯誤，只糾正非常明顯的錯誤即可，例如：將 he go 糾正為 he goes，informations 糾正為 information。
4. 利用重複、換句話說和上面提到的技巧來糾正錯誤，使回答顯得自然而輕鬆。

　　記住：評分人不會去數你犯了多少處錯誤，他們更關注語言的前後銜接和連貫性。

▶ 模擬試題①

　　請回答下題。回答時，可嘗試使用下面列出的實用答題範本。

Narrator: Read the article in the newspaper about fall classes which have been canceled. You will have 45 seconds to read the article. Begin reading now.
Reading Time: 45 Seconds

Cancellation of Fall Courses

The university does not like to cancel courses, but sometimes it is unavoidable. There are numerous reasons why a class may not be offered, including insufficient enrollment, lack of qualified instructors and lack of classroom space. Students who have signed up for a fall class that is canceled will be notified at least two days before the class was scheduled to begin.

Students can then request a full refund of tuition or transfer to another course, space permitting. A list of the university's classes that have been canceled for the fall semester can be found on the Registrar Office's web page.

Narrator: Now listen to two students discussing the announcement.

🎧 *Track 084* （播放錄音檔 084，錄音原文見特別收錄 2 的 P.296）

The woman expresses her opinion of the university's policy. State her opinion and explain the reasons she gives for holding that opinion.

Preparation Time: 30 Seconds
Response Time: 60 Seconds

實用答題範本　　　*Track 085* 聽聽看！別人的高分回答！（高分回答原文請見 P.283）

Not surprisingly, one of her main criticisms is that...
The woman also takes issue with the fact that...

得分考技：美國人用哪些動詞片語來表示支持與反對

　　第三題要求考生告訴評分人聽力對話中表達觀點的學生是否支持學校的某項計畫或政策，因此，考生應該會用多種表示支援或反對的動詞片語。

　　可以使用以下幾種基本的結構：

　　1. 主詞 + 簡單動詞 + 受詞，例如：He supports the plan.
　　2. 主詞 + 片語動詞 + 受詞，例如：He agrees with the plan.
　　3. 主詞 + be 動詞 + 受詞，例如：He is for the plan.
　　4. 主詞 + 表達觀點的動詞 + that 補語（子句），例如：He thinks (that) the plan is reasonable.

　　下表列出了可以用在每種模式中的動詞：

主詞 + 簡單動詞 + 受詞

支持	反對
He supports the plan.	He doesn't support the plan.
He backs the plan.	He opposes the plan.
He endorses the plan.	He rejects the plan.
He advocates the plan.	He dislikes the plan.

主詞 + 片語動詞 + 受詞

支持	反對
She agrees with the plan.	She disagrees with the plan.
She expresses support for the plan.	She expresses dissatisfaction about the plan.
She approves of the plan.	She disapproves of the plan.
She argues in favor of the plan.	She argues against the plan.

主詞 + be 動詞 + 受詞

支持	反對
He is for the plan.	He is against the plan.
He is in favor of the plan.	He is not in favor of the plan.
He is delighted with the plan.	He is disappointed with the plan.
He is behind the plan.	He is opposed to the plan.
He is comfortable with the plan.	He is uncomfortable with the plan.
He is pleased with the plan.	He is displeased with the plan.

主詞 + 表達觀點的動詞 + that 補語（子句）

支持	反對
She accepts that the plan is a good idea.	She questions that the plan is necessary.
She thinks the plan is reasonable.	She thinks the plan is unreasonable.
She believes the plan is well-designed.	She believes the plan is misguided.
She thinks the plan has benefits.	She thinks the plan has weaknesses.

托福總監帶你練

聽下列句子錄音，句子中包含表達支持和反對的動詞片語或一般動詞，已用底線標出。
反覆聽錄音，然後跟著讀。

🎧 *Track 086*

1. The woman is displeased with the university's plan to put a committee in charge of campus art.
2. The man thinks that the university's plan for first-year students to live in the new dorm is reasonable.
3. The woman expresses support for the university's new grading policy.
4. The man believes the proposal in the letter is a bad idea.
5. The woman approves of the new pricing plan for printing documents at the computer lab.

• 想用表示支援或反對的動詞組織句子，可以運用以下策略：

1. 多練習支持或反對的動詞片語的基本文法結構。
2. 牢記哪些動詞後不加介系詞，哪些動詞後需要加介系詞用作片語動詞，如：approve of sth.
3. 練習時，措辭、句型和動詞儘量多樣化。例如，不要總是用這樣的句子：The student thinks the plan is good.

▶模擬試題②

請回答下面關於大學課程設置的問題。回答時，可嘗試使用下面列出的實用答題範本。

Narrator: The university is establishing a new degree program in the School of Music. Read the article about these plans. You will have 45 seconds to read the article.

Reading Time: 45 Seconds

New Degree Program in Music Theory

The School of Music recently announced the addition of a new graduate program, a master's degree in Music Theory. According to the Dean of the School of Music, this program allows students to study music theory at a more advanced level and offers an alternative for students who do not wish to pursue a master's degree in Music Performance. As part of the Music Theory M.A. application package, candidates must submit a composition such as a short sonata or a modern academic piece. A formal performance audition is not required; however, applicants must satisfy a basic proficiency requirement in piano.

Narrator: Now listen to two students discussing the article.

🎧 *Track 087* （播放錄音檔 087，錄音原文見特別收錄 2 的 P.296）

The man expresses his opinion about the university's plan. State his opinion and explain the reasons he gives for holding that opinion.

Preparation Time: 30 Seconds
Response Time: 60 Seconds

實用答題範本 🎧 *Track 088* 聽聽看！別人的高分回答！（高分回答原文請見 P.284）

The man praises the university's new plan to VERB...
The man endorses...as well.

• 最後再練習一下「大學課程設置相關話題」最實用的答題模板！

1. The man is not in favor of the university's new practice of VERBing...

例 • The man is not in favor of the university's new practice of giving classes online.

• The man is not in favor of the university's new practice of requiring a foreign language.

2. He disagrees with the letter writer and says that serious students won't like VERBing...

例 • He disagrees with the letter writer and says that serious students won't like learning this way.

- He disagrees with the letter writer and says that serious students won't like taking physical education.

3. His other point is that certain classes are especially unsuited for...

例 • His other point is that certain classes are especially unsuited for online lectures.

- His other point is that certain classes are especially unsuited for humanities majors.

4. He can learn...from his textbook, but he wonders how students can learn to VERB...if they're not able to VERB...

例 • He can learn economics from his textbook, but he wonders how students can learn to actually speak Spanish if they're not able to practice talking in a classroom.

- He can learn theories from his textbook, but he wonders how students can learn to apply those theories if they're not able to discuss them in a classroom.

5. The university has released an announcement regarding...

例 • The university has released an announcement regarding the cancellation policy for fall classes.

- The university has released an announcement regarding prerequisites for architectural design courses.

6. The woman is disgusted with the policy, especially since...

例 • The woman is disgusted with the policy, especially since her Honors Seminar in World History was one of the classes that was suddenly canceled.

- The woman is disgusted with the policy, especially since she thinks the tuition is already too high.

7. Not surprisingly, one of her main criticisms is that...

例 • Not surprisingly, one of her main criticisms is that the classes are canceled very late—after the schedule is already in place.

- Not surprisingly, one of her main criticisms is that she feels the list in the course catalog is not accurate.

8. The woman also takes issue with the fact that...

例 • The woman also takes issue with the fact that the university advertises many elective classes, but then doesn't feel it has to actually give the classes.

- The woman also takes issue with the fact that she'll probably have to take a class she doesn't want to take.

9. This is, in the woman's opinion, ..., and is not fair.

例 • This is, in the woman's opinion, "false advertising," and is not fair.

• This is, in the woman's opinion, irresponsible behavior, and is not fair.

10. The man praises the university's new plan to VERB...

例 • The man praises the university's new plan to add a new music theory program to the School of Music.

• The man praises the university's new plan to increase the number of chemistry courses.

11. The man thinks this is a good idea, his rationale being that...

例 • The man thinks this is a good idea, his rationale being that the ability to write music is related to the knowledge of music theory.

• The man thinks this is a good idea, his rationale being that Advanced Seminars in Anthropology will prepare students for graduate work.

12. The man endorses...as well.

例 • The man endorses this requirement as well.

• The man endorses the new online tutorial as well.

Student Affairs
學生活動

在本章，你將學到……

★如何運用換句話說將聽到的材料自信、流利地說出來
★如何掌握複合詞的重讀技巧，使回答更清晰易懂

解讀常考題

　　雖然學生活動並非第三題最常考的話題，但總是不時地出現。因此，考生需要掌握與學生社團、體育和音樂活動等相關的重點以及文化背景，為考試做好準備。

　　一般來說，和學生活動相關的情境會涉及學生的官方組織，包括學生會、競技和休閒運動、學生的戲劇和音樂表演、學生報刊、學生社團和學生活動中心。有些學生活動涵蓋社區服務、其他一些志工專案以及海外留學專案。另外一些活動主題可能會涉及針對新生和轉學生開設的新生訓練。

　　第三題一般不會涉及「校友會」和「大學中的兄弟會或姊妹會」這樣的場景，因為這些是個別機構的活動，帶有一定的文化背景，即使對於一些母語為英語的人來說也不一定好理解。

　　現在，看一道關於學生活動的例題。

▶舉例試題

Narrator: Read a student letter in the newspaper about changes in class times. You will have 45 seconds to read the letter. Begin reading now.

Reading Time: 45 Seconds

Class Times and Rehearsals

State University is considering a new plan which will allow music ensembles a designated time to practice. Currently, bands, choirs and small ensembles hold rehearsals late afternoons. Students frequently miss these rehearsals due to science labs that run overtime. In addition, no athletes are able to take part in music ensembles due to their training schedules. I think the plan to reserve one hour midday is just what we need. With no regular classes allowed to take place during that window, 12:00 to 13:00 will be free and everyone, including non-music majors, will be able to attend rehearsals.
Vera King

Narrator: Now listen to two students discussing the letter.

🎧 *Track 089* （播放錄音檔 089，錄音原文見特別收錄 2 的 P.297）

> **A letter has been written to the newspaper about the plan to change class times. State the man's opinion of the letter and explain the reasons he gives for that opinion.**
>
> Preparation Time: 30 Seconds
> Response Time: 60 Seconds

Narrator: You have 30 seconds to prepare.
Narrator: Begin speaking after the beep.

策略：找到能流利表達自己想法的方法

　　很多英語學習者認為背單字就可以快速提高口語技巧，但事實上，短時間內提高語言技巧的方法是培養和訓練換句話說的能力。為什麼？因為學會用另外的措辭來表達同一個意思，考生就會有信心總能找到方法流利表達自己的想法。培養和訓練換句話說能力的另一個好處是：能夠讓你學習並鞏固詞彙的用法，因為通過這個過程你將能完全掌握該詞彙和其用法。

高分回答

注意看，仔細聽，這裡面標上粗體的地方都要發重音才道地喔！　🎧 *Track 090*

The **man**, who is a **music major**, be**lieves** the **student plan isn't** practical. **Chang**ing **regular class periods** to cre**ate** a **window** of **free time** during the **middle** of the **day** is a **lot** of **trouble** and it **won't** prevent people from **having conflicts** with re**hear**sals. He **thinks** they're **going** to a **lot** of **trouble** for **nothing**, **basically**. He **also thinks** the **conflicts mostly occur** with **people** who **aren't** music **majors**. He be**lieves** a **better** solution to the **problem** would be to **form** ensembles for **non-majors** and **then hold** re**hear**sals in the **evening** for **those music** ensembles, the **ones** that **non-**majors **belong** to. **If** they're **really interested, non**-majors will at**tend evening** re**hear**sals. And **evening** re**hear**sals have the **added advantage** that they can **last two** or **three hours**, giving the **groups** a **good chance** to **practice**.

　　來看上面這個回答中所做的換句話說：

對話中所用的措辭	回答中所做的換句話說
there is no realistic way to avoid schedule conflicts	the student's plan isn't practical
having the university formally change class times is pointless	they're going to a lot of trouble for nothing
start up more ensembles for non-majors	form ensembles for non-majors
Plus evening rehearsals can run two—even three hours. So you get quality practice.	And evening rehearsals have the added advantage that they can last two or three hours, giving the groups a good chance to practice.

托福總監為什麼覺得這是高分回答？

　　當然，要抓住對話中的所有關鍵片語是不可能的。但即使只把一兩個單字換句話說，評分人還是會注意到，並很可能因為你能組織出「和原文不一樣的」語言而給你加分（根據官方的評分準則，要想得到滿分，這一能力是必不可少的）。如果考前經常做一些換句話說練習，你的聽說能力會有大幅度的提高。

要能把聽力文章中的語句換句話說，可運用以下策略：

1. 考試前，練習把小文章和對話（或第四題和第六題中的講座）中的句子換句話說。如果想不出同義詞，可以查英英詞典。
2. 考試中，找到小文章中的關鍵片語，做好充分的準備，這樣在聽錄音的時候就能辨別出來。
3. 在聽對話（或講座）時儘量記下關鍵字和關鍵片語。
4. 回答問題時，至少換句話說一次，就算只有一兩個字也是有用的，例如：將 is not realistic 改說為 is not practical。這樣你的分數一定會有所提高。

▶模擬試題①

　　請回答下題。回答時，可嘗試使用下面列出的實用答題範本。

Narrator: The university recently announced a requirement to complete a community service project. Read about the new requirement. You will have 45 seconds to read the announcement. Begin reading now.

Reading Time: 45 Seconds

Community Service Requirement
　　There is a world that exists beyond textbooks, and the university works to foster a sense of social responsibility in students. Consequently, the completion of 20 hours of community service will now be a requirement for graduation. The requirement must be completed before the end of the student's second year. Each student should submit a brief proposal of where the volunteer work will be done, including briefly describing the nature of the work. Failure to complete community service could result in the withholding of grades, or not being granted a diploma until expectations are met.
Narrator: Now listen to two students discussing the announcement.

🎧 *Track 091* （播放錄音檔 091，錄音原文見特別收錄 2 的 P.297）

The woman expresses her opinion about the university's plan. State her opinion and explain the reasons she gives for that opinion.

Preparation Time: 30 Seconds
Response Time: 60 Seconds

實用答題範本　　　🎧 *Track 092* 聽聽看！別人的高分回答！（高分回答原文請見 P.284）

The woman is not pleased with the university's new plan requiring that...
That is all the more reason why...

得分考技：複合詞的重音就是華人考生最怕的地方！

複合詞有三種形式：

1. 獨立詞，如 textbook
2. 用連字號連起來的詞，如 editor-in-chief
3. 兩個或多個片語形成的詞，如 air conditioning。

複合詞一般很容易理解，但是卻不容易發音。很多考生不知道複合詞重音的位置。實際上，由單音節片語合成的複合詞的重音規則並不難：複合名詞的重音通常在第一部分的母音上，而複合動詞和複合形容詞的重音通常落在第二部分的母音上，如下表所示：

複合詞類型	重音	舉例
名詞	第一部分	**back**ground, **lap**top, **hand**book
動詞	第二部分	fore**warn**, up**root**, under**stand**
形容詞	第二部分	over**due** (book), hands-**on** (skill), warm-**bloo**ded (animal)

當然，這些規則也有例外。另外，對於由多音節片語成的複合詞，這些規律並不適用，例如 com**pu**ter **pro**grammer 和 aca**de**mic concen**tra**tion。其部分原因是：多音節詞中的主要重音落在一個音節上，而次要重音落在其他音節上。這樣，針對多音節詞，最好將其當做實意詞，根據一般的重音規則來發每個音節，例如 com**pu**ter 和 aca**de**mic。純粹的複合動詞一般很少。

一定要記住，複合詞重音落下的位置很容易影響到詞義。例如：Small particles make up the product. 如果説成了 **make**-up, 聽者會將這個詞理解成名詞，可能認為你在談論某種化妝品。如果你的發音為 make **up**，將重音放在 up 上，聽者就會知道這是個片語動詞，意思是「組成」。這兩者的區別很大。下一章會提供一些技巧，學習像 make up 和 take out 這樣的片語動詞的用法和發音。

托福總監帶你練

聽下列句子，注意複合詞中重音的位置。複合詞已用底線標出。反覆聽錄音，然後跟著讀。

🎧 *Track 093*

1. **Be**cause of over**flo**wing capacity, the **dead**line for **law** school applicants is in **late fall**.
2. There **seems** to be wide**spread** su**pport** for the university's **new plan**.
3. **Stu**dents who seek a cross-**dis**ciplinary de**gree** should **con**tact their academic advisors.
4. The **head**line in the **news**paper announced the new "need-**blind**" admissions policy.
5. **State** University is known for its **cutting-edge**, state-of-the-**art** technology.

• 想掌握複合詞的重音位置，可運用以下策略：

1. 記住，重音的音節要比前後的音節念得響亮、長久。我們在重音音節中會突出母音的發音。
2. 複合名詞，尤其是單音節片語成的複合名詞，重音通常都落在第一部分，如 lifetime。
3. 複合形容詞和複合動詞，如 old-**fashioned** 和 foretell，重音通常落在第二部分。
4. 使用正確複合名詞的重音，有利於聽者理解說話人的意思。例如，a photo of the white house（白色房子的照片）和 a photo of the **White** House（白宮的照片）中的不同重音。後面一句的 White House 是複合詞；而前面一句只是用形容詞 white 來描述 house。
5. 應對由多音節片語成的複合名詞的方法是：觀察每個單字的重讀音節，然後在每個詞間簡短停頓，讓聽者能夠理解你所表達的意思。
6. 複合詞的發音越準確，評分人就越容易理解你的意思，這樣他們才有可能給你打更高的分數。

▶ 模擬試題②

請回答下面關於學生活動的問題。回答時，可嘗試使用下面列出的實用答題範本。

Narrator: The university has decided to repeat the student council election. Read the article about the election in the university newspaper. You will have 45 seconds to read the announcement.

Begin reading now.

Reading Time: 45 Seconds

Another Election Scheduled

The student council election held last week resulted in widespread confusion. In the switch to a new voting system, somehow a portion of students did not receive e-mail ballots. Although the winning candidates won by a substantial margin, several students have formally complained, saying the process was unfair. The Dean of Student Affairs told reporters she agreed that the glitch did not seem to have a significant impact on election results. Nevertheless, a repeat election has been scheduled for next week. IT personnel have assured university administrators that student lists and voting software will be fully functional at that time.

Narrator: Now listen to two students discussing the article.

🎧 *Track 094* （播放錄音檔 094，錄音原文見特別收錄 2 的 P.297）

The woman expresses her opinion about the university's plan. State her opinion and explain the reasons she gives for holding that opinion.

Preparation Time: 30 Seconds
Response Time: 60 Seconds

實用答題範本　　　　🎧 *Track 095* 聽聽看！別人的高分回答！（高分回答原文請見 P.284）

She bases her opinion on the fact that...
The other, more important, reason she holds this opinion is that...

• 最後再練習一下「有關學生活動」最實用的答題模板！

1. The man, who is a(n)..., believes the university's plan isn't practical.

> 例 • The man, who is a music major, believes the university's plan isn't practical.
> • The man, who is a basketball player, believes the university's plan isn't practical.

2. He thinks they're VERBing...for nothing, basically.

> 例 • He thinks they're going to a lot of trouble for nothing, basically.
> • He thinks they're changing the schedule for nothing, basically.

3. He believes a better solution to the problem would be to VERB...

> 例 • He believes a better solution to the problem would be to form ensembles for non-majors and then hold rehearsals in the evening for those music ensembles, the ones that non-majors belong to.
> • He believes a better solution to the problem would be to create a chess club for amateurs.

4. If they're really interested, non-majors will VERB...

> 例 • If they're really interested, non-majors will attend evening rehearsals.
> • If they're really interested, non-majors will join one of the music ensembles.

5. The woman is not pleased with the university's new plan requiring that...

> 例 • The woman is not pleased with the university's new plan requiring that all students complete twenty hours of community service as a graduation requirement.
> • The woman is not pleased with the university's new plan requiring that first-year students take physical education.

6. She thinks that...should be optional for students, not required.

例 • She thinks that volunteer work should be optional for students, not required.

• She thinks that going to football games should be optional for students, not required.

7. That is all the more reason why...

例 • That is all the more reason why she considers the time she has left to study precious.

• That is all the more reason why she wants to change her major to international studies.

8. The woman thinks the plan to VERB...is a waste of time.

例 • The woman thinks the plan to hold a new election is a waste of time.

• The woman thinks the plan to create a gardening club is a waste of time.

9. She bases her opinion on the fact that...

例 • She bases her opinion on the fact that only a few students didn't get ballots.

• She bases her opinion on the fact that students aren't really interested in learning Greek.

10. Moreover, in her experience, not very many students VERB...anyway—so...were probably not going to make a difference.

例 • Moreover, in her experience, not very many students vote in the student council elections anyway—so those few votes were probably not going to make a difference.

• Moreover, in her experience, not very many students have motorcycles anyway—so a few motorcycle riding lessons were probably not going to make a difference.

11. The other, more important, reason she holds this opinion is that...

例 • The other, more important, reason she holds this opinion is that the candidates who came out as winners in the first election won by a substantial percentage—by forty percent.

• The other, more important, reason she holds this opinion is that the exercise classes are given on the other side of campus, which is very far away.

Student Employment and Internships
打工與實習

在本章，你將學到……

★如何讓冠詞加強語言的緊密性
★熟練使用片語動詞，讓口語更自然、流利

解讀常考題

　　新托福考試中常常會出現有關助教職務和校園內外多種兼職工作的問題，家教工作和實習也是常見話題。談論學生兼職的問題，涉及雇用條件、工資甚至面試過程。此外，因為雇主想直接瞭解求職者，實習對於用人單位來說就成為了選擇合適人才越來越重要的一種手段。所有專業的學生都會申請實習機會，這一趨勢在新托福考試中也有所體現。

　　現在，看一道關於學生打工的例題。

▶舉例試題

Narrator: The university has agreed to let students operate a used bookstore. Read a student letter in the newspaper about the bookstore. You will have 45 seconds to read the letter. Begin reading now.

Reading Time: 45 Seconds

Student-run Used Bookstore

It is an excellent thing that students will now have a new place to buy books. A student-operated used bookstore has been formally approved, which we can now use to get inexpensive books. And, because the bookstore will be student-run, students in the School of Business who hope to become managers or entrepreneurs will get hands-on experience in operating a business. The word is that the bookstore will buy and sell used medical books and law books, as well as a variety of other textbooks and reference books. Let's all go out and support this new venture!
Kelly Thomas

Narrator: Now listen to two students discussing the letter.

Track 096 （播放錄音檔 096，錄音原文見特別收錄 2 的 P.298）

> **A letter has been written to the newspaper about a student-operated bookstore. State the man's opinion of the letter and explain the reasons he gives for that opinion.**
>
> Preparation Time: 30 Seconds
> Response Time: 60 Seconds

Narrator: You have 30 seconds to prepare.
Narrator: Begin speaking after the beep.

策略：小冠詞，大作用

如果使用正確，冠詞能夠增強語言的前後銜接。冠詞的使用看似微妙且難以把握，但是評分人卻能注意到這一點，從而影響他們的評分。

冠詞的一個重要作用是能夠指示資訊是新的還是舊的。不定冠詞 a 或 an 表示新的資訊，定冠詞 the 則表示該資訊之前已經給出，目前正在談論的事和之前說的事情是同一件事。

以口語考試第三題為例，看一看這個原則是怎樣在實際中發揮作用的。在第三題中，小文章第一次給考生呈現了資訊。上面講學生經營書店的例題中，一個學生寫了一封關於學生經營書店的信函登在校園報紙上。第二句使用了不定冠詞，因為寫信的人正在呈現新資訊：

<u>A student-operated used bookstore</u> has been formally approved, ...

然後，下一句使用了定冠詞：

And, because <u>the bookstore</u> will be student-run, ...

第二次提起同一家書店時用到 the bookstore，寫信的人通過 the 使自己的文章前後銜接更緊密。同樣，後面再提到這個概念時，都用了 the bookstore，因為 bookstore 是一個已知的舊資訊。

再來看看這道題的對話。女生第一次提到書店的時候，用了定冠詞。很明顯，她這麼用是假設男生已經知道她指的是什麼。

(woman) Student: Mac, are you going to be part of the used bookstore?

但在她給出的評論中，該女生問男生：

(woman) Student: Do you think a student-run business will be able to compete?

在這種情況下，這位女生使用了不定冠詞 a，因為她泛指學生做生意這件事。如果她使用 the，那就不正確了，因為她指的是「任何學生經營的生意」是否會成功，而不是詢問「那個學生經營的生意會成功嗎？」

最後，看看題幹中所使用的冠詞。題幹中的資訊是：有人寫了一封關於某家由學生經營的書店（a student-operated bookstore）的信，要求考生「陳述這個男生的觀點」（state the man's opinion）。

根據小文章、對話和題幹，考生就瞭解了完整的背景，知道了有關書店的所有事實，那麼回答時就應該用對冠詞。

高分回答

注意看，仔細聽，這裡面標上粗體的地方都要發重音才道地喔！ *Track 097*

The **man** was de**ligh**ted to **see** a **stu**dent had **wri**tten a **le**tter of su**pport** for the **new** **stu**dent-operated **bu**siness, a **used book**store. As a **bu**siness **ma**jor, **he** him**self hopes** to **work** at this **book**store. **He** be**lieves** that the **book**store will be **ve**ry **po**pular with **stu**dents, since **stu**dents are **al**ways **ha**ppy to **buy books** at **low pri**ces. The **man** is **con**fident that the **used book**store will **make mo**ney, **e**ven **though** the **pro**fit on **each book** will be **small**. He's **al**so **ve**ry ex**cit**ed about the **fact** that **stu**dents in the **School** of **Bu**siness will be able to **gain** ex**pe**rience in **o**perating a **bu**siness. Al**though** it is **po**ssible that **stu**dents will at **times** have **ques**tions about **ma**naging the **book**store, the pro**fe**ssors at the **School** of **Bu**siness will be able to ad**vise** them. **That way**, the **stu**dents will **gain** a **great deal** of **know**ledge about **ru**nning a **bu**siness.

托福總監為什麼覺得這是高分回答？

　　看看第一句中考生的冠詞使用情況：The man was delighted to see a student had written a letter of support for the new student-operated business, a used bookstore. 從題幹中可知 the man 的所指，所以一定要用定冠詞。考生說到 a student，使用了不定冠詞，是因為寫信的 Kelly Thomas 並不重要，只要知道是某個學生寫了一封信即可。

　　a letter of support 用了不定冠詞，因為這是要說給聽者的新資訊。the new student-operated business 中用了定冠詞是因為說話人和聽者都知道了這個特定的生意指什麼。同義語 a used bookstore 使用了不定冠詞，因為它作為一個注釋，定義並解釋了這項生意具體指的是什麼。

　　注意，定義本質上針對的是普遍概念，所以要用不定冠詞，例如：A chair is a piece of furniture consisting of a seat, legs and a back.

　　繼續看回答範例，後文再次提到這一概念時用的是 the used bookstore 或 the bookstore。但要注意，考生首次談到商學院的學生時，不用任何冠詞：He's also very excited about the fact that students in the School of Business will be able to gain experience in operating a business. 在這個句子中，考生本可以說 the students，因為談及了一個特指的事物，但是，此處不用任何冠詞也沒有任何問題。在最後一句中，考生用了定冠詞來強調：That way, the students will gain a great deal of knowledge about running a business.

　　很多考生覺得冠詞的用法很難把握，但是在準備新托福口語考試過程中，你對冠詞的運用會越來越熟練，因為特定的模式總是重複出現。通過有針對性的練習和強化，就能掌握什麼時候使用定冠詞、不定冠詞或不用冠詞，從而使語言的前後銜接更緊密。

想通過冠詞加強前後銜接，可運用以下策略：

1. 不定冠詞用於不明確的指代。通常，不定冠詞表示該資訊對於講話者和聽者都是新的。定冠詞用於特定的指代，通常指舊資訊。

2. 如果小文章、對話和題幹中提到過某個名詞，可以用 the 來進行指代，如：The man is happy about the new plan.

3. 下定義時（同位語中）用不定冠詞，如：As a business major, ...

4. 在總結觀點、指代一群學生或其他群體時，使用不帶冠詞的複數形式，如：It is possible that students will at times have questions about managing the bookstore. 雖然使用 the 通常也是正確的，但在這種情況下不用冠詞更加保險。

5. 用本書準備考試時，注意實用答題範本和回答範例中的冠詞。背範本時，冠詞的用法要記正確。

6. 使用冠詞的首要目的不是為了準確，而是在回答中構建緊密的前後銜接。評分人一定會注意到語言的銜接性和邏輯連貫性，然後據此評分。

▶模擬試題①

　　請回答下題。回答時，可嘗試使用下面列出的實用答題範本。

Narrator: State College recently announced internships with a nearby law firm. Read about the internships. You will have 45 seconds to read the article. Begin reading now.

Reading Time: 45 Seconds

Law Internships Announced

The renowned firm Smith & Larson plans to offer several paid intern positions for law students at State College who specialize in tax law. Students who have taken any tax law course will be eligible for the internships. A shortlist of candidates will be invited to interview. For students interested in a career in tax law, this is a major opportunity to experience the practice at the highest level. As a reminder, State College policy is that at least one internship is necessary for any law student who wishes to be formally listed with Job Placement Services.

Narrator: Now listen to two students discussing the article.

🎧 *Track 098* （播放錄音檔 098，錄音原文見特別收錄 2 的 P.298）

The woman expresses her opinion about the college's plan. State her opinion and explain the reasons she gives for holding that opinion.

Preparation Time: 30 Seconds
Response Time: 60 Seconds

實用答題範本　　　　🎧*Track 099* 聽聽看！別人的高分回答！（高分回答原文請見 P.284）

She tells the man that, based on her experience last summer, ...is/are a waste of time.
Not only are the three months a waste of time, they keep students from VERBing...

得分考技：標準英語口語中常用片語動詞的用法

　　很多考生認為片語動詞是一種類似中文的成語、很生硬的東西。但實際上，只有一些片語動詞比較生硬，剩下的都屬於標準的英語口語。另外，如果放在情境裡當做語塊進行記憶，片語動詞是很好用的！

　　考生應掌握片語動詞的正確發音和用法。首先，組成片語動詞的通常是既常用又好理解的詞彙。例如，片語動詞 make up（組成；編造）由動詞 make 和介系詞 up 組成。這兩個詞都很簡單，但是組合在一起後意思發生了很大的變化。不過，如果將 make up 當做一個語塊來記憶，就可以很容易地記住並正確使用它。

　　其次，片語動詞在口語中很常見。因此，新托福口語、聽力和寫作部分的對話或小講座中都有可能會出現。另一方面，回答中片語動詞使用得越多，你的表達就越自然、流利。

　　一些片語動詞被認為是像成語一樣困難的「俚語」，例如：The man wanted to veg out.。veg 是 vegetable 的縮寫。veg out 是俚語，表示「悠閒度日，無所事事，懶惰得像植物一樣」。口語考試中最好避免用這樣的困難俚語，但比較口語的片語動詞用在考試中是合適的。例如：The student handed in her work late. 和 The woman backed up her data daily.

　　在一本好的英語字典中，俚語是會標出來的。所以如果有疑問，可以查字典。在考試中，只用符合正規口語習慣用法的動詞片語。

　　很多學習者不太瞭解片語動詞的重音。實際上，規則十分簡單：在片語動詞中，重音通常落在介系詞或副詞上，而不在動詞上。如：

The man needs to <u>check out</u> a book at the library.
The university <u>called off</u> the trip due to the weather.

　　這一重音規則和複合詞的重音規則剛好相反，複合詞的重音通常落在第一部分。記住，這一點很重要！因為很多組成複合詞的詞和組成片語動詞的詞是相同的。例如，正確的說法：

The woman will print **out** her term paper tonight, but she won't give the **print**out to the professor until tomorrow.

托福總監帶你練

聽下列句子，注意片語動詞中重音的位置。片語動詞已用底線標出。反覆聽錄音，然後跟著讀。
🎧*Track 100*

1. The **man** has to <u>figure out</u> how to find an **internship** in a **nearby town**.
2. **Undergraduate students** need to <u>face up</u> to the fact that **good-paying part-time jobs** are **scarce**.

3. A **student** wrote a **letter** to the editor complaining that university **shuttle** buses were frequently <u>breaking down</u>.
4. The **woman** be**lieves** that the university should <u>do away with</u> the **language** requirement.
5. The university has **announced** that it will <u>look into</u> the matter of overcrowded **dormitories**.

• **想在回答中把握好片語動詞的用法和發音，可運用以下策略：**

1. 多掌握片語動詞，在情境中將它們當做語塊記憶。
2. 片語動詞的重音通常落在介系詞或副詞上。如果出現多音節的介系詞或多個詞彙組成的片語動詞，重音則通常落在第二個詞的第一個音節上，如：The man suggested getting **rid** of the recycling bins 中的 get **rid** of。
3. 不能因為組成片語動詞的詞都是簡單的詞，就認為評分人會輕視片語動詞的表達。相反地，片語動詞能加強表達的流利程度，也代表較高的口語熟練水準。
4. 在整個新托福考試中都要避免使用深難的俚語，口語也不例外。

▶模擬試題②

請回答下面關於學生打工的問題。回答時，可嘗試使用下面列出的實用答題範本。

Narrator: Central University recently changed its policy for hiring at the Math Center. Read the announcement about the new policy. You will have 45 seconds to read the notice. Begin reading now.

Reading Time: 45 Seconds

New Hiring Policy at Math Center

For the coming school year, the Math Center at Central University is changing its hiring policy to provide better services to students. Undergraduates who are able to demonstrate advanced competency in mathematics will now be eligible to apply for tutor positions. Previously, only graduate students were permitted to apply. The Math Center provides free support for students who are taking mathematics and statistics classes at Central University. Math Center tutors all have some experience in the mathematics and statistics courses supported. Tutoring is provided on a firstcome, first-served basis in half-hour increments.

Narrator: Now listen to two students discussing the announcement.

🎧 *Track 101* （播放錄音檔 101，錄音原文見特別收錄 2 的 P.299）

The man expresses his opinion about the university's plan. State his opinion and explain the reasons he gives for that opinion.

Preparation Time: 30 Seconds
Response Time: 60 Seconds

實用答題範本 🎧 *Track 102* 聽聽看！別人的高分回答！（高分回答原文請見 P.284）

The man, who is a(n)...himself, is sorry to hear this news.
He thinks that, generally speaking, graduate students are...

• **最後再練習一下「有關學生打工與實習」最實用的答題模板！**

1. The man was delighted to see a student had written a letter of support for...

例 • The man was delighted to see a student had written a letter of support for the new student-operated business, a used bookstore.

• The man was delighted to see a student had written a letter of support for the new Employment Center.

2. As a business major, he himself hopes to VERB...

例 • As a business major, he himself hopes to work at this bookstore.

• As a business major, he himself hopes to go into business.

3. He's also very excited about the fact that...

例 • He's also very excited about the fact that students in the School of Business will be able to gain experience in operating a business.

• He's also very excited about the fact that big companies are recruiting at the university.

4. The woman thinks that...at State College is unnecessary.

例 • The woman thinks that the law internship requirement at State College is unnecessary.

• The woman thinks that the job training program at State College is unnecessary.

5. She tells the man that, based on her experience last summer, ...is/are a waste of time.

例 • She tells the man that, based on her experience last summer, internships are a waste of time.

• She tells the man that, based on her experience last summer, sending out online resumes is a waste of time.

6. **Not only are the three months a waste of time, they keep students from VERBing...**

例 • Not only are the three months a waste of time, they keep students from earning real money, money that could be saved for tuition and housing.

• Not only are the three months a waste of time, they keep students from learning real engineering skills.

7. **She explains to the man that even though the companies say…, …is very small.**

例 • She explains to the man that even though the companies say the intern positions are "paid," the salary is very small.

• She explains to the man that even though the companies say they have lots of intern positions, the number of positions is very small.

8. **The university has changed its policy of VERBing...**

例 • The university has changed its policy of using only graduate students as tutors in the Math Center.

• The university has changed its policy of hiring foreign students.

9. **The man, who is a(n)...himself, is sorry to hear this news.**

例 • The man, who is a graduate student himself, is sorry to hear this news.

• The man, who is an English major himself, is sorry to hear this news.

10. **The man's second point relates to...**

例 • The man's second point relates to the quality of instruction at the Math Center.

• The man's second point relates to the salary paid to student workers.

11. **He thinks that, generally speaking, graduate students are...**

例 • He thinks that, generally speaking, graduate students are better qualified to serve as tutors in the various types of math and statistics.

• He thinks that, generally speaking, graduate students are more experienced.

Task 5 Communicating a Solution
第五題 討論解決方法

口語考試第五題要求考生就大學生遇到的問題提出解決辦法。

考生將聽到一段對話，但不用讀小文章。對話時長為 60～90 秒（180～220 個單字）。一般來講，對話者是兩名學生，但有時也可能是學生與教授，或學生與教職員。對話內容通常涉及其中一位學生遇到的問題，但偶爾問題對雙方均有影響，兩人須合作找到解決辦法。

和第三題一樣，對話雙方為一男一女。考生要準確把握男女雙方究竟誰遇到了麻煩。有時，遇到麻煩的學生會傾聽另一名學生提出的兩種解決辦法。也有些時候，遇到問題的學生會自己想出兩種解決辦法，另外一名學生給出回饋。但是不管是哪種情形，考生都將聽到兩種解決問題的辦法及其各自的利弊。考生一定要快速記下具體情形及各種要素，以便在回答問題時更充分地論證自己的觀點。

▶提問形式

對話結束後，考生將聽到一個問題，該問題同時也會出現在電腦螢幕上。題目通常會要求考生：（1）簡要總結問題；（2）快速列舉出兩種解決辦法；（3）選擇自己認為比較好的一種解決方法；（4）就自己的選擇給出原因。考生有 20 秒的準備時間和 60 秒的答題時間。

第五題的提問形式大同小異，通常是如下形式：

1. The students discuss two possible solutions to the woman's problem. Describe the problem. Then state which of the two solutions you prefer and explain why.

2. Briefly summarize the problem the speakers are discussing. Then say which solution you would recommend. Explain the reasons for your recommendation.

▶第五題的評分方式

和第三題一樣，第五題會按照綜合型題目評分準則評分。評分時主要考慮考生的語言表達能力、語言運用能力和話題展開能力三個方面。考生回答時必須「涵蓋題目要求提供的相關資訊」。如果給出的資訊不完整或有錯誤，那麼，即使語言流利、文法正確，也會被扣分。

　　第五題討論的話題也很好理解。話題背景也都是校園生活。與第三題不同之處在於，第五題不涉及政策，而是探討學生個人遇到的問題。要拿到高分，考生僅需要理解對話內容，然後對該內容進行簡要總結，選出自己覺得最好的解決方法並給出一個清晰易懂、有理有據的解釋。

▶第五題的六個主要情境

　　第五題中最常見的情境可分為六類：

1. 學校活動的期限
2. 時間衝突
3. 交通和房屋問題
4. 失誤與意外
5. 財政與其他資源的短缺
6. 人事問題

　　接下來的章節會分別講解以上每一種情境，並給出多道題目、回答範例和實用答題範本。通過在情境中練習這些題目，你可以更容易地記住考試中會用到的語言。

⑲ School Deadlines 學校活動的期限

❝ 在本章，你將學到……❞

★如何組織第五題的答題思路
★位於音節末尾的 /l/ 如何發音

解讀常考題

　　第五題中出現的很多問題都和大學生遇到的學校活動的截止日期有關。例如：無法按時完成學期論文或實驗專案的問題、申請研究所或者獎學金的期限問題等。解決方法包括重新安排任務或者按輕重緩急將任務重新排序，或者請求放寬任務期限等等。

　　現在，看一道關於學校活動期限的例題。

▶舉例試題

Narrator: In this question, you will listen to a conversation. Then you will be asked to talk about the information in the conversation and give your opinion. After the question you will have 20 seconds to prepare and 60 seconds to respond.

Narrator: Listen to a conversation between two students.

Track 103 （播放錄音檔 103，錄音原文見特別收錄 2 的 P.299）

> **Briefly summarize the problem the speakers are discussing. Then say which solution you would recommend. Explain the reasons for your recommendation.**
>
> Preparation Time: 20 Seconds
> Response Time: 60 Seconds

Narrator: You have 20 seconds to prepare.
Narrator: Begin speaking after the beep.

策略：第五題的答題思路

　　回答上題只需四個步驟：

1. 邊聽邊做筆記。仔細聽談話人遇到的問題及兩種解決方法。
2. 回答時先描述問題。不用過多描述細節，只要能讓聽者瞭解問題的大致情形即可，用時不超過 20 秒鐘。
3. 簡要列舉兩種解決方法，越簡短越好。
4. 選擇你認為較好的解決方法並解釋原因。

高分回答

注意看，仔細聽，這裡面標上粗體的地方都要發重音才道地喔！

The **man's problem** is that he **doesn't know where** he will **live** in the **fall**. （←先描述問題）

He did **not submit** his application for **housing on time** because he'd been **busy working**. Even though he's on the **waiting list** for **dorms**, **just** in **case**, he's **thinking** about **two options**. The **first** option is for **him** to **live** with his **parents**, but **they** live **far away** and he'd **have** to **make** a **long drive**. As an **alternative**, **he** could **rent** an apartment **near campus** and **pay** about **one thousand** dollars a **month**. Of the **two** solutions, I would **choose** renting an apartment **near campus** （←選擇一種你認為較好的解決方法） because commuting **back** and **forth** to his **parents'** house would take **way** too much **time**. Compared to **driving so far**, renting an apartment would **save** a **lot** of **time**. （←解釋選擇原因）

Because the **rent** for the **apartment** is **quite** expensive, I would find a **roommate** to **share** expenses.

托福總監為什麼覺得這是高分回答？

　　回答第五題時，對問題的概述越簡練越好。例如：The man's problem is that he... 或者 The man has a problem in that... 然後，應簡要敘述兩種解決方法。記住不要在這裡過多描述細節，只需提供足夠的資訊，使聽者明白事情的大致背景即可。

　　簡潔地敘述完問題後，確定一種你認為更好的解決方法。表明傾向的好句型如：Of the two solutions, I would choose... / Of the two options, I prefer... 然後在剩下的時間裡為自己的選擇做出清晰、令人信服的解釋。有一條經驗是，應為這一部分留出約 20 秒的時間，以便完成論證，否則就會有丟分的風險。

　　時間有限，應儘快在兩種解決方法中做出選擇並解釋原因。如出現下列情形，將被扣分：

1. 總結問題及兩種解決方法所用的時間太多；
2. 語意含糊，未能將概述或提出的解決方法表達清楚；
3. 對情景中的事實理解有誤，導致陳述時出現錯誤；
4. 回答時前後銜接不暢，缺乏連貫性；
5. 基本文法和詞彙沒掌握好；
6. 發音不標準，致使評分人難以理解。

要答好第五題，可運用以下策略：

1. 聽對話時，注意聽說話人遇到的問題。如果一開始無法確定問題是什麼，不必驚慌，繼續聽下去，你會漸漸搞清楚具體情形。
2. 做筆記，標出是男方還是女方遇到了問題。

3. 在 20 秒的準備時間裡，腦海中要快速回顧兩種解決方法。

4. 開門見山地陳述對話所圍繞的問題及兩個解決方法。這一部分的表述儘量簡練。只有這樣，才能留出 20~25 秒的時間就自己的選擇進行解釋。

5. 語速不宜過快，否則評分人可能無法聽懂。但如果語速過慢或中間有較長停頓，就無法完成回答。最佳方法是保持均勻的速度，句子之間或表達完一個完整意思之後稍作停頓。

6. 解釋自己的選擇原因時，對話雙方提及的資訊均可使用。例如：在談論住宿問題的對話中，女方說 All that driving! 你就可以使用 all that driving 或者 so much driving 作為選擇不住在家裡的原因。

7. 你也可以補充原因來解釋自己為什麼選擇某個解決方法。例如：I would rent an apartment near campus because I like to be where the action is. 雖然對話中並未提及 where the action is（熱鬧的地方），但卻是一個非常合理的理由。

8. 沒必要花時間反駁你不贊成的解決方案。反駁當然是可以的，但時間可能不會允許你這麼做。集中精力論證自己贊成的方案就好。

9. 在支援自己的選擇時，提供的細節越多越好。但要保證語言銜接流暢、連貫，這樣評分人才能跟上你的思路。

記住：在回答第五題時要針對對話提到的問題表達自己的看法。這一點與第三題不同。在回答第三題時，只需總結他人觀點即可。

▶模擬試題①

請回答下面關於期限的題目。回答時，可嘗試使用下面列出的實用答題範本。

Narrator: Listen to a conversation between two students.

🎧*Track 105*（播放錄音檔 105，錄音原文見特別收錄 2 的 P.299）

> **The students discuss two possible solutions to the woman's problem. Describe the problem. Then state which of the two solutions you prefer and explain why.**
>
> Preparation Time: 20 Seconds
> Response Time: 60 Seconds

實用答題範本　　　🎧*Track 106* 聽聽看！別人的高分回答！（高分回答原文請見 P.285）

The woman is worried that she won't be able to finish...on time.
If it were me, I would VERB...

得分考技：發好位於音節末尾的 /l/ 音

若考生無法正確發出位於音節末尾的 /l/ 的發音，評分人就會很難理解。對於有些亞洲國家的考生而言，末尾的 /l/ 音確實很有挑戰性。有些英語學習者將 /l/ 音發得太短，有些人則發得太長，也有些人會在音的末尾加上一個母音。

要正確發出這個音，需要在 /l/ 之前加上一個非常短的 /ə/ 音。例如：讀 tell 時，可以說 [tɛəl]，不然 /l/ 就會發得太短。為改善這個發音，可以嘗試將以 /l/ 結尾的單字和以母音開頭

的單字連讀。例如：先說 school_activity，再說 schoollllll__activity，然後說 schoollll。練習時末尾的 /l/ 可以發得誇張一些，反覆練習幾次。

有時 /l/ 會跟在 d 或者 t 之後的非重讀音節裡，這種發音也需要多加練習。這種情況下，需要發一個更短的 /ə/ 音，或者根本不發。例如：little 及 middle。

托福總監帶你練

聽對話，練習位於音節末尾的 /l/ 的發音。含有位於音節末尾的 /l/ 的單字已用底線標出。反覆聽錄音，然後跟讀。 🎧 *Track 107*

1. **(woman) Student:** Hey Ken. Have you applied to graduate <u>school</u> yet?
   (man) Student: I'm right in the <u>middle</u> of one; the deadline's tomorrow. <u>All</u> the <u>schools</u> seem to have slightly different requirements.
2. **(man) Student:** Did you <u>tell</u> anybody you were changing your major?
   (woman) Student: Not yet. I <u>will</u> in a <u>couple</u> days. I've been waiting to get a confirmation of my new <u>schedule</u>.
3. **(woman) Student:** Do you think <u>you'll</u> do <u>well</u> on your physics <u>final</u> exam?
   (man) Student: It's <u>possible</u>. I <u>still</u> have a lot of <u>material</u> to review, though.

• 要掌握 /l/ 的發音，使自己的回答更易使人理解，可運用以下策略：

1. 先通過聽錄音或有發音功能的線上詞典學習位於音節末尾的 /l/ 的發音，然後重複誦讀。錄下自己的發音，聽一聽自己的 /ə/ 音是否發得夠長。
2. 單獨練習含有位於音節末尾的 /l/ 的單字，也要練習將之與其後的單字連讀。
3. 將一個以 /l/ 結尾的單字和以母音開頭的單字連讀時，如 full answer，在發母音之前，要保證之前的 /l/ 已經發得夠長。
4. 讀諸如 little、cattle、riddle 等包含 d 或者 t 的單字時，/ə/ 音可以發得短一些，有時根本不用發。

記住：如果 /l/ 的發音可以讓評分人聽懂，那麼你的分數會更高。發 /l/ 音時不要敷衍了事，也不要發得太短。

▶模擬試題②

請回答下面關於期限的題目。回答時，可嘗試使用下面列出的實用答題範本。

Narrator: Listen to a conversation between two students.

🎧 *Track 108* （播放錄音檔 108，錄音原文見特別收錄 2 的 P.300）

The students discuss two possible solutions to the man's problem. Describe the problem. Then state which of the two solutions you prefer and explain why.

Preparation Time: 20 Seconds
Response Time: 60 Seconds

實用答題範本 🎧**Track 109** 聽聽看！別人的高分回答！（高分回答原文請見 P.285）

The woman offers two solutions.
Her first suggestion is for him to VERB...

• **最後再練習一下「有關學校活動的期限問題」最實用的答題模板！**

1. The man's problem is that...

例 • The man's problem is that he doesn't know where he will live in the fall.

• The man's problem is that he has too much work.

2. The man has a problem in that...

例 • The man has a problem in that he needs housing.

3. The woman could VERB...

例 • The woman could find a roommate.

• The woman could live at home.

4. He's thinking about two options.

5. He's considering two options.

6. As an alternative, he could VERB...

例 • As an alternative, he could rent an apartment near campus.

• As an alternative, he could see if he gets on the waiting list.

7. Of the two solutions, I...

例 • Of the two solutions, I would choose renting an apartment near campus.

• Of the two solutions, I prefer living at home.

8. Compared to driving so far, VERBing...would VERB / is...

例 • Compared to driving so far, renting an apartment would save a lot of time.

• Compared to driving so far, living in town is more convenient.

9. The woman is worried that she won't be able to finish...on time.

例 • The woman is worried that she won't be able to finish her history paper on time.

10. She missed the deadline.

11. She forgot about the deadline.

12. One solution to this problem is that she can get an extension.

13. The other thing she can do is...

例 • The other thing she can do is staying up working all night.

14. If it were me, I would VERB...

例 • If it were me, I would ask my coach to explain the situation to the professor.

• If it were me, I would ask my coach to help me.

15. The woman offers two solutions.

16. The woman suggests two solutions.

17. Her first suggestion is for him to VERB...

例 • Her first suggestion is for him to take the online exam the second time it's administered.

Scheduling Conflicts
時間衝突

❝ 在本章，你將學到…… ❞

★第五題如何記筆記
★如何用情態動詞 could 和 should 表達可能性與建議

解讀常考題

　　第五題中經常出現的一個情境是時間衝突。大學生通常很忙，白天要上課、打工、健身或參加其他體育運動及各種社交活動，晚上要熬夜做作業、寫報告。因此新托福口語考試中會出現各種情境，要求考生回答如何安排時間，避免活動衝突。此外，當學校教務主任或某位教授臨時決定安排一堂課或者舉辦某項活動時，就會與學生的原計劃衝突。這類情況在大學校園裡司空見慣，也正是第五題中會出現的情境。

　　一般來說，第五題中出現的時間衝突問題通常和大學生的社交活動有關，例如：到底要去看電影還是留在宿舍等室友？班機延誤導致學生趕不上某一堂課這類狀況也可能出現。不管哪種時間衝突，考生都應快速找出問題所在，說明自己贊同對話中某一方提出的解決方案，然後給出理由。

　　現在，看一道關於時間衝突的例題。

▶舉例試題

Narrator: Listen to a conversation between two students.

🎧 *Track 110*（播放錄音檔 110，錄音原文見特別收錄 2 的 P.300）

Briefly summarize the man's problem. Then state which solution you would recommend. Explain the reasons for your recommendation.

Preparation Time: 20 Seconds
Response Time: 60 Seconds

Narrator: You have 20 seconds to prepare.
Narrator: Begin speaking after the beep.

策略：第五題記筆記的訣竅

　　記筆記對第五題而言非常重要，因為這道題目沒有文章可供閱讀。此外，第五題不僅要求考生闡述他人遇到的問題，還要說出提到的解決方法，這與第三題有著本質上的區別。

第五題中，考生有 20 秒的準備時間，這比第三題的準備時間少 10 秒，原因是考生不必考慮閱讀材料的內容。

做第五題筆記需要以下幾個步驟：

1. 聽對話，瞭解問題所在，也就是「到底是什麼樣的時間衝突」。用縮寫形式將其快速記下。

2. 聽清兩種解決方案並記下來。若時間充裕，記下兩種解決方法中存在的問題。當然，筆記需要採用縮寫形式。

3. 快速在筆記中標出你贊成的解決方案，如畫圓圈或畫底線。

高分回答

注意看，仔細聽，這裡面標上粗體的地方都要發重音才道地喔！　 *Track 111*

The **problem** the **student faces** is that he's **promised** his **good friend Bob** he'd **attend** his **solo violin** recital. However, he's been **asked** to do **extra work** that day for the **law firm** where he's an **intern**. The **woman suggests** that he go into the **law firm early** to **finish up** the **work** and **come back** to **campus in time** for the concert. However, the **firm** is **far** and he has a **class** in the **morning**. The **woman then** asks if he can **get** another **intern** to do the work **for** him. The **man** doesn't **know whether** another **intern** would **help out**; moreover, the **man doesn't want** to anger the **lawyers**. To **solve** the **problem, I** think the **man** should **call** his **boss** at the **law firm right** away and **ex**plain the situation. He should volunteer to **go in very early, skip** his **morning class**, and **get** the **work done**. He could **also ask** her if **she** had any **other** idea for **how** he might be able to **help them**—at a **time** that **didn't conflict** with **Bob's concert**.

托福總監為什麼覺得這是高分回答？

下面來分析這一答案，看看什麼樣的筆記可以幫助考生做出如此嚴密的回答。前兩句明確陳述具體的時間衝突問題：這位學生的好朋友 Bob 將舉辦一場個人音樂會，但是這位學生需要在實習單位加班，因而不確定能否出席音樂會。第三句提出了第一個解決方案，即他可以早點去工作。第五句提出了第二個解決方案，即找他人代班。最後三句是考生提議的解決方案：跟實習單位的老闆聯繫，說明情況，然後自己儘早完成工作，以便擠出時間參加音樂會。

做這道題目的筆記時，可記下如下單字及縮寫：

```
concert
Bob
M can't go
frds
xtra wk - intern
1. in early? but class
2. s.o. else? but rep
```

前文說過，記下的筆記內容越多越好。但上述單字及其縮寫已經足夠考生組織出一個出色的回答。concert 一詞可幫助考生回憶起要出席的活動。Bob 是人名，M 是 man 的縮寫，frds 是 friends 的縮寫，表示說話者和 Bob 是好朋友。xtra wk–intern 表示說話者需要在實習單位加班（extra work）。

之後的兩行筆記以 1. 和 2. 開頭，說明這是兩種解決方案。在第一個解決方案的筆記中，「in early?」的意思是「他可以早點上班嗎？」，而「but class」說明他明天早上還有課，和實習時間衝突。第二種解決方案中，「s.o. else?」的意思是：「Can someone else do the work?」，「but rep」是縮寫，意思是：「But the man is worried about his reputation as a good worker, and doesn't want to be seen to be unwilling to help out.」第一種解決方案下畫了橫線，表示這是考生贊成的解決方案。

筆記中不可能記下很多內容。考生應憑藉記憶和常識填補細節的空白。簡潔的筆記只是一個邏輯框架，讓考生可以集中思路，為考生回答問題提供指導。如果考生能記住並練習使用本章結尾提供的實用答題範本，考試中必能借助範本填補記憶的空白。

回答第五題時，要記好筆記，可使用下列策略：

1. 注意聽，然後判斷是男性還是女性遇到了問題，以 M 或者 F 標示。
2. 既要留意遇到問題的一方，也要留意提供兩種解決方案的另一方。事實上，任何一方都有可能提出解決方案，將這些資訊分兩點以縮寫形式記下。
3. 如果時間充裕，記下實施兩種方案時存在的困難。
4. 圈出或者畫出你贊成的解決方案。
5. 用這些筆記組織成一個連貫、有條理的回答。

▶模擬試題①

請回答下面關於時間衝突的題目。回答時，可嘗試使用下面列出的實用答題範本。

Narrator: Listen to a conversation between two professors.

🎧 *Track 112* （播放錄音檔 112，錄音原文見特別收錄 2 的 P.301）

Briefly summarize the problem the professors are discussing. Then say which solution you would recommend. Explain the reasons for your recommendation.

Preparation Time: 20 Seconds
Response Time: 60 Seconds

實用答題範本 🎧 *Track 113* 聽聽看！別人的高分回答！（高分回答原文請見 P.285）

While chatting with..., she considers two possible solutions.
The second option is for her to VERB...

得分考技：用 could 和 should 表達可能性與建議

could 除了用作 can 的過去式，還表示「推測某人或許可以做某事」。

句型說明	例句
固定句型：主詞 + could + 動詞原形	1. The man could buy used textbooks from other students. 2. The woman could hire a moving company to help her move.
變形句型 1：在上述固定句型之前或之後加上一個 if 引導的子句，解釋必要條件	1. The man could get a ride home with his roommate if he finished his paper. 2. If her boss approved, the woman could skip work and attend the lecture.
變形句型 2：在上述兩個句型中加入副詞，如 maybe 和 possibly 等	1. The man could possibly rent a laptop computer for a day. 2. If the library was open, maybe the woman could go there to work, where it was quiet.

should 除了用作 shall 的過去式，還表示「建議某人做某事」。

句型說明	例句
固定句型：主詞 + should + 動詞原形	1. The man should take the chemistry class next semester. 2. The woman should teach the review class first and then go to the party.
變形句型：在上述固定句型前加上 I think (that)	I think (that) the man should take the chemistry class next semester.

口語中，含 should 的句子裡有沒有 I think (that)，意思不會有差別，因為含 should 的句子就表達了這是說話者的觀點。但想著重強調某一觀點時可以加上 I think (that)。

托福總監帶你練

聽聽看下列含有情態動詞 could 和 should 的句子。情態動詞已用底線標出。反覆聽錄音，然後跟讀。

🎧 *Track 114*

1. The **man** could **go** home to **attend** his **family** reunion and **rewrite** his **report** at **home**.
2. If there's **enough time**, the **man** should **make** a **new sculpture**.
3. The **woman** could **possibly** persuade the professor that she overslept.
4. The **university** should **publish** the **newspaper once every two months**.
5. I think the **woman** should **take** the **literature class** at a **nearby** community college.

• 要想恰當使用情態動詞 could 和 should，可運用以下策略：

1. 掌握用 could 表達可能性的基本文法句型。練習第五題時注意用上這種句型。如：The man could ride his bicycle to campus to save money.
2. 掌握用 should 表達建議的基本文法句型。練習第五題時注意用上這種句型。如：The woman should explain to her roommate that she cannot attend the play.
3. 偶爾可以在 could 句型中加上 maybe 或者 possibly，這樣會使回答的句型顯得更豐富。
4. 希望強調某一觀點時，可以在 should 前面的部分加上 I think (that)。

▶模擬試題②

　　請回答下面關於時間衝突的題目。回答時，可嘗試使用問題下面列出的實用答題範本。

Narrator: Listen to a conversation between two students.

🎧**Track 115**（播放錄音檔 115，錄音原文見特別收錄 2 的 P.301）

The speakers discuss two possible solutions to the man's problem. Briefly summarize the problem. Then state which solution you recommend and explain why.

Preparation Time: 20 Seconds
Response Time: 60 Seconds

實用答題範本　　　　🎧**Track 116** 聽聽看！別人的高分回答！（高分回答原文請見 P.285）

The other possibility is for the man to VERB...
Personally, I would VERB...

• 最後再練習一下「表達時間衝突」最實用的答題模板！

1. The problem the student faces is that he's VERBed...

　例 • The problem the student faces is that he's promised his good friend Bob he'd attend his solo violin recital.

　　　• The problem the student faces is that he's supposed to tutor a student.

2. To solve the problem, I think the man should VERB...

　例 • To solve the problem, I think the man should call his boss at the law firm right away and explain the situation.

　　　• To solve the problem, I think the man should ask a friend to teach his class for him.

3. The woman just became aware that…

　例 • The woman just became aware that she has a scheduling conflict.

　　　• The woman just became aware that she has a meeting tomorrow.

4. While chatting with..., she considers two possible solutions.

例 • While chatting with the man, she considers two possible solutions.

5. The second option is for her to VERB...

例 • The second option is for her to find another professor to teach the class on Friday.

• The second option is for her to audit the Spanish class.

6. My choice would be to VERB...

例 • My choice would be to find a replacement teacher who knows some archaeology.

• My choice would be to do a take-home exam.

7. The reason I wouldn't try to schedule the class over the weekend is that...

例 • The reason I wouldn't try to schedule the class over the weekend is that it would be very difficult to get everybody together then.

• The reason I wouldn't try to schedule the class over the weekend is that students probably wouldn't come.

8. The first (solution) is to VERB...

例 • The first is to switch class times with a student in another lab section.

• The first solution is to persuade the professor to give a make-up exam.

9. The problem with that option is that…

例 • The problem with that option is that the professor doesn't like students to trade places.

10. The other possibility is for the man to VERB...

例 • The other possibility is for the man to wait for someone to drop out of organic chemistry and then take his place.

• The other possibility is for the man to ask for an extension.

11. Personally, I would VERB...

例 • Personally, I would find a student to switch places with and then start going to the lab section.

• Personally, I would choose to audit the course.

Problems with Transportation and Buildings
交通及房屋問題

在本章，你將學到……

★回答第五題時如何表明個人立場
★如何發對 can、can't、have、have to 的音

解讀常考題

　　交通及房屋問題是大學生日常生活的一部分，因而頻頻出現於第五題中。常考的交通問題例如：汽車拋錨，某學生希望搭便車回家；某學生要搬到校外住，但自己沒有汽車，因此需要解決上學的交通問題等。

　　關於房屋問題的題目涉及：教學大樓過於擁擠；學生分配到的房間太小，無法懸掛某件藝術品；水管漏水；學校宿舍寒假不開放；宿舍年久失修等。

　　回答與這些話題相關的題目時，要想有出眾的表現，考生應該能夠談論交通工具、宿舍以及教室可能會引起的各種麻煩。

　　現在，看一道關於交通問題的例題。

▶舉例試題

Narrator: Listen to a phone call between two students.

🎧 *Track 117*（播放錄音檔 117，錄音原文見特別收錄 2 的 P.302）

> **The speakers discuss two possible solutions to the woman's problem. Describe the problem. Then state which of the two solutions you prefer and explain why.**
>
> Preparation Time: 20 Seconds
> Response Time: 60 Seconds

Narrator: You have 20 seconds to prepare.
Narrator: Begin speaking after the beep.

策略：表明個人立場的三個步驟

　　第 10 章介紹了如何在回答第二題時快速表明立場，但是，第五題這樣的綜合口語題比第二題這種獨立口語題更為複雜，回答問題的時間也延長為 60 秒。此外，儘管第二題和第五題均要求考生從兩種選擇中做出一種選擇，但第五題要求考生先聽一段內容詳細的對話，然後再闡釋自己為什麼選擇某一解決方案。由此可見，第五題的回答更長、更複雜，因而考生表明自己立場時使用的策略也必須與第二題有所不同。

在第五題中，表明個人立場需要以下三個基本步驟：

1. 闡述題目中學生的具體情況。
2. 說明自己知道有哪兩種解決方案。
3. 在此基礎上表明個人立場，注意使用連貫技巧。
下面來看看在前面這道例題中如何應用上述步驟。

高分回答

注意看，仔細聽，這裡面標上粗體的地方都要發重音才道地喔！　*Track 118*

The **situation** is that the **woman** is **responsible** for **driving** a **van** full of geology **students up** to the **mountains** for a **field** trip. When she picked **up** the van, however, she **noticed** that a **red light** went on, so she's **worried**. She **wonders** if there's a **problem** with the van's **engine**. Her **friend** su**gg**ests that she **call** her advising **professor** to see if **he** can **help** her find a**n**other **van** or come **up** with another sug**g**estion. He **also** su**gg**ests just **driving** the **van** as it **is**, because the **red light** may **just** be a **minor problem**. The van's **engine** may be **fine**. If **this** were my **decision**, **I** would **choose** the **first** option, that is, **I** would **call** my ad**v**ising pro**f**essor. (←表明個人立場)

The **main** reason I pre**f**er **this** option is that I'd **want** to have a **senior person take** the responsi**b**ility for the situa**t**ion. **Furthermore**, the ad**v**ising professor is **more** experienced and will **probably know** of a **good way** to **quickly** re**s**olve the **problem**. (←解釋自己立場的原因)

托福總監為什麼覺得這是高分回答？

　　注意，上述回答只有九句，但考生直到第七句話才表明自己的立場。表明立場的句子為：If this were my decision, I would choose the first option, that is, I would call my advising professor. 最後兩句話解釋自己持該立場的原因。前六句話都在闡述基本情況：描述問題，說明對話提到的兩種解決方案。

　　還要注意，考生僅描述問題就用了三句話。這種答題方式和之前所說的第二題的答題策略大不相同。在回答第二題時，必須很快表明自己的偏好，例如，是選擇 the city 還是 the countryside。但是在第五題，花一些時間描述一個複雜的情況並不浪費時間，因為有了這些鋪墊，之後在選擇一種解決方案並解釋原因時，就可以直接闡述自己的觀點，不必擔心評分人不理解。看看本回答最後兩句話，考生陳述了兩個理由：

　　The main reason I prefer this option is that I'd want to have a senior person take the responsibility for the situation. Furthermore, the advising professor is more experienced and will probably know of a good way to quickly resolve the problem.

　　這兩句話清楚地解釋了考生為何選擇給指導教授打電話求助。考生無需進一步闡釋，因為前六句話已經將具體情況描述得非常清楚了。最終，考生通過先陳述事實，再表明立場的方式，給出了一個連貫而有條理的回答。但是，巧妙運用這種答題方式的關鍵之一是要注意合理安排答題時間，只有這樣，才能在 60 秒內自如地表明立場並闡明原因。

更多可用來表明立場的例句：
The solution I prefer is to call the advising professor.
I think the woman should call her advising professor.
To solve the problem, I think the woman should first call her advising professor.

答第五題時，要清楚表明立場，可運用以下策略：

1. 表明立場之前，先用一些時間描述清楚具體情況，即應先描述問題及兩種解決方案。
2. 若時間充裕，可簡要提及兩種解決方案在實施過程中的潛在障礙。但是，要言簡意賅，使用一個子句或者一個短句即可。例如，在 The woman could contact her professor, <u>although he might be annoyed</u> 中，第一個分句描述解決方案，畫線句子則解釋了該方案的潛在障礙。
3. 在充分陳述了事件之後，簡潔明瞭地表明自己的立場。
4. 表明立場時，考生應使用連貫技巧，引用之前說過的句子，幫助評分人理解論證過程。例如：I would choose the first option, that is, I would contact my professor 中，the first option 就起到了增進上下文連貫性的作用，因為它指代之前說過的第一個解決方案。
5. 合理安排答題時間，在規定的時間內陳述自己選擇的解決方案並講出兩個原因。

▶模擬試題①

　　請回答下面關於租場地問題的題目。回答時，可嘗試使用下面列出的實用答題範本。
Narrator: Listen to a conversation between two students.

 Track 119 （播放錄音檔 119，錄音原文見特別收錄 2 的 P.302）

Briefly summarize the problem the students are discussing. Then say which solution you would recommend. Explain the reasons for your recommendation.

Preparation Time: 20 Seconds
Response Time: 60 Seconds

實用答題範本　　　　　*Track 120* 聽聽看！別人的高分回答！（高分回答原文請見 P.286）

The man has to figure out how to VERB...
Although I'd have to VERB..., I would not VERB...

得分考技：不容小覷的常見發音錯誤（can、can't、have、have to）

情態動詞的發音不正確是個不容小覷的問題。考生說的是 can 還是 can't？是 have 還是 have to？造成這種理解混亂的原因是母音的發音太短、重音及聲調不正確以及忽略尾音 t，如 can't。試想，如果評分人不確定考生說的是 can 還是 can't，考生的分數當然會受影響啊！意思完全相反耶！

導致情態動詞發音不正確的原因之一是，考生沒有意識到：根據 can 和 have 在句中的用法不同，它們的發音也會發生變化。

1. can 和 can't

肯定句中，can 只當情態動詞用時，不發重音。這是最常見的用法，如：

The **man** can (/kən/) **get** to **campus** by **taking** a **bus**.

但是，當 can 表示一種能力，強調儘管他人的期望不高，但某人實際上能夠做某事時，應該重讀，如：

Woman: It's not **true**! Students **can't** park their cars on campus.

Man: Oh, but they **can** (/kæn/)! They **just need** the **right kind** of **permit**.

而 can't 很少有不發重音的情況。和許多否定形式一樣，否定式 can't 和 cannot 與其肯定式 can 相比，重音更明顯，母音更長。這是為了強調說話者要表達的意思。正因如此，尾音 t 也經常需要發重音。考生要在尾音 t 的發音上多下工夫，如：

Man: So, they're **not** going to **renovate** the **dorm** this **fall**. They **can't** (/kænt/) do any construction **work** while **students** are **living** there.

2. have 和 have to

have 不做情態動詞時，一般不發重音，如：

I have (/həv/) a **problem with my car**.

The **man** has (/həz/) a **meeting** with his de**partment chair** tomorrow.

但 have to 中的 have 經常需要發重音，以強調主詞必須做某事，如：

I **have to** (/hæf tə/) find a **way** to **transport** the **soccer team** to the **match**.

The **woman has to** (/hæs tə/) **take** a **train** to **get** to her **internship job**.

記住，have to 中的 to 是清音，無需發重音。因為 to 是清音，have 中的 v 也變成了清音。也就是說，v 發 /f/ 的音。同樣，has to 中 has 也從 /hæz/ 變成 /hæs/。

托福總監帶你練

聽下列句子中 can、can't、have 和 have to 的發音，自己練習。can、can't、have 和 have to 及其後的動詞已用底線標出。反覆聽錄音，然後跟著讀。 🎧**Track 121**

1. As **one** option, the **man** <u>can tell</u> his **roommate** there'll **be** a **surprise** party.
2. The **student** <u>has to sign up for</u> a **different lab** section.
3. **Unless more students** submit **poems**, the **poetry contest** <u>can't be held</u>.
4. The **woman** <u>has</u> a **nice apartment**, so she **doesn't want** to **move**.
5. **Starting next year**, university **clubs** <u>have to find</u> their own **funding**.

• **要準確地發 can、can't、have 和 have to 這幾個音，可運用以下策略：**

1. 情態動詞 can 的肯定形式不發重音。
2. 想要強調某人有能力做某事時，can 可以發重音，如：My teacher said I **can't** sing very well; but I know I **can!** 此時，要拉長 a 的發音。
3. can't 要發重音（此外，所有否定的縮寫形式也都應發重音），如：doesn't、hasn't 和 wouldn't。
4. 除「have to + 動詞原形」的結構中之外，其他情況下 have 都不發重音。
5. 「have to + 動詞原形」結構中，have 發重音，如：If I got into an Ivy League school, I would **have** to borrow money.

▶模擬試題②

請回答下面關於房屋問題的題目。回答時，可嘗試使用下面列出的實用答題範本。

Narrator: Listen to a conversation between a student and a repairman.

🎧*Track 122*（播放錄音檔 122，錄音原文見特別收錄 2 的 P.303）

> **The speakers discuss a problem and two possible solutions. Briefly summarize the problem. Then state which of the two solutions you prefer and explain why.**
>
> Preparation Time: 20 Seconds
> Response Time: 60 Seconds

實用答題範本　　🎧*Track 123* 聽聽看！別人的高分回答！（高分回答原文請見 P.286）

...makes two suggestions to her.
I think the woman should VERB...and VERB...

• **最後再練習一下「陳述交通與房屋問題」最實用的答題模板！**

1. **The situation is that the woman is responsible for VERBing...**
   例 • The situation is that the woman is responsible for driving a van full of geology students up to the mountains for a field trip.

2. **She wonders if there's a problem with...**
   例 • She wonders if there's a problem with the van's engine.
   • She wonders if there's a problem with the lease.

3. **If this were my decision, I would choose the first option, that is, I would VERB...**
   例 • If this were my decision, I would choose the first option, that is, I would call my advising professor.
   • If this were my decision, I would choose the first option, that is, I would give the landlord a call.

4. The main reason I prefer this option is that I'd want to VERB...

例 • The main reason I prefer this option is that I'd want to have a senior person take the responsibility for the situation.

• The main reason I prefer this option is that I'd want to have a good relationship with the landlady.

5. The man has to figure out how to VERB...

例 • The man has to figure out how to handle the situation.

• The man has to figure out how to deal with the problem.

6. He talks about two possible...

例 • He talks about two possible actions.

• He talks about two possible solutions.

7. My reasoning is that...

例 • My reasoning is that there are lots of good bands.

• My reasoning is that students like to listen to a variety of bands.

8. Although I'd have to VERB..., I would not VERB...

例 • Although I'd have to do some last-minute advertising, I would not waste the money I paid to the concert hall.

• Although I'd have to pay the plumber for the house call, I would not have to pay for the actual repairs.

9. X and Y have major problems.

例 • The kitchen sink and the bathroom have major problems.

• The carpet and the refrigerator have major problems.

10. ...makes two suggestions to her.

例 • The repairman makes two suggestions to her.

11. First, he suggests that she VERB...and VERB...

例 • First, he suggests that she call the landlord and persuade him to pay the bill for the repairs.

• First, he suggests that she contact the university mediator and explain the situation.

12. I think the woman should VERB...(and VERB...)

例 • I think the woman should call the university mediator and ask for advice.

• I think the woman should speak with the landlord directly.

22 Mistakes and Accidents
犯錯與意外

> ❝ 在本章，你將學到…… ❞

★ 如何通過使用指示詞加強回答的前後銜接
★ 如何用 what 引導的名詞性子句提出建議

解讀常考題

　　常出現在第五題中的犯錯類情形如：忘記帶筆電出門；因睡過頭而曠課；開學第一天不知道教室在哪裡；把包包掉在圖書館，背包裡有硬碟，裡面存著論文……

　　第五題中的意外類情形如：因扭傷腳踝或者手骨折而無法參加舞蹈表演；不小心毀壞某件物品，例如不小心把一桶黑漆倒在一件完工的藝術品上，或者失手讓一個建築模型掉進水溝。

　　回答失誤及意外事件類題目時，考生應從對話提到的兩個解決方案中選擇一個，然後闡述自己將如何補救失誤或意外所造成的後果。一段出色的回答通常會闡明應如何向教授或同學解釋問題所在。

　　現在，看一道關於失誤的例題。

▶舉例試題

Narrator: Listen to a conversation between two students.

🎧 **Track 124** （播放錄音檔 124，錄音原文見特別收錄 2 的 P.303）

Briefly summarize the problem the speakers are discussing then state which solution you would recommend. Explain the reasons for your recommendation.

Preparation Time: 20 Seconds
Response Time: 60 Seconds

Narrator: You have 20 seconds to prepare.
Narrator: Begin speaking after the beep.

策略：怎麼發揮四個指示詞的作用

　　前面的章節探討過如何在口語考試中提高語言的前後銜接，例如怎麼使用代名詞、連接詞以及冠詞連接動詞和片語，並使觀點的表達更連貫。下面將探討最後一個銜接手法：指示詞。

指示詞用來特指某一個詞或某一事物，分為兩種：指示代名詞和指示形容詞，其中指示形容詞又叫做指示限定詞。這兩種指示詞都是指代前文所述內容的好方法，能提高考生回答的銜接性。

大家耳熟能詳的四個指示代名詞就是：this、that、these 和 those。這四個指示代名詞可用來指代前文提到過的某一名詞或代名詞，如：The man can persuade the professor to give a make-up exam. This will allow him to pass the course.

這一例句中，指示代名詞 this 指勸說教授這一行為。this 和 these 指代時間或者空間上距離較近的事物，而 that 和 those 則指代時間或者空間上距離較遠的事物。

指示形容詞與片語或名詞連用，如 this plan 和 those students。這種名詞片語和指示代名詞的作用相同，都用來指代特定的人、物或觀點。如：The woman applied for a job in research. This job is perfect for her, because it allows her to work in biochemistry.

指示詞的用法非常簡單！考生只需注意單複數的一致即可。

高分回答

注意看，仔細聽，這裡面標上粗體的地方都要發重音才道地喔！ **Track 125**

The **man is** in **trou**ble because he **oversle**pt and **missed** a **math exam**. He **isn't sure** **what** to **say** to his pro**fess**or, who is **strict**. His **first thought** is to **e**-mail her and **tell** her the **reason** he **missed** the **test** is that he was **sick**. The professor **might** ask for a **sick** note, but he **doesn't know** for **sure**. The **other** way of **handling** this situation is to **go into** the pro**fess**or's office and **tell** her the **truth**—that he **stayed** up **late** and **overslept**. The **risk** with **that** approach is that she **might think oversleeping** is a **poor excuse** and **not allow** him to **make up** the **test**. **My** solution would be to **go to** the professor im**med**iately and **say** I was **read**y to **take** a **make-up exam**. If she **asked** me **why** I **missed** the **test**, I would **tell** the **truth**. **Then** I'd **try** to per**suade** her to **let** me **take** the **test**, saying I'd **take** it **right away**, if she **agreed**.

托福總監為什麼覺得這是高分回答？

下面來看這一回答範例中兩個指示詞的例子，研究一下指示詞如何加強句子的銜接性：

The other way of handling <u>this situation</u> is to go into the professor's office and tell her the truth—that he stayed up late and overslept.

該句中，this situation 指代考生之前描述過的情境。通過使用這一指示詞，考生的回答顯得非常緊湊。同樣，下面這個例子中，that approach 指代該男生找教授坦白事實這一解決方案：The risk with <u>that approach</u> is that she might think oversleeping is a poor excuse and not allow him to make up the test.

在新托福口語考試中，指示形容詞（名詞片語）比簡單的指示代名詞（this、that 等）用處更大，因為指示形容詞（名詞片語）的特指意味更強。使用指示詞是一個簡單而有效的方法，可以使論述更加緊湊，從而在考試中拿到更高的分數。

要更好地使用指示詞，加強回答的前後銜接，可運用以下策略：

1. 使用指示代名詞和指示形容詞時，記住要保持指示詞與被指代事物的單複數一致，並注意是「近指」還是「遠指」。
2. 指示代名詞可用來替代名詞和名詞片語。
3. 指示形容詞特指在文段別處提到的某個具體的人、物或觀點。
4. 要增強前後銜接，可使用定冠詞（the project）或指示形容詞（this project、that project），兩者都能起到加強句子前後銜接的作用。原則是：在通常情況下使用定冠詞或指示代名詞；當表示強調意味時再使用指示形容詞，如：this project。

▶模擬試題①

請回答下面關於意外事件的題目。回答時，可嘗試使用下面列出的實用答題範本。

Narrator: Listen to a conversation between two students.

🎧 *Track 126*（播放錄音檔 126，錄音原文見特別收錄 2 的 P.304）

> **The students discuss two possible solutions to the woman's problem. Briefly summarize the problem. Then state which of the two solutions you prefer and explain why.**
>
> Preparation Time: 20 Seconds
> Response Time: 60 Seconds

實用答題範本 🎧 *Track 127* 聽聽看！別人的高分回答！（高分回答原文見 P.286）

However, the woman is not convinced that...
The second course of action is for her to VERB...

得分考技：口語中的萬能句型，what 名詞子句作主詞

綜合口語評分準則規定的最高級別（滿分標準）中提到：考生的回答要「能體現考生對基本文法結構和複雜文法結構良好的把握能力，從而能連貫、有效地表達相關觀點」。在回答中包含複雜結構的方法之一就是使用名詞性子句作主詞。

在新托福口語考試中，用名詞性子句作主詞可以組合出非常簡練的複合句。這類句子在闡述具體情形時不僅非常到位，而且也能傳達觀點，如：What I think he should do is to ask his landlord to repair the damage.

請看 what 名詞性子句作主詞的例子：

What the man said is that he would make a new drawing.
What the woman should do is to explain the situation to the professor.
What I think the man ought to do is to wait till his arm has healed.
What the roommate did was not fair.

疑問詞 what 可引導名詞性子句。在上述例句中，子句作主詞。可以看出，名詞性子句

中詞的順序與疑問句中詞的順序並不相同。新托福口語考試中非常適宜使用 what 引導的名詞性子句作主詞，因為這類句子的語言不會太正式，也很容易理解。此外，由這類子句組合而成的句子會顯得句型多變、複雜。

托福總監帶你練

聽下列 what 名詞性子句作主詞的句子並練習。what 名詞性子句已用底線標出。反覆聽錄音，然後跟著讀。 🎧 *Track 128*

1. <u>What the woman actually wanted</u> was for the reporter to write a review.
2. <u>What happened</u> was that the woman lost her laptop.
3. <u>What the man did</u> was this: He overslept and missed his final exam.
4. <u>What the woman should do</u> is to be patient and perform when she's healthy.
5. <u>What I suggest</u> is that the man revise his term paper to make it better.

• 要使用由 what 引導的名詞性子句作主詞，可運用以下策略：

1. 名詞性子句是流暢的複合句的重要組成要素。
2. 用由疑問詞引導的名詞性子句作主詞，特別是 what 引導的名詞性子句，非常適合用於新托福口語考試中。
3. 名詞性子句的語序不能倒裝成疑問句語序。名詞性子句中，主詞必須在動詞之前。
4. 使用以 what 名詞性子句作主詞的句子來闡述事實、表達觀點。

▶模擬試題②

　　請回答下面關於意外事件的題目。回答時，可嘗試使用下面列出的實用答題範本。

Narrator: Listen to a conversation between two students.

🎧 *Track 129* （播放錄音檔 129，錄音原文見特別收錄 2 的 P.304）

Briefly summarize the man's problem. Then state which solution you would recommend. Explain the reasons for your recommendation.

Preparation Time: 20 Seconds
Response Time: 60 Seconds

實用答題範本 　　🎧 *Track 130* 聽聽看！別人的高分回答！（高分回答原文請見 P.286）

On top of that, he's a(n)...student and his building is...
If I were the man, I would explore the possibility of VERBing...

• 最後再練習一下「失誤和意外的表達」最實用的答題模板！

1. The man is in trouble because...and...

例 • The man is in trouble because he overslept and missed a math exam.

• The man is in trouble because he lost his keys and can't get into his apartment.

2. His first thought is to VERB...and tell her the reason he VERBed...is that…

例 • His first thought is to e-mail her and tell her the reason he missed the test is that he was sick.

• His first thought is to talk with her and tell her the reason he didn't come to class is that his car broke down.

3. The other way of handling this situation is to VERB...

例 • The other way of handling this situation is to go into the professor's office and tell her the truth—that he stayed up late and overslept.

• The other way of handling this situation is to have his roommate bring his laptop to the library for him.

4. The risk with that approach is that...

例 • The risk with that approach is that she might think oversleeping is a poor excuse and not allow him to make up the test.

• The risk with that approach is that the professor might start thinking he was a troublemaker.

5. The problem the woman has is that...

例 • The problem the woman has is that her landlord believes her cat has stained the carpet in her apartment.

• The problem the woman has is that she forgot to do her assignment.

6. However, the woman is not convinced that...

例 • However, the woman is not convinced that the stains were from her cat.

• However, the woman is not convinced that she was the one who broke the refrigerator.

7. She discusses two...with her friend.

例 • She discusses two courses of action with her friend.

• She discusses two alternatives with her friend.

8. The second course of action is for her to VERB...

例 • The second course of action is for her to go to court.

• The second course of action is for her to hire a lawyer.

9. The man has VERBed...and is going to have trouble VERBing...

例
- The man has sprained his ankle and is going to have trouble getting around.
- The man has lost his keys and is going to have trouble getting into his room.

10. On top of that, he's a(n)...student and his...is...

例
- On top of that, he's an engineering student and his building is quite far away.
- On top of that, he's an art student and his studio is on the other side of campus.

11. This would be convenient, but… and VERBing...is a hassle.

例
- This would be convenient, but a room might not be available and moving is a hassle.
- This would be convenient, but renting a car is expensive and walking is a hassle.

12. If I were the man, I would explore the possibility of VERBing...

例
- If I were the man, I would explore the possibility of moving into Miller Dorm.
- If I were the man, I would explore the possibility of making a new sculpture.

13. If I could persuade the university to VERB..., I would VERB...

例
- If I could persuade the university to let me move there, I would get one of my classmates to help me move.
- If I could persuade the university to postpone the date, I would dance the part myself.

23 Financial and Other Resource Shortages
資金與其他資源的短缺

在本章，你將學到……

★如何描述假設情形
★如何正確地發 /ɛ/ 和 /æ/ 的音

解讀常考題

　　儘管資金問題並不是第五題中最常見的情境，但還是有出現的機會，要注意一下。具體情境包括：學生無力支付旅行費用；大學預算縮減給教授或學生帶來影響等。有些題目會問：某位學生暑假期間應該待在實驗室還是去書店打工？有的題目會討論學校廣播站設備老化、故障頻傳，但學校無力支付維修費用，面對這種情況該如何處理。還有一些題目會討論諸如大學財政預算縮減導致某位學生的補助金減少這類的情況。

　　現在，看一道關於資金短缺的例題。

▶舉例試題

Narrator: Listen to a conversation between two students.

🎧 **Track 131** （播放錄音檔 131，錄音原文見特別收錄 2 的 P.305）

> **The students discuss a problem and two possible solutions. Briefly summarize the problem. Then state which of the two solutions you prefer and explain why.**
>
> Preparation Time: 20 Seconds
> Response Time: 60 Seconds

Narrator: You have 20 seconds to prepare.
Narrator: Begin speaking after the beep.

策略：掌握描述假設情形的句型

　　掌握描述假設情形的技巧很有用，因為第五題有兩種解決方案可供選擇。

　　第五題中，考生會聽到一段對話，關於一個具體問題及其兩種解決方案。有些題目會問：Which option do you prefer? 有些則問：Which solution would you recommend? 在談論這些假設性選擇的優缺點時，考生可使用條件句。第一條件句和第二條件句都適合考生描述選擇、闡述其贊成的解決方案。使用第一條件句，表示考生談論的解決方案有可能實現或者實現的可能性非常大；使用第二條件句則表明兩種解決方案不太可能實現，僅在理論和假設意義上才具有可行性，採用虛擬語氣。

第一條件句的結構為：

If + 主詞 + 動詞的一般現在式，主詞 + 動詞的一般現在式，如：

If the man gets a part-time job, he can pay the tuition.

If + 主詞 + 動詞的一般現在式，主詞 + 動詞的一般未來式，如：

If the woman borrows money from her friend, she will feel bad.

第二條件句的結構為：

If + 主詞 + 動詞的一般過去式，主詞 + would + 動詞原形

If + 主詞 + 動詞的一般過去式，主詞 + could + 動詞原形

If + 主詞 + 動詞的一般過去式，主詞 + should + 動詞原形，如：

If the woman borrowed money from her friend, she would feel bad.

注意，雖然兩種條件句中，主句和子句的位置可以互換，如：The woman would feel bad if she borrowed money from her friend. 但是，在新托福口語考試中，用 if 條件句開頭，考生的意思會表述得更清楚。

下表是描述假設情形的幾個例子：

第一條件句	第二條件句
If the man gets a scholarship, he can go to State College.	If the man got a scholarship, he could go to State College.
If the woman quits her lab job, she will be unhappy.	If the woman quit her lab job, she would be unhappy.
If the man takes fewer classes, his tuition will be less.	If the man took fewer classes, his tuition would be less.
If the university expands the chemistry department, there can be more assistantship positions.	If the university expanded the chemistry department, there might be more assistantship positions.
If the newspaper is published online, the university will reduce costs.	If the newspaper were published online, the university would reduce costs.

回答第五題時，第一條件句和第二條件句均可以使用，但是考生在選擇使用某一條件句後，注意保持前後一致，不能將兩種條件句混著用。另外應注意，在第二條件句的子句中，如果動詞是 be 的形式，其過去時態一律用 were，不用 was。

高分回答

注意看，仔細聽，這裡面標上粗體的地方都要發重音才道地喔！ *Track 132*

The **problem** is that the university **news**paper is facing a financial **crisis**. The **cost** of **newsprint paper** is **too high** and they're **losing money**. The **man** makes **two** **suggestions** to the **woman**:

First, he **suggests** the university **news**paper **add** a **classified advertisement section**. **If** they **did that**, he says, the **newspaper** could **bring** in **more money** and it would **help pay** for the **paper** they buy.（←使用條件句説明選擇優缺點）

The **second** sug**ges**tion the **man** makes is to be**gin** **p**ub**lish**ing the **news**paper in electronic **form**. **I** think the **news**paper should **go** with the **latter** sug**gest**ion—begin **p**ub**lish**ing the paper **online**. **If** they published **online**, **this** would sub**stan**tially re**duce** the **costs**, especially the **cost** of **news**print.（←使用條件句支持自己的選擇）
Readers would get **used** to **rea**ding the paper **online** eventually. Adding a **cla**ssified advertisement **section** would **bring in** a little **money**, but **probably** **not enough**.

托福總監為什麼覺得這是高分回答？

上面回答範例中的畫線句子均使用了第二條件句：

If they did that, he says, the newspaper could bring in more money and it would help pay for the paper they buy.

If they published online, this would substantially reduce the costs, especially the cost of newsprint.

可以看出，回答第五題時，恰當運用條件句描述假設情形可充分展現考生對複雜多樣的文法結構擁有良好的駕馭能力，可以藉此拿到高分。

要描述假設的情形，可運用以下策略：

1. 使用第一條件句或者第二條件句都可以，例如在回答第五題時，可以說：If the man finds a roommate, he can save money on housing. 也可以說：If the man found a roommate, he could save money on housing.
2. 回答問題時，不能將第一條件句和第二條件句混著用，注意保持一致性。

▶ 模擬試題①

請回答下題。回答時，可嘗試使用下面列出的實用答題範本。
Narrator: Listen to a conversation between two professors.

🎧 *Track 133*（播放錄音檔 133，錄音原文見特別收錄 2 的 P.305）

Briefly summarize the problem the speakers are discussing. Then state which solution you would recommend. Explain the reasons for your recommendation.

Preparation Time: 20 Seconds
Response Time: 60 Seconds

實用答題範本　　　　🎧 *Track 134* 聽聽看！別人的高分回答！（高分回答原文請見 P.287）

The man comes up with two ways of VERBing...
This is a tough choice, but if it were mine to make, I'd VERB...

得分考技：/ɛ/ 和 /æ/ 發錯音，意思差很大！

　　men 中的母音 /ɛ/ 和 man 中的母音 /æ/ 看似非常簡單，但是，當考生在考場上集中精力思考並快速回答問題時，便無暇顧及到發音，因而這兩個音經常區別不清。但若發不準這些母音，考生的回答便會讓評分人困惑不解！

　　實際上，發這兩個音時，口型是完全不同的。/æ/ 是 /ɑ/ 和 /ɛ/ 兩個音的結合。發 /æ/ 音時，可先説 father，下顎下沉，嘴巴張大，像在看牙醫那樣，説「啊」。保持這樣的口型，試著同時發 father 和 feather。若能將這兩個母音結合起來，就能正確地發出 /æ/ 這個音。

　　發 /ɛ/ 時，嘴巴不用張得像發 /æ/ 時那樣大，此時口型閉合一些。此外，發 /ɛ/ 的時候，嘴角咧開，呈微笑狀。

托福總監帶你練

聽下列句子，注意 /ɛ/ 和 /æ/ 的發音。含有 /ɛ/ 和 /æ/ 的詞已用底線標出。反覆聽錄音，然後跟著讀。　🎧 *Track 135*

1. The **man** should **ask** his advisor if there's a **chance** for a **scholarship**.
2. **Graduating** early would be a **better** option for the **woman**.
3. If the **man** buys a new **laptop**, he'll **have** to **use** his **credit** card.
4. **After** the woman **takes** her **last exam**, she should **get** a **cheaper** apartment.
5. If the **man** with**draws** some **cash** from the **ATM** machine, he can **take** his **professor** to a **nice** **restaurant**.

• 要掌握 /ɛ/ 和 /æ/ 這兩個發音，可運用以下策略：

1. 聽錄音及網路字典中這兩個音的發音，然後反覆練習。錄下自己的發音，聽聽每個母音是否發得夠長。
2. 發 /ɛ/ 和 /æ/ 時，要保證每個母音的發音足夠長。如果母音只發到一半便停止，那麼別人就有可能聽不懂你在説什麼。想一想，如果發錯了音，bed 和 bad 的意思差別是多麼大！
3. 對於含有 /ɛ/ 或 /æ/，以輔音結尾的單字，發音時可以將末尾的輔音稍微拉長。這樣評分人會更容易理解。
4. 重讀音節和重讀詞彙中的母音要比非重讀的情形下發得更長。
5. 考試中不要太匆忙！有些單字需要重讀，有些不用，要確保每一個母音都能發清楚，以便於評分人的理解。

▶ **模擬試題②**

　　請回答下面關於資金短缺的題目。回答時，可嘗試使用下面列出的實用答題範本。
Narrator: Listen to a conversation between two students.
🎧 *Track 136*（播放錄音檔 136，錄音原文見特別收錄 2 的 P.306）

Briefly summarize the woman's problem. Then state which solution you would recommend. Explain the reasons for your recommendation.

Preparation Time: 20 Seconds
Response Time: 60 Seconds

實用答題範本　　　　　　🎧 *Track 137* 聽聽看！別人的高分回答！（高分回答原文請見 P.287）

The woman's problem is that she has to make a choice between X and Y.
If she goes to..., she won't VERB..., but she might not VERB...

・最後再練習一下「資金與資源短缺的表達」最實用的答題模板！

1. The problem is that...is facing a financial crisis.

例　・The problem is that the university newspaper is facing a financial crisis.

　　・The problem is that the graduate school is facing a financial crisis.

2. I think...should go with the latter suggestion—VERB...

例　・I think the newspaper should go with the latter suggestion—begin publishing the paper online.

　　・I think the School of Engineering should go with the latter suggestion—offer scholarships to students with needs.

3. ...would get used to VERBing...eventually.

例　・Readers would get used to reading the paper online eventually.

　　・Students would get used to paying higher tuition fees eventually.

4. VERBing...would bring in a little money, but probably not enough.

例　・Adding a classified advertisement section would bring in a little money, but probably not enough.

　　・Asking for corporation donations would bring in a little money, but probably not enough.

5. The man comes up with two ways of VERBing...

例　・The man comes up with two ways of cutting costs.

　　・The man comes up with two ways of raising money.

6. The first way is to VERB...

例　・The first way is to shorten the camp from four weeks to three.

　　・The first way is to take out a student loan.

7. This is a tough choice, but if it were mine to make, I'd VERB...

例　• This is a tough choice, but if it were mine to make, I'd shorten the camp period to three weeks.

• This is a tough choice, but if it were mine to make, I'd wait to take the class next year.

8. Perhaps...could be done in the classroom, using computers.

例　• Perhaps some of the original activities that are omitted could be done in the classroom, using computers.

• Perhaps the testing could be done in the classroom, using computers.

9. The woman's problem is that she has to make a choice between two... / X and Y.

例　• The woman's problem is that she has to make a choice between two universities.

• The woman's problem is that she has to make a choice between an excellent engineering school and an ordinary one.

10. The problem is that X did not offer her any money, whereas Y offered her a full scholarship.

例　• The problem is that the top-tier school did not offer her any money, whereas City College offered her a full scholarship.

• The problem is that the Ivy League university did not offer her any money, whereas a community college offered her a full scholarship.

11. If she goes to..., she won't VERB..., but she might not VERB...

例　• If she goes to City College, she won't have any debts, but she might not learn as much.

• If she goes to work, she won't have to pay tuition, but she might not be as happy later on.

12. Moreover, because...is a practical field, I think that a(n)...degree from a less prestigious university like...is still very valuable.

例　• Moreover, because engineering is a practical field, I think that an engineering degree from a less prestigious university like City College is still very valuable.

• Moreover, because nursing is a practical field, I think that a nursing degree from a less prestigious university like City University is still very valuable.

People Problems
人際關係問題

66 在本章，你將學到…… 99

★增強邏輯連貫性的技巧：講故事
★在句首使用介系詞片語，闡述具體情境

解讀常考題

　　第五題常涉及人際關係問題。經常出現在題目中的有同學、室友之間的摩擦，如：有的室友太吵、不衛生或者做事不負責任。要解決這些問題就需要讓這位室友糾正自己的行為。人際關係問題還有學生與老師或其他教職員工之間的爭執，如：學校後勤主管突然告知學生體育館閉館時間變為晚上 9 點。還有時會出現如某學生要搬出宿舍，給室友帶來諸多不便這樣的問題。

　　第五題的對話裡，兩位學生會針對這些情況探討化解爭執的對策，包括勸說對方採取一些行動，或者改變最初的計畫。考生需理解問題的實質，然後選擇一種容易討論的解決方案。考生需要牢記的一點是，在回答人際關係問題時一般要談及當事人的感受。也就是說，考生要提前準備一些描述情緒的英語詞彙，如闡述某個男同學為何「不開心」，或某個女生想怎樣「改善自己和游泳隊其他隊員之間的關係」。

　　現在，看一道關於人際關係的例題。

▶舉例試題

Narrator: Listen to a conversation between two students.

🎧 *Track 138* （播放錄音檔 138，錄音原文見特別收錄 2 的 P.306）

> **The speakers discuss two possible solutions to the man's problem. Briefly summarize the problem. Then state which solution you recommend and explain why.**
>
> Preparation Time: 20 Seconds
> Response Time: 60 Seconds

Narrator: You have 20 seconds to prepare.
Narrator: Begin speaking after the beep.

策略：像講故事一樣回答第五題

　　回答第五題時，想答得有連貫性，就要講究講故事的技巧。先告訴聽眾主要人物是誰，核心事件是什麼。當聽眾對情境有所瞭解之後，再具體講述主角面臨的難題。第五題的故

事情節總會輔以兩個可能的「次要情節」。而考生，也就是講故事的人，要在兩個「次要情節」之間做出選擇，使得主角最終能有完美的結局。最後，考生還要給出至少兩個理由來說明為什麼這才是最好的結局。

　　將第五題的答題看做是在講述一個連貫、流暢的故事有什麼好處呢？首先，如果考生將題目中的人物想成是故事裡面的「主角」（通常至少有兩名學生，其中一人遇到麻煩問題），題目本身就不再那麼可怕了。緊張情緒有所緩解，才更容易集中精力，像在聊家常一樣從容地描述一個事件，如：A student I know has a real problem—she doesn't get along with her roommate. 其次，講故事是我們的習慣，我們經常跟朋友和同事講故事：發生了什麼事、背景是什麼、後續情況如何等等，這種描述的順序大部分人都非常熟悉。說完故事，就可以說：She wants to move out but she doesn't know if she can. Her lease lasts through the year, but she's working on some ways to deal with her situation... 我們還可以一直講下去。考生若能把回答問題看做是簡簡單單地講個故事，自然就不緊張了。

　　當然，即使是簡單地講故事也有提高的空間，這就要運用一些基本的語言技巧，這些技巧能保證考生的觀點表達地流暢、連貫，讓評分人更容易理解。

　　講述一個連貫的故事需要以下幾個步驟：
1. 故事的開頭使用現在式（一般現在式或現在進行式均可）。即假設故事發生在當下。
2. 描述主角的感受，如：The woman is worried that... 或者 The man is unhappy about...
3. 要清晰地呈現事件發生的前後順序，可使用時間副詞，如 first 和 later。

高分回答

注意看，仔細聽，這裡面標上粗體的地方都要發重音才道地喔！ *Track 139*

The **man** is **working** on an English **paper** in the **dorm's** computer lab because his **laptop** broke **down**. Unfortunately, **one** student is being **really loud**, so the **man** is having **trouble concentrating**. The **woman first** suggests that he **go find** the Resident Assistant and have **her talk** to the student. The **man doesn't** know if the **RA** is **awake** this **late**, and he's **also nervous** about getting the **student** in **trouble**. The **woman then suggests** that he **go back** to his **room** and **borrow** his **roommate's laptop**. The **man** says his **roommate** was using the **laptop** the **last time** he **saw** him, but that he **might** be **asleep** now. I would **resolve** this situation by **seeing** if my **roommate** was **still** using his **laptop**. If he **wasn't**, I would **wake** him **up** and borrow it for the **rest** of the **night**. If he was **still** using it, I would go **back** to the computer lab to **check**. Hopefully, the **noisy student** would be **quiet** by then.

托福總監為什麼覺得這是高分回答？

　　第一句話用現在進行時介紹主角（一位男生）在哪裡、在做什麼：他的筆電出了問題，只能在宿舍大樓的電腦室裡唸書。第二句話告訴我們，這位男生真正的困擾是，電腦室裡有一位同學在大聲喧嘩，完全不顧其他人正在看書。注意第二句話以

一個副詞 Unfortunately 開頭，這是講好一個故事的關鍵技巧之一，因為這類帶有感情色彩的副詞能讓聽眾更容易體會情境，同時也能達到句子之間的巧妙過渡。第三句話介紹第三位「故事人物」，一位想幫助這位男生的女生。第三句和第四句講述了第一個「次要情節」，即第一個解決方案：男生可以向宿舍管理員反映這個問題。考生說這位男生不太願意將此事告知宿舍管理員，因為他擔心這會給這位大聲喧嘩的同學帶來麻煩。聽眾由此瞭解到了這位男生的想法，通過考生的論述對事件有了更進一步的理解。第五句和第六句講述了另外一個「次要情節」，即女生建議男生回到宿舍，看看能否借室友的電腦用。注意，在描述兩個「次要情節」時，考生使用了帶有時間副詞的平行結構：The woman first suggests that he... 和 The woman then suggests that he... 這種技巧使考生將觀點表述得非常清晰。

最後四句話，考生提出了解決方案並闡明了理由。當然，這僅僅是對可能出現的情況進行設想，但是闡述得非常清楚。最後一句話同樣以副詞開頭，起到了圓滿結尾的作用。

要掌握講故事的技巧，以有效增強回答的連貫性，可運用以下策略：

1. 開頭要簡潔明瞭，用現在時態介紹主要人物，如：男生、女生、指導教授等。故事的開頭先介紹問題，接下來的內容便會自然而然地引出來。
2. 回答問題時，要想辦法讓評分人瞭解主要人物的感受。使用形容詞是一種方法，如：The woman was worried she wouldn't pass the exam. 使用副詞發表評論也可以，如：Unfortunately, the man doesn't get along with his boss. 在回答人際關係問題的題目中，這種技巧對描述具體情境非常有用。
3. 要清晰地呈現事件發展的前後順序，可使用時間副詞，如 first、soon、later。
4. 運用平行結構增強敘述的連貫性，如兩句話可以用相似的片語開頭：<u>The man could apologize</u> to his current lab partner and they might be able to finish the experiment. Alternatively, <u>the man could find</u> another lab partner to step in, though that might be complicated.
5. 要闡述自己選擇的解決方案會產生「圓滿」的結局，給自己的「故事」下個結論，這會讓回答的組織結構更為緊湊。
6. 考前，練習在 60 秒時間內講述第五題的「故事」。考試時要合理安排答題時間，以便在規定時間內傳達出所有的關鍵資訊。

▶模擬試題①

請回答下題。回答時，可嘗試使用下面列出的實用答題範本。

Narrator: Listen to a conversation between two students.

🎧 **Track 140** （播放錄音檔 140，錄音原文見特別收錄 2 的 P.307）

The students discuss two possible solutions to the woman's problem. Describe the problem. Then state which of the two solutions you prefer and explain why.

Preparation Time: 20 Seconds
Response Time: 60 Seconds

The advisor says the only other option is to VERB..., using...

Furthermore, she's knowledgeable about...

得分考技：介系詞片語置於句首——闡釋細節的第一法寶

　　新托福口語考試的六道題目常常要求考生闡述一個觀點或者總結某種想法，然後做進一步的解釋。這些都需要對細節進行描述。回答問題時描述細節的方法之一就是巧妙地運用介系詞片語來解釋某人「如何」做某事、「為何」做某事。介系詞片語可充當介紹成分置於句首，修飾其後的分句，也可以幫助達到句子之間的自然過渡，增強連貫性和條理性。

　　許多考生不會想到在句首使用介系詞片語，而只是使用一個副詞性的連接詞，例如 consequently 或 thus。介系詞片語並不是非常難掌握的文法結構，但很少有考生在考試中用上這一招，因而能夠展現考生的能力。

　　下面列舉了一些可以引導解釋性語句的介系詞片語：

介系詞片語	解釋性語句
In this way, ...	The man will be able to find a new roommate.
By doing this, ...	The student can finish her paper on time.
To avoid spending any money, ...	The woman will stop going out to coffee shops.
To solve this problem, ...	I would persuade my professor to give me an extension.
Using this approach, ...	I could focus on my paper.

托福總監帶你練

聽聽看下列可以用來引入含有解釋性資訊的句子。介系詞片語已用底線標出。反覆聽錄音，然後跟著讀。　🎧 **Track 142**

1. The **woman** should be **friendli**er to her **roommate**. **That** way, they would communicate **better**.
2. With his professor's recommendation, the **man** could **apply** to **work** in a **different lab**.
3. The **mountain climbing club doesn't** have **enough members** to continue. To solve this problem, I would send text messages to a lot of students.
4. The **clerk wouldn't** let the **man into** the **library** because it was **closing**. To get the book he needed, the **man** could **ask** his professor for a **copy**.
5. **One** option is for the **dance** ensemble to **schedule** the performance on a **later date**. By doing this, the **woman's ankle** would have **time** to **heal**.

• **使用介系詞片語做介紹性副詞，可運用以下策略：**

1. 在句首使用介系詞片語引出接下來的闡述。
2. 使用介系詞片語銜接上文，如 In this way, the man...，這樣可增強回答的連貫性和條理性。
3. 解釋 how 和 why 的時候更應該注意使用介系詞片語。介系詞片語可用於闡述過程和目的。

▶模擬試題②

請回答下面關於人際關係問題的題目。回答時，可嘗試使用下面列出的實用答題範本。

Narrator: Listen to a conversation between two students.

🎧 *Track 143* （播放錄音檔 143，錄音原文見特別收錄 2 的 P.307）

The students discuss two possible solutions to the man's problem. Describe the problem. Then state which of the two solutions you prefer and explain why.

Preparation Time: 20 Seconds
Response Time: 60 Seconds

實用答題範本 🎧 *Track 144* 聽聽看！別人的高分回答！（高分回答原文請見 P.287）
The woman recommends the man VERB...as he's...
The man wonders if the director will stay...

• **最後再練習一下「人際關係方面的表達」最實用的答題模板！**

1. Unfortunately, one student is VERBing..., so...is having trouble VERBing...

例 • Unfortunately, one student is being really loud, so the man is having trouble concentrating.

• Unfortunately, one student is not being cooperative, so the team is having trouble getting along.

2. The man doesn't know if..., and he's also nervous about (VERBing)...

例 • The man doesn't know if the RA is awake this late, and he's also nervous about getting the student in trouble.

• The man doesn't know if his roommate will loan him a laptop, and he's also nervous about the time.

3. I would resolve this situation by VERBing...

例 • I would resolve this situation by seeing if my roommate was still using his laptop.

• I would resolve this situation by texting the Resident Assistant.

4. If he was still..., I would VERB...

例 • If he was still using it, I would go back to the computer lab to check.

• If he was still unwilling to cooperate, I would go talk to the professor.

5. The woman is disappointed to learn that...

例 • The woman is disappointed to learn that her master's thesis advisor is going to Hong Kong for one year.

• The woman is disappointed to learn that her roommate is moving out.

6. The advisor mentions two...to the woman.

例 • The advisor mentions two possibilities to the woman.

• The advisor mentions two options to the woman.

7. The advisor says the only other option is to VERB..., using...

例 • The advisor says the only other option is to advise the woman over the Internet, using e-mail and other electronic means.

• The advisor says the only other option is to complete her thesis within a month, using the winter holiday.

8. If this were my choice, I would continue to VERB...

例 • If this were my choice, I would continue to work with Doctor Anderson while she was overseas.

• If this were my choice, I would continue to discuss the problem with the landlady.

9. Furthermore, she's knowledgeable about...

例 • Furthermore, she's knowledgeable about my field, computer translation.

• Furthermore, she's knowledgeable about job opportunities in interior design.

10. The man has VERBed...and doesn't know what to do.

例 • The man has written this play for his senior thesis and doesn't know what to do.

• The man has gotten into an argument with his teacher and doesn't know what to do.

11. The woman recommends the man VERB...as he's...

例 • The woman recommends the man direct the play himself as he's familiar with the play.

• The woman recommends the man go see his family as he's got some vacation time.

12. The man wonders if the director will stay...

例 • The man wonders if the director will stay calm.

• The man wonders if the director will stay focused.

13. Personally, I would choose the latter option, VERBing...

例 • Personally, I would choose the latter option, getting the director to stay on.

• Personally, I would choose the latter option, asking the professor to provide another Teaching Assistant.

Section 4

Academic Subjects: Tasks 4 and 6

第 4 部分
第四題 & 第六題：
命題總監教你，學術問題小意思！

Task 4 ▶ Synthesizing a Text and a Lecture

第四題 整合文章及講座資訊

第四題的題目要求如下：首先，閱讀一段關於某學術話題的小文章。該話題取自某一學術領域。然後，聽一位教授的講座，教授會簡要談論該學術話題的某一方面。講座結束後，考生需要就該教授的講座回答問題。總之，第四題要求考生將一篇文章和一個講座的資訊加以整合。

要在第四題中拿到高分，考生要盡可能多地、準確地聽懂並傳達講座的關鍵要點。

▶小文章

小文章篇幅為 75～100 個單字，大約為新托福考試閱讀部分文章長度的六分之一。要想在規定的時間內讀完小文章，應在平時多加練習，達到每分鐘閱讀 120 個單字的速度。小文章前通常會有一句說明，告知這篇文章屬於哪類主題，如生物學或心理學。許多小文章都是對某個學術概念的大致介紹，提供足夠的資訊，使考生能對接下來的學術講座有大體的認識。也就是說，小文章會提供簡單的定義和描述，幫助考生對學術概念形成初步的認識，例如：一條科學原理，一種假設，或者對某概念或現象的描述性概覽或暫行定義。考生最好能從文章中記下一到兩個語塊，這有助於接下來有重點地聽講座，也便於在回答問題時引用。和新托福口語考試所有的閱讀和聽力材料一樣，最好的策略就是儘快抓住其主要意思。

▶小講座

閱讀時間結束後，文章將從電腦螢幕上消失，切換成一位教授的圖像，電腦開始播放一段講座錄音。講座中，教授談論的話題和小文章相關，但更具體，會提供例證或案例分析。偶爾，教授會給出一個與小文章的觀點相反的論點或者反例，所以考試中心才把第四題稱做「概括與具體」型題目（文章＝概括；講座＝具體）。小講座時間長度 60～90 秒。和其他題目的聽力材料一樣，小講座開講之前會有一句說明，告知考生將會聽到某一堂課的部分內容，例如：生物學課、心理學課等。教授的講座經常以 An example of this can be seen in... 開頭，這種類型的開頭最容易理解。有時候，教授則會由講述個人經歷開始，例如：The other day I experienced this at home, with my son. 或者，教授會直接開始談論學術內容：This happens with babies when they are very young. 實際上，上述每一個介紹性語句中都有 this，指代閱讀材料介紹的概念。考生需要快速辨別出 this 指代的內容，以及例子或者故事講的是什麼，這樣才能記筆記。記筆記時要注意，第四題會就教授舉的例子提問，而閱讀材料中的資訊不會直接考。

小講座結束後，考生將聽到一個問題，該問題也會出現在電腦螢幕上。提問會涉及小講座所討論概念的某個或某兩個方面，要求考生對其進行解釋。考生有 30 秒的準備時間思考並瀏覽筆記，標出重點詞彙。聽到「嗶」的聲音後，將有 60 秒時間作答。

▶提問形式

第四題題目的措辭有很多種，最常見的形式如下：

1. Using the examples from the lecture, explain what...is and how it works.
2. Using the examples from the lecture, explain the concept of...
3. Explain what is meant by "...," using the examples provided by the professor.
4. Explain how the example from the professor's lecture illustrates the concept of...

▶考官會怎麼對第四題評分？

第四題的評分標準仍依照綜合型題目評分準則。考生需要充分展示自己的語言表達（發音）和語言運用（文法及詞彙）能力，同時還需要「完整地回答問題」。也就是說，考生先要給沒讀過文章、也沒聽過講座的人快速、清晰地介紹主要概念。然後，必須談論講座中的具體觀點，並在 60 秒時間內完成回答。許多考生在總結閱讀內容時花了太多時間，結果 60 秒時間內沒能敘述完整。若回答時遺漏關鍵點或沒有對重要資訊展開論述，那麼評分人會只給 2 分。

記住：第四題要想拿高分，考生的回答要持續（很少或者沒有不恰當的停頓）並且連貫（邏輯流暢），容易使人理解。個別小錯誤不會影響得分。

第四題中最難的部分是學術概念和專業術語。若不瞭解文章或者講座中出現的詞彙，怎麼能談論這些內容呢？所以瞭解第四題中的學術類情境非常重要。

▶第四題的四個主要情境

和另外一道學術類題目一樣，第四題的情境主要來自以下四個領域：

1. 物理科學
2. 人文藝術
3. 生命科學
4. 社會科學

接下來的章節會分別講解以上每一種情境，並給出多道題目、回答範例、實用語塊和實用答題範本。通過在情境中練習這些題目，你將更加熟悉考試中會用到的文字。

Physical Sciences
物理科學

❝ 在本章，你將學到⋯⋯ ❞

★如何組織第四題的答題思路
★怎麼發好以 ed 結尾的單字

解讀常考題

　　在新托福考試口語部分中，物理科學類情境有以下相關話題：天氣、海洋、地震、沙漠、天文學、光與聲、環境，以及化學、地質學和自然地理學中與物理學相關的原理。考試中出現的概念不會很高深，毫無相關背景的考生也能理解。

　　現在，看一道有關物理科學的例題。

▶舉例試題

Narrator: You will now read a short passage and then listen to a talk on the same academic topic. You will then be asked a question about them. After you hear the question, you will have 30 seconds to prepare your response and 60 seconds to speak.

Narrator: Now read the passage about echolocation. You will have 45 seconds to read the passage. Begin reading now.

Reading Time: 45 Seconds

Echolocation

Some animals, such as bats and whales, have the ability to navigate and find prey by using a system called "echolocation." In this system, animals emit high-pitched sounds which travel as waves through the air and bounce off any objects they encounter. When the echoes are reflected, the animals process the information and learn about the objects. A relatively loud echo means the object is relatively large. The time it takes for the echo to come back is an indication of how far away the object is. By repeatedly sending out signals and processing the echoes, animals are provided with a continuous picture of their surroundings.

Narrator: Now listen to part of a lecture on this topic in an acoustics class.

🎧 *Track 145*（播放錄音檔 145，錄音原文見特別收錄 2 的 P.307）

Explain how the example from the professor's lecture illustrates the principle of echolocation.

Preparation Time: 30 Seconds
Response Time: 60 Seconds

Narrator: You have 30 seconds to prepare.
Narrator: Begin speaking after the beep.

策略：第四題的答題思路

回答這道題目只需簡單的三步：
1. 閱讀和聽錄音時記筆記。小文章會包含核心的學術概念。
2. 回答時先概括核心概念。提供的資訊足以使評分人大致瞭解此概念即可。
3. 然後，解釋教授舉出的例子。在時間允許的範圍內提供的具體要點越多越好。

高分回答

注意看，仔細聽，這裡面標上粗體的地方都要發重音才道地喔！ *Track 146*

In describing echolocation, the professor provides the example of bats. When bats hunt for food, they send out high-pitched sound waves. These waves bounce against objects and come back as echoes, and the bats use that information in their searches.（←概括核心概念，提供背景資訊）
Scientists know that bats can recognize certain plant species to help find insects, but they've been puzzled just how bats process echoes reflected off vegetation—these echoes are very complex due to the many leaves and branches. That's why scientists conducted an experiment, generating sound waves at bat frequency and bouncing them off five kinds of plants. From this experiment, the scientists learned that a plant echo, although complex, was easily recognizable as being from a certain species. Thus bats can use echoes to identify the plants they want without much effort.

托福總監為什麼覺得這是高分回答？

　　第四題的理想回答是：快速提供核心概念的背景資訊，給出適當的情境使不熟悉該領域的聽者也能理解。因此，考生需要具備良好的轉述要點的能力。
　　不要浪費時間解釋閱讀文章裡的細枝末節。因為在 60 秒作答時間內，至少要花 30 秒來闡述題目要求解釋的例子。如果有兩個例子，每個例子應至少花 15~20 秒的時間。好好算算吧！考場上分秒必爭，浪費不得。
　　回答第四題的策略就是儘快開始解釋教授舉出的例子，在規定的時間內完成題目要求。

實用語塊

echolocation system where animals make sounds and use their echoes to determine such things as the direction and distance of objects 回聲定位

navigate find one's way 找到方向，找到路

find prey find food 捕獵；覓食

emit... send out... 排出，排放……

high-pitched sound sound at a high frequency 聲調高的聲音；尖叫聲

echo reflection of sound 回聲

reflect... throw back... 將……反射回去

process information gain an understanding of information 處理資訊

signal a quantity representing information 信號

continuous picture frequently updated image 連續圖像

acoustics study of sound 聲學

myth popular belief that is untrue（許多人相信的）錯誤觀念

(send out) pulses send out bursts of sound energy（發送）脈衝

vegetation plants 植物，植被

dense bushes thick bushes, many short shrubs close together 茂密的灌木叢

acoustical echo sound echo 回聲

different angles different perspectives 不同角度

frequency the rate at which a sound wave, light wave, or radio wave vibrates（聲波、光波或無線電波的）頻率

(plant's echo) "signature" distinctive characteristics (of the plant's echo)（植物回聲的）特徵

要答好第四題，可運用以下策略：

1. 仔細閱讀小文章的標題，這很可能就是要談論的關鍵概念。
2. 閱讀文章和聽錄音時都要記筆記。記下主要觀點和一些重要的次要觀點。預測一下答題時需要哪些語塊，並寫下來。
3. 不要等提示音響了之後才開始準備，要邊閱讀邊思考。
4. 語速不宜過快，不要遺漏對意思表達非常重要的詞彙。
5. 回答時要重讀重要詞彙，尤其是實詞。
6. 不要浪費時間重複文章中的所有觀點。評分人不會被這種伎倆欺騙，會扣考生的分數。
7. 儘量進行改述，而不要一字不漏地照搬自己讀到或者聽到的句子。學術概念和專業術語可以照搬，但是其他內容要用自己的話表達。
8. 不要使用超出自己語言能力所及的語句。清晰、準確要比花俏卻毫無連貫性好得多。如果回答中有大的錯誤，或者內容不易理解，就會被扣分。
9. 說話時不要吞吞吐吐。長時間或不合時宜的停頓肯定會被扣分。語速不用很快，但必須保持平穩。
10. 即使是在概述，也要使用恰當的具體詞彙來闡述觀點。不要使用含義模糊的表達，例如：The professor is describing a physical process. 注意回答的邏輯和所表達的意思。如果使用花俏的詞但表意含糊或不準確，那麼評分人就會扣分。
11. 借助筆記以避免離題，嚴格按照題目要求完成回答。
12. 精確掌握答題時間。

記住：回答第四題時不能夾帶個人觀點。若談論了個人看法，得分將大大降低。只有在回答第一題、第二題和第五題時才需要發表個人觀點。

▶模擬試題①

請回答下題。回答時，可嘗試使用下面列出的實用答題範本。

Narrator: Now read the passage about irrigation systems. You will have 45 seconds to read the passage. Begin reading now.

Reading Time: 45 Seconds

Irrigation Systems

Irrigation is the controlled application of water to the soil through systems designed to supply water when there is not enough rainfall. Thousands of years ago, civilizations used irrigation to grow more food, allowing people to survive periods of bad weather and expand in number. In modern times, the advanced irrigation of crops has provided nourishment for evergrowing populations, especially in dry, arid regions. Irrigation systems can be used on the surface of the soil or under it. Flood irrigation is a type of surface irrigation. In drip irrigation, water can be applied under the surface, near the root.

Narrator: Now listen to part of a lecture on this topic in a physical geography class.

🎧*Track 147*（播放錄音檔 147，錄音原文見特別收錄 2 的 P.308）

Using the professor's examples, explain the potential problems associated with flood irrigation and drip irrigation.

Preparation Time: 30 Seconds
Response Time: 60 Seconds

實用答題範本　　　🎧*Track 148* 聽聽看！別人的高分回答！（高分回答原文請見 P.288）

The first example of...that she mentions is...
One possible problem with...is that...

實用語塊

---

irrigation supplying water for agricultural purposes by means of ditches, pipes and streams 灌溉

rainfall amount of rain that falls 降雨量

expand in number multiply 大量增加

provide nourishment for... give nutrition for... 給……施肥

ever-growing populations continuously increasing populations 不斷增長的人口

arid regions extremely dry regions, where trees have trouble growing 乾旱地區

flood irrigation application of water over an area of level soil 漫灌
drip irrigation application of water slowly to the roots of plants, by dripping the water on the soil surface or directly to the root zone 滴灌
mechanics of (moving water) technical aspects of (moving water)（引水）機制
elevation height 海拔
sophisticated system complicated system 複雜系統
environmental impact affect of something on the environment 環境影響
pose (different) problems create (different) problems 產生（不同的）問題
level basin area flat, low-lying area 中部平坦的盆地地區
evaporation conversion from a liquid to a gas state 蒸發
seep into the soil leak into the soil 滲入土壤
intended area targeted area 目的地區域
subsurface drip drip underneath the surface 地下滴灌
accumulation of (salts) buildup of (salts)（鹽類）積累
root zone area where the root is 根帶，根區

得分考技：簡單但容易發錯的 ed 結尾音

　　以 ed 結尾的單字易讀易懂，但考試中不少考生卻會發錯音。把音發清楚讓自己的話容易被理解是很重要的，若忽略了詞尾的 t 或者 ed 音，經常就是遺漏了這個詞的「過去時態」，這樣，評分人就有理由認為考生不知道如何運用動詞的一般過去式。

　　評分準則中規定，考生「對文法的瞭解程度和掌握能力有限」時，只能拿 2 分。因此，當你沒有發 t 或者 ed 時，評分人就有可能以為你不懂過去式，只能拿 2 分。口語考試中，涉及過去時態的概括和敘事非常多，因此回顧並練習詞尾 ed 的發音，必能助你提高口語分數。

　　下面是詞尾 ed 發音必須遵守的規則：

1. 動詞原形的最後一個音是 /k/, /s/, /tʃ/, /ʃ/, /f/, /p/, /ð/，則結尾的 ed 發 /t/。
    例如：Before graduate school, I worked in a medical laboratory for a year.
2. 動詞原形的最後一個音是 /t/, /d/，則結尾的 ed 發 /ɪd/。
    例如：The students wanted to better understand sound waves.
3. 其他情況下，結尾的 ed 發 /d/。
    例如：The professor described two irrigation systems.

托福總監帶你練

聽下面幾個學術類句子，注意以 ed 結尾的單字如何發音，以 ed 結尾的單字已用底線標出。反覆聽錄音，然後跟著讀。　　🎧 *Track 149*

1. In the early 1800s, scientists noted that sedimentary layers in widely distant areas could be <u>distinguished</u> by their distinctive fossil content.

2. The research assistants <u>washed</u> the laboratory and <u>sterilized</u> the equipment before they began the experiment.
3. The final stage of a high mass star is <u>reached</u> when it begins producing iron.
4. A neutron star then evolves, <u>formed</u> when it collapses under the crunch of its own gravity.
5. Marine scientists in the arctic <u>observed</u> that, in winter, whales <u>breathed</u> by smashing through the ice with their snouts.

• **要在口語考試中發好 ed 音，可運用以下策略：**

1. 記住上述三條發音規則，分辨單字末尾的 ed 發音為 /t/, /ɪd/ 還是 /d/。
2. 記住發 /t/ 音時聲帶不振動，只是氣流從口腔中送出；發 /d/ 音時聲帶要振動。發這兩個音均需要氣流的停頓。
3. 發 /ɪd/ 音時，在 /d/ 音之前要發一個非常短促的母音 /ɪ/，或將 /ɪ/ 弱化為 /ə/。
4. 聽錄音或帶發音功能的線上字典學習這些單字的發音，然後重複誦讀。錄下自己的發音，聽一聽自己的發音是否正確。
5. 考試中不要著急！每一個詞尾的 ed 都要發清楚。

▶模擬試題②

　　請回答下題。回答時，可嘗試使用下面列出的實用答題範本。

Narrator: Now read the passage about sound waves. You will have 45 seconds to read the passage. Begin reading now.

Reading Time: 45 Seconds

Sound Waves and Glass

The laws of physics make it possible for a human voice to break glass. That is because every object has its own "frequency"—the speed at which the object vibrates when disturbed, for example, when disturbed by a sound wave. Crystal wine glasses have a high frequency vibration, and so crystal glasses make a ringing sound when tapped gently. If a singer sings the same tone as that ringing tone, her sound waves will vibrate the air molecules at the glass's frequency, causing the glass to vibrate as well. If she sings loudly enough, the glass will shatter.

Narrator: Now listen to part of a lecture on this topic in a physics class.

🎧 *Track 150* （播放錄音檔 150，錄音原文見特別收錄 2 的 P.308）

The professor talks about an experiment using sound waves to break glass. Explain how the results of the two student lab groups were different.

Preparation Time: 30 Seconds
Response Time: 60 Seconds

實用答題範本　　　🎧**Track 151** 聽聽看！別人的高分回答！（高分回答原文請見 P.288）

In his lecture, the professor talks about...

To do this, the students needed to VERB...

實用語塊

sound wave longitudinal pressure wave of sound 聲波

vibrate shake, oscillate 使振動

disturb physically touch 干擾；外力作用

crystal wine glass goblet made of a special type of glass 水晶玻璃酒杯

ringing sound resonant sound 清脆的聲響

tap gently hit something, usually with one's fingers 用手指輕敲

air molecule smallest unit of air 氣體分子

shatter break into tiny pieces 破碎

property (scientific property) quality, attribute（科學屬性）性質；屬性

match ... to ... to make ... the same as ... 使……符合……

natural frequency frequency at which an object vibrates when hit or otherwise disturbed by some stimulus 固有頻率

lab assignment class assignment to be done in the lab 實驗室作業

manipulate carefully adjust up or down 小心地調整

adjust change slightly 調整

pitch relative position of a tone as determined by its frequency (in physics, pitch is called "frequency") 音高（在物理學中，被稱為「頻率」）

tone the pitch of a note 音調

speaker loudspeaker; device that converts electric signals to sound 喇叭；揚聲器

violently forcefully 劇烈地

hypothesize that... guess that... 假設……（例：Scientists hypothesize that the Sun formed 4.5 billion years ago.）

• 最後再練習一下「有關物理科學方面的表述」最實用的答題模板！

1. In describing..., the professor provides the example of...

　　例　• In describing echolocation, the professor provides the example of bats.

　　　　• In describing volcanoes, the professor provides the example of magma.

2. First of all, the professor VERB...

　　例　• First of all, the professor describes how bats hunt.

　　　　• First of all, the professor discusses the properties of waves.

3. In the lecture, the professor gives two examples to illustrate...

例 • In the lecture, the professor gives two examples to illustrate echolocation.

• In the lecture, the professor gives two examples to illustrate irrigation.

4. From this experiment, the scientists learned that...

例 • From this experiment, the scientists learned that echoes could be recognized.

• From this experiment, the scientists learned that bats recognized plant echoes.

5. The first example of...that she mentions is...

例 • The first example of irrigation that she mentions is flood irrigation.

• The first example of igneous rock that she mentions is granite.

6. One possible problem with...is that...

例 • One possible problem with drip irrigation is that salts will accumulate.

• One possible problem with the irrigation system is that water is lost.

7. In his lecture, the professor talks about...

例 • In his lecture, the professor talks about two properties of sound waves.

• In his lecture, the professor talks about earthquakes.

8. To do this, the students needed to VERB...

例 • To do this, the students needed to determine the frequency of glass.

• To do this, the students needed to build a model irrigation system.

9. They broke the glass by VERBing...

例 • They broke the glass by adjusting the pitch of the singer's voice.

• They broke the glass by increasing the sound volume.

10. That's why scientists conducted an experiment, VERBing...

例 • That's why scientists conducted an experiment, generating sound waves.

• That's why scientists conducted an experiment, trying to break glass.

11. Both X and Y are...but they differ in that...

例 • Both erosion and weathering are geological processes, but they differ in that erosion transports the decomposed earth.

12. Whereas X is..., Y is not.

例 • Whereas friction is always opposed to movement, inertia is not.

Humanities and the Arts
人文藝術

26

66 在本章，你將學到…… 99

★第四題如何記筆記
★如何用動詞片語闡釋細節

解讀常考題

　　新托福口語考試中，人文藝術類問題涵蓋的範圍非常廣泛，包括建築與設計、工作室藝術與藝術史、紡織與手工藝、音樂與音樂史以及舞蹈等。此類問題還包括攝影與新聞、文學（包括小說、詩歌、戲劇以及如浪漫主義和現代主義等各種藝術流派）以及美國歷史與世界歷史。和其他學術類情境一樣，人文藝術類題目的閱讀及聽力材料不會涉及高深概念，毫無相關背景的考生也能理解。

　　現在，看一道有關人文藝術的例題。

▶舉例試題

Narrator: Now read the passage about method acting. You will have 45 seconds to read the passage. Begin reading now.

Reading Time: 45 Seconds

Method Acting

Method acting developed in the 1950s as an alternative to traditional technical acting. "The Method," as it is called, actually includes many different techniques, many of which encourage actors to draw upon personal experiences while portraying their characters. The goal is to achieve psychological realism; consequently, method actors probe deeply into a character's day-to-day life. While reading through the script, the actor asks the constant question: "If I were living in the character's circumstances, how would I behave?" After this methodical preparation, a method actor then draws boldly and spontaneously from his or her emotions to deliver a realistic performance.

Narrator: Now listen to part of a lecture on this topic in a theater class.

🎧 *Track 152*（播放錄音檔 152，錄音原文見特別收錄 2 的 P.309）

Explain how the examples given by the professor illustrate the techniques of method acting.

Preparation Time: 30 Seconds
Response Time: 60 Seconds

Narrator: You have 30 seconds to prepare.
Narrator: Begin speaking after the beep.

策略：第四題記筆記的訣竅

　　對第四題、第六題這類學術題目而言，記筆記至關重要，必須做好。原因在於：一方面，這兩道題目含有專業術語，既不容易記憶，也不容易掌握發音。另一方面，這類題中的學術概念和事件比校園生活類題目會涉及的情景要複雜得多。記下這些概念和術語，即使用縮寫，都能幫助考生構思、清晰地説出專業術語。

　　和所有的口語題目一樣，做筆記時要預測題目會問到什麼問題。如上述關於 method acting 的例題要求解釋 the examples given by the professor 如何闡釋了 the techniques of method acting。當然，只有在小講座結束後才能在電腦螢幕上看到這個問題。正因如此，需要學會怎樣預測問題並在筆記中記下相關資訊。通過多做練習題以及在聽小講座時自問「問題會是什麼？我應該記下什麼？」，就可以漸漸掌握預測的技能。

　　和第三題相同，第四題會給出 30 秒準備時間，這期間你可以查看自己的筆記。

　　要記好第四題的筆記，只需簡單的三步：

1. 記下關鍵術語，通常都是標題，並記下足夠的單字以幫助自己定義這個術語。
2. 用縮寫從小文章和小講座中摘取一些描述性片語。在闡述教授的例子時會用到這些片語。
3. 使用圓圈、箭頭、底線、數位等畫出筆記結構並做些註解，這些能幫助你答題。

高分回答

注意看，仔細聽，這裡面標上粗體的地方都要發重音才道地喔！

 Track 153

Method acting helps actors take advantage of **personal experiences** so they can por**tray** their **characters** more realistically. **Research is** important for **method acting**, because **actors need** to under**stand** the psychology of their **characters**. The pro**fessor** cites the **movie** *Jaws*, a movie about a **great white shark**. The **scene is the one** in which the **shark** fisherman **tells** the **story** of the **sinking** of a **U.S. ship** during World War II. To **do** this **scene**, the **actor** who **played** the old **fisherman** spent a **lot** of **time** researching his **part**. For e**xample**, he **met** a **real fisherman** and **talked** with him. He **paid** attention to the **fisherman's** behavior and **studied ways** to include it in his performance. When the **actor** gave the **monologue** about the **sinking** of the **ship**, he was able to **draw upon** the **things** he had **learned**. The **second example also relates** to *Jaws*. In **real life**, the **actors** who **played** the **shark fisherman** and the **young scientist** did **not like** one another. They were able to **draw upon** these **hostile feelings** during **filming**.

托福總監為什麼覺得這是高分回答？

　　下面來看看什麼樣的筆記可幫助考生給出如此縝密的回答。第一句定義了關鍵術語：method acting（方法派演技）。接著第二句補充了相關資訊：方法派演技要研究角色的心理。第三句開始談論小講座中的相關內容，即電影《大白鯊》的例子。第四句進一步展開，描述了《大白鯊》中的場景：老漁民講述二戰時期群鯊圍繞在一艘正在沉沒的艦艇四周。第五句到第八句則闡明老漁民的扮演者如何研究角色：他與真正的漁民深入交談並模仿這位漁民的言行舉止。第九句描述了《大白鯊》中方法派演技的第二個例子：兩位演員之間的關係很僵。最後一句解釋了這兩位演員在拍攝過程中如何運用兩人間真實的衝突來使表演更加真實。

　　為這道題記筆記時，可記下如下單字及縮寫：

小文章的筆記
methd actg (method acting)
many tech (many techniques)
psych realsm (psychological realism)
probe deep
draw emot (draw emotions)

小講座的筆記
apprch role (approach a role)
Jaws
shrk fishrmn actr (actor who played the shark fisherman)
1. WWII story, methd actg (World War II story, method acting) 　　talk w real fishrmn (talked with a real fisherman)
2. tension w biologist (interpersonal tension with a marine biologist) 　　used real feelgs (used real dislike for each other in their roles)

托福總監為什麼覺得這是高分筆記？

　　正如之前提過的，記下的筆記越多越好。而從上述筆記可看出，小文章的筆記中的縮寫能幫助考生定義 method acting。然後，聽小講座時，考生恰當地記下了教授所舉例子中的一些關鍵字，如電影名稱 *Jaws*，並分序號 1 和 2 記錄了電影中方法派演技的兩個例子。

　　要在這道例題拿到高分，必須給方法派演技一個恰當的定義，闡述《大白鯊》中用到的方法派演技，簡要概括教授舉的兩個例子。

實用語塊

method acting techniques that allow actors to understand the inner psychology of characters 方法派演技，體驗派表演方法

draw upon/on... make use of... 利用……

portray (their characters) play the part of (their characters) 扮演（角色）

psychological realism artistic concept focusing on a character's "interior"; what seems "real" to an audience is based on psychological perception 心理現實主義

probe (deeply) into... carefully study...; delve into... （深入）探究……

day-to-day life everyday life 日常生活

script text of a play or film 劇本

ask the constant question ask the same question again and again 重複問同一個問題

circumstances (always plural) standard of living 生活境況（通常用複數）

methodical preparation painstaking preparation 周密準備

draw from... dip into...to use it 從……中獲得；取材於……

boldly unrestrainedly 大膽地

spontaneously freely 自發地

deliver a performance perform on stage; give a performance 表演

flesh...out add more detail and substance to... 充實……，使……更有血有肉

epic film heroic film 史詩電影

hunt down... / hunt...down track down something to catch it 追捕……

great white shark large shark that grows to 23 feet 大白鯊

sink go under (water) 沉沒

native to... originally comes from... (place) 來自於……

famed well-known 著名的

monologue long speech made by one actor 獨白

shark-filled waters area of sea that contains many sharks 有大量鯊魚出沒的海域

subtle tension faint signs of friction between people 小摩擦

marine biologist scientist who studies life in the ocean 海洋生物學家

...and...get along ...and...are hospitable with one another ……與……相處融洽

underlying hostility feelings of dislike beneath the surface 暗地裡相互敵視

做第四題時，想充分利用筆記，可運用以下策略：

1. 仔細看小文章的標題，這極可能是將要談論的關鍵概念。讀小文章時，搜尋這個標題術語的定義。用英語記下該標題及其他有助於定義這一術語的詞語。
2. 記下一兩個描述關鍵概念的形容詞。但回答問題時，盡可能換用其他詞來替代這些形容詞，例如：文章中使用修飾語 intense 來形容某一畫作，你可以用其同義詞 powerful。
3. 記下小講座的前兩句話，因為這有可能就是回答中將要用到的具體例子。如果教授的開場白是 We see <u>this</u> a lot in expressionist paintings. 你就需要記下 this 指代的內容。this 可能指某一藝術作品表現出的強烈感情（intense emotion），這時可記下 intense emot。

4. 除了記下例子外，還應記下支持例子的兩個關鍵細節。這類細節包括：事實、說理或其他更多的例子。

5. 聽小講座時，記下所有新介紹的專業術語。標注其正確的發音（重讀音節、母音），以便知道怎麼讀這些詞。準備期間，可以默讀這些不熟悉的單字，練習其發音。

6. 特別注意看起來非常重要的專有名詞，如地名與人名。如果這些名詞在小講座中重複出現，也要記下來。

7. 聽錄音時確實需要記筆記，但不要讓記筆記妨礙了聽力。聽清整段講座的內容要比只記下一小部分內容的筆記重要得多。

　　可以看出，與第三題和第五題這種校園生活類題目相比，做第四題這種有文章、有講座的學術類題目時，記筆記更有難度。要給出一個完整的回答，需要整合許多零散資訊。但是，如果練習使用上述策略記筆記，並借助筆記給出一個有條理的回答，考試時就一定會成功。

▶模擬試題①

　　請回答下題。回答時，可嘗試使用下面列出的實用答題範本。

Narrator: Now read the passage about medieval romances. You will have 45 seconds to read the passage. Begin reading now.

Reading Time: 45 Seconds

Medieval Romances

In medieval times, a "romance" initially meant a work written in Old French, as opposed to Latin. But because French works were tales of knights and their heroic deeds, the term soon referred only to such tales. The heroes of romances were knights surrounded in mystery who embarked on adventures. Knights would often appear in disguise. One quality of the knight-hero was chivalry—he had to demonstrate courtesy, courage and honor. Many medieval romances were based on the tales of King Arthur and his many Knights of the Round Table, for example, the knight Sir Gareth.

Narrator: Now listen to part of a lecture on this topic in a literature class.

🎧 *Track 154*（播放錄音檔 154，錄音原文見特別收錄 2 的 P.309）

Explain why the tale of Sir Gareth is typical of a medieval romance.

Preparation Time: 30 Seconds
Response Time: 60 Seconds

實用答題範本　　　　🎧 *Track 155* 聽聽看！別人的高分回答！（高分回答原文請見 P.288）

In his lecture, the professor points out...
The focus of the romances was...

實用語塊

medieval related to the Middle Ages 中世紀的	
romance a narrative that tells of heroic adventures 傳奇文學，冒險故事	
Old French early French spoken in northern France and elsewhere from the 9th to the 14th centuries 古法語	
knight (in medieval times) person of noble birth trained to fight on horseback 騎士	
heroic deeds brave acts 英雄事蹟	
surrounded in mystery be in a strange situation 謎團重重	
embark on an adventure set off an unknown journey 開始冒險	
appear in disguise dress in a way so that you cannot be recognized 喬裝；偽裝	
knight-hero main heroic character in medieval romances 騎士英雄	
chivalry (in medieval times) code of honor, bravery, and courtesy 騎士精神	
courtesy polite etiquette 禮節，禮貌	
King Arthur legendary leader in the mythology of Britain 亞瑟王	
Knights of the Round Table knights of King Arthur's court 亞瑟王的圓桌武士	
Sir Gareth gentle and honorable knight under King Arthur 加雷思爵士	
We see this happening with... This phenomenon can be observed in... 在……中可看到此現象	
be born a nobleman have aristocratic blood 出身貴族	
on a mysterious quest on a mission which isn't clear 執行神秘任務	
be disguised as a... dress up as a... 偽裝成……	
treat...badly be mean to someone 欺負……	
pretend to be (weak) put on an act of being (weak) 假裝（很弱）	
reveal (his) true identity show people who (he) really is 揭露（他的）真面目	
pursue (his) quest try to reach (his) goal of obtaining someone or something 追求	

得分考技：動詞片語──闡釋細節的第二法寶

　　在學術類題目中，通常都會先籠統介紹一個學術概念，然後舉出具體例子和其他支持主題的細節。考生必須能夠概述小文章和小講座中討論的這些或籠統或具體的概念。

　　許多考生發現，他們能夠介紹某一學術話題，但卻無法從概念介紹過渡到細節描述。無論是描述事物還是闡述觀點，用英語解釋相關學術細節非常困難，特別是在時間有限的情況下。其實，你不必擔心！即使學術語言很難，通過記憶一些動詞片語，你就能克服障礙，順利完成題目。

下表列舉了一些實用的動詞片語，可以用來解釋細節：

動詞片語	例句
elaborate on...by VERBing...	The professor elaborated on the Knights of the Round Table by giving details about Sir Gareth.
elaborate on...	In his lecture on Greek sculpture, the professor elaborated on the sculpture's sense of freedom.
expand upon/on...	After the professor defined ergonomic design, she expanded on how it has made people's lives more comfortable.
provide additional insights into...by VERBing...	The professor provided additional insights into method acting by describing how one actor in *Jaws* prepared for his role.
This means that...	In silent films, there is no recorded dialog. This means that some form of live or recorded music must be used.
That is to say, ...	Many inventions in history have not been a result of hard work. That is to say, people sometimes produce an invention by accident.

托福總監帶你練

聽下面幾個學術類句子，注意這些句子是如何用動詞片語來說明細節的。動詞片語已用底線標出。反覆聽錄音，然後跟著讀。 🎧 *Track 156*

1. The professor <u>elaborated on</u> the role of the steam engine in the Industrial Revolution by explaining how energy helped develop transportation.
2. The professor <u>provided additional insights into</u> color theory <u>by describing</u> two rules for mixing colors.
3. In the middle of the nineteenth century, Navajo rug designs became more varied. <u>That is to say</u>, weavers began to use more patterns and colors.
4. Modern architecture is characterized by a functional approach. <u>That means</u>, when people designed buildings, they were thinking about how materials would be used, not just how they would look.
5. The professor defined an opera as a play set to music. However, <u>this does not mean that</u> a character's lines are always sung in an opera.

• 要學會用動詞片語解釋細節，可運用以下策略：

1. 做好筆記，這樣才能把專業術語和描述性片語用在自己的話中。
2. 記住上頁表格中列出的動詞片語。練習使用這些片語造句，直到能熟練運用。
3. 注意上頁表格中列出的片語中的介系詞。例如：elaborate on... 中的 on。多記憶本書所提供的實用語塊列表中的介系詞搭配，以避免一些不必要的錯誤。
4. 用這些動詞片語實現從概念介紹向舉例說明和細節描述之間的過渡。

熟練掌握了動詞片語的用法，可幫助你在做學術類題目時流利地給出細節說明。這些細節說明將向考官展示你連貫、有條理地回答問題的能力，從而增加拿高分的機會。

▶模擬試題②

請回答下題。回答時，可嘗試使用下面列出的實用答題範本。

Narrator: Now read the passage about installation art. You will have 45 seconds to read the passage. Begin reading now.

Reading Time: 45 Seconds

Installation Art

Beginning in the 1970s, artists began to experiment with three-dimensional works which were "installed," or arranged, in a certain place—either indoors or outdoors. Installations, both temporary and permanent, are now very common in the art world. Installation artists try to transform viewers' perceptions by tapping all their senses. The artists use a broad range of materials, which are chosen for their suggestive qualities. Industrial materials and even garbage can be combined in unusual juxtapositions to affect viewers, challenging them to think about their relationship with the art and the space. Viewers often leave installations with new ideas about society.

Narrator: Now listen to part of a lecture on this topic in an art history class.

🎧 *Track 157* （播放錄音檔 157，錄音原文見特別收錄 2 的 P.309）

【下圖為播放錄音期間螢幕上顯示的圖像】

Will Ryman

Using the example of Will Ryman, explain what installation art is and how it is supposed to affect viewers.

Preparation Time: 30 Seconds
Response Time: 60 Seconds

實用答題範本　　　🎧 *Track 158* 聽聽看！別人的高分回答！（高分回答原文請見 P.288）

Installation art is a type of art in which...
Ryman's exhibit illustrates how...

實用語塊

installation art large work of art with "installed objects," which alters the way a space is experienced 裝置藝術

transform viewers' perceptions change the way people look at things 改變觀賞者對事物的看法

tap all their senses making people use all their senses (sight, sound, etc.) 讓人們動用各種感官

suggestive quality characteristic that evokes feelings or thoughts 引起聯想的特性

juxtaposition interesting combination 並置

gallery art gallery, where art is displayed and sold 畫廊

scale relative size 比例

over-sized larger than normal size 大號的

cigarette butt leftover piece of cigarette 煙蒂

crumpled can smashed can 被壓扁的罐子

litter objects thrown on the ground (illegally) in public spaces 垃圾

wire mesh woven metal used in sculpture and construction 金屬絲網，鐵絲網

plaster mixture used to coat walls and ceilings 灰泥，泥漿

skyscraper tall building 摩天大樓

• 最後再練習一下「有關人文藝術的表達」最實用的答題模板！

1. Method acting helps actors VERB...

例　• Method acting helps actors take advantage of personal experiences.
　　• Method acting helps actors play more diverse roles.

2. Research is important for method acting, because...

例　• Research is important for method acting, because actors need to understand the psychology of their characters.
　　• Research is important for method acting, because it allows actors to learn.

3. The professor cites the movie Jaws, a movie about...

例　• The professor cites the movie Jaws, a movie about a great white shark.
　　• The professor cites the movie Jaws, a movie about an obsessed fisherman.

4. When the actor VERBed..., he was able to VERB...

例 • When the actor gave the monologue about the sinking of the ship, he was able to draw upon the things he had learned.

• When the actor spoke with the fisherman, he was able to learn a lot.

5. The second example also relates to...

例 • The second example also relates to Jaws.

• The second example also relates to installation art.

6. In his lecture, the professor points out...

例 • In his lecture, the professor points out several characteristics of medieval romances.

• In his lecture, the professor points out that installation art makes people think.

7. The focus of the romances was...

例 • The focus of the romances was usually a mysterious knight who was on a quest and who was performing heroic deeds.

8. The heroes in medieval romances were supposed to be both...and...

例 • The heroes in medieval romances were supposed to be both courteous and brave.

9. The professor says the tale of Sir Gareth is typical of...because...

例 • The professor says the tale of Sir Gareth is typical of a medieval romance because it contains many of these characteristics.

10. This...is also typical of...

例 • This sense of fairness is also typical of knights in medieval romances.

11. Installation art is a type of art in which...

例 • Installation art is a type of art in which objects are arranged in a space.

12. The artist uses installation art to make viewers...

例 • The artist uses installation art to make viewers interact with the objects and think.

13. The example of Will Ryman is...

例 • The example of Will Ryman is his installation of a city garden.

14. That means when people go to the exhibit, they feel...

例 • That means when people go to the exhibit, they feel smaller, as if they were rats in the garden.

15. Ryman's exhibit illustrates how...

例 • Ryman's exhibit illustrates how an installation artist can change the perspectives of a viewer.

Life Sciences
生命科學

❝ 在本章，你將學到⋯⋯ ❞

★遇到聽不懂的專業術語怎麼辦
★學術性的名詞片語怎麼念

解讀常考題

　　新托福考試的口語部分中有許多題目都和生命科學相關，尤其是動物學和植物學。生命科學還包括生態學、微生物學、公共衛生、解剖學和生理學等。典型的情境是：小文章描述某一種動物行為，小講座則具體以某動物為例闡釋這種行為。

　　動植物的種類繁多，有各種各樣的名字和行為方式，因此有些生命科學類的講座會令人覺得恐怖，畢竟生物相關的單字背都背不完。雖然學術類題目中的原理和定義不會太過專業，但聽到用英語講出的生命科學類術語，有時候還是會讓人感到壓力很大。但是不要驚慌，一般來說，到小講座結束時，你還是可以理解大部分重要的生命科學概念。

　　現在，看一道有關生命科學的例題。

▶舉例試題

Narrator: Now read the passage about predator-prey interactions. You will have 45 seconds to read the passage. Begin reading now.
Reading Time: 45 Seconds

Predator-prey Interactions

In nature, the populations of predators and their prey are closely connected. This is especially true when the predator feeds mainly on one species of prey. If the food supply of the prey is increased, there is often an increase in the prey population. This increase is then often followed by an increase in the predator population because it becomes easier for predators to locate prey. Correspondingly, when fewer prey are available, the number of predators will eventually drop. With few predators around, the prey population begins to increase once again and the process repeats itself in a cycle.

Narrator: Now listen to part of a lecture on this topic in an ecology class.

🎧*Track 159* （播放錄音檔 159，錄音原文見特別收錄 2 的 P.310）

Using the examples from the lecture, explain what predator-prey interactions are and how they are different in the arctic zone and the tropical zone.

Preparation Time: 30 Seconds
Response Time: 60 Seconds

Narrator: You have 30 seconds to prepare.
Narrator: Begin speaking after the beep.

策略：怎麼猜測讓人抓狂的專業術語

　　小文章或小講座中可能會有一些陌生的專業詞彙和片語。這可能會讓你抓狂，尤其在聽錄音時，但是還是有辦法解決這個難題。

　　應對未知的專業術語，只需簡單的三步：
　　1. 閱讀小文章時，尋找可以提供線索的定義。
　　2. 利用一切你所知的專業知識來猜測詞義。
　　3. 不要驚慌！繼續聽錄音，尋找線索和解釋。

高分回答

注意看，仔細聽，這裡面標上粗體的地方都要發重音才道地喔！ *Track 160*

Predator-prey inter**ac**tions are the **ways** that **predator** and **prey** populations influence **one** another. In the **simple** model, when the population of the **prey** de**clines**, the population of **predators** will **also** go **down**, because there's **not enough** to **eat. Then**, the number of **prey** starts to go **up. This** model is **most ob**vious when a **single predator species feeds on** a **single prey species.** It is **seen** in the **arctic zone**, where there are **few animals.** For **example, polar bear** and **seal** populations directly a**ffect** one another. However, predator-**prey** interactions in the **tropical zone** are **more** complex. **That's** be**cause predators** have **choices of which** prey to eat, and the **prey** can be eaten by **many** animals as **well.** For **example, tropical frogs** eat **various types** of insects. **So** if the **ant** population becomes **smaller**, you **can't assume** that the **frog** population will **also** become **smaller.**

托福總監為什麼覺得這是高分回答？

　　學術類問題裡，小文章幾乎都會給出術語的定義，許多時候小講座中也會有定義。牢記這一點很重要，因此如果不理解某個詞或者某個術語，很可能可以在定義中找到答案。

　　例如，在關於捕食動物與獵物的小文章中，你可能不會立即明白 predator 或者 prey 的意思。因此看到標題 Predator-prey Interactions 後，第一反應是驚慌！但繼續讀下去，就會在第二句中發現線索：This is especially true when the predator feeds mainly on one species of prey. 從這句話中可以看出，predator 會吃某一種 prey。啊！現在就能猜出這些術語的意思了：predator 是以其他動物為食的動物，prey 則是被捕食的動物！通過定義和情境，就能快速應對專業術語，繼續做題。

　　做題過程中要保持冷靜並利用常識。一開始看起來很難的術語和概念之後會有幾句相對直白的語言表述。繼續聽下去並做筆記。一般來說，小講座結束後，你便可以理解材料中提到的大部分關於生命科學的概念。

實用語塊

predator animal that attacks and kills others for food 捕食性動物	
prey animal that is hunted and eaten 獵物，捕食對象	
population number of specific group of organisms that live in a certain habitat 種群數量	
feed on... eat... 以……為食	
process repeats itself process is cyclical 循環過程	
It makes sense. The idea is logical. 這很有道理。	
hold true for... be the case for... 適用於……	
arctic related to the North Pole 北極的	
arctic zone region north of the Arctic Circle 北極地區	
community a group of organisms living in the same region （動植物的）群落	
North Pole most northern point on the Earth's axis 北極	
polar bear white bear that lives in the arctic zone 北極熊	
seal an aquatic mammal living mainly in the Northern Hemisphere 海豹	
predictable pattern behavior that recurs 可預見的行為模式	
tropical zone region between the Tropic of Cancer and the Tropic of Capricorn, characterized by a hot climate 熱帶地區	

做學術類題目時，要對付未知專業術語，可運用以下策略：

1. 小文章中，單字的構成是猜測生字含義的線索之一，例如：字根、字首、字尾。也可以聯繫上下文來猜測詞義。
2. 小文章和小講座中，要特別注意解釋術語意思的句子。
3. 在有較難專業術語的聽力文段中，命題人會故意「囉唆」，對專業術語使用不同的語言解釋兩遍，再輔以一個專業性不強的例子。應注意講座中的這種重複並加以利用。
4. 利用你所掌握的知識猜測專業術語的含義。例如：教授在講述一種有許多條腿的海洋生物，立即想一想你所知的一切關於海洋生物的知識。會不會是章魚？

▶模擬試題①

請回答下題。回答時，可嘗試使用下面列出的實用答題範本。

Narrator: Now read the passage about seed dormancy. You will have 45 seconds to read the passage. Begin reading now.

Reading Time: 45 Seconds

Seed Dormancy

Plants which reproduce through seeds produce a surplus of food that is stored in the seeds or fruit. This helps the embryonic plant get a good start in life. However, even with this extra food, most seeds need to go through a period of inactivity, or dormancy, before germinating. Seed dormancy is regulated internally by chemicals in the seed's inner tissues. During the dormant period—which lasts from a few days to several months—biological activity slows dramatically until the seed is ready to germinate. Many seeds break their dormancy only when certain external conditions are met.

Narrator: Now listen to part of a lecture on this topic in a botany class.

🎧 *Track 161* （播放錄音檔 161，錄音原文見特別收錄 2 的 P.310）

Using the example of the dogwood tree, explain what seed dormancy is and why it is important.

Preparation Time: 30 Seconds
Response Time: 60 Seconds

實用答題範本　　　　🎧 *Track 162* 聽聽看！別人的高分回答！（高分回答原文請見 P.289）

Seed dormancy refers to the period of inactivity that...
The professor talks about her dogwood tree to illustrate how...

實用語塊

seed plant embryo inside its covering(s) 種子

dormancy biological rest or inactivity 休眠

embryo / embryonic plant plant in the early stages of development 胚，胚胎

germinate sprout 發芽

tissues units of similar, specialized cells that perform a common function （生物）組織

slow dramatically slow down radically 顯著減慢

break dormancy leave the dormant state 結束休眠狀態，蘇醒

conditions (are) met requirements (are) satisfied 滿足條件

undergo dormancy go through dormancy 休眠中

full-blown complete 具有全部特徵的；充分發展的

dogwood tree small ornamental tree with clusters of showy flowers 梾木

greenhouse building where the temperature is controlled for growing plants out of season 溫室

ripe fully mature 成熟的

得分考技：準確讀出專業術語

　　小講座的語言很有趣，是科學界術語與日常英語口語的混合體。例如，在小講座中教授會説：Now let's talk a little bit about crop rotation, a practice where we plant different crops in a certain section of the farm. We rotate them. 儘管上述句子中的大部分詞語都相對簡單，但是 crop rotation 是農業領域的專業術語，考生之前可能沒有見過。雖然可以從情境和釋義中瞭解這個術語的意思，但還需要在回答問題時將這個術語清晰地説出來。

　　下面是學術語言中一些典型名詞的重音位置：

development	argument	amendment	temperament	treatment	retirement
hydration	oxidation	germination	mutation	population	gestation
absorption	reaction	function	reproduction	suction	interaction
characteristic	unrealistic	materialistic	nationalistic	pessimistic	individualistic

　　注意：字尾為 -ment, -ation 和 -tion 的單字，字尾不發重音。在字尾 -istic 中，則要在 –is 發重音，其之前的輔音也要發重音，如 characteristic 中的 r 和 is。要記住這些發音規律。

　　許多這樣的名詞會組合在一起構成較長的名詞片語，例如：the development of the brain / the gradual absorption of water。在這類名詞片語中，要記住實詞的發音，實詞要發重音，虛詞不用。

托福總監帶你練

聽下面幾個學術類句子，注意其中專業術語的發音。關鍵的專業術語已用底線標出。反覆聽錄音，然後跟著讀。　🎧 *Track 163*

1. In underline{individualistic cultures}, children are encouraged to form and express their own opinions.
2. Genetic mutation is a permanent change in the DNA sequence of a gene.
3. In bats, as in birds, the function of wings is to allow flight.
4. The production of spores is characteristic of most fungi.
5. The interaction between doctors and patients has been the subject of much research.

• 要掌握專業術語的發音，可運用以下策略：

1. 考試前，要熟悉以 -ment、-ation、-tion 和 -istic 等字尾結尾的常見學術詞彙的音節重音讀法。
2. 讀小文章時記下一兩個關鍵片語。然後在聽小講座時注意聽其發音，記下重讀音節。
3. 讀學術性名詞片語時不要太快，要確保讓考官聽清楚關鍵性的實詞。
4. 讀每一個學術性名詞片語時，記住要重讀實詞，不要重讀虛詞，例如：the development of the young turtle。
5. 把每一個學術性名詞片語作為一個整體，前後留有簡短的停頓。

6. 語速不要太快！學術性名詞片語通常傳達著複雜的含義，要給考官充裕的時間理解單字及你要表達的意思。

▶模擬試題②

請回答下題。回答時，可嘗試使用下面列出的實用答題範本。

Narrator: Now read the passage about the social order in wolves. You will have 45 seconds to read the passage. Begin reading now.

Reading Time: 45 Seconds

Social Order in Wolves

Wolves live in groups called "packs" averaging about six to eight animals. Within each pack, wolves have a rank order—a hierarchy which helps keep peace within the pack. Because there are separate ranking lines for males and females, an alpha male and alpha female each sit atop a dominance hierarchy. Good communication between pack members also promotes stability. Subtle signals convey the hierarchy and allow wolves to settle their differences with shows of dominance or submission rather than with physical confrontation. Because all pack members are vital to the pack's survival, each wolf tries to prevent injury to its packmates.

Narrator: Now listen to part of a lecture on this topic in a biology class.

🎧 *Track 164* （播放錄音檔 164，錄音原文見特別收錄 2 的 P.310）

Explain how the examples of dominant alpha wolves demonstrate the principle of social dominance in wolf packs.

Preparation Time: 30 Seconds
Response Time: 60 Seconds

實用答題範本　　🎧 *Track 165* 聽聽看！別人的高分回答！（高分回答原文請見 P.289）

The hierarchy of wolf packs is based on...
For example, the lecturer talks about how alpha wolves VERB...

實用語塊

---

social order ranking in a group of animals where the most dominant one is in the top position 社會秩序

(wolf) pack group of animals such as wolves that hunt together（狼）群

---

rank order sequenced order of the social rank or position 社會等級秩序

---

hierarchy system of persons or things arranged in a sequenced order 等級制度

---

keep peace prevent conflict 維持和睦

---

alpha male/female most dominant male/female 雄、雌性首領

---

dominance control 主導

communication between... information sharing between... ……間的交流

pack members wolves belonging to the pack（狼）群成員

promote the stability of... help...have order and strength 維護……的穩定

subtle signal understated gesture 微弱的信號

vital to... very important for... 對……很重要

prevent injury keep someone from harm 防止受傷

packmate fellow pack member 群體成員

have a set place have a fixed social position 有固定的社會地位

cross paths encounter one another 相遇

high in status have a high social position 社會地位高

be submissive to... be subservient to... 屈服於……

act self-confidently act with assurance 表現得自信

adopt a (neutral) pose act (neutrally; neither aggressively nor passively) 保持（中立）

crouch down lie down low 趴下

be in charge of... exercise leadership over... 掌管……

the right to do what (one) wants the privilege of doing as one pleases 隨心所欲做（自己）想做的事的權利

home territory area where (the wolves) are based 領地

take the lead in VERBing... be the first to do... 帶頭做……

• **最後再練習一下「有關生命科學的表達」最實用的答題模板！**

1. Predator-prey interactions are the ways that predator and prey populations VERB...

　　例 • Predator-prey interactions are the ways that predator and prey populations influence one another.

　　　　• Predator-prey interactions are the ways that predator and prey populations affect each other.

2. In the simple model, when the population of the prey declines, ...

　　例 • In the simple model, when the population of the prey declines, the population of predators will also go down.

　　　　• In the simple model, when the population of the prey declines, the population of predators declines as well.

3. It is seen in the arctic zone, where...

　　例 • It is seen in the arctic zone, where there are few animals.

　　　　• It is seen in the arctic zone, where predators don't have many choices.

4. **That's because predators VERB..., and the prey VERB...**

   例 • That's because predators have choices of which prey to eat, and the prey can be eaten by many animals as well.

   • That's because predators eat diverse animals, and the prey is eaten by diverse animals.

5. **Seed dormancy refers to the period of inactivity that...**

   例 • Seed dormancy refers to the period of inactivity that a seed goes through before germinating.

   • Seed dormancy refers to the period of inactivity that protects a seed.

6. **The professor talks about her dogwood tree to illustrate how...**

   例 • The professor talks about her dogwood tree to illustrate how some seeds need to be exposed to certain conditions before they leave the dormant period.

   • The professor talks about her dogwood tree to illustrate how cold and moisture are sometimes necessary to break dormancy.

7. **To do this, she needed to VERB...**

   例 • To do this, she needed to allow the seeds to be dormant.

   • To do this, she needed to make the seeds break dormancy.

8. **In this way, she made the seeds VERB...**

   例 • In this way, she made the seeds break dormancy so they could germinate in her greenhouse.

   • In this way, she made the seeds think it was safe to germinate.

9. **Wolves live in packs which have...**

   例 • Wolves live in packs which have a specific social order.

10. **The hierarchy of wolf packs is based on...**

   例 • The hierarchy of wolf packs is based on social dominance.

   • The hierarchy of wolf packs is based on a social hierarchy.

11. **The professor describes how the alpha wolves behave when VERBing...**

   例 • The professor describes how the alpha wolves behave when interacting with the other wolves.

   • The professor describes how the alpha wolves behave when hunting.

12. **For example, the lecturer talks about how alpha wolves VERB...**

   例 • For example, the lecturer talks about how alpha wolves sometimes decide to go hunting for prey and the rest of the pack follows.

   • For example, the lecturer talks about how alpha wolves stare directly at another wolf.

Social Sciences
社會科學

在本章，你將學到……

★如何給專業術語下定義
★用於舉例的最常用片語

解讀常考題

第四題中，社會科學類情境經常出現，心理學和社會學更是常考學科。社會科學類題目有時還涉及人類學、考古學、商業經營與管理、傳播學、教育學和經濟學等。社會科學領域的專業術語會涉及人類行為，即人類在社會中為何會有這樣或那樣的行為。

現在，看一道有關社會科學的例題。

▶舉例試題

Narrator: Now read the passage about assimilation and accommodation. You will have 45 seconds to read the passage. Begin reading now.
Reading Time: 45 Seconds

Assimilation and Accommodation

When the scientist Piaget worked in a school for boys, he noticed patterns in the wrong answers the younger boys gave. This stimulated him to study learning skills in children of many ages. As children observed their environment and reacted to it, they seemed to rely on certain mental processes. One of these was "assimilation," which occurred when a child incorporated a new concept into a pre-existing knowledge category. Another process was "accommodation," which occurred when the child had to change the category, or add a new one. These processes allowed a child's mental framework to stay consistent with external reality.

Narrator: Now listen to part of a lecture on this topic in a psychology class.

Track 166 （播放錄音檔 166，錄音原文見特別收錄 2 的 P.311）

Explain how the example given by the professor illustrates the mental processes of assimilation and accommodation.

Preparation Time: 30 Seconds
Response Time: 60 Seconds

Narrator: You have 30 seconds to prepare.
Narrator: Begin speaking after the beep.

策略：超恐怖的專業術語怎麼定義

　　口語部分的小文章和小講座都不長，因此只能集中講述一個核心概念。第四題的核心概念通常都是小文章的標題，而這個概念的定義會出現在文章的首句或第二句。總結第四題的觀點時，也應遵循同樣的模式，最好的開場白是介紹核心概念並為其下定義。

高分回答

注意看，仔細聽，這裡面標上粗體的地方都要發重音才道地喔！ *Track 167*

There are **two mental processes** used to **learn** and under**stand new concepts. These**
are assimi**lation** and accommo**dation.** （←介紹核心概念）
Assimilation **takes place** when we encounter **something new** and **put it** into a **pre-**
existing **category.** Accommo**dation** is when we encounter a **new concept** that **doesn't**
fit into a **pre-existing category,** so we **have to** create a **new category.** （←下定義）
The professor illustrates these in a **story** about a little **girl** named Sally. **Sally** has
never seen a **ze**bra before, so when she **sees** a **pic**ture of one, she **calls it** a
"**horse.**" **That's** assimi**lation. After** she learns **more** about **ze**bras and the **fact** that
zebras always have **black** and **white stripes,** she's able to create a **new category**
for zebras. **That's** accommo**dation. Then,** when she **sees** a butterfly with **black** and
white stripes, she uses assimi**la**tion to **la**bel the butterfly a "**zebra butterfly.**" She has
success**fully linked** the **know**ledge **cat**egories for "zebra" and "**butterfly.**"

托福總監為什麼覺得這是高分回答？

　　第一句說明學習和理解新的概念有兩種心理過程，然後指出是哪兩種。第三句和第四句話給出了這兩種過程的定義。給出定義後，再通過教授舉的例子對兩個概念進行進一步闡述。

　　專業術語的定義有幾種類型：有些定義非常籠統；有些定義描述性很強，使用了一連串的形容詞或名詞片語；許多措辭嚴謹的專業術語定義會指出概念所屬的類型或分類；還有些定義會列舉被定義事物的組成部分；有些定義甚至從功能角度出發，描述被定義事物是做什麼用的。考生可以根據要定義的概念的特點從上述類型中選擇合適的一種運用在自己的回答中。

實用語塊

assimilation taking in new information or experiences and incorporating them into our
existing knowledge categories (schema) 同化

accommodation altering our existing knowledge categories in light of new information 順應

pattern in... special way that...is structured ⋯⋯的規律（模式）

stimulate...to VERB... motivate someone to do... 激勵某人做⋯⋯

mental process process used in the brain 思維過程

incorporate...into... put...inside of... 把⋯⋯歸併入⋯⋯

pre-existing... ...that existed beforehand 已存在的⋯⋯

knowledge category grouping used in categorizing knowledge; schema 知識結構

mental framework how knowledge is structured in the brain 思維框架

...be consistent with... ...be in harmony with... ⋯⋯和⋯⋯一致

complement one another work with each other in a system, to complete the system 相互補充

categorize... classify... 把⋯⋯分門別類

label... give a name to... 給⋯⋯命名

fit into... match... 符合⋯⋯

make sense of... understand... 理解⋯⋯

Take the case of... Take the example of... 以⋯⋯為例

stripes pattern of parallel bands 條紋

下表列舉了基本定義類型的句型和例子：

類型	句型	範例
總體性	某概念 + is defined as...	Inflation is defined as the upward movement in the average level of prices.
	某概念 + refers to a...	Self-efficacy refers to a person's confidence in accomplishing tasks or handling problems.
	某概念 + is when...	Kinesthetic learning is when learners assimilate new knowledge through movement.
描述性	某概念 +is a+ 形容詞 + 名詞 +with a+ 名詞片語	Sweat is a colorless fluid with a distinctive odor secreted by glands within the skin.
說明功能	某概念 +is a...whose objective is to...	Relationship marketing is a marketing strategy whose objective is to create a long-term relationship with each customer.
	某概念 +is a...that can...	Money is a medium that can be exchanged for goods and services.
說明類別	某概念 + is a form of + 分類 + that...	Human capital is a form of capital that is "owned" by a human.
	某概念 + is a type of + 分類 + that...	Emotional intelligence is a type of social intelligence that enables a person to be very aware of emotions.

説明組成	某概念 + is a...that consists of...and...	Culture is a complex heritage of a society that consists of its knowledge, beliefs, art and habits.

要更好地進行學術定義，可運用以下策略：

1. 考試前，熟悉基本定義類型，多記一些句型。
2. 做練習時，嘗試使用不同的句型，找到適合不同概念的定義方式。同時，最好找到自己得心應手的句型，經過反覆實踐，這將成為你真正的「武器」。
3. 考試中使用自己最擅長的句型來闡述專業術語的概念。
4. 記住，給出嚴謹的學術定義，就等於是向評分人展示自己對語言掌握得有多熟練。能給出嚴謹的學術定義，往往表示你的回答具有良好的銜接性和連貫性。

▶模擬試題①

請回答下題。回答時，可嘗試使用下面列出的實用答題範本。

Narrator: Now read the passage about buzz marketing. You will have 45 seconds to read the passage. Begin reading now.

Reading Time: 45 Seconds

Buzz Marketing

When a marketing agency seeks to create a sense of excitement about a product or service, they will often use buzz marketing as one of their tactics. Buzz marketing is a type of promotion that relies on untraditional channels such as blogs, online postings and special events, designed to generate a "buzz" in networking communities. A buzz marketing approach is most effective when consumers perceive that the message about a product has "social authority" and is coming from everyday people. In peer-to-peer buzz marketing initiatives, ordinary citizens become brand ambassadors and promote products and services throughword of mouth.

Narrator: Now listen to part of a lecture on this topic in a marketing class.

🎧 *Track 168* （播放錄音檔 168，錄音原文見特別收錄 2 的 P.311）

Using the examples from the lecture, explain what buzz marketing is and how it works.

Preparation Time: 30 Seconds
Response Time: 60 Seconds

實用答題範本　　🎧 *Track 169* 聽聽看！別人的高分回答！（高分回答原文請見 P.289）

In his first example, he talks about a(n)...which/who...
The impact on the company was...

實用語塊

buzz marketing creating a "buzz" to get people to do word-of-mouth marketing 口碑行銷

marketing agency business which plans and sometimes implements marketing strategies for client companies 行銷代理公司

create a sense of excitement make people feel excited 使人興奮

tactics plans of action 手段，策略

promotion advertising 宣傳，推廣

untraditional channel unorthodox way of communicating 非傳統管道

blog shared online journals 部落格

online posting electronic message on forums 網路文章

social authority when an individual or organization gains influence and respect within a given field or social network 社會威信

peer-to-peer initiative activity organized by everyday people 點對點行動

brand ambassador person representing the company's brand 品牌形象大使，廣告代言人

word of mouth when a message is spread by people telling other people 口耳相傳

No press is bad press. Even bad PR about someone or something has good media value. 沒有新聞就是負面新聞。

ice cream cone scoops of ice cream in a sugar cone 冰淇淋甜筒

ripple effect spreading influence 連鎖反應；漣漪作用

brand awareness level of awareness that consumers have about a brand 品牌知名度

social media Internet applications that allow creation and exchange of content 社群媒體

drawn from... taken from... 來自⋯⋯的

fake identity pretending to be someone else 虛假身份

得分考技：美國人最常用於舉例的動詞片語

　　新托福考試口語部分的六道題目都會要求考生以不同的方式舉例。第一題和第二題這類日常話題中，要舉親身經歷或身邊發生的事為例子；第三題和第五題這類校園生活題目中，不管是概述學生觀點還是表達自己的觀點，都要根據對話場景舉例；第四題和第六題這樣的學術類題目中，要引用教授在小講座中舉的例子。根據情境的不同，教授舉的例子也會有很大的不同：物理科學的例子也許是一個物體或一塊岩石；人文藝術學科的例子可能是作家或藝術品；生命科學的例子可能是一種昆蟲或樹木；社會科學的例子也許是人類、人類行為或社會活動。

　　即使是舉不同類型的例子，用到的文法結構可以是一樣的，都可以用動詞片語來談論概念和事物！

下表是舉例時最常用的一些動詞片語：

動詞片語	範例
give an example of...	The professor gives an example of how his daughter learned to talk.
provide an example of a(n) ...	The lecturer provides an example of an important Romantic composer.
cite...as an example of...	The student cites Miller Hall as an example of the problem.
use the example to show that / how...	The professor uses the example to show that sedimentary rocks have layers.
demonstrate...with...	The professor demonstrates moral suasion with a recycling campaign.
illustrate this by VERBing...	The professor illustrates this by mentioning two specific causes.
compare...to..., illustrating...	The professor compares Baroque music to a conversation, illustrating how the voice shifts from person to person.

托福總監帶你練

聽下面學術類句子，注意如何用動詞片語來舉例。動詞片語已用底線標出。反覆聽錄音，然後跟著讀。

🎧 *Track 170*

1. The professor cites drying as an example of a technique for storing food.
2. The professor illustrates displacement by telling a story of a student who becomes frustrated at school and is mean to his dog.
3. In the lecture, the professor provides an example of Baroque music.
4. The professor demonstrates non-verbal communication with a story about his daughter.
5. The student uses the example of students preparing for exams to show that playing music is a bad idea.

• **使用動詞片語來舉例，可運用以下策略：**

1. 考試前，熟悉並記住舉例時最常用的動詞片語。
2. 練習時，嘗試使用不同的動詞片語來舉例，至少要學會熟練運用兩到三種動詞片語。
3. 考場上，用自己掌握得最好的動詞片語來舉例。

▶模擬試題②

　　請回答下題。回答時，可嘗試使用下面列出的實用答題範本。

Narrator: Now read the passage about tool use. You will have 45 seconds to read the passage. Begin reading now.
Reading Time: 45 Seconds

Tool Use

The use of tools has traditionally been cited as evidence of intelligence. Based on bones with cutting marks found in Africa, scientists hypothesize that early humans were using stone tools more than 3 million years ago. These tools may simply have been sharp rocks that our ancestors chose to pick up. The ability to actually manufacture tools probably came thousands of years later. Animals also use tools. Increasingly, studies are designed to probe how tools are used and created by primates and non-primates. In particular, the remarkable cognitive abilities underlying tool use in New Caledonian crows have attracted much attention.

Narrator: Now listen to part of a lecture on this topic in a cognitive psychology class.

🎧 *Track 171*（播放錄音檔 171，錄音原文見特別收錄 2 的 P.311）

Using the examples from the lecture, explain how crows use and create tools.

Preparation Time: 30 Seconds
Response Time: 60 Seconds

實用答題範本　　🎧 *Track 172* 聽聽看！別人的高分回答！（高分回答原文請見 P.289）

These crows live...and have special abilities to VERB...
In several settings, the crow demonstrated it could VERB..., including...

實用語塊

be cited as evidence of... be referred to as proof of... 被引用來證明⋯⋯

cutting mark trace of having been cut with a sharp object 切痕

probe... investigate... 研究⋯⋯

primate animal that belongs to the group of mammals which includes humans, apes and monkeys 靈長目動物

cognitive abilities abilities such as learning and thinking 認知能力

New Caledonian crow a species of crow found only on several islands in New Caledonia 新卡里多尼亞烏鴉

manipulate objects move and control things 操控物體

accomplish tasks achieve goals 完成任務，達成目標

have fallen by the wayside no longer be done 已經半路放棄	
pass on... teach...to subsequent generations 將……傳承給下一代	
beak (birds) bill（鳥類）嘴，喙	
wire strand of metal 金屬絲	
aluminum bendable metal 鋁	
bucket pail 桶子	

• 最後再練習一下「有關社會科學」最實用的答題模板！

1. There are two mental processes used to VERB...

例 • There are two mental processes used to learn and understand new concepts.

• There are two mental processes used to acquire a second language.

2. The professor illustrates these in a story about...

例 • The professor illustrates these in a story about a little girl named Sally.

• The professor illustrates these in a story about when he was a little boy.

3. That's...

例 • That's assimilation.

• That's short-term memory.

4. She has successfully linked the knowledge categories for "X" and "Y."

例 • She has successfully linked the knowledge categories for "zebra" and "butterfly."

• She has successfully linked the knowledge categories for "computer" and "laptop"—meaning "small and portable."

5. The professor says it's very important to VERB...and gives examples of a good way and a bad way to VERB...

例 • The professor says it's very important to use buzz marketing correctly and gives examples of a good way and a bad way to use this technique.

• The professor says it's very important to understand niche marketing and gives examples of a good way and a bad way to do market research.

6. In his first example, he talks about a(n)...which/who...

例 • In his first example, he talks about an ice cream company which had a special event called "free ice cream day."

• In his first example, he talks about a buyer who regretted having purchased a new car.

7. The impact on the company was...

例　• The impact on the company was positive.

　　• The impact on the company was huge.

8. The other example was an example of...

例　• The other example was an example of a failed buzz marketing campaign.

　　• The other example was an example of what psychologists call projection.

9. These crows live...and have special abilities to VERB...

例　• These crows live on islands in the South Pacific Ocean and have special abilities to solve problems.

　　• These crows live in New Caledonia and have special abilities to use tools.

10. They could VERB..., showing a skill in...

例　• They could choose sticks of the right width and length, showing a skill in using tools.

　　• They could make tools out of wire, showing a skill in problem-solving.

11. In another experiment, researchers observed...

例　• In another experiment, researchers observed the crows actually creating tools.

　　• In another experiment, researchers observed children memorizing words.

12. In several settings, the crow demonstrated it could VERB..., including...

例　• In several settings, the crow demonstrated it could customize tools made of different materials, including tools of leaves and metal.

　　• In several settings, the crow demonstrated it could make the tool fit the task, including tasks such as picking up a small bucket of meat.

Task 6 ▸ Summarizing a Lecture
第六題 概括講座內容

　　口語部分第六題要求考生概述從講座中獲取的資訊，題目形式是：先播放一段關於某學術話題的小講座，要求考生概述話題（某個科學概念或現象）。

▶小講座

　　小講座中，教授會先介紹一個概念或現象，然後通過舉兩個例子或者強調兩個重要方面來進行深入解釋。小講座時長為 90 ～ 120 秒，有時候更長。有關某一物理過程的講座可能會描述這一過程的兩個變數。在關於某社會科學理論的講座中，教授會舉出一些例子說明這一理論如何在日常生活中起作用。講述某一歷史事件的講座可能會描述這一事件的前因後果。

　　由於第六題中沒有閱讀材料，講座通常會在第一句話中點明主要內容。有時教授會非常直接地點明話題，例如：Today we'll talk about different ways in which sculpture is created. 有時教授會提一個有關核心內容的問題來作為開場白，例如：If a buyer has to choose between two stores, what determines the choice? 然後，教授會講述主要概念涉及的運作過程或者基本原理並舉例。

　　要想快速抓住核心概念、兩個原理或要點，就需要速記筆記。記筆記時，記住第六題總是要求考生「使用講座中的要點和例子解釋……」，所以這樣的要點和例子記得越多越好。

　　小講座結束後，考生將聽到並在電腦螢幕上看到題目。第六題的題目會要求考生解釋小講座所討論的核心概念。準備時間為 20 秒，在此期間，考生可以思考並瀏覽筆記，標出重要詞彙。聽到「嗶」的聲音後，考生將有 60 秒的作答時間。

▶提問形式

第六題最常見的提問形式如下：

1. Using points and examples from the lecture, explain the...strategies described by the professor.
2. Using points from the lecture, explain how A and B defend themselves from predators.
3. Using the examples of A and B, describe two kinds of camouflage and the benefits they provide.
4. Using points and examples from the talk, explain the concept of...

▶考官如何對第六題評分？

第六題的評分標準是：考生需要充分展示自己的語言表達（發音）和語言運用（文法及詞彙）能力，能「完整地回答問題」。許多考生在規定時間內無法完成回答，因為他們在概念總結上花費了太多時間。若回答「遺漏關鍵資訊」或「沒有對重要資訊展開論述」，那評分人會只給 2 分。記住，第六題要想拿高分，考生的回答要持續（很少或者沒有不恰當的停頓）並且連貫（邏輯流暢），容易使人理解。

▶概括講座內容的四種語言技巧

首先，聽小講座時需要記好筆記；其次，你需要在自己的語言「工具箱」中裝備好兩種能力：理解能力和通過轉述學術概念或術語進行概括的能力；第三，你需要具備能流暢地將思路串聯起來的能力；最後，你要有快速思考的能力（最好是用英語思考）以便能在規定時間內完成回答。如果先將小講座譯成母語，用母語思考如何概括概念，再將思考的結果譯成英語，那麼你不僅浪費了寶貴的時間，也有可能在回答時吞吞吐吐，說出一些令人費解的、不自然的英語。

▶第六題的四個主要情境

和第四題一樣，第六題的情境也可以歸為以下四個領域：

1. 物理科學
2. 人文藝術
3. 生命科學
4. 社會科學

接下來的章節會分別講解以上每一種情境，並提供多道題目、回答範例、實用語塊和實用答題範本。通過在情境中練習這些題目，你將更加熟悉考試中會用到的語言。

Physical Sciences
物理科學

66 在本章，你將學到……99

★如何組織第六題的答題思路
★怎麼處理虛詞的發音，使口語更加流暢自然

解讀常考題

　　和第四題一樣，第六題的物理科學類問題可能會與天氣、海洋、地震、沙漠、天文學、光與聲、環境、化學、地質學、自然地理學等相關。考題內容不會很深奧，所以理論上沒有相關背景的考生也能理解。

　　現在，看一道有關物理科學的例題。

▶舉例試題

Narrator: In this question you will listen to part of a lecture. Then you will be asked a question about it. After the question you will have 20 seconds to prepare and 60 seconds to respond.

Narrator: Now listen to part of a talk in a geology class.

🎧 *Track 173* （播放錄音檔 173，錄音原文見特別收錄 2 的 P.312）

> **Using the points and examples in the lecture, explain how weathering occurs in rocks.**
>
> Preparation Time: 20 Seconds
> Response Time: 60 Seconds

Narrator: You have 20 seconds to prepare.
Narrator: Begin speaking after the beep.

策略：第六題的答題思路

　　回答這道題只需要簡單的三個步驟：

1. 講座一開始，要注意聽核心概念，記下專業術語及支持核心概念的要點和例子。
2. 回答時，先概括核心概念。提供的細節足以使評分人大致瞭解此概念即可。
3. 然後，開始闡述題目要求的要點和例子。在時間允許的範圍內提供的具體要點越多越好。

高分回答

注意看，仔細聽，這裡面標上粗體的地方都要發重音才道地喔！

Weathering in **rocks** falls into **two basic categories**. The **first** is physical **weathering**, and the **second** is chemical **weathering**.（←概括核心概念）
Physical weathering is described as the **breaking down** of **rocks** by physical **forces** such as **heat** and **water**. The professor gives the **example** of **frost** action to illustrate **physical** weathering. **Frost** action is found in **cold climates** where the **temperatures** go **down** below freezing point and then back **up** again. Water gets **into** the **cracks** of the **rock** when it is **above** freezing point, then ex**pands** when it **freezes**. Over **time**, the **freezing** and **thawing** process **breaks** down the **rocks**.（←題目要求的回答要點之一）
Chemical weathering is when a **substance** re**acts** with the **rock** in a **chemical reaction**; for example, **oxygen** or **carbon** dioxide. The professor de**scribes how plants** such as **moss** can **also** cause **chemical** weathering by releasing **acid** into the **rock** and causing the **particles** to become **loose**. Water can **serve** as **both** a physical and a chemical weathering agent.

托福總監為什麼覺得這是高分回答？

　　回答第六題時，要先提供核心概念的背景資訊，給出適當的情境使非本專業的聽者也能理解。因此，考生需要具備良好的轉述能力。
　　在 60 秒作答時間內，至少要花 30 秒來闡述題目要求解釋的例子。如果有兩個例子，每個例子應至少花 15 ～ 20 秒的時間。回答第六題的策略就是儘快開始解釋教授舉出的例子。

實用語塊

weathering processes that cause rocks to break down 風化；侵蝕	
break down separate into pieces 破裂，破碎	
to simplify things, ... to make things easier, ... 簡單來說，……	
divide...into two categories categorize...into two groups 把……分成兩類	
mechanically through physical force（ 通過物理作用）機械地	
frost action weathering caused by cycles of freezing and thawing of water 冰凍風化作用	
fluctuate vary greatly 波動，起伏	
trickle down into... drip into... 滲入……	
drip slowly fall in drops 滴下	
freezing and thawing process cycle of a substance repeatedly freezing and thawing, due to temperature changes 凍結和融化過程	
chemical composition chemical make-up 化學成分	

molecular level combination of materials at the atomic level 分子能階

agent thing acting on something else, causing change 因素；作用劑

moss small, velvety plants 苔蘚

lichen fungus that grows on rocks 地衣

nutrients source of nourishment 營養物質

loosen its particles somewhat separate the particles 分解物質

...react chemically with... ...and...are transformed into a new substance ……與……發生化學反應

be responsible for... cause...to happen 是……發生的原因

要答好第六題，可運用以下策略：

1. 不要等提示音響了之後才開始準備答題，要邊聽錄音邊思考。
2. 注意聽概念、定義、要點和例子。
3. 預測會用到哪些語塊並寫下來。
4. 回答時儘量採取換句話說的方式。除專業術語外，其他說法都用自己的話表達。
5. 長時間或不合時宜的停頓肯定會被扣分。語速不用很快，但要保持平穩，回答要有條理。
6. 不理解某個單字或片語時，不必驚慌，繼續說自己理解的內容。
7. 即使是在概述，也要使用恰當的詞彙來闡述觀點。如果使用花俏的詞但表意含糊或不準確，那麼評分人就會扣分。
8. 嚴格按照題目要求完成回答，精確掌握答題時間。

　　記住：回答第六題時不能夾帶個人觀點。

▶模擬試題①

　　請回答下題。回答時，可嘗試使用下面列出的實用答題範本。

Narrator: Now listen to part of a lecture in a meteorology class.

🎧 *Track 175*（播放錄音檔 175，錄音原文見特別收錄 2 的 P.312）

Using points and examples from the talk, explain the phenomena of sea breezes and land breezes.

Preparation Time: 20 Seconds
Response Time: 60 Seconds

實用答題範本　　　🎧 *Track 176* 聽聽看！別人的高分回答！（高分回答原文請見 P.290）

The professor introduces two types of...
There are two reasons why...

實用語塊

meteorology study of weather and atmospheric conditions 氣象學

coastal winds wind activity that occurs along shorelines 沿海風

in a predictable fashion in a consistent way 以可預測的方式

sea breeze coastal wind that moves from ocean to land, during the day 海風

flow in the reverse direction move in the opposite direction 反向流動，逆流

land breeze coastal wind that moves from land to ocean, at night 陸風

heat capacity amount of heat required to raise the temperature of a substance 熱容量

heat up become hotter 升溫

air pressure weight of the atmosphere pushing down on Earth 氣壓

hot air balloon balloon for travel, powered by a bag of heated air 熱氣球

air mass uniform body of air 氣團

reverse process opposite action 逆過程

得分考技：說得快≠清晰流利，小虛詞幫你解決大問題

　　許多考生認為如果語速很快，就會聽起來「很流利」，能說更多的東西，由此拿到更高的分數。事實上，加快語速並非明智之舉，因為說得越快，就越有可能語意不清。口語考試中，質比量更重要。

　　其實，如果注意英語的節奏，不用說得很快就能讓人聽起來清晰流利。要掌握正確的節奏，一個簡單的方法就是掌握虛詞中 /ə/ 的發音。中性母音，即非重音母音 /ə/ 是美式英語中最常見的音，通常出現在非重音的音節中，在虛詞中尤其常見。

　　為什麼要注意虛詞呢？虛詞是英語中功能極廣的詞，包括冠詞、介系詞、代名詞和助動詞，往往含有在句子中讀作 /ə/ 的母音。

　　看看下列新托福考試中的原句，句子中都包含帶 /ə/ 的虛詞：

虛詞	發音（非重音）	例句
冠詞		
a	/ə/	A (/ə/) **fault** is a (/ə/) **fracture** in the **Earth's crust**.
the	/ðə/	The **area seen** as (/əz/) a (/ə/) **dark spot** on the (/ðə/) **Sun** is called a (/ə/) **sunspot**.
an	/ən/	**Water** in an (/ən/) artesian **well rises above** the (/ðə/) surrounding **water table**.
介系詞		
of	/əv/	The **atmosphere** is a (/ə/) **mass** of (/əv/) **air** surrounding the **Earth**.
at	/ət/	**Mist refers** to (/tə/) the (/ðə/) **very fine droplets** at (/ət/) **ground level** as (/əz/) a (/ə/) **result** of (/ə/) condensation.
to	/tə/	I think the (/ðə/) **solution** to (/tə/) the (/ðə/) **problem** is to (/tə/) **change** the (/ðə/) **bus** routes.

for	/fə/	The (/ðə/) **student** is **looking** for (/fə/) a (/ə/) **new room**mate.
代名詞		
him	/əm/	I'd **tell** him (/əm/) to (/tə/) **take** the (/ðə/) **class next** semester.
them	/əm/	**After lecturing** to (/tə/) the (/ðə/) **students**, the (/ðə/) **professor asked** them (/əm/) to (/tə/) **write** a (/ə/) **term** paper.
her	/hɚ/	The (/ðə/) **student** left her (/ə/) **laptop somewhere** in the (/ðə/) **library**.
助動詞		
can	/kæn/	We can (/kən/) **see** where **mountains** have (/əv/) **formed**.
have	/ə/	The (/ðə/) **club** members have (/əv/) **organized** a (/ə/) **ski** trip.

托福總監帶你練

聽聽下列談論學術話題的句子，含 /ə/ 虛詞已用底線標出。反覆聽錄音，然後跟著讀。

 Track 177

1. As acid **rain falls** on **trees**, it can **make** them **lose** their **leaves**.
2. **Saturn** has been **visited** by **several probes** from **Earth**.
3. The **lead** that is **present** in discarded electronics can be extracted for other uses.
4. The **lecture** described **two ways** that gravity has an **effect** on us.
5. **Sandstones** are made of **sand grains** that have been cemented together.

• 要掌握含 /ə/ 音的虛詞的發音，可運用以下策略：

1. 説話節奏比語速更重要。抓到這種節奏的重點包括實詞發重音、虛詞不發重音。要逐漸領會英語口語中單字及音節重音的節奏。
2. 由於虛詞不發重音，所以這些詞中許多母音應被讀作 /ə/。
3. 即使 /ə/ 是美式英語中最常見的音，也不可能只看拼寫就辨別出其是否要發 /ə/ 音，應想一想該詞的作用和重要性。
4. 不讀重音的母音比讀重音的母音發音更短、更輕，有時甚至不發音。

　　記住：若能熟練掌握需要重音的實詞和不重讀的虛詞，將得到更高的分數！

▶模擬試題②

　　請回答下題。回答時，可嘗試使用下面列出的實用答題範本。

Narrator: Now listen to part of a talk in a physical geography class.

 Track 178（播放錄音檔 178，錄音原文見特別收錄 2 的 P.313）

Using the points from the lecture, explain the natural aging process of a lake.

Preparation Time: 20 Seconds

Response Time: 60 Seconds

實用答題範本　　🎧 *Track 179* 聽聽看！別人的高分回答！（高分回答原文請見 P.290）

As the lecture points out, ...

This cycle repeats itself, so that finally...

實用語塊

body of water accumulation of water that is a geographic feature 水體

permanent fixture on... lasting feature on... ⋯⋯的固定地貌

extended period prolonged time 長期

shallow not deep 淺的

glacier large mass of ice flowing over a land mass 冰川

come and go be transient 轉瞬即逝的

aging process how something or someone becomes older 衰老過程

organic matter material from once-living organisms that are capable of decaying 有機物

swamp lowland saturated with water 沼澤

wetland lowland partly covered with water or wet most of the time 濕地

meadow grassland 草地

choke (a lake) fill up and eventually "kill" (a lake) 塞滿（湖泊）

devoid of... lack... 缺乏⋯⋯

algae simple aquatic, photosynthetic organisms 藻類

bacteria very small and simple organisms 細菌

decompose rot 腐爛

thrive on... love..., do well with... 喜愛⋯⋯

take over dominate 佔領

decay decompose 腐爛，腐朽

layer of sediment deposited material that settles to the bottom of a liquid 沉積層

chemical fertilizers chemicals given to plants to promote growth, such as nitrogen and phosphorus 化肥

• 最後再練習一下「有關物理科學的表達」最實用的答題模板！

1. ...is described as...

例　• Physical weathering is described as the breaking down of rocks by physical forces.

　　• The atmosphere is described as an envelope of air surrounding the Earth.

• An oasis is described as a fertile area in the desert where the water table is near the surface.

2. The professor gives the example of...to illustrate...

例 • The professor gives the example of frost action to illustrate physical weathering.

• The professor gives the example of hurricanes to illustrate extreme weather.

3. ...is when a substance...

例 • Chemical weathering is when a substance reacts with the rock in a chemical reaction.

• Boiling is when a substance changes from a liquid to a gas.

4. The professor describes how plants such as...can...

例 • The professor describes how plants such as moss can cause chemical weathering.

• The professor describes how plants such as willows can help reduce greenhouse gas.

5. The professor introduces two types of...

例 • The professor introduces two types of wind: Sea breezes and land breezes.

6. There are two reasons why...

例 • There are two reasons why this happens.

• There are two reasons why this is a problem.

7. When X..., Y..., making Z...

例 • When the Sun shines, the land heats up faster than the water, making the air on land get hotter, too.

• When land is over-irrigated, the soil can accumulate too many salts, making it difficult for crops to grow.

• When pollutants are in the air, acid rain may fall, making the soil undergo chemical changes.

8. At night, it's the opposite—X...and Y...

例 • At night, it's the opposite—the land air gets cool and the sea air stays warm.

9. As the lecture points out, ...

例 • As the lecture points out, lakes have a natural aging process.

• As the lecture points out, a lake gradually accumulates plant nutrients.

10. This cycle repeats itself, so that finally...

例 • This cycle repeats itself, so that finally the lake turns into a wetland.

• This cycle repeats itself, so that finally a steady state is achieved.

11. Humans cause...to take place more...

例 • Humans cause the natural aging process to take place more rapidly.

• Humans cause erosion to take place more easily.

30 Humanities and the Arts 人文藝術

66 在本章，你將學到…… 99

★第六題如何記筆記
★引出兩個要點的最佳片語和句型

解讀常考題

第六題涉及的學科較廣泛：建築與設計、工作室藝術與藝術史、紡織與手工藝、音樂與音樂史以及舞蹈等，還包括攝影與新聞、文學（包括小説、詩歌、戲劇以及如浪漫主義、現代主義等各種文學流派）以及美國歷史和世界史。和其他題目一樣，這一類情境的聽力材料不會涉及高深的概念，沒有相關背景的考生也能理解。

現在，看一道有關人文藝術的例題。

▶舉例試題

Narrator: Now listen to part of a talk in a design class.

🎧 **Track 180** （播放錄音檔 180，錄音原文見特別收錄 2 的 P.313）

Using points and examples from the lecture, explain how static movement and dynamic movement affect the way we view an artist's composition.

Preparation Time: 20 Seconds
Response Time: 60 Seconds

Narrator: You have 20 seconds to prepare.
Narrator: Begin speaking after the beep.

策略：第六題記筆記的訣竅

由於沒有閱讀材料，又是學術類題目，對第六題而言，記筆記至關重要，必須掌握。一方面，題目含有專業術語，考生不熟悉，也不容易記住；另一方面，這類題涉及的學術概念和事件要比校園生活類題目複雜得多。記下這些概念或術語，即使是用非常簡略的形式，也有助於組織思路並清晰地説出專業術語。

和第五題相同，第六題的準備時間也是 20 秒，期間可查看筆記。

做第六題時，從題目解說者（Narrator）開始說話時就應該做筆記，因為解說者會說明這是哪門課，甚至可能會提及講座的具體話題。然後，一定要抓住小講座首句話的中心意思：第一句話至少會說明主要話題，有時甚至會是一句完整的主題句。

做好第六題的筆記，只需要簡單三個步驟：

1. 聽小講座時，注意記下關鍵術語（關鍵術語也可能出現在題目解說者的說明中），還要記下足夠的資訊來幫助自己定義這一核心概念。
2. 用縮寫快速記下和例子相關的詞和片語，以便之後用這些詞語來說明例子是如何闡明核心概念的。
3. 使用圓圈、箭頭、底線、數位等標出筆記的結構並做好注解，以便組織語言回答問題。

高分回答

注意看，仔細聽，這裡面標上粗體的地方都要發重音才道地喔！　　　*Track 181*

In **this** **design** **class**, the professor **explains** how an **artist** can make a composition have **movement** and **guide** the **viewer's** **eyes**. There are **two** **basic** **types** of **movement**, **static** and **dynamic**. When a composition has **static** **movement**, **that** means the **viewer's** **eyes** **jump** from **object** to **object**. The professor **illustrates** **static** **movement** by **describing** a composition that has **many** **white** **balls** and a **few** **black** balls in it. The **viewer's** **eyes** move to the **black** **balls** **first** and **then** to the **white** **balls**, because of the **contrast**. When a composition has dynamic **movement**, **that** means the **viewer's** **eyes** go **smoothly** **across** the composition; for **example**, **following** **lines**. The professor's **example** of a composition with dynamic **movement** is a **drawing** of a **winding** **road** that goes **up** into the **mountains**. The **viewer's** **eyes** **follow** the **lines** of the **road** up to the **mountains**.

托福總監為什麼覺得這是高分回答？

　　下面來分析這個回答。第一句定義了核心概念：movement in a composition。第二句立即列舉了兩種移動方式。第三句中，該考生定義了第一種移動方式：static movement。第四句和第五句舉了一個 static movement 的例子。第六句接著定義了 dynamic movement。最後兩句舉了一個 dynamic movement 的例子，即通往山頂的公路。

　　由於第六題的小講座通常會舉兩個例子，因此做筆記時要有所預測：教授通常會先講述學術概念的大致背景，包括定義，然後可能會舉兩個例子，分別闡釋核心概念的不同方面。

　　為這道題記筆記時，可記下如下單字或縮寫：

design（科目名稱）
movement
how?
def (definition) - eyes follow comp movt
by comp's arrangmt
2 types
1. static → eyes, jump frog → white balls w/ blk
2. dynamic → eyes mv smoothly, linear → lines, mtns and road, energy

托福總監為什麼覺得這是高分筆記？

　　第六題的成敗比其他任何一道題更依賴筆記。此時，既要注重筆記的質，也要注重筆記的量。更重要的是，要知道教授是如何組織內容的，例如：static movement 和 dynamic movement 是 compositional movement 的兩種類型。在上面的筆記中，static movement 和 dynamic movement 之後的箭頭「→」指的，就是對這兩種移動類型的描述，而每一種類型的例子緊隨其後，並用圓圈圈出。

　　這道例題要求考生使用「要點」和「例子」解釋 static movement 和 dynamic movement 如何影響觀賞者欣賞藝術作品的方式。「要點」就是對 movement 類型的定義；「例子」就是白球中的黑球和通往山頂的公路。那麼，要回答這個問題，只需瀏覽筆記中的詞語，並將其串聯成一個緊湊、連貫的回答即可。

實用語塊

two-dimensional work art in which the elements are organized on a flat surface 平面作品

composition work of art 藝術作品

elements design components 設計項目

static movement when a viewer's eyes jump between isolated parts of a composition 靜態視力（目光在兩點之間跳動）

dynamic movement when a viewer's eyes move smoothly and in a linear fashion from one part of the composition to another 動態視力（目光連續線性移動）

stationary fixed; unmoving 固定的，靜止的

isolated parts parts that are separated by distance 孤立的幾部分

linear fashion approximating a line 線性方式

value relative lightness or darkness （色彩的）明度

做第六題時，想充分利用筆記，可運用以下策略：

1. 仔細聽題目解説，因為它常常包含對學科和具體話題的説明。
2. 講座的第一句話可能會包含具體的講座主題，要特別注意聽並用縮寫形式記下來。
3. 聽定義，盡可能多地抓住定義資訊。
4. 考場上，要時刻準備著記下解釋核心概念的例子。通常會有兩個例子，但也有例外。
5. 如果沒聽懂某一術語，而該術語又多次出現，不管用什麼方法，儘量先將其大致記下來，該術語有可能會在螢幕上的題目要求中以文字方式出現。記下一兩個可在描述「要點」和「例子」時使用的片語。
6. 記下所有新介紹的專業術語，標注其正確的發音（重音音節、母音），以便知道怎麼讀這些詞。準備期間，可以默讀這些不熟悉的單字，練習其發音。
7. 使用任何你可以看懂的記號（直線、箭頭、圓圈等）來標注筆記。

8. 不要讓記筆記妨礙了聽。聽講座時重在理解，尤其是理解教授如何組織觀點，理解講座的邏輯連貫性，這比記筆記更重要。

▶模擬試題①

請回答下題。回答時，可嘗試使用下面列出的實用答題範本。

Narrator: Now listen to part of a lecture in a history class.

🎧 *Track 182*（播放錄音檔 182，錄音原文見特別收錄 2 的 P.314）

Using points and examples from the talk, explain the two ways the River Thames influenced the formation of the city of London.

Preparation Time: 20 Seconds
Response Time: 60 Seconds

實用答題範本　　　🎧 *Track 183* 聽聽看！別人的高分回答！（高分回答原文請見 P.290）

The professor emphasizes two ways in which rivers...
The Romans were able to get into London by VERBing...

實用語塊

transportation route regular line of travel 交通路線	
mode of transportation method of travel (ship, train, etc.) 交通方式	
get loaded onto... be put onto... 被裝載在……上	
facilitate land travel make land travel easier 促進陸路運輸	
transportation hub center of activity for travel or shipping 交通樞紐	
marketplace place where goods and services are bought and sold 市場；市集	
flourish prosper 繁榮	
take them over occupy them 佔領	
think of rivers strategically think of ways to use rivers advantageously 從策略的角度考慮如何利用河流	
boundary border 邊界	
defensive barrier something that obstructs the aggressor 防禦屏障	
keep intruders from VERBing... keep attackers from doing... 阻止入侵者做……	
withstand the attack of... be able to defend against... 抵擋住……的進攻	
invader conqueror 入侵者	
the River Thames river in England that flows through London to the North Sea 泰晤士河	
ocean tides rise and fall of sea level 潮汐	
navigable (of waters) wide or deep enough for a ship to travel 適於航行的	

thriving doing very well 興旺的	
Roman troops Roman soldiers 羅馬軍隊	
gain access into... get into... 進入……	
fort fortress 堡壘；要塞	
take shape develop and become more complete 成形	

得分考技：引出要點——最不易失手的動詞片語和句型

　　第六題的小講座通常會用兩個要點來解釋或説明核心概念。如前面關於泰晤士河的例題，要求考生「解釋」在倫敦發展為都市的過程中，泰晤士河產生影響的兩種方式。其他題目也可能會要求談談「兩種類型」或「兩個因素」。儘管各個話題會存在一定的差異，但第六題的題目形式大體相似，因此應該準備好用於引出這兩點的片語或句型，告訴聽者：小講座講述的對象包含兩個方面。通過這種方式，可為後面更具體地陳述原理、過程和事實做好過渡和鋪墊。

　　下表列舉了一些可以用來引出兩個要點的常用動詞片語和句型：

動詞片語／句型	範例
There are two methods that can be used to...	There are two methods that can be used to make etchings.
Two different approaches are possible in...	Two different approaches are possible in news interviews.
...appear as two types, X and Y.	Monkey flowers appear as two types, yellow and red.
There were two parts to the experiment on...	There were two parts to the experiment on piano playing.
..can VERB...in two ways, by VERBing...and by VERBing...	Creatures can camouflage themselves in two ways, by changing their color and by staying in certain environments where they blend in.
...distinguish between two types of...	Psychologists distinguish between two types of motivation.
...describes two steps in the...process.	The professor describes two steps in the weaving process.

　　一般來講，上述句型最適用於學術類問題，尤其是第六題。但是，將上述句型變形後也可以用於其他題目，包括第四題和第五題。如回答第五題時，可以用 ...can VERB...in two ways, by VERBing...and by VERBing... 這個句型，説：The student can solve the problem in two ways, by working overtime and by borrowing money.

托福總監帶你練

聽下列談論學術話題的句子，注意如何引出兩個要點。動詞片語和常用句型已用底線標出。反覆聽錄音，然後跟著讀。

🎧 *Track 184*

1. <u>The professor discusses **two possible approaches**</u> for setting prices.
2. **Plants** can de**fend** themselves <u>in **two ways**</u>, by using **physical means** and **chemical means**.
3. <u>**Two basic principles are**</u> important in any de**sign**.
4. <u>There were **two main factors**</u> driving the Industrial Revolution.
5. The professor <u>**distinguishes between two types** of</u> software, the operating system and applications.

• 要掌握引出兩個要點的方法，可運用以下策略：

1. 考試前，記住一些可用來引出兩個要點的動詞片語及句型。
2. 做練習時，嘗試使用不同的形式，找到適合不同情況的不同範本。例如，應注意：There were two steps in the experiment 和 The professor distinguished between two types of memory 這兩句所適用的情境並不相同。
3. 把這些片語和句型當做情境中的語塊來記憶，尤其要注意有沒有介系詞，如果有，要注意是哪個介系詞。例如：在 Animals can reproduce in two ways, **by** VERBing...and VERBing... 中應使用介系詞 by，但在 Two types of reproduction are possible in animals, sexual and asexual 這一句中則沒有介系詞。
4. 注意片語和句型中單字和音節的重音。例如，應注意：説到 two types 時，two 和 types 都要發重音，two factors 中的兩個詞也都要發重音，而且 factors 的重音音節是 fac。
5. 考場上，描述完教授對話題的總述後，要緊接著使用這類片語或句型引出下文。

▶模擬試題②

請回答下題。回答時，可嘗試使用下面列出的實用答題範本。

Narrator: Now listen to part of a talk in a studio art class.

🎧 *Track 185* （播放錄音檔 185，錄音原文見特別收錄 2 的 P.314）

> **Using the points from the talk, describe the coiling and wheel methods of making pottery and compare their advantages and disadvantages.**
>
> Preparation Time: 20 Seconds
> Response Time: 60 Seconds

實用答題範本　　🎧 *Track 186* 聽聽看！別人的高分回答！（高分回答原文請見 P.290）

X and Y are two different methods for making pottery.
The disadvantage of...is that it's a slow process.

實用語塊

clay fine-grained material that becomes plastic when moist but hardens on heating 黏土；陶土
pottery ware shaped from moist clay and hardened by heat 陶器
coiling method of creating pots by placing one coil on top of another 泥條盤築法（陶器成型技法之一）
hand-building method of creating pots by hand, as compared to by wheel 手工成形法
wheel work artwork created on a pottery wheel 在陶輪上製成的作品
potter's wheel revolving wheel on which clay is shaped 陶輪；拉坯輪
throw a pot form a pot on a potter's wheel 拉坯
coils concentric rings 盤繞的（泥）條
stack... pile up...neatly 將……堆疊整齊
turntable flat circular table that rotates around its center 轉盤
rotate turn on one's axis 旋轉
hollow shape form that is empty inside 空心的形狀
fire... bake... 烤……，焙……
kiln oven for baking pottery 窯爐
offer (several) advantages be superior (in several ways)（在一些方面）有優勢
exercise a lot of control over... completely manipulate... 熟練地操控……
studio potter potter who creates pots in a workshop 工作室裡製作陶器的陶工
pride oneself that... feel proud that... 為……而自豪
one of a kind completely unique 獨一無二的
tableware dishes used in setting a table 餐具
spinning force force that causes something to rotate quickly 旋轉力

• 最後再練習一下「有關人文藝術的表達」最實用的答題模板！

1. In this design class, the professor explains how...

> 例 • In this design class, the professor explains how an artist can make a composition have movement.
>
> • In this design class, the professor explains how an artist can guide a viewer's eyes.

2. There are two basic types of...

> 例 • There are two basic types of movement, static and dynamic.
>
> • There are two basic types of literature, fiction and non-fiction.

3. The professor illustrates static movement by describing...

例 • The professor illustrates static movement by describing a composition that has many white balls and a few black balls in it.

4. When a composition has dynamic movement, that means...

例 • When a composition has dynamic movement, that means the viewer's eyes go smoothly across the composition.

5. In this lecture, the River Thames is used as an example of how...

例 • In this lecture, the River Thames is used as an example of how a river influences the development of a city.

• In this lecture, the River Thames is used as an example of how geography influences cities.

6. The professor emphasizes two ways in which...

例 • The professor emphasizes two ways in which rivers influence cities.

• The professor emphasizes two ways in which rivers attract settlers.

7. The Romans were able to get into London by VERBing...

例 • The Romans were able to get into London by building a bridge.

8. X and Y are two different methods for making pottery.

例 • Using coils of clay and using a potter's wheel are two different methods for making pottery.

• Coiling and throwing pots are two different methods for making pottery.

9. ...is another way that artists create pots.

例 • The potter's wheel is another way that artists create pots.

• Hand-building is another way that artists create pots.

10. The disadvantage of...is that it's a slow process.

例 • The disadvantage of coiling is that it's a slow process.

• The disadvantage of hand weaving is that it's a slow process.

Life Sciences
生命科學

❝ 在本章，你將學到…… ❞

★口語考試中應該用什麼風格的語言
★如何運用重音突出對立概念，強調重點

解讀常考題

　　第六題生命科學類情境涉及的範圍很廣，包括動物學、植物學、生態學、生物進化學和與人類健康相關的話題，有時還會涉及微生物學、公共衛生、解剖學和生理學等。

　　第六題中沒有閱讀材料，因此對於不同生命體的具體名稱，不管是動物還是植物，理解起來都很有挑戰性。幸好，小講座中的教授會「囉唆」一些，會用不同的詞語、舉不同的例子來重複說明同一個事物。此外，即使無法正確讀出動植物的名稱，也不見得會失分。評分人知道生命科學類問題所涉及的名稱很難，他們不會在這個問題上太過苛刻。通常，命題人會將相對較難的名稱寫在會顯示在螢幕上的題目中，這樣考生在準備時就可以看到拼寫方式。

　　現在，看一道有關生命科學的例題。

▶舉例試題

Narrator: Now listen to part of a talk in a physiology class.

🎧 **Track 187**（播放錄音檔 187，錄音原文見特別收錄 2 的 P.315）

Using the points and examples from the lecture, describe the two types of tears described by the professor.

Preparation Time: 20 Seconds
Response Time: 60 Seconds

Narrator: You have 20 seconds to prepare.
Narrator: Begin speaking after the beep.

策略：語言要正式還是隨意？

　　不管是大學生還是研究生，參加新托福考試的學生大都是為了申請國外的學校，因此有人認為應該在口語考試中使用高深、花俏的 GRE 詞彙。然而，也有人認為英語口語只有一種模式，即會話式口語，也就是要使用很多流行詞語，語速很快，用很多 I mean 這類的口頭禪。其實，這兩種看法都不可取。新托福口語考試的語言應定位於上述兩者之間：應

該有禮貌，即要比較正式；但有時可選用比較隨意的語言，如使用 talk about 來表示「談論」而不用 discuss。

為什麼要注意語言風格呢？因為人們會視不同情形而使用不同的語言。例如，若是對一個龐大的科學家協會做報告，就要使用相對正式的語言，不用像學術寫作那麼正式，但比和朋友聊天正式得多。

不管是機器考試還是和考官面對面，要當做正在與一位你所尊敬的老師交談。一方面，要表現出禮貌謙恭；另一方面，作為學生，你知道你的老師希望你能展現出自己最好的一面。

在回答第一題和第二題這樣談論個人經歷的題目時，使用的語言較為隨意；而回答第四題和第六題這類學術問題時，用語則較為正式。

如前所述，口語考試中不必使用花俏的連接詞，例如：Nevertheless, ... / To recapitulate, ... 等。使用下列詞彙或者片語即可：Still, ... / In other words, ... 另外，在回答學術類問題時，如果談論的是科學原理或歷史事件，就要注意用詞準確，包括專業術語的正確使用。

高分回答

注意看，仔細聽，這裡面標上粗體的地方都要發重音才道地喔！　　*Track 188*

Tears are pro**duced** in **glands** to help pro**tect** and **clean** the **eyes**. The professor discusses **two types** of **tears**—constant **tears** and reflex **tears**. Constant **tears** are pro**duced** continuously, even in **sleep**. **These tears** have an **oily layer** on **top** of them to **keep** the eyeball from **drying out**. In ad**dition** to **salt** and **water**, **constant tears** also con**tain** antibodies which help **fight off** disease. The **other type** of **tears** mentioned is **reflex tears**. **Reflex tears** are pro**duced** in re**sponse** to an **outside** stimulus. The ex**amples** in the **lecture** are **chopping onions** and **frying red chili** peppers. **These** foods can **cause** a **person's eyes** to cre**ate** re**flex** tears. Their **purpose** is to **flood** the **eye** with **lots** of **water** so the irritant will go **away**. There are **more reflex tears** than **constant tears** and they are **more watery**.

托福總監為什麼覺得這是高分回答？

從上述答案可以看出，該考生使用了相對常見的動詞，例如：produce、protect、clean。這些詞都不算花俏，但是，該考生用這些詞為眼淚下定義時的用語屬於非常典型的學術語言，不管是用於口語還是書面語。另外要注意，使用 constant tears 和 reflex tears 這樣的專業術語時，要非常準確。

實用語塊

physiology study of body functions 生理學

tears fluid secreted by some gland of the eye for lubrication and cleansing 眼淚

sweat perspiration 汗

constant tears tears that are continuously produced by the eye 基本的淚液分泌

fluid substance that can flow 液體

gland organ that secretes a substance for use in the body 腺

blink to shut and open your eyes quickly 眨（眼）

eyelid fold of skin and muscle that cover the eyeball 眼瞼

film coating 膜，薄層

lubricated made slippery and smooth 潤滑過的

evaporate change from a liquid state to a gas 蒸發

antibody substance that fights off disease, helping the immune system 抗體

enzyme protein that acts as a catalyst 酶

reflex tears tears that are produced when the eye is irritated 反射性眼淚

produce...as a reflex create...in response to something 因反射作用產生……

external stimulus outside factor causing something to happen 外部刺激

irritant something that causes pain or annoyance 刺激物

foreign body entity in the body that has come from the outside 異物

chop up... cut up...into pieces 將……剁碎

shed tears create tears 流眼淚

eyes water eyes create many tears 眼睛流淚

watery containing water 含水的

要想在考試中用對語言，可運用以下策略：

1. 第一題、第二題、第三題和第五題使用的語言可以比第四題和第六題稍微非正式一點。
2. 考試中不要大量使用華麗的詞，把這些詞留到寫作時用吧！而且，如果作答時突然說出一個不常用的詞彙，會顯得很突兀。這就像是一個人上身穿西裝、打領帶，但下半身卻穿了一條運動短褲。
3. 口語考試中不要使用 guys 和 kids 這樣的俚語，這在考試中是不禮貌的。
4. 口語考試中不要將 going to 說成 gonna，或把 want to 說成 wanna，這也是不禮貌的。
5. 語氣要恭敬。對著麥克風講話時，要把它想像成一位自己非常喜歡但又很嚴格的老師。
6. 不要表現得很輕率，更不要在考試中開愚蠢的玩笑。
7. 考試中可自由使用縮寫形式，例如：can't、doesn't、I'd、I've、could've、would've 等，這些都是非常典型的常見會話用語。
8. 第四題和第六題中，描述科學現象時要保證用詞準確。例如：可以說 Tears are produced in glands，但不要說 Tears flow in the eyes。儘管後者文法上沒有錯誤，但並沒有傳達出學術情境。

　　總而言之，考試中要放鬆，說話要自然，就像在用英語和一位備受尊敬的老師交談一樣，不必太正式，但也不能太隨便。使用恰當的語言，可以避免在社會文化方面失禮，讓評分人覺得不舒服。使用恰當的語言可以給評分人留下好印象，增加拿高分的可能性。

▶模擬試題①

請回答下題。回答時，可嘗試使用下面列出的實用答題範本。

Narrator: Now listen to part of a lecture in a marine biology class.

🎧 *Track 189*（播放錄音檔 189，錄音原文見特別收錄 2 的 P.315）

Using points from the lecture, explain the two aspects of the seahorse body shape that evolved in response to a changed environment.

Preparation Time: 20 Seconds
Response Time: 60 Seconds

實用答題範本　　🎧 *Track 190* 聽聽看！別人的高分回答！（高分回答原文請見 P.291）

Seahorse bodies had two major changes from...
The other aspect of the seahorse that evolved was...

實用語塊

seahorse small fish with a horse-like head 海馬	
marine creature sea animal 海洋動物	
upright standing up 直立的	
evolve into... develop into...through evolution 進化成……	
fossil record total number of fossils that have been discovered 化石記錄	
disintegrate break down into tiny particles 分解；粉碎	
forces be at play operating forces 產生作用的力量	
collide into one another come together（大陸）碰撞	
floor of the ocean bottom of the ocean 海底	
vast expanses of... large stretches of... 一望無際的……	
seagrass type of seaweed that grows in shallow water 海草	
clumps of... masses of... 大量的……	
pipefish fish with a tubelike snout and a long body 海龍	
swim horizontally swim parallel to the (ocean) floor 水平地游泳	
vertical swimmer swimming upright, with the head up and feet or tail beneath 直立游泳者	
attach itself to... hold on to... 依附於……	
adaptation adjustment in body or behavior, in response to the environment 適應	
shape of an "S" looks like an "S" S 形	
extend its neck stretch out its neck 伸長頸部	
sneakier hunter craftier hunter 更狡猾的獵人	
strike out at... suddenly attack... 突然襲擊……	

得分考技：美國人怎麼用重音突出對立概念，強調重點

談論不同的事物時，人們會自然而然地強調這些相互對立的詞和概念。這種強調能使聽者清楚地抓住說話者要突出的重點或要傳達的觀點。

在新托福考試的口語部分中，考生在比較兩種事物或從兩種事物中選出自己較喜歡的一種時，就可使用重音來強調兩種對立事物之間的區別，或強調自己比較喜歡的那種事物。

請看下頁在不同題目中使用的句子，注意句子中的重音。含對立意思的成分已用底線標出：

第一題	Of <u>all the sports</u> to <u>choose</u> from, I prefer <u>tennis</u>.
第二題	Parents should <u>monitor</u> what their **children watch** on **TV**, <u>not</u> let them turn to any channel they want.
第三題	The **man** says that **students don't** have **time** to <u>do community service</u> because they're <u>busy studying</u>.
第四題	They put a **scent** that was **attractive** to <u>women</u> at the entrance to a <u>women's</u> clothing **store** and a **scent** that was **attractive** to <u>men</u> at the entrance to a <u>men's</u> clothing **store**.
第五題	The **man can't wait** to take **out** the library **book** <u>next week</u> because his **paper** is due <u>this week</u>.
第六題	There are **two types** of advertisements, <u>positive</u> and <u>negative</u>.

可以看出，很多口語題目都要用到「對立重音」，如上表最後一句話中的 positive 和 negative 是反義詞，考試中，可以通過用重音發這些單字的音來強調它們之間的對立關係。由於 positive 和 negative 是多音節詞，可以重讀第一個音節的母音，而這種重音會使這種對立更鮮明。

對立重音經常出現在含有如 this、that、these、those 這類限定詞的語塊中。有時，對立重音會出現在兩個不同的時間片語之間，如上表第五題例句中的 next week 和 this week。

托福總監帶你練

聽下列句子，注意重音的位置。含對立重音的詞語已用底線標出。反覆聽錄音，然後跟著讀。

🎧 *Track 191*

1. I <u>used to</u> play <u>table tennis</u>, but <u>now</u> I like <u>basketball</u>.
2. **Quite frankly, I** would rather be a <u>follower</u> than a <u>leader</u>.
3. The **woman doesn't** want <u>undergraduate</u> students to take <u>graduate</u> courses.
4. When we **look** at a kitchen **plate** <u>from above</u>, it **appears** to be a <u>circle</u>; however, <u>from the side</u>, it **appears** to be an <u>oval</u>.
5. <u>Most frogs</u> <u>don't change color</u> and rely on <u>the kind of protective resemblance</u> where animals remain in a **constant** environment; <u>tree frogs</u> have <u>another kind</u>, as **they change colors** to blend in with <u>brown bark</u> or <u>green leaves</u>.

• 要掌握對立重音的用法，可運用以下策略：

1. 要強調對立成分，可將相關音節讀得更大聲、音調更高、發音時間更長。
2. 說完含有對立成分的語塊時，應有短促的停頓，以進一步強調其重要性。
3. 語言越複雜，強調對立概念的作用越重要。

▶ 模擬試題②

請回答下題。回答時，可嘗試使用下面列出的實用答題範本。

Narrator: Now listen to part of a talk in an ecology class.

🎧 *Track 192* （播放錄音檔 192，錄音原文見特別收錄 2 的 P.316）

Using the points and examples from the lecture, describe the two benefits that fires have in the ecology of Northern Forests.

Preparation Time: 20 Seconds
Response Time: 60 Seconds

實用答題範本　　🎧 *Track 193* 聽聽看！別人的高分回答！（高分回答原文請見 P.291）

Fires can have a positive influence on...
The Jack pine is an example of this kind of...

實用語塊

destructive forces forces which cause great damage 破壞力量

play a (constructive) role in... help (benefit)... 對……有（積極）作用

habitat environment where organisms usually live 棲息地

periodic fires fires that take place from time to time 週期性大火

...serve different purposes ...have several functions ……有不同作用

open up space free up an open area 開闊空間

eliminate get rid of 消除；消滅

nutrient-rich full of nutrients 營養豐富的

Northern Forests Boreal Forests; large forests located below the arctic tundra 北方針葉林

arctic tundra cold, treeless area in northern regions just below the icecap 北極苔原

leave behind... cause...to appear as a result of certain actions 遺留……

left untouched not influenced 未受影響的

mosaic of... pattern made of many small pieces of... 由……構成的馬賽克圖案

patchwork of... collection of miscellaneous...parts ……的拼湊物

sunlit areas places where the Sun shines down directly 光照地區

thrive do extremely well 茁壯成長

Jack pine evergreen tree of northern North America 短葉松

pine cone in pine trees, the cone-like structure containing seeds 松果

flames burn down fire dies down 火焰熄滅

come popping out are ejected 蹦出，迅速脫落

reproductive cycle cycle of producing babies, young animals or plants 繁殖週期

ecosystem community of interacting organisms 生態系統

overhead vegetation plants growing above the ground, including all the way up the tree canopy 表層植被

ash powdery remains from a fire 灰燼

chock-full of... very full of... 裝滿⋯⋯的

• 最後再練習一下「有關生命科學的表達」最實用的答題模板！

1. Tears are produced in glands to help VERB...and VERB...

例 • Tears are produced in glands to help protect and clean the eyes.

• Tears are produced in glands to help lubricate and clean the eyes.

2. The professor discusses two types of tears—X and Y.

例 • The professor discusses two types of tears—constant tears and reflex tears.

3. In addition to salt and water, constant tears also contain...which help(s) VERB...

例 • In addition to salt and water, constant tears also contain antibodies which help fight off disease.

• In addition to salt and water, constant tears also contain an oily layer which helps prevent evaporation.

4. The other type of tears mentioned is...

例 • The other type of tears mentioned is reflex tears.

5. Their purpose is to VERB...so the...will VERB...

例 • Their purpose is to flood the eye with lots of water so the irritant will go away.

• Their purpose is to coat the eye with oil so the eye will stay moist.

6. These conditions were good for...

例 • These conditions were good for seagrass.

• These conditions were good for small animals who wanted to graze.

7. Seahorse bodies had two major changes from...

例 • Seahorse bodies had two major changes from pipefish.

• Seahorse bodies had two major changes from its ancestor.

8. The other aspect of the seahorse that evolved was...

例 • The other aspect of the seahorse that evolved was the S-shape of its body.

• The other aspect of the seahorse that evolved was its ability to attack its prey.

9. Fires can have a positive influence on...

例 • Fires can have a positive influence on an ecosystem.

• Fires can have a positive influence on a forest.

10. For one thing, they VERB... In addition, fires can VERB...

例 • For one thing, they open up space for new plants to grow. In addition, fires can improve the soil.

• For one thing, they allow diverse species to survive. In addition, fires can release minerals that are trapped in dead vegetation.

11. The Jack pine is an example of this kind of...

例 • The Jack pine is an example of this kind of plant.

• The Jack pine is an example of this kind of fire-dependent species.

12. Fires also benefit...

例 • Fires also benefit the soil in Northern Forests.

• Fires also benefit wild birds, by allowing shrubs with berries to grow.

Social Sciences
社會科學

★如何使回答富有邏輯性
★使役動詞的妙用

解讀常考題

第六題的社會科學類問題通常涉及人類學、經濟學、社會學等，而最常考的是心理學的諸多分支，教授常常會討論某種人類行為或描述某個心理學實驗。有的小講座會涉及社會科學的其他學科，例如：兒童發展、商業、管理和廣告宣傳、傳播學研究和教育學等等。

現在，看一道有關社會科學的例題。

▶舉例試題

Narrator: Now listen to part of a talk in an economics class.

 Track 194（播放錄音檔 194，錄音原文見特別收錄 2 的 P.316）

> **Using the points and examples from the lecture, explain the two types of economic utility described by the professor.**
>
> Preparation Time: 20 Seconds
> Response Time: 60 Seconds

Narrator: You have 20 seconds to prepare.
Narrator: Begin speaking after the beep.

策略：輕鬆給出邏輯清晰的回答

要想在口語部分的六道題中得到高分，邏輯非常重要。不管是獨立型題目還是綜合型題目，評分人都會仔細聽考生怎麼展開主題，以確定考生是否能給出「清晰的觀點闡述」。但是，在學術類問題中，要保證思路的連貫性可能會非常困難。需要反應敏捷，才能給出一個組織嚴密、連接恰當的回答。

下表列出了回答缺乏連貫性和連貫性強的區別：

連貫性弱	連貫性強
組織結構鬆散混亂	結構清晰
內容極為籠統	有實質性內容

意識流	邏輯思維
毫無意義的空話	有意義的連接詞語

　　在第六題中，最常用的邏輯關係就是用於解釋學術原理和事件的邏輯關係。介紹完一個概念的定義之後，教授會説明這一概念為什麼重要、怎麼重要。教授通常會描述這一概念或事件的影響、結果及目的。因此，還應熟練掌握描述原因與結果、影響因素與後果、問題與產生問題的原因、目的與結果等邏輯關係的表達。

高分回答

　　注意看，仔細聽，這裡面標上粗體的地方都要發重音才道地喔！　 *Track 195*

The professor gives a **broad** definition of economic utility and then goes **on** to de**scribe** some spe**cific types** of utility. Utility is de**fined** as the satis**faction** a **cus**tomer gets when **buy**ing a **pro**duct or **service**. **One** type of economic utility is **place** utility. In **this** type of utility, the **cus**tomer is pro**vided products** or **services** at con**venient places**. The pro**fessor** uses the **banking** industry for his e**xample**. **Some** banks put little **branches** in **supermarkets**, where **people** are al**ready shopping**. **This** makes it **easy** for **shoppers** to **quickly** do some **bank**ing.（←因果邏輯關係）
The **other** type of utility mentioned is **time** utility. **Time** utility is when the **customers gets value** from the **time** that the **product** or **service** is provided. **So**, in the e**xample** of **banking**, **some banks** offer **late hours** on Friday **nights** and ATMs with **24-hour service**. **This** flexibility in **time** is convenient for **busy people** and **people** who **work** at **night**.

托福總監為什麼覺得這是高分回答？

　　在上述回答中，第一句為引出經濟效用的多種類型進行了鋪陳。第二句給出了效用的寬泛定義。然後從第三到五句，該考生解釋了什麼是空間效用並引出了教授舉的例子。在這裡，邏輯變得非常其重要。注意該考生在第六句和第七句中是怎麼説的：Some banks put little branches in supermarkets, where people are already shopping. This makes it easy for shoppers to quickly do some banking. 考生透過舉例和推理論證，解釋了在超市設立銀行分支機構的內在邏輯，即 makes it easy for shoppers to quickly do some banking。在這裡，考生使用使役動詞片語 makes it easy for 進行邏輯展開，表達簡潔自然，且非常有效。與 Because the bank is in the supermarket, it is convenient 相比，這種説法邏輯性更強。

　　接著，在第八至十句中，考生定義並解釋了時間效用：Time utility is when the customers gets value from the time that the product or service is provided. So, in the example of banking, ... 這裡使用了連接詞 so 來描述「影響因素與後果」這種邏輯關係。提供服務的時間是影響因素，而給消費者帶來的好處，即 time utility，就是後果。最後一句進一步解釋了前後邏輯，注意這一具有邏輯性的陳述如何成為一個有效的結尾句。

實用語塊

economic utility ability of a product or service to satisfy the desires of a consumer 經濟效用
place utility providing value to the consumer by locating products or services in convenient locations 空間效用
supermarket large grocery store selling food and other items 超市
buy groceries purchase food supplies 採購食品
teller bank cashier 銀行出納員
make another stop go to another place 去別的地方
time utility providing value to the consumer by offering products or services at convenient times 時間效用
branch local office 分支機構
ATM electronic banking machine that allows customers to take out money from their accounts 自動提款機

　　除上文提到的技巧外，在回答口語題目時，可以使用片語和連接詞增加觀點的邏輯性。下表列舉了一些最常用的片語和連接詞：

目的與結果	原因與結果
use...to VERB...	As a result, ...
try VERBing...to VERB...	So, ...
planned to VERB...by VERBing...	The outcome was...
...did...in order to VERB...	For this reason, ...
...did...so that...	...causes...
To do..., the scientist VERBed...	...leads to...
One's goal was to VERB...	...happens because of...
decide to VERB...to be able to VERB...	This is why...VERB...

要想在考試中把握邏輯關係，可運用以下策略：

1. 對觀點的展開要沿著一條思路進行，貫穿整個回答。
2. 有意識地將各個想法前後連接起來，而且要保證句子之間的連續性。
3. 考試前多練習各種加強邏輯關係的技巧。
4. 想一想自己希望表現哪種邏輯關係。例如：原因與結果？影響因素與後果？還是問題與產生問題的原因？或者目的與結果？例如上題：空間效用的定義解釋了空間效用的影響和重要性，即為什麼要注重空間效用？空間效用有何作用？空間效用如何實現這一作用？
5. 使用恰當的連接詞和片語解釋邏輯關係。不要只用 Because..., ... 這種過於簡單的邏輯結構。
6. 不要把 you know 和 that is 這類口頭語當成邏輯連貫性和語言銜接性的替代品。
7. 不要用 and 作為句子的開頭。口語考試中，句子開頭使用 and 會讓意思含糊不清，不能

讓評分人瞭解句子間的邏輯關係。想一想自己想表達的邏輯關係，使用一個能表現這種關係的連接詞，例如：So, ... / However, ... / But, ... / In addition, ...

8. 邏輯連接詞會幫助評分人瞭解你要表達的意思，甚至預測你將要説什麼。不管是採用迂迴方式説明因果關係，如先舉出一個例子，再説 This is why...is effective，還是順承表達，如使用 As a result 這樣的連接詞，回答問題時展開並保持清晰的邏輯線索都有助於提高分數。

　　警告！口語考試和寫作考試中使用邏輯連接詞的方式大不相同。在新托福考試的寫作部分中千萬不要以 So, ... 作為句子的開頭！

▶模擬試題①

　　請回答下題。回答時，可嘗試使用下面列出的實用答題範本。

Narrator: Now listen to part of a lecture in a sociology class.

🎧**Track 196**（播放錄音檔 196，錄音原文見特別收錄 2 的 P.317）

Using points and examples from the lecture, explain the importance of symbols in culture. Preparation Time: 20 Seconds Response Time: 60 Seconds

實用答題範本　🎧**Track 197** 聽聽看！別人的高分回答！（高分回答原文請見 P.291） The professor says the most important symbols are those in... Red ties send a message of X, whereas dark blue neckties send a message of Y.

實用語塊

button-up shirt dress shirt with a collar that buttons up to the top （扣子扣到領口的）襯衫

mainstream professional white-collar worker in generally respected fields 主流行業的職業人士

dress code required etiquette for clothing 著裝規定

necktie tie worn around the neck in formal menswear 領帶

"power tie" necktie whose style or color sends out a message of authority 「彰顯威嚴的領帶」

seriousness of purpose diligent and task-oriented 工作認真

得分考技：回答學術類題目的用詞武器

　　在學術類文章和講話中，使役動詞片語這樣較為複雜的文法結構很常見。這是因為使役動詞和動詞片語能幫助人們解釋科學過程或科學事件中的細節。要在第四題和第六題中表現卓越，你應該熟練掌握一些「使役武器」。

看下列從新托福考試回答範例中摘錄的一個關於廣告的句子。注意其中的使役動詞結構：

Good advertising causes people to talk about a product's name.

該句的主詞 good advertising 並不是動作 talk about a product's name 的直接執行者，people 才是，但是歸根結底，good advertising 是導致這一動作發生的源頭。

回答新托福考試口語題目時最常用的使役動詞有：

cause, make, allow, enable, have, help, require, motivate, get, convince, assist, encourage, permit

下表列舉了一些實用的使役動詞片語：

使役動詞片語	範例
cause...to VERB...	Advertisements using catchy tunes can cause viewers to desire the product.
make possible...	An investment in education makes possible the economic mobility of the poor.
make it easy for...to VERB... make it possible for...to VERB...	There are nutrients in the ash left from the fire, which make it easier for new plants to grow.
make it possible to VERB...	Advances in technology make it possible to photograph brain waves.
allow...to VERB... enable...to VERB...	Fieldwork allows anthropologists to understand many cultural belief systems.
have...VERB... had...VERBed...	The professor had his students conduct an experiment on peer influence.

托福總監帶你練

聽聽下列句子，注意如何在回答學術類問題時運用使役動詞片語。使役動詞片語已用底線標出。反覆聽錄音，然後跟著讀。 🎧 *Track 198*

1. **Episodic memory** makes it possible for a **person** to keenly remember certain experiences which occurred at a specific time.
2. **Brain** development allows a baby to develop the abilities to eat, crawl and speak.
3. A good business plan helps companies target repeat customers.
4. Virgil was unhappy with his epic poem *The Aeneid* and tried to have it destroyed.
5. The study showed that strong emotional intelligence enabled people to perform well in sales positions.

• 要恰當運用使役動詞片語回答學術類題目，可運用以下策略：

1. 考試前，記住一些使役動詞片語。
2. 在練習時，嘗試使用多種不同的使役動詞片語，找到自己用起來最得心應手的表達方式。

例如：可以從 make it easy for...to VERB... 和 make it possible to VERB... 這兩種類似的説法中選一個。

3. 以語塊的方式記憶這些片語結構，特別要注意片語中有沒有介系詞。例如：The heat caused the rock to crack 中有介系詞 to，而 The heat made the rock crack 中則沒有。

4. 在説話時，使役動詞很少讀成重音。例如下面從本章「托福總監舉例」的回答範例中摘錄的句子：

This makes it **easy** for **shoppers** to **quickly** do some **banking**. 其中的 makes 不發重音。

▶模擬試題②

請回答下題。回答時，可嘗試使用下面列出的實用答題範本。

Narrator: Now listen to part of a talk in an advertising class.

🎧 *Track 199* （播放錄音檔 199，錄音原文見特別收錄 2 的 P.317）

Using the points from the lecture, explain what factors influence the effectiveness of celebrity advertisements.

Preparation Time: 20 Seconds
Response Time: 60 Seconds

實用答題範本　　　🎧 *Track 200* 聽聽看！別人的高分回答！（高分回答原文請見 P.291）

It is generally recognized that...can cause viewers to VERB...
Whether a customer...is more important than whether the spokesperson...

實用語塊

public's fascination with... people's intense interest in... 大眾對⋯⋯的強烈興趣
celebrity famous person, especially in the entertainment industry 名人
entertainer performer in the arts 藝人
spokesperson person who speaks on behalf of a product or service 代言人
wide range of... diverse kinds of... 多種多樣的⋯⋯
subconsciously in the back of our minds 下意識地
consumer customer 顧客，消費者
VIP abbreviation for "very important person" 貴賓
endorse... appear in advertisements and say that you use and like... 在廣告中宣傳⋯⋯
trust belief that the other person has good judgment and will not lie 信任
trustworthiness honesty, credibility 可靠性，可信賴度
place confidence in... trust... 信任⋯⋯
potential customers people who might buy products or services in the future 潛在客戶
viewer person watching the advertisement 觀眾

highly opinionated message communication that directly expresses an opinion 非常主觀的信息

superiority of the brand clear advantages of the brand 品牌的優越性

expertise knowledge about something 專業知識

attractiveness good looks 吸引力

make an endorsement support a product or service 宣傳推薦

effective in VERBing... influential in successfully doing... 對……有效

positive associations thinking good things when thinking about something 正面的聯想

purchase intentions plans to buy something 購買欲

• 最後再練習一下「有關社會科學的表達」最實用的答題模板！

1. The professor gives a broad definition of X and then goes on to describe some specific types of X.

例 • The professor gives a broad definition of economic utility and then goes on to describe some specific types of utility.

• The professor gives a broad definition of inflation and then goes on to describe some specific types of inflation.

2. The professor uses the...industry for his example.

例 • The professor uses the banking industry for his example.

• The professor uses the entertainment industry for his example.

3. In this type of..., the customer is provided...

例 • In this type of utility, the customer is provided products or services at convenient places.

• In this type of market, the customer is provided services by only one company.

4. This makes it easy for...to quickly VERB...

例 • This makes it easy for shoppers to quickly do some banking.

• This makes it easy for companies to quickly promote their brands.

5. We learn ideas and experiences from previous generations through...

例 • We learn ideas and experiences from previous generations through symbol systems.

• We learn ideas and experiences from previous generations through the language of our culture.

6. The professor says the most important symbols are those in/of...

例 • The professor says the most important symbols are those in language.

• The professor says the most important symbols are those of spoken and written language.

7. Here, the professor gives the example of..., including...

例 • Here, the professor gives the example of clothing, including the style and colors of clothing.

• Here, the professor gives the example of language, including spoken and written forms.

8. Red ties send a message of X, whereas dark blue neckties send a message of Y.

例 • Red ties send a message of power, whereas dark blue neckties send a message of being serious.

• Red ties send a message of dominance, whereas dark blue neckties send a message of conscientiousness.

9. It is generally recognized that...can cause viewers to VERB...

例 • It is generally recognized that advertisements using famous spokespersons can cause viewers to want the product or service.

• It is generally recognized that television can cause viewers to change their buying behavior.

10. The professor talks about several factors that make...effective.

例 • The professor talks about several factors that make celebrity advertisements effective.

• The professor talks about several factors that make marketing campaigns effective.

11. Whether a customer...is more important than whether the spokesperson...

例 • Whether a customer has trust in the celebrity is more important than whether the spokesperson seems to know a lot about the product.

• Whether a customer has low self-esteem is more important than whether the spokesperson speaks passionately about the product.

12. However, just because viewers VERB...does not mean they'll decide to buy the product.

例 • However, just because viewers like these spokespersons does not mean they'll decide to buy the product.

• However, just because viewers have a lot of money does not mean they'll decide to buy the product.

Appendices

特別收錄

Appendix I ▸ The Scoring of the TOEFL® iBT

特別收錄 1 新托福考試的評分

★ 新托福考試成績概述

新托福考試為決策機構提供了兩套分數：總分和各部分得分。各部分的分數由「標準分」組成，標準分由原始分根據一個通用比例轉換而來。標準分很重要，因為它可讓決策者對學生進行更為公平的比較。

新托福考試成績的滿分如下：

閱讀：	30
聽力：	30
口語：	30
寫作：	30
總分：	120

考生會收到被稱為「成績回饋」的資訊。該資訊旨在告訴考生該如何瞭解自己的整體表現。例如在閱讀和聽力部分，考生得分情況有 Low（0～13）、Intermediate（14～21）或 High（22～30）。口語部分，考生得分情況有 Weak（0～9）、Limited（10～17）、Fair（18～25）或 Good（26～30）。寫作部分，考生得分情況有 Limited（1～16）、Fair（17～23）或 Good（24～30）。

但是請注意，提交給大學的成績單中不會有該成績回饋資訊。只有考生個人會收到此資訊。

★ 新托福考試口語部分的評分

1. 評分人

將有多名評分人對一個考生所答的六道題目進行評分，每道題目至少由兩個人進行評分。所以說在新托福考試的口語部分中，對考生的評估是相當客觀的，並非僅基於某個人的主觀意見。

2. 怎樣對考生的回答進行評分？

在考生完成新托福考試之後，記錄了口語回答錄音的數位檔就會被送往 ETS。在那裡，每份回答錄音會通過評分系統分配給評分人員。評分人會根據新托福考試口語部分的評分準則來給分。共有兩套不同的準則：一套適用於獨立型題目，即第一題和第二題；另一套則適用於綜合型題目，即第三題到第六題。這兩套準則實際上有很多相似之處，都會全面考查三個方面的語言技能：表達（包括發音和流利程度）、語言運用（包括詞彙和文法）和主題展開（包括內容的組織和綜合型題目中回答的完整程度）。

　　兩套準則的另一個相似之處是每個評分人給每道題評分的範圍都是 0 到 4 分。評分人一般很少會打出 0 分，除非出現下列情況：1）沒有答題；2）離題；3）有抄襲嫌疑。

　　那麼，兩套準則最大的區別在哪裡呢？區別在於：對於綜合型題目，即第三題到第六題，準則要求考生傳達「題目要求的相關資訊」，即必須準確地從小文章和小講座中抓住相關資訊，並在回答中傳達出來。如果只傳達出題目要求的部分資訊，沒有完整回答題目，那麼就只能得 2 分或 3 分，對於語言的其他方面，兩套準則是相同的。

　　大多數題目的得分會在 1 ～ 3 分之間。在得 1 分的回答中，考生通常只說了幾個詞語，並重複了題幹的措辭，得 3 分的回答則「具有較好的連貫性」。2 分和 3 分的分水嶺則在於：2 分回答的前後銜接不是很緊湊，或邏輯連貫性不是很好，而 3 分回答的前後銜接較緊湊且連貫性較好。能得到 4 分的回答則進一步展現出「清晰的觀點闡述」和準確的語言運用。正因如此，本書一直在努力敦促考生去學習能夠加強前後銜接和邏輯連貫性的策略，因為這可是關係到能得 2 分還是能得 3 分耶！當然，表達、語言運用和主題展開（包括前後銜接和連貫性）

　　這些要素也都是能幫你得 4 分的堅實基礎。如果抓住這些關鍵，就算犯一點點小錯誤，你仍然可以得到 4 分。

　　評分人在給每道題目打完分數後，所有評分的平均分會加起來，並轉換為 0 到 30 分的標準分，這就是官方成績單上的最終分數。

3. 口語各類題目的評分資訊

　　在兩周之內，官方的口語分數（在 0 ～ 30 之間）就會和閱讀、聽力及寫作分數一同寄給考生以及考生要求寄往的所有院校。另外，考生還會收到口語考試各類題目的得分資訊，通常包括：

Speaking about familiar topics (Tasks 1 and 2)
對日常話題的回答（第一題和第二題）
Speaking about campus situations (Tasks 3 and 5)
對校園情景問題的回答（第三題和第五題）
Speaking about academic course content (Tasks 4 and 6)
對學術課程內容的回答（第四題和第六題）

　　在上面的每一項中，考生都會得到如 Fair、Good 這樣的回饋，代表了在每種類型兩道題目上的平均表現。

★其他重要資訊

1. 成績單

　　考生可在完成考試兩週後線上查看成績單，郵寄成績單的耗時則會更長一些（一週到一個月）。每位考生都會收到成績單，同時考試機構會將最多四份成績單的正本寄往考生所選定的教育機構。成績單上只顯示一次考試的成績，如果你以前參加過新托福考試，以前的成績將不會出現在最新的成績單上。新托福成績的有效期是參加考試後的兩年之內。

2. 所需的最低總分

許多考生問：「需要在新托福考試中得多少分才能被大學錄取？」答案是：「視大學而定；視級別（大學或研究生）而定；有時還會視大學裡的某個系而定」。目前，很多公認較有名的教育機構要求新托福總分最低為 80 分。頂尖學院，如哈佛大學、麻省理工學院和芝加哥大學，總分可能至少需要 100 分，尤其當該考生申請的是商業、法律或傳播學這類科系時更需要高分。相反地，理工科的學生可能只需要 80 分，甚至更低。也有院校總分只需 69 分便可入學。

3. 各部分所需的最低分數

有些大學對新托福考試各部分的最低分沒有要求，但有些大學會要求，也會規定最低總分。還有些大學雖然對各部分的最低分有要求，但沒有單獨列出最低總分。舉例來說，你可能會發現你要申請的學校要求你閱讀最低 21 分、聽力最低 18 分、口語最低 23 分、寫作最低 22 分。如果考生滿足上述最低要求，則考生的總分至少為 84 分。

4. 如何查詢你的目標大學對新托福成績的要求

如果你正在申請出國留學或獎學金，想瞭解你想去的學校對英文能力的要求，必須到目標大學的網站上查看是否規定了最低托福分數。查找此類資訊的最好方法是：先點擊 Admissions（招生），再點擊 International（國際），然後查找 English language proficiency（英語語言能力）或類似這樣的標題。

Appendix II ▶ Sample Responses and Transcripts
特別收錄 ❷ 回答範例與聽力錄音原文

1～32章　模擬試題高分回答範例

1 Describing a Favorite Person 描述一個你最喜歡的人

模擬試題① 🎧 *Track 002*

The celebrity I most admire is Jackie Chan. One reason that I admire him is that he is humble. He has a great sense of humor and often makes fun of himself. Although he was born poor, he was able to become skilled at martial arts. It took many years of hard work, but ultimately Jackie Chan succeeded in the movie business and he's now an international celebrity. Another reason I admire him is that he often uses his fame to do charity work. For instance, he has given time and money to help the victims of natural disasters. Jackie Chan's example inspires people to work harder and give generously.

模擬試題③ 🎧 *Track 005*

It's difficult to define good leadership, but we all recognize it when we see it. In my mind, one of the most important characteristics of a good leader is the ability to inspire others. Even when times are tough, good leaders can motivate their people. Another fundamental quality is the ability to lead through example. Many leaders try to get people to follow them by telling them what to do, and sometimes this works. But the leaders who "walk the talk" are the leaders who truly earn respect and loyalty.

2 Describing a Memorable Past Experience 描述一次難忘的經歷

模擬試題① 🎧 *Track 007*

My grandfather's seventieth birthday party was the best celebration I've ever attended because it brought so many people together. Before the party, we created a large photo album with pictures of my grandfather when he was younger. In it, all the guests wrote words of congratulation. At the party, we had a jazz band. Friends and family came in from all over the country, and everyone got up and danced. But the most special part was when my grandfather gave a speech, talking about his life and telling us how much he loved us.

模擬試題③ 🎧 *Track 010*

When I was in junior high school, I decided to run for class president. I was determined to become a student leader. For weeks I prepared flyers advertising my candidacy and put them up around school. On the afternoon before the election, the three candidates gave speeches. My speech was a disaster, and I received the fewest votes of all. I felt totally humiliated and wanted to hide. Fortunately, my best friend was there to console me. He took me out for a snack after school and tried to make me laugh. Although the memory of that election is still painful, the memory of my friend's kindness is strong.

3 Describing a Favorite Activity in the Present 描述最喜愛的活動

模擬試題① 🎧 *Track 012*

One of the parks I go to a lot is a city park in my hometown. In this park is a large lake with footpaths that wind around it. Also, there are several little islands in the lake, which can be reached by bridges. I usually go to this park on Sunday afternoons with friends. In the summer, sometimes we rent a boat and paddle around to different spots in the lake. Most of the time, however, we just sit on the benches, talking as we watch people go by. Because the park is downtown, there's always an interesting mix of people, from grandfathers to babies. Every visit is a little different.

模擬試題③ 🎧 *Track 015*

I have to say that I find trains the most civilized way to travel. You don't have to go through long security lines to get on a train. Once you're on board, you can relax because you don't have to worry about traffic. If you want to take a nap, you can. Trains can be very romantic if you are crossing through interesting scenery, and if you have a good companion—or even a good book to read. The service is usually good, and some trains have a cafe car where you can get snacks. If you need to stretch your legs, you can walk around. No matter what you do, you can look outside at the scenery rushing by.

4 Describing Something You Want in the Future 描述要做的某件事

模擬試題① 🎧 *Track 017*

I believe that the world will be vastly different ten years from now. With global warming, I think that we'll begin to see the sea level gradually rise. We'll see increasingly extreme weather events, as well as changes in the patterns of precipitation. All of this will affect how well our crops grow and the price of food. Global warming will affect which animals will become extinct and will probably also lead to the spread of new diseases. At the same time, I believe that we're advancing in technology and medicine. I would not be surprised if, in ten years, we'll have found a new mode of transportation or a cure for cancer.

模擬試題③ 🎧 *Track 020*

If I were to buy a gift, I would give it to my boyfriend. That's because he's been with me through thick and thin for the last three years—the most difficult period in my life. During this period, my mother passed away and I had my own health problems. Every day was a struggle. He was always there to give me advice when I was confused and to give me support when I was sad. I can't imagine how I could have pulled through without him. If I could afford it, I would buy him something special to show him how much I love him. Otherwise, I'd probably just make something for him, like a wool scarf.

5 Describing Something Special in Your Culture 描述本國文化的特色

模擬試題① 🎧 *Track 022*

The bus is by far the most efficient transportation in my country. Most cities have large fleets of city buses covering extensive webs of routes. In the city of Chengdu, where I live, you can go literally anywhere by bus. Buses can travel in dedicated bus lanes during the rush hour, so at peak traffic times it is actually faster to take a bus than to drive a car. Additionally, many long-distance bus lines connect regional cities that are otherwise unreachable by rail or by air. I can easily get to the suburbs and even small towns outside Chengdu. Oh, I should also mention that the bus fares are dirt cheap!

模擬試題③　🎧 *Track 025*

I am from Italy and what I miss the most is the little cafes. Cafe culture in Italy is hard to describe, but if you ever visit, you'll understand. The atmosphere in the cafe is very relaxed. People stand at the bar and don't sit down at tables. The waiter behind the counter is always very friendly. Because most people come in to their neighborhood cafe every day, he remembers what everyone likes to drink. So when I go in, for example, I'm handed an espresso. I like to stand at the bar and watch the people come in and out. Although there are coffee shops in many countries, they can't compare with Italy's cafes.

6 Describing a Thing That Has Profoundly Affected You　描述對你影響深遠的某物

模擬試題①　🎧 *Track 027*

Two things are important to me when it comes to my place of residence. First is the view. If it's a house we're talking about, preferably it should have a nice yard, so when I look out the window I can enjoy the view of trees and flowers, or maybe even watch birds flying around. If it's a high-rise apartment building, then I prefer to live on higher floors so I can have an unobstructed view of the cityscape. The second important thing is that the neighborhood needs to be quiet. Home is a place for rest. And it's also a place where I do some of my most creative work. So I need an absolutely quiet place to live.

模擬試題③　🎧 *Track 030*

The Internet is the resource that has helped me the most. I used to spend a great deal of time at the school library, poring over the few reference books in the school's collection. It was frustrating because half the time I couldn't find the information I needed. When I started to do my research online, I was amazed to find there were many articles I could have used. Now I wonder how I ever lived without the Internet. I also rely heavily on chat software to stay in touch with friends and family. People may think that I'm addicted to the Internet, but I'd like to think my life has become much more efficient because of it.

7 Communication and the Media　交流與媒體

模擬試題①　🎧 *Track 032*

In general, I don't think it's a good idea to give advice to friends, even if we have good intentions. When we tell our friends what to do, it's easy for them to become angry. No matter how close the friend is, there's a chance that he or she will take our advice the wrong way. And there's also a risk that we won't give good advice because we don't fully understand the situation. Of course, if our friend specifically asks us for advice, that's different—in that kind of situation, we should tactfully offer one or two suggestions. But we need to be careful.

模擬試題③　🎧 *Track 035*

In this day and age, mobile phones are everywhere, and so of course young people carry them to school. I disagree with the statement that students shouldn't be allowed to use phones in class. My reasons are as follows: First, students need to check their messages between classes, and it's inconvenient not to have a phone. Second, if students don't power off their phones during class, teachers can confiscate them. In other words, there's no need to forbid students from bringing phones to school, as long as nobody's using them during actual class time. That's a practical solution.

8 Food, Travel and the Arts 餐飲、旅行和藝術

模擬試題① 🎧 *Track 037*

When I'm on a vacation I like to stop along the way and visit many places of interest. That is why my favorite trip was when I drove across the country with my best friend. The two of us drove from New York to California. Originally we planned to fly directly to Los Angeles and stay there for a week, but then we realized that we had time to drive. We took our time, driving through gorgeous scenic landscapes, exploring many small towns. We met some of the most amazing people. By choosing to stop at little, out-of-the-way places on our way, we had the chance to experience so much more than if we'd flown directly to Los Angeles.

模擬試題③ 🎧 *Track 040*

Given a choice between fiction and non-fiction, I prefer to read novels, especially science-fiction and fantasy. I find that when I read works of fiction, they take me to another world and my imagination can run free. For example, when I read Harry Potter, I am transported to a land where witches and wizards fly on brooms and cast spells with their magic wands. Visiting other worlds by reading novels can be incredibly entertaining. What's more, I'm able to leave all my troubles behind. And still another reason I would rather read fiction is that I usually get inspired—I want to go out and do great things. For some reason, when I read a good author's creative account, I find I become more creative in my own life.

9 Work and Money 職業與金錢

模擬試題① 🎧 *Track 042*

People aren't necessarily successful when they have money and power. True success encompasses much more than wealth and status. One example of success is sticking through a tough math class until the end of the year, because you are up for the challenge. Another measure of success is how much experience you gain in life, and how much you learn from your experiences, year by year. A "successful" person will set new goals as soon as he or she has achieved the old ones. And a successful person takes time to teach his or her children and help others. A powerful person who has billions of dollars but has never helped anyone else—that person is not a success in life.

模擬試題③ 🎧 *Track 045*

I prefer to work in the office. The nature of my work is such that I need to interact with my colleagues frequently. We work in teams in our office. If all the members of our team are there on site, we can easily communicate with each other and quickly resolve any issues that might have cropped up. I guess we could use the phone and the Internet to communicate with each other, but meeting face to face in a conference room and using the whiteboard to brainstorm ideas has proven to be the most efficient way for us. Working at home is not very convenient for me because I still live with my parents in a small apartment. They spend a lot of time in the living room, watching TV or having conversations. And their friends and neighbors often drop by. So I'm always forced to retreat into my cramped little bedroom, which is really not a nice place to work. That's why working in the office is much better.

10 Education—Primary and Secondary 教育——初等和中等教育

模擬試題① 🎧 *Track 047*

I don't think it's a good idea for parents to dictate what career their children should pursue. Many of my friends have complained to me how unhappy they are with their jobs. And more than a few have blamed the problems on their parents. For example, one friend says she dreads going to work every morning. She is employed by one of the "Big Four" accounting firms, earns very good money and works with world-class corporate clients. But the long hours and tedious nature of auditing work don't suit her at all. She says she took the job only to please her parents. Parents often place more importance on the financial aspect of a job. Luckily, my parents are more open-minded. They allow me to explore my own interests and they never give me any pressure.

模擬試題③ 🎧 *Track 050*

I think students should study during weekends. In fact, out of necessity, they have to. Nowadays, there is too much competition. We need to spend as much time as possible preparing for exams. At some point, we need to compete to get into a good school and compete in the job market. To succeed, we have to study a lot. Moreover, whenever possible, it's good to do extracurricular activities. These shape our character and give us skills not found in textbooks. Extracurricular activities often take up evening hours on weekdays, eating into our time for homework and pre-class preparation. Quite frankly, there's no way for me to finish all my homework by Friday night. I usually end up studying on Saturday and Sunday because there's so much to do. This is not to say I never spend time with my family. I try to see them once a month.

11 Education—University 教育──大學教育

模擬試題① 🎧 *Track 052*

I agree that students who go to faraway universities can benefit from the experience. Although it's not easy to leave behind friends and family, at a distant university you can learn about the geography and culture of the new place. For example, if my home is in the South and I go to university in New York, I'll be surrounded by New Yorkers who eat East Coast food and speak East Coast slang. But I think living and studying in an unfamiliar place helps people better understand themselves and grow up faster. Of course, students who go to faraway universities might be lonely at first. They have to make a whole new set of friends. Unlike students who live nearby, they don't get to go home on weekends. Nevertheless, as a result of living far away, students become stronger and tougher.

模擬試題③ 🎧 *Track 055*

Well, I'm afraid I disagree with the statement. Being a professor may be hard in the sense that one needs to have certain qualifications. But once a person becomes a professor, the hardest part is over. He or she can go on to enjoy a life of research and teaching. Being a student, on the other hand, is extremely challenging, to say the least. Personally, the hardest part is the uncertainty about one's future. I don't know if my education will adequately prepare me for a successful career. The other problem is the expectation of one's parents. Parents make a lot of sacrifices so that we can concentrate on our studies. So we push ourselves really hard, to the point where it seems life is only work and no fun. That's why I think it's much more difficult to be a student.

12 Life Choices and Life Lessons 生活中的抉擇和經驗教訓

模擬試題① 🎧 *Track 057*

I agree that people can learn from their mistakes. We learn more about ourselves. Basically, we learn what it is that we don't know, or what we can't do. For example, learning how to cook a stew. I probably had seen my mother make beef stew hundreds of times, and so I thought I knew how to make it. But when I actually tried making stew by myself, it tasted wrong. I didn't brown the beef cubes long enough in the pan before adding water. This mistake taught me that I actually didn't know as much as I thought I did. In this fashion, every time we make a mistake, we are given an opportunity to reflect on what we did wrong—what we didn't know, what false assumptions we had. If we identify the problem, we have learned more about ourselves.

模擬試題③ 🎧 *Track 060*

I am a young person, and so I like to live where the action is. That's why I would definitely choose to live in a big city. Cities are often noisy and dirty, but I love the energy. I also love the opportunities that cities offer to young people. For example, many big companies have offices in downtown areas. This is especially true for marketing and advertising companies, and I would like a job in one of those companies. In cities, there are also lots of places where people can find good food and good entertainment. Although young people don't have a lot of money, they can always find places to get together, grab a bite to eat and listen to good music. Suburbs are probably OK for old married people; however, for me, the city is the only place to be.

13 University Investments and Expenditures 大學的投資與支出

模擬試題① 🎧 *Track 064*

The man is happy about the news that the university radio station is going to expand. He believes that when the station adds new types of programs—so that they're not just playing classical music, but also jazz and folk music—university students will have more opportunities to work in the radio business. For example, they can learn how to be DJs. In addition, the man says he supports the plan to add more transmitters so that the broadcasting area will be widened. The man predicts that many young people in neighboring counties will listen to the station. He thinks the station will help bring the university community closer to the people in surrounding areas. He also thinks the new transmitters will create student jobs in technical production.

模擬試題② 🎧 *Track 067*

The student's letter proposes a solution to the university's housing shortage. What the student recommends is taking the lounges and study areas in the main dorms and converting these spaces into dorm rooms that would each hold three first-year students. The woman, however, doesn't like this proposal. She thinks dormitories need to keep lounges and study rooms so students can have quiet places to escape to. When roommates get noisy, it's hard to study for exams in one's own room. That's why she's against converting those rooms into big dorm rooms. The other point the woman makes is that, although she is opposed to converted rooms, if there must be converted rooms, they shouldn't be given to first-year students because they're located in isolated parts of the building. First-year students should be assigned regular rooms so that they can meet people and have a normal experience. Second-year students can volunteer to stay in the converted rooms.

14 University Services—Health Center, Cafeteria and Library
大學服務——健康中心、餐廳和圖書館

模擬試題① 🎧 *Track 071*

A student named Mark has written a letter to the college newspaper, praising the food in the new food court. In the letter, the student talks about how popular the food court is and how it's a "win-win" project for the administration and students. From the conversation, we know that the woman doesn't share Mark's point of view. She admits that many students will find the food court's food choices attractive. However, she has two criticisms. First, she thinks the vendors at the food court are providing food that isn't healthy. For example, fried foods that are high in fat. Second, she suspects that the college administration and vendors care mostly about bringing in money, and so are not thinking about nutrition. She believes that the college should hire a nutrition expert. This expert could work with food court vendors.

模擬試題② 🎧 *Track 074*

The woman is not at all happy with the new library policy. She believes that reducing the borrowing period to one month is unwise. In her opinion, if the problem is there aren't enough books for all the undergraduate students, that problem won't be solved by buying multiple copies of books for the core subjects. Her reasoning is that there are just too many branches of academic knowledge. The library can't possibly get multiple copies of all the books on specialized topics. The woman's other point is that the new borrowing period is not practical and won't be obeyed. One month is too short. She predicts that, in the future, students will simply ignore a book's due date and keep the book till they're through using it. When students start ignoring the due date, it will become difficult for everyone to keep track of the books.

15 University Services—Housing, Transportation and Facilities Management
大學服務──住宿、交通和設施管理

模擬試題① 🎧 *Track 078*

A student has written a letter in order to address the parking problem on campus. She describes how the main parking lot, which is close to campus buildings, is always full, while B-Lot, the far parking lot, is always empty. She questions the logic of charging the same monthly fee for both parking lots. Her proposal is to charge more for the nearby main lot, and less for the far lot. The man, who is a commuter student, supports this proposal. First, he thinks having a different fee structure makes economic sense. A nearby parking spot is more convenient and so should be more expensive. Second, he thinks resident students will be willing to park far away because they don't use their cars that often. If the fee is low, they won't mind walking to their cars. The man adds that he thinks resident students should have to pay a little more for parking than commuter students, no matter what lot.

模擬試題② 🎧 *Track 081*

The woman is critical of the university's plan for building maintenance. Her biggest concern is that an eight-year plan is too long a plan. She believes the scale of the problem is very large, and so more should be done in a shorter period of time. For example, the university plans to do maintenance work on only two buildings next year. And one downside of waiting so long to fix all the old buildings is that emergency repairs will have to be done. Emergency repairs are more expensive and more disruptive to people's lives. In addition to this criticism, the woman thinks the proposed plan does not consider energy use. In other words, they're not thinking about the energy that will be wasted in the old buildings. She believes the university should do the necessary maintenance on all the buildings in just two years to save on the cost of energy.

16 University Course Offerings 大學課程設置

模擬試題① 🎧 *Track 085*

The university has released an announcement regarding the cancellation policy for fall classes. The woman is disgusted with the policy, especially since her Honors Seminar in World History was one of the classes that was suddenly canceled. Not surprisingly, one of her main criticisms is that the classes are canceled very late—after the schedule is already in place. This makes it extremely difficult to find a suitable replacement. The woman also takes issue with the fact that the university advertises many elective classes, but then doesn't feel it has to actually give the classes. This is, in the woman's opinion, "false advertising," and is not fair. She's afraid she'll now have to take a class that she really doesn't like simply because it fits into her schedule.

模擬試題② 🎧 *Track 088*

The man praises the university's new plan to add a new music theory program to the School of Music. He believes that the requirements for this master's degree are appropriate. For example, one of the requirements for the master's degree in Music Theory is that candidates submit a musical work that they have composed. The man thinks this is a good idea, his rationale being that the ability to write music is related to the knowledge of music theory. The other requirement for the new program is basic proficiency in piano. The man endorses this requirement as well. Even if a person excels at theory, he or she needs to play piano. For example, when music theory specialists teach theory, they need to be able to illustrate examples on the piano. Moreover, the man says that having basic skills in piano is necessary for any person studying music.

17 Student Affairs 學生活動

模擬試題① 🎧 *Track 092*

The woman is not pleased with the university's new plan requiring that all students complete twenty hours of community service as a graduation requirement. She thinks that volunteer work should be optional for students, not required. In her own case, she doesn't think she has the time for community service because she works so many hours in her part-time job. She works this job because tuition costs are high and she owes money. That is all the more reason why she considers the time she has left to study precious. She wants to spend her few free hours studying so that she can get good grades, and also so she can learn as much as she can during her college years.

模擬試題② 🎧 *Track 095*

In the first student council election, some students didn't get ballots e-mailed to them, so the university is holding a new election. The woman thinks the plan to hold a new election is a waste of time. She bases her opinion on the fact that only a few students didn't get ballots. Moreover, in her experience, not very many students vote in the student council elections anyway—so those few votes were probably not going to make a difference. The other, more important, reason she holds this opinion is that the candidates who came out as winners in the first election won by a substantial percentage—by forty percent. This was confirmed by the Dean of Student Affairs. For these reasons, the woman thinks holding a new election is not going to be a meaningful activity.

18 Student Employment and Internships 打工與實習

模擬試題① 🎧 *Track 099*

The woman thinks that the law internship requirement at State College is unnecessary. She tells the man that, based on her experience last summer, internships are a waste of time. She says that interns are only given basic tasks like filing and data entry. As a result, interns don't learn anything important. Her other criticism of the internship requirement is that it takes up too much time. Not only are the three months a waste of time, they keep students from earning real money, money that could be saved for tuition and housing. She explains to the man that even though the companies say the intern positions are "paid," the salary is very small. The only reason she did her law internship was to be eligible for using the Job Placement Services at State College.

模擬試題② 🎧 *Track 102*

The university has changed its policy of using only graduate students as tutors in the Math Center. Now they will start hiring undergraduate students as well. The man, who is a graduate student himself, is sorry to hear this news. His line of reasoning is as follows. First, he thinks that graduate students should have priority for jobs like this because it's not easy to find appropriate jobs. He thinks that undergraduate students should take jobs off campus. The man's second point relates to the quality of instruction at the Math Center. He thinks that, generally speaking, graduate students are better qualified to serve as tutors in the various types of math and statistics. With undergraduate tutors, students may not learn as much.

19 School Deadlines 學校活動的期限

模擬試題①　🎧 *Track 106*

The woman is worried that she won't be able to finish her history paper on time. The deadline is two days from now, but because she has to be in a basketball game out of town, she'll be busy. One solution to this problem is that her basketball coach can talk to her professor, to help her get an extension for the paper. The other thing she can do is staying up working all night, so she can turn in the paper before she leaves. If it were me, I would ask my coach to explain the situation to the professor, so I could get more time. Because the playoffs are important to the university, the professor should be willing to let her turn in her paper a little bit late.

模擬試題②　🎧 *Track 109*

The man's problem is that he missed a deadline to sign up for an online math test. He needs to take the test in order to take a business economics class. The woman offers two solutions. Her first suggestion is for him to take the online exam the second time it's administered, which will be in the summer. Her second suggestion is to talk with a professor in the Business School to see if he can take a pencil and paper math test instead of the computer test. I think the man should try to take a pencil and paper test before summer. That way, he won't have to make an extra trip back to campus from his hometown just to take the test. Also, when he talks with the professor, he can learn more about the business economics seminar and see if the professor can give him other advice.

20 Scheduling Conflicts 時間衝突

模擬試題①　🎧 *Track 113*

The woman just became aware that she has a scheduling conflict. She's scheduled to give a paper in New York next Friday, but on that same day she's supposed to teach an honors class in archaeology. While chatting with the man, she considers two possible solutions. First, she can reschedule the archaeology class for sometime over the weekend—before their midterm the following week. The second option is for her to find another professor to teach the class on Friday. My choice would be to find a replacement teacher who knows some archaeology. I would write down a detailed lesson plan so that teacher could know exactly what to do during the class. The reason I wouldn't try to schedule the class over the weekend is that it would be very difficult to get everybody together then. A lot of students have part-time jobs or other commitments on weekends.

模擬試題②　🎧 *Track 116*

The man registered for classes online but now there's a time conflict between two of his classes. His organic chemistry lab section and his required writing class are at the same time, so he needs to change his schedule. He's considering two possible solutions. The first is to switch class times with a student in another lab section. The problem with that option is that the professor doesn't like students to trade places. Also, the man has to get the professor's signature before he can change sections. The other possibility is for the man to wait for someone to drop out of organic chemistry and then take his place. However, this is very risky and students usually wait until after the first exam. Personally, I would find a student to switch places with and then start going to the lab section. After the first week, I would go with the other student and beg the professor for permission to trade places.

21 Problems with Transportation and Buildings 交通及房屋問題

模擬試題① 🎧 *Track 120*

The man's problem is that the rock band that was supposed to perform this weekend at the concert hall has just canceled. The man has to figure out how to handle the situation. He talks about two possible actions. The first alternative is to reschedule the rock band for a later date and offer the ticket buyers refunds. However, he would still have to pay the concert hall a fee for this weekend. The second alternative is to quickly find another band to perform this weekend, instead of the original band. The solution I prefer is to contact an agent and try to book another band for this weekend. My reasoning is that there are lots of good bands. As long as the band is fairly popular, students who've already bought tickets will probably come to the concert. Although I'd have to do some last-minute advertising, I would not waste the money I paid to the concert hall.

模擬試題② 🎧 *Track 123*

The woman has recently moved into a new apartment and she's discovered that there are a lot of problems with the plumbing. The kitchen sink and the bathroom have major problems. The plumber, who has made a house call to the apartment, tells her how much the repairs will cost, including the fee for making a house call. The woman doesn't want to pay the bill herself. The repairman makes two suggestions to her. First, he suggests that she call the landlord and persuade him to pay the bill for the repairs. The repairman's second suggestion is for her to call a mediator at the university to help resolve the dispute. I think the woman should call the university mediator and ask for advice. The mediator may know the landlord and be able to persuade him better than she could.

22 Mistakes and Accidents 失誤與意外

模擬試題① 🎧 *Track 127*

The problem the woman has is that her landlord believes her cat has stained the carpet in her apartment. She is moving out and the landlord wants her to pay for replacing the carpet. However, the woman is not convinced that the stains were from her cat. She discusses two courses of action with her friend. The first is to tell the landlord to take her deposit and apply it to cleaning the carpet. The second course of action is for her to go to court. She could ask for proof of inspection reports and carpet receipts. I would choose the former course of action, because it is quicker and less hostile. Even though I'd be giving up my four hundred dollars, I would hopefully be saving myself— and the landlord—a lot of time and trouble. If the carpet wasn't especially new, he would probably be happy to take the deposit money and be done with the issue.

模擬試題② 🎧 *Track 130*

The man has sprained his ankle and is going to have trouble getting around. Midterm exams are next week, so it's an important time for studying. On top of that, he's an engineering student and his building is quite far away. The man thinks that one solution might be to use a motorized cart. He could put his crutches and books in it and drive the cart to class. But he doesn't know if a cart is available. The woman suggests he consider moving into Miller Dorm, which is very close to the engineering building. This would be convenient, but a room might not be available and moving is a hassle. If I were the man, I would explore the possibility of moving into Miller Dorm. If I could persuade the university to let me move there, I would get one of my classmates to help me move. That way, I could spend more time focusing on studying and recovering, without having to worry about transportation.

23 Financial and Other Resource Shortages 資金與其他資源的短缺

模擬試題① Track 134

The two professors are concerned about the rising cost of the marine biology field camp. The camp is a required activity, and they are afraid that some students won't be able to afford the fees. The man comes up with two ways of cutting costs. The first way is to shorten the camp from four weeks to three. This would be cheaper, but would impact some of the experiments. The other idea is to not rent research boats, which are expensive. However, then students couldn't do deep water activities. This is a tough choice, but if it were mine to make, I'd shorten the camp period to three weeks. It's important to rent the research boat, so students can see deep water marine life. This is a rare opportunity for young scientists. Perhaps some of the original activities that are omitted could be done in the classroom, using computers.

模擬試題② Track 137

The woman's problem is that she has to make a choice between two universities. She's been accepted to two engineering schools—one at a top-tier university and the other at City College, a school that isn't very famous. The problem is that the top-tier school did not offer her any money, whereas City College offered her a full scholarship. If she goes to the top-tier school, she might be able to get a better job, but she'll owe a lot of money. If she goes to City College, she won't have any debts, but she might not learn as much. If this were my decision, I would take the full scholarship at City College. This way, I could graduate without owing any money. Moreover, because engineering is a practical field, I think that an engineering degree from a less prestigious university like City College is still very valuable.

24 People Problems 人際關係問題

模擬試題① Track 141

The woman is disappointed to learn that her master's thesis advisor is going to Hong Kong for one year. She's afraid that it will make it very difficult to communicate with her about her thesis. The advisor mentions two possibilities to the woman. She has spoken with a colleague, who's agreed to take on the woman as a student. However, his specialty is networking, which is not the same as hers. The advisor says the only other option is to advise the woman over the Internet, using e-mail and other electronic means. But the woman isn't sure if this would be enough to really help her. If this were my choice, I would continue to work with Doctor Anderson while she was overseas. I would do this because we know each other and I trust her. Furthermore, she's knowledgeable about my field, computer translation. I would find a way to make technology work—perhaps through video-conferencing.

模擬試題② Track 144

The problem the man faces is the student director of his play has suddenly walked out on the play. The man has written this play for his senior thesis and doesn't know what to do. The woman recommends the man direct the play himself as he's familiar with the play. The man would like to direct the play, but is nervous about taking on more work. The woman then recommends that he persuade the student director to come back. The man wonders if the director will stay calm. Personally, I would choose the latter option, getting the director to stay on. For one thing, the student director is the more talented director, even if he's moody. Using this approach, I could focus on my paper. I'd probably also meet with the actors and urge them to act more professionally.

25 Physical Sciences 物理科學

模擬試題① 🎧 *Track 148*

The professor talks about some of the problems caused by irrigation systems. The first example of irrigation that she mentions is flood irrigation, in one form of which farmers quickly cover the entire surface of the soil by water, as if the soil were under a pond. One problem with flood irrigation is that a lot of water is wasted—when water evaporates and when it soaks into the soil outside the growing area. The other type of irrigation that the professor mentions is drip irrigation, irrigation that takes place under the surface of the ground. One possible problem with drip irrigation is that it can cause the salts in the soil to increase, especially around the root area. This problem with salt concentration is particularly serious in arid climates.

模擬試題② 🎧 *Track 151*

In his lecture, the professor talks about two properties of sound waves. One property is related to loudness and the other is frequency—how fast waves move. He asked two groups of students to do an experiment, to use sound waves to make a wine glass break. To do this, the students needed to determine the natural frequency of the wine glass. Then they were supposed to use a recording of a singer's voice and adjust it. Group One was successful. They broke the glass by adjusting the pitch of the singer's voice and then playing it loud enough. However, Group Two failed to break the glass. Group Two thought the glass might have been too thick. But the professor said maybe they did not set the singer's voice at the correct frequency.

26 Humanities and the Arts 人文藝術

模擬試題① 🎧 *Track 155*

In his lecture, the professor points out several characteristics of medieval romances. The focus of the romances was usually a mysterious knight who was on a quest and who was performing heroic deeds. The knight was often in disguise. The heroes in medieval romances were supposed to be both courteous and brave. The professor says the tale of Sir Gareth is typical of a medieval romance because it contains many of these characteristics. For example, Gareth disguised his identity. Even though Gareth had noble blood, he pretended to be a beggar. Gareth's quest was that he wanted to become a knight. He defeated many knights but was always fair to them. This sense of fairness is also typical of knights in medieval romances.

模擬試題② 🎧 *Track 158*

Installation art is a type of art in which objects are arranged in a space. The installations can be permanent or temporary, indoors or outdoors. The artist uses installation art to make viewers interact with the objects and think. Installation artists use non-traditional materials, including everyday objects and industrial materials. The example of Will Ryman is his installation of a city garden. A key point was that the roses in the garden were very large, larger than scale. That means when people go to the exhibit, they feel smaller, as if they were rats in the garden. The installation also had ugly objects like old cigarettes that had been thrown away. Ryman's exhibit illustrates how an installation artist can change the perspectives of a viewer. In addition, it illustrates how installations use industrial materials to make viewers think about what a city garden really is. Many rose sculptures were unfinished and raw. This makes viewers think about the process of art and the process of construction in the city.

27 Life Sciences 生命科學

模擬試題① 🎧 *Track 162*

Seed dormancy refers to the period of inactivity that a seed goes through before germinating. Seeds contain extra food and have a dormant period to protect them. The professor talks about her dogwood tree to illustrate how some seeds need to be exposed to certain conditions before they leave the dormant period. In the case of the professor, she wanted to grow baby plants from the seeds of her dogwood tree. To do this, she needed to allow the seeds to be dormant. But she also needed to expose the seeds to moisture and cold, to imitate winter. She put her dogwood seeds into moist sand and then put them in the refrigerator. In this way, she made the seeds break dormancy so they could germinate in her greenhouse. The professor showed that seed dormancy often includes requirements that protect seeds from extreme climates.

模擬試題② 🎧 *Track 165*

Wolves live in packs which have a specific social order. The hierarchy of wolf packs is based on social dominance. The alpha wolves—a dominant male and a dominant female—are the most dominant wolves in the pack. The professor describes how the alpha wolves behave when interacting with the other wolves. Alpha wolves are not dominant because they are bigger or stronger, but because of their confident attitude. When other wolves meet the alpha wolves, they must communicate signals that they are submissive to the alpha wolves. A dominant wolf will stand up straight, and a submissive one will crouch down. Even though the dominant alpha wolf has the power to choose what he or she wants to do, the alpha wolves don't always exercise those rights. For example, the lecturer talks about how alpha wolves sometimes decide to go hunting for prey and the rest of the pack follows, but at other times, the alpha wolves do not act as leaders and it's the younger members of the pack who decide to go hunting.

28 Social Sciences 社會科學

模擬試題① 🎧 *Track 169*

Buzz marketing is a marketing activity that uses social networks and everyday people to create excitement about a product or service. Examples are blogs and special events. The professor says it's very important to use buzz marketing correctly and gives examples of a good way and a bad way to use this technique. In his first example, he talks about an ice cream company which had a special event called "free ice cream day." This event created a lot of buzz, so that people started talking to each other about it and the media wrote about it. The impact on the company was positive. The other example was an example of a failed buzz marketing campaign. A cleaning products company wanted to promote its products. It created a false identity for a man, who pretended to be a normal person sending posts to others about personal problems. However, the public found out it was fake and got really angry. This buzz marketing campaign had a negative impact on the company.

模擬試題② 🎧 *Track 172*

Human beings are not the only ones who can use and make tools, as scientists are discovering more and more. The professor gives an example of a series of research experiments being done with New Caledonian crows. These crows live on islands in the South Pacific Ocean and have special abilities to solve problems. Researchers have observed these crows using tools in an experiment where the crows had to choose the right-sized stick to get food. They could choose sticks of the right width and length, showing a skill in using tools. In another experiment, researchers observed the crows actually creating tools. For example, a crow could create a hook out of a piece of wire so it could get some meat in a bucket. In several settings, the crow demonstrated it could customize tools made of different materials, including tools of leaves and metal.

29 Physical Sciences 物理科學

模擬試題① 🎧 *Track 176*
The professor introduces two types of wind: Sea breezes and land breezes. Sea breezes blow from the ocean to land during the day. Land breezes blow from the land out to the ocean at night. There are two reasons why this happens. First, the heat capacity of land and water is different. When the Sun shines, the land heats up faster than the water, making the air on land get hotter, too. That's the second reason why the two winds act differently—air temperature and pressure. Hot air rises, so in the daytime, the land air rises and the cooler sea air comes over to land, causing sea breezes. At night, it's the opposite—the land air gets cool and the sea air stays warm. When the warm sea air rises, the land air moves toward the sea, causing land breezes.

模擬試題② 🎧 *Track 179*
Lakes last a relatively short time compared to other water bodies. As the lecture points out, lakes have a natural aging process. When a lake is new, the water is clear because there aren't many nutrients for plants to live on. But later on in the lake's development, algae grow in the warm, shallow parts of the water. Then bacteria start to grow because they feed on dead algae. The bacteria use up most of the oxygen so the plant matter can't completely decompose, and it sinks, becoming sediment. That provides lots of nutrients for other plants, which grow and die. This cycle repeats itself, so that finally the lake turns into a wetland. Sometimes the wetland will turn into a meadow. Humans cause the natural aging process to take place more rapidly.

30 Humanities and the Arts 人文藝術

模擬試題① 🎧 *Track 183*
In this lecture, the River Thames is used as an example of how a river influences the development of a city. The professor emphasizes two ways in which rivers influence cities. The first factor is that rivers are usually places where marketplaces exist. For example, a city may be built where shipped goods are being handed off to smaller boats or where bridges are built. Ever since the Romans occupied London, the Thames has been used to ship goods in and out. The market activity has led to a good economy. The second important factor the professor points out is that rivers serve as boundaries or borders. Because invaders want to occupy the prosperous cities by rivers, the residents need to find ways to defend themselves. The Romans were able to get into London by building a bridge. Later, they built forts and defensive walls in London, which became the boundaries of the city for many years.

模擬試題② 🎧 *Track 186*
Using coils of clay and using a potter's wheel are two different methods for making pottery. Coiling is an ancient method. In coiling, the artist takes rolls of clay and piles them on top of each other. Then the artist blends the coils together. The potter's wheel is another way that artists create pots. The potter puts a ball of clay in the middle of the wheel and turns it. Then the clay is squeezed up until a pot forms. The disadvantage of coiling is that it's a slow process. However, because it's slow, the artist can control the process better. Another advantage is that each pot is a unique work of art. For the potter's wheel, one advantage is that an artist can work very efficiently. In addition, because of the spinning force, the artist can create pots that look like one another. This is ideal for artists who want to make matching dishes.

31 Life Sciences　生命科學

模擬試題① 🎧 *Track 190*

Scientists believe that seahorses appeared about 25 million years ago, after two continents collided. At that time, the floor of the ocean was raised and the water became shallow. These conditions were good for seagrass. Seahorses evolved at that time from pipefish. Seahorse bodies had two major changes from pipefish. First, seahorses developed tails which could grab onto the seagrass. This means that seahorses could stay in the grass and wait for food to swim by. In this way, seahorse bodies started being vertical. The other aspect of the seahorse that evolved was the S-shape of its body. Because of the S-shape, the seahorse was able to reach its neck out farther than the pipefish. This allows the seahorse to attack its prey quickly and from far away.

模擬試題② 🎧 *Track 193*

Fires can have a positive influence on an ecosystem. For one thing, they open up space for new plants to grow. In addition, fires can improve the soil. The professor illustrates these two points by using the example of the Northern Forests. The Northern Forests are big forests located under the arctic tundra. Fires burn the trees in the Northern Forests to different degrees, but some trees are completely destroyed. This creates spaces and allows species that need sun to grow. The Jack pine is an example of this kind of plant. Furthermore, the Jack pine needs fire to reproduce because its seeds won't come out unless there's a very hot fire. Fires also benefit the soil in Northern Forests. The soil in the open spaces gets more light, so it's warmer in the daytime. More rain can get in as well. Also, there are nutrients in the ash left from the fire, which make it easier for many new plants to grow.

32 Social Sciences　社會科學

模擬試題① 🎧 *Track 197*

Symbols are of great importance in culture. We learn ideas and experiences from previous generations through symbol systems. Each culture shares symbols and communicates through them. The professor says the most important symbols are those in language. Words like "chair" are symbols for the actual objects. But everyone in the culture understands the meaning of "chair." The professor also talks about symbols that are objects. Here, the professor gives the example of clothing, including the styles and colors of clothing. In some cultures, men wear suits and ties. This dress code has meaning because the suits and ties are symbols, meaning that the men are important professionals. Another example of symbols in clothing is the color of the neckties. Red ties send a message of power, whereas dark blue neckties send a message of being serious. These symbols are shared by the wearers and the people who see the clothing.

模擬試題② 🎧 *Track 200*

Celebrity advertisements are very common nowadays. It is generally recognized that advertisements using famous spokespersons can cause viewers to want the product or service. The professor talks about several factors that make celebrity advertisements effective. The first factor is the trustworthiness of the celebrity. This is the most important factor in making people change their opinions and think positively about a product. Whether a customer has trust in the celebrity is more important than whether the spokesperson seems to know a lot about the product. The other factor mentioned by the professor is the attractiveness of the celebrity. Researchers have proven that attractive celebrities cause viewers to think positively about the spokesperson and the brand. However, just because viewers like these spokespersons does not mean they'll decide to buy the product.

13 ～ 32 章 聽力試題錄音原文

13 University Investments and Expenditures 大學的投資與支出

舉例試題 🎧 *Track 061*

(man) Student: I can't wait till the new wing of the library gets completed!

(woman) Student: Hey, don't hold your breath! It's two years away from now. Anyway, personally, I think the whole expansion concept is misguided.

(man) Student: Really? I thought it sounded pretty cool.

(woman) Student: Here's the problem—investing in hard-copy books is essentially an outdated concept. Most libraries nowadays are building up their electronic resources.

(man) Student: Yeah, I didn't hear anything about them acquiring e-books.

(woman) Student: Electronic books and journals wouldn't require any more physical shelf space. And they're easily upgraded!

(man) Student: I see your point.

(woman) Student: Plus, to tell you the truth, instead of more study space at the library, I'd rather see the university invest money in an addition to the student cafeteria! We need a place to study in that part of campus, and we could get food at the cafeteria during study breaks.

(man) Student: You should've shared your ideas with the planners before they finalized their plan!

模擬試題① 🎧 *Track 063*

(man) Student: Did you see the news about WXY-2—City University's radio station?

(woman) Student: No, what are they up to? I don't enjoy rock and roll that much.

(man) Student: Well, you should start listening! They're expanding their programming to other kinds of music—like jazz and folk music.

(woman) Student: Nice! I love jazz piano.

(man) Student: Think of all the opportunities that'll be created for students who want to learn how to be DJs and host radio programs!

(woman) Student: Yeah, you're probably right.

(man) Student: And with the expanded distribution to other communities, the station will need more work-study students to do the technical production work.

(woman) Student: But do the you think these new audiences—the non-university people in other listening areas—will actually listen to our station?

(man) Student: Definitely. What's more, I think this initiative will create a sense of unity between college students and the young people in the new listening areas. This will definitely bring our communities closer together.

模擬試題② 🎧 *Track 066*

(man) Student: Sally, you're a first-year student. What do you think of this letter?

(woman) Student: Frankly, I think it's a terrible idea.

(man) Student: Why's that?

(woman) Student: OK, it's true that there aren't enough dorm rooms. But we shouldn't take away lounges and study areas from the dorms. Students need those open rooms so they can get away from their roommates when it's noisy.

(man) Student: Yeah, especially when you have an exam and everyone else is in a party mood.

(woman) Student: Exactly. Or even if you just want to read quietly. It's quiet there.

(man) Student: Quiet is good.

(woman) Student: And the other thing is that the incoming first-year students shouldn't be put off in a corner, where those lounges are. More than anyone else, newcomers should be allowed to have normal experiences.

(man) Student: So are you saying that first-year students shouldn't be the ones to be assigned to converted rooms?

(woman) Student: Exactly. I mean, ideally, no one should have to stay in a converted room—it's an inferior situation. But it's especially bad for first-year students to have to stay there. If we really have to have converted spaces, we should ask for volunteers from second-year students, students who have already made a lot of friends and know their way around campus.

14 University Services—Health Center, Cafeteria and Library
大學服務──健康中心、餐廳和圖書館

舉例試題　🎧 *Track 068*

(woman) Student: Hey Peter. Been at the gym?

(man) Student: Yeah, I was playing a little basketball with my roommate.

(woman) Student: Speaking of sports, did you see the article about the health center?

(man) Student: On sports medicine? Yeah. I think the new policy's pretty reasonable, actually.

(woman) Student: Really! I'm surprised.

(man) Student: Hey, athletics are important to this university. They want the players to be successful.

(woman) Student: It's true—our teams always seem to be ranked pretty high.

(man) Student: Right. Well, if we want to keep recruiting elite athletes, we need to give them top sports medicine facilities when they come.

(woman) Student: That makes sense.

(man) Student: Plus, these days everyone's doing some sort of physical exercise. Whether it's running or working out. And then they get injured. The Sports Medicine Clinic probably couldn't handle all the patients.

(woman) Student: Hmm, maybe.

(man) Student: Anyway, I think it's natural for a large university like ours to reserve its best sports medicine facilities for team athletes.

模擬試題① 🎧 *Track 070*

(woman) Student: Hey Ed. Wanna grab a bite?

(man) Student: I've already eaten—fried chicken and French fries over at the food court.

(woman) Student: Not you, too! You probably agree with the guy who wrote the letter in today's newspaper.

(man) Student: What, you don't like the food court?

(woman) Student: OK, the new eating area is shiny and beautiful. And they've contracted with lots of vendors. But very few of the food choices are healthy.

(man) Student: Burgers and pizza seem to be what the market wants, though. That place is always buzzing.

(woman) Student: Just because people like junk food doesn't mean that it's good for them. All that grease and salt...

(man) Student: So, you don't think students should be able to choose what they eat?

(woman) Student: Put it this way—I think the college has the responsibility to provide healthy choices: lean meats, fruit salads, yogurt...

(man) Student: You sound like my mom: "Watch what you eat!"

(woman) Student: [laughing] Seriously. But another thing—I feel like the administration and the vendors are working together just to make money.

(man) Student: So, you think the college only cares about profit?

(woman) Student: Maybe they're just trying to balance the budget. But at minimum they should hire a nutrition expert to work with the vendors—to make sure students are offered a balanced diet that's low-fat, low-salt and low-sodium.

模擬試題② 🎧 *Track 073*

(man) Student: Laura, did you happen to read the announcement about the library lending period being shortened?

(woman) Student: I did, and I'm still fuming.

(man) Student: The library director seems to think it's a good thing.

(woman) Student: Of course that's what she's saying. But one month isn't enough time to use a book to research a term paper. It can take a couple weeks just to plough through a book on an unfamiliar subject.

(man) Student: Hmm. They're supposedly buying more books in the core subjects—I guess that means books related to required undergraduate courses, like psychology.

(woman) Student: Supplying multiple copies of a few titles won't address the need. Just think of all the specialized subjects a student might want to write on! Even in psychology, there's just too many branches of academic research.

(man) Student: So you don't think acquiring multiple copies is the answer, huh.

(woman) Student: It'll help in some cases, but not all. Besides, I think a one-month borrowing period is so unrealistic that it'll create more problems.

(man) Student: What do you mean?

(woman) Student: We all know what students do when they seriously need a library book. They ignore the due date and keep it till they've finished the paper. Trust me, the library's gonna start seeing a lot more overdue books—and no one'll ever know when the book is really coming back.

15 University Services—Housing, Transportation and Facilities Management
大學服務——住宿、交通和設施管理

舉例試題 🎧 *Track 075*

(man) Student: Hi Tiffany. How's everything?

(woman) Student: Not great. Did you read that announcement about the housing lottery?

(man) Student: Yeah, the deadline is coming up.

(woman) Student: The lottery's supposed to be fair. But personally I think the idea is really poorly conceived.

(man) Student: Really? Aren't they just trying to take care of the incoming freshmen—the ones who don't know the way around?

(woman) Student: Saving some rooms for freshmen is fine. But having a lottery for returning students creates chaos. It's impossible to plan ahead. Take my roommate Susan and me for example.

(man) Student: Do you two want to share a dorm room again?

(woman) Student: If possible. But, let's say Susan gets an early lottery space and chooses one dorm, but I end up getting a bed space in another dorm. There's no good way that she and I can coordinate under this system.

(man) Student: Yes, that's awkward.

(woman) Student: And, even if I wasn't trying to room with somebody specific, I'd still be in trouble if I got put on the waiting list.

(man) Student: Why is that?

(woman) Student: If you're lucky, waiting doesn't matter. But what if I wait till summer for some student to forfeit her space—and it doesn't happen? By that time, all the good, cheap apartments will be rented out.

(man) Student: So you'd be stuck. You'd have to rent a really expensive room.

(woman) Student: Yeah! Or a horrible, cheap room. It's not worth the risk. I'd be better off looking for a nice cheap room with a compatible roommate starting now...

模擬試題① **Track 077**

(woman) Student: Hey Mike. How come you were late to class?

(man) Student: I couldn't find a parking place in the main lot. I don't mind commuting to school, but parking's always a hassle.

(woman) Student: So what did you think of the letter in the newspaper—proposing changing the fees?

(man) Student: I'm in total favor of it.

(woman) Student: How come? I'd have thought you'd be concerned about any fee increase.

(man) Student: For one thing, having a different fee structure makes sense from an economic perspective. I mean, a convenient nearby parking spot is worth more! And it's a waste of university resources to have those hundreds of spots in B-Lot go unused.

(woman) Student: Yeah, but nobody wants to walk all the way from the far lot.

(man) Student: That's just the thing. A lot of student cars are owned by resident students—many of whom don't use their cars very often. Their cars just sit there most of the time.

(woman) Student: You think those guys are gonna be willing to park out in B-Lot?

(man) Student: Definitely, if the monthly fee is attractive enough. And quite frankly, I don't think resident students should be paying the same fee as commuter students anyway.

(woman) Student: What do you mean?

(man) Student: If I had my way, I'd make both the main lot and the far lot cheaper for commuters than for residents. We have to use cars every time we come to class.

模擬試題②  **Track 080**

(woman) Student: Did you see this article? What a joke.

(man) Student: Well, the buildings are all pretty old. The basement in the Humanities Building flooded just last week.

(woman) Student: Right! The infrastructure is crumbling and there's a huge need. But did you notice? They're only fixing two buildings next year.

(man) Student: Yeah, I guess you're right. They're just scratching the surface.

(woman) Student: So my biggest criticism of the plan is that it's spread over eight years. That's just too long, and a lot of the pipes will break.

(man) Student: Well, they can always fix them after they break...

(woman) Student: Bad idea. If you wait till there's an emergency, repairs always cost more. And emergencies make everyone's lives crazy.

(man) Student: That's true.

(woman) Student: And my other complaint about this plan is that it doesn't take sustainability into consideration. These old buildings waste an awful lot of energy. You can't say they support sustainability.

(man) Student: You mean the fact that these buildings aren't energy efficient... The windows and heating systems and stuff aren't good in winter.

(woman) Student: Right. These old buildings waste a ton of energy. If the university borrowed money to make the infrastructure repairs in all the buildings in, say, two years, the savings in energy costs alone would be worth it.

16 University Course Offerings 大學課程設置

舉例試題  **Track 082**

(woman) Student: Oliver, you're taking a class online, aren't you?

(man) Student: Yeah, macroeconomics. I hate the fact that there are fifteen hundred of us sitting in our dorms, listening to the professor go on about inflation.

(woman) Student: Oh, I suppose you must disagree with the letter in today's newspaper then.

(man) Student: The person who wrote that obviously isn't a very serious student. I mean, there's a lot more to learning than just taking notes. Face-to-face contact is important.

(woman) Student: I know. I enjoy being able to interact with my teachers.

(man) Student: Not to mention the personal interactions with other students. It's very motivating.

(woman) Student: But you're learning from your online class, aren't you?

(man) Student: Yeah, I guess, but only 'cause I've been studying the economics textbook. But Spanish is a language—how are people supposed to learn to actually speak it without having other people around?

(woman) Student: Well...

(man) Student: There's no way that you can practice conversational Spanish sitting at your laptop. University language courses just shouldn't be taught online.

(woman) Student: You have a point there, Oliver.

模擬試題① 🎧 *Track 084*

(man) Student: Did you register yet?

(woman) Student: I did, but then I was told my Honors Seminar in World History got canceled! And classes start in two days!

(man) Student: Yeah, I saw the announcement today. That's tough.

(woman) Student: The way they handle cancellations is worse than awful. It's just sad. I was gonna use that world history class for one of my electives.

(man) Student: It's kinda inconvenient at this late date.

(woman) Student: [sarcastically] Well, yeah! The university can suddenly cancel a class for any reason they want. Then we have to scramble to find another class that fits in our schedule.

(man) Student: Yeah, you're sort of locked in.

(woman) Student: And what really irritates me is that the course catalog contains this impressive, long list of all these great classes to choose from. It's false advertising, in a way.

(man) Student: [in disbelief] You think?

(woman) Student: I guess what I'm saying is, I don't think the university is truly committed to offering most electives. They don't seem to take course selection seriously.

(man) Student: I hear ya.

(woman) Student: So now I'm probably going to end up taking some stupid class I'm not even interested in, just because it's on Tuesday and Thursday afternoons.

模擬試題② 🎧 *Track 087*

(woman) Student: So what do you think of the new master's degree program?

(man) Student: In Music Theory? It's about time! This music school needs a program specializing in theory.

(woman) Student: You think it'll attract any students? The requirements are pretty tough.

(man) Student: Students studying music theory need to know how to write music. Music composition and music theory are closely related.

(woman) Student: They are?

(man) Student: Of course. No one can create a complex piece of music without knowing—and applying—the rules of music theory.

(woman) Student: And what about the piano requirement? That's not excessive?

(man) Student: No, it's completely reasonable.

(woman) Student: But, say, what if I'm brilliant in music theory, I know all the rules, but I can't play piano very well? That seems wrong.

(man) Student: It doesn't matter how brilliant you are. Every music student, no matter what level or what specialization, needs basic piano skills. How can a teacher demonstrate theory principles to students if he or she can't play the musical examples?

(woman) Student: I guess those music theory majors had better start practicing then.

17 Student Affairs　學生活動

舉例試題　🎧 *Track 089*

(woman) Student: Rick, you're a music major. What was your take on the letter in the newspaper?

(man) Student: [disgusted] Please. That student is so naive.

(woman) Student: You're not good with the new plan?

(man) Student: No. No way. First of all, there is no realistic way to avoid schedule conflicts. So having the university formally change class times is pointless.

(woman) Student: Hmm.

(man) Student: During the day, everybody's busy—music majors and people who join the music ensembles for fun.

(woman) Student: But what happens when people can't come to practice?

(man) Student: Hey, most of the conflicts are with non-music majors. So in my opinion, the best solution is for the university to start up more ensembles for non-majors—and they can rehearse after dinner.

(woman) Student: In the evenings, you mean?

(man) Student: Yeah. Non-majors should be free then. Plus evening rehearsals can run two—even three hours. So you get quality practice.

(woman) Student: And the people who have to work at nights?

(man) Student: We all have to make choices. If somebody really wants to play—or sing—in an ensemble, they'll find a way.

模擬試題①　🎧 *Track 091*

(woman) Student: I really was not overjoyed to hear that we're gonna have to do community service. I do enough work at my part-time job at the coffee shop.

(man) Student: I know—you put in a lot of hours. But don't you think volunteering is important?

(woman) Student: Helping people is fine, but volunteering should be optional. I mean, the tuition rate is skyrocketing!

(man) Student: I guess you're right.

(woman) Student: I've got student loans to pay back. That's just a fact.

(man) Student: You work really hard, I know.

(woman) Student: And because I put in so many hours on my part-time job, in the precious time remaining, I need to focus on my studies.

(man) Student: To keep your grade point average up?

(woman) Student: Yeah, that. And like, to just learn stuff. To take full advantage of my time in college.

(man) Student: Well, unfortunately, you're gonna have to squeeze in the time for community service now—or you won't be able to graduate.

模擬試題②　🎧 *Track 094*

(man) Student: Hey, congratulations on getting elected to the student council!

(woman) Student: Didn't you hear? They're holding new elections. It's so ridiculous.

(man) Student: The vote didn't count?

(woman) Student: But it should have! It's like this: A few students didn't get ballots.

(man) Student: Uh oh.

(woman) Student: Wait. You need to know that very few students actually vote in elections. So most of those students probably wouldn't have voted anyway!

(man) Student: Could be.

(woman) Student: And listen, this is even more important: The margins of victory for all the winning candidates—including me—were very high. Like forty-percent higher than the other candidates.

(man) Student: Sounds rather conclusive.

(woman) Student: Exactly. Which is why even the Dean of Student Affairs said the winners won by a "substantial margin."

(man) Student: [pause] But they're still reholding the election...

(woman) Student: Yeah. What a big waste of time.

18 Student Employment and Internships 打工與實習

舉例試題 🎧 *Track 096*

(woman) Student: Mac, are you going to be part of the used bookstore?

(man) Student: Yeah, I signed up to work there. I was really happy to see the letter of support in the paper today.

(woman) Student: Do you think a student-run business will be able to compete?

(man) Student: Absolutely.

(woman) Student: Even with the prices of books so low?

(man) Student: The bookstore won't make as much of a profit on each book, but they'll make it up in volume. I'm sure they'll get lots of customers. Students love bargains.

(woman) Student: I'll buy my textbooks there! Anything that helps to save money...

(man) Student: Hey, thanks! Everyone in the School of Business is really determined to make this little bookshop a success.

(woman) Student: Hmm... I wonder if students will have enough experience to make the right decisions. You know, judgment calls.

(man) Student: I'm sure there'll be moments when they need help. But the business professors will be acting as advisors, especially at the beginning.

(woman) Student: For free?

(man) Student: Of course! They want their students to learn as much as they can about business—in the classroom and in the real world.

模擬試題① 🎧 *Track 098*

(man) Student: I just signed up for the internship with Smith & Larson. Are you interested in that one, Nora?

(woman) Student: I did an internship last summer—thank god that requirement is over.

(man) Student: Why? It's supposed to be a great experience.

(woman) Student: The law companies always make it sound that way. But I did, like, nothing at that job. The work I got was basically filing and data entry.

(man) Student: You didn't learn anything?

(woman) Student: Not really. Certainly nothing remotely related to law. And that's the other thing—I feel like those three months could have been put to so much better use.

(man) Student: Oh yeah?

(woman) Student: Yeah. Like earning some real money. If I had worked as a waitress at a nice restaurant for all that time, I could have made a lot of money in tips.

(man) Student: You mean, to pay for tuition?

(woman) Student: Right. You'll soon find out that those so-called "paid internships" never pay very much.

(man) Student: So tell me again why you bothered doing an internship in the first place?

(woman) Student: Because I wanted to be able to use the college's Job Placement Services when it's time to find a job. That's the only reason.

模擬試題②  *Track 101*

(man) Student: I think this new hiring policy at the Math Center is so unwise.

(woman) Student: You do? If they expand the hiring pool, there'll be a lot more tutors available when students come in at peak times.

(man) Student: Hey! Think about it. You're a graduate student, like me! The Math Center has always been one of the ways for us to get financial aid.

(woman) Student: Even if the Math Center can't find enough tutors?

(man) Student: It's just not fair to give these money-making chances away to undergraduates.

(woman) Student: It's true that there aren't a lot of jobs for graduate students.

(man) Student: And another thing—the quality of teaching at the Center. I'm telling you, with this new approach, the university's going to end up with a lot of unqualified tutors.

(woman) Student: Some juniors and seniors really know their stuff.

(man) Student: Yes, a few. But not in all aspects of math and statistics.

(woman) Student: Well. We all have to pay our tuition.

(man) Student: Undergraduates should find other jobs, jobs off campus. Those jobs may even pay more, and employers in town are always looking for people.

19 School Deadlines 學校活動的期限

舉例試題  *Track 103*

(woman) Student: Hey Sam. How's your part-time job going? The weather's been so hot, I'll bet everybody's lining up to buy ice cream.

(man) Student: Yeah, it's been crazy. I've been working a lot of extra hours. In fact, I've been so busy that I totally forgot to send in my dorm application for the fall semester.

(woman) Student: Oh no! You missed the deadline for housing?

(man) Student: Yeah, can you believe it? The cut-off date for online applications was June first, and they're very strict. The housing people said they'd put me on the waitlist for dormitories, but I'm not optimistic.

(woman) Student: So what are you gonna do about housing in September?

(man) Student: Well, I was thinking I might just live at home next year. With no rent, I could save some money.

(woman) Student: I wonder... Your house is a two-hour drive to State College! All that driving! And with the price of gas as high as it is; that's a lot of money.

(man) Student: I know, I know.

(woman) Student: So do you have any other option?

(man) Student: Well, the university has a list of apartments near the campus, and so I called up a few places. Know what? They want over a thousand dollars a month for one of those!

(woman) Student: And I'll bet that's just the rent, without utilities like electricity and water.

(man) Student: Yeah, in some cases. Any way you spread it, it's a pain. And I don't have much time to make a decision.

模擬試題① *Track 105*

(man) Student: Hi Molly. How's it going?

(woman) Student: Things could be better. I've got a history paper to finish by Thursday morning—two days from now. I'm afraid I won't make the deadline.

(man) Student: Why not? You've got the rest of the day today and all tomorrow to finish it.

(woman) Student: Well, you may know that I'm on the women's basketball team and our team has advanced to the regional playoffs. So I have to travel out of state tomorrow to compete. I won't get back until late tomorrow night.

(man) Student: That's so exciting! But you do have a lot on your plate. Hmm. Can't you have your basketball coach talk to your professor? Have the coach ask him for an extension?

(woman) Student: I thought about that, but you know, the university policy about sports is that we're supposed to plan ahead and get our assignments done in advance.

(man) Student: But these are the playoffs—I mean, a competition like this is a special case. The university is proud of its sports successes.

(woman) Student: Yeah, but I don't think my history professor cares about sports. The other thing I thought of doing is staying up all night tonight and finishing the paper. If I keep working, I might be done by tomorrow morning.

(man) Student: I guess that's a possibility. But then you'll be exhausted. How will you be able to play basketball if you're all worn out?

(woman) Student: Maybe I can sleep on the bus on the way to the game.

(man) Student: Well, no matter what you decide, good luck!

模擬試題② 🎧 *Track 108*

(woman) Student: Hey John. How are things?

(man) Student: I thought I was so organized, but...

(woman) Student: What's wrong?

(man) Student: I didn't sign up to take the online mathematics test, and the deadline was yesterday. You know, everyone who wants to enroll in the business economics seminar is required to pass that test.

(woman) Student: Right. A friend of mine registered for that. The course will be offered in the fall, right? So, is this going to be a major problem for you?

(man) Student: I called the Business School departmental office, and they told me that they'll offer a second online exam this summer. The problem is, I wasn't planning on being here then—I'll be in my hometown working in a bank over the summer.

(woman) Student: Can't you travel back to campus just to take the test?

(man) Student: Maybe. But it's not really convenient. And ideally, I'd like to register for that business economics class before summer. It gets pretty full.

(woman) Student: Well, maybe you can talk with one of the professors in the Business School. See if you can find another way to demonstrate your competency in math.

(man) Student: Like what?

(woman) Student: I don't know—um, maybe you can take some sort of paper and pencil test as a make-up exam.

(man) Student: Huh. I hadn't thought of that. But I wonder if the paper and pencil test would be harder than the regular online one? I don't want to do badly.

(woman) Student: Yeah, it's a risk. On the other hand, it might be easier than the online test!

(man) Student: I'll just have to get more information before I make my decision.

20 Scheduling Conflicts 時間衝突

舉例試題 🎧 *Track 110*

(woman) Student: You're not eating any of your lunch—is something wrong?

(man) Student: Yeah, I'm trying to figure out what to do. Y'know how Bob has his big violin concert tomorrow evening?

(woman) Student: His solo recital at the Hall of Music. Everybody's going!

(man) Student: [awkwardly] Uh... everybody but me...

(woman) Student: What?! He's counting on you to be there. You two have been best friends forever.

(man) Student: I had every intention of going—and still want to, but my boss at the law firm told me this morning she wants me to do extra work. There's a client coming next Monday and they need me to pull together some materials.

(woman) Student: Why don't you go in to work early tomorrow, and get everything done in the afternoon? That way you'll be done and can go to the concert.

(man) Student: I don't know if that'd work. The law office where I work as an intern is all the way downtown, and the traffic is really bad Friday afternoons. [short pause] And I have a class in the morning.

(woman) Student: Or, you could find someone else to do this stuff. There must be other interns at this place.

(man) Student: Yeah, there's another guy on an internship from City College. I don't know if he'd be able—or willing—to do this work. And the other thing—I hate even saying this—I really want the lawyers at this firm to think highly of me.

模擬試題① 🎧 *Track 112*

(man) Professor: Diane, hello. You look stressed.

(woman) Professor: I just realized I've got a scheduling conflict and I'm not sure what to do about it.

(man) Professor: Anything serious?

(woman) Professor: Sort of. I'm supposed to give a paper in New York next Friday at a regional conference. I completely forgot about that commitment.

(man) Professor: That sounds important... So what's the conflict?

(woman) Professor: I teach my honors seminar Friday afternoons, in archaeology.

(man) Professor: Can you reschedule with them? That class can't be very large.

(woman) Professor: There are 15 students, so I could probably try to contact everybody. The problem is that their midterm exam is the following week, and that date is firm.

(man) Professor: I see. You'd have to offer the class over the weekend to give them enough time to study. Say, on Saturday afternoon?

(woman) Professor: Maybe, but they'd hate that. [short pause] One thing's for sure: I can't not go to New York!

(man) Professor: I hear you. Hey, have you thought about asking someone else to teach your honors class for you that day?

(woman) Professor: I'm not sure who'd be able to do this at the last minute. Are you volunteering? [laughing]

(man) Professor: No. [embarrassed] To be honest, I'm not comfortable teaching an honors-level class in archaeology. That's not really my field and those students must be pretty advanced. Anyone else you can call?

(woman) Professor: I'll have to think about it.

模擬試題② 🎧 *Track 115*

(woman) Student: Hey Mark! What's up?

(man) Student: Things are crazy. Yesterday I registered for classes online and everything was fine. But today I got an e-mail saying I have scheduling conflict.

(woman) Student: What! How is that even possible?

(man) Student: Apparently, this happens all the time—the chemistry department changes the times of lab sections at the last minute, which is why I suddenly have a conflict.

(woman) Student: Oh! Which of your courses overlaps with the organic chemistry lab?

(man) Student: A technical writing class I need to take in order to graduate. [pause] This is so annoying.

(woman) Student: For sure.

(man) Student: Maybe I could fix this situation by finding someone who's enrolled in a different lab section—and switch with them.

(woman) Student: So do it! Fast! Classes start next week!

(man) Student: Here's the thing: You can't swap sections without the professor's sign-off. All the lab sections are completely full and this professor hates it when students start switching back and forth.

(woman) Student: Hmm. Any other option?

(man) Student: Well, one of the Teaching Assistants told me there are usually a couple people who drop out of organic chemistry right after the first exam. I guess they can't handle it.

(woman) Student: So, you could wait and try to go into that open lab section when a slot opens up. Still, that way you'd miss several weeks of lab work.

(man) Student: Right. Or I'd have to skip my technical writing class for the first couple weeks. And who knows if the section I want will open up...

(woman) Student: Well, good luck, Mark. I'm sure things will work out.

21 Problems with Transportation and Buildings 交通及房屋問題

舉例試題 🎧 *Track 117*

(woman) Student: [in a phone call] Hello, Mark?

(man) Student: Ellen! You're calling really late. Aren't you going on a geology field trip early tomorrow morning?

(woman) Student: That's why I'm calling—I need your advice. I'm supposed to drive the geology department van for the trip—up into the mountains.

(man) Student: Ha! So, you're the lucky Teacher Assistant who gets to take the undergraduates to look at rocks.

(woman) Student: [laughing] Yeah. Well, I picked up the van this afternoon and packed up all the geology equipment.

(man) Student: OK. And?

(woman) Student: But on the way home, I had the air conditioner on and a red light went on. You know, the light that tells you when the engine is getting hot?

(man) Student: So you're concerned about the van overheating?

(woman) Student: It may be nothing serious, but I can't stop worrying. It's been so hot outside, and it's a long drive to the mountains.

(man) Student: [thinking] Hmm. What about calling up your advising professor? Maybe he can help you find another vehicle. Or at least give you some advice.

(woman) Student: I thought about that. But he's already up on the mountain, getting the geology lab ready. And it's late, he's probably already gone to bed.

(man) Student: Well, it could be just a problem with the light. Maybe there's nothing wrong with the engine. Maybe you can drive the van just the way it is and hope things are fine.

(woman) Student: That's definitely an option. But I feel like I'm responsible. And if the van breaks down, we'll lose a lot of time doing geology work on the mountain.

(man) Student: Well, get some sleep. I'm sure you'll do the right thing.

模擬試題① 🎧 *Track 119*

(woman) Student: Larry, what's up?

(man) Student: I just got some bad news. The rock band scheduled to perform on campus this weekend just canceled.

(woman) Student: Oh no! That concert was sold out months ago!

(man) Student: Exactly. I have to figure out really fast what to do. What to tell the concert hall. And what to tell the public.

(woman) Student: What do the university lawyers say?

(man) Student: The band is allowed, legally, to cancel any time if there is a serious illness. But after that, we have to decide if we want to book with them for another time.

(woman) Student: You mean, reschedule for next month?

(man) Student: Yeah. But even if we reschedule, we have to offer refunds to everyone who bought tickets. And we have to pay the concert hall for this weekend, even if we don't use it.

(woman) Student: Yikes!

(man) Student: The band that just canceled is really popular. But, maybe one way of handling this would be to find another good band to come and perform. I could call an agent today.

(woman) Student: Find someone else to play? Instead of the original band?

(man) Student: Yeah. That way we'd be able to provide entertainment and not waste the fee to the concert hall. The problem with that option is that we'd have to tell everyone we've made the switch.

(woman) Student: Which means a lot of PR, really fast.

(man) Student: Plus, we'd still have to give the ticket buyers the option of refunds, just in case they don't want to hear the new band. So, it's complicated.

模擬試題② 🎧 *Track 122*

(man) Repairman: So how long have you been living in this apartment? There's a lot wrong with it.

(woman) Student: I moved in a couple weeks ago, before classes started. Needless to say, when I signed the lease I had no idea there would be so many problems with the plumbing.

(man) Repairman: That's an understatement. The kitchen sink is leaking badly. The unit needs to be replaced. And the toilet pipes are totally rusted through.

(woman) Student: I know, I know. It's a disaster area. So how much will fixing all this stuff cost?

(man) Repairman: Well, it's seventy dollars for today's house call: Me being here today.

(woman) Student: What?!

(man) Repairman: And then to repair the kitchen sink and the toilet, let's see, materials and labor... Probably another six hundred dollars.

(woman) Student: I can't pay that. I mean, the landlord should have to pay for that. [nervous pause] Right?

(man) Repairman: I don't know the terms of your lease agreement...

(woman) Student: Gosh, I'm not sure what to do.

(man) Repairman: Um, well, I can't do any repairs till I find out who's going to pay me. So my first suggestion is that you call up your landlord and persuade him to give me the money.

(woman) Student: Maybe I'll be able to persuade him, but who knows? I mean, he let me move into the place this way.

(man) Repairman: And, well, there's another thing you can do. I've heard from other customers, in similar situations, that there's a mediation program at the university.

(woman) Student: You mean, someone who helps out with disputes between landlords and tenants?

(man) Repairman: Yup. So you might want to call that office.

(woman) Student: Oh. That's a possibility, I guess. But I don't wanna make the landlord angry if I can help it.

22 Mistakes and Accidents 犯錯與意外

舉例試題 🎧 *Track 124*

(woman) Student: You look terrible. Are you feeling OK?

(man) Student: No. I stayed up till 4 a.m. last night, studying for my math exam. Then I slept so hard that I overslept and woke up half way into the class.

(woman) Student: Oh no! That's not good.

(man) Student: Seriously! And I think I could have got an A on that thing. Should I shoot my professor an e-mail saying that I was sick and unable to attend class?

(woman) Student: You mean, flat-out lie?

(man) Student: Well, she has a strict policy about there not being any make-up exams for people who miss tests. So maybe if I tell her I had the flu, she'd be more sympathetic.

(woman) Student: I wonder if she'd ask you for a note from the doctors.

(man) Student: Hmm. Not every kid goes to a doctor every time they're sick.

(woman) Student: I'm just saying.

(man) Student: The other thing I thought I could do is to go and see her in person. Maybe during her office hours.

(woman) Student: And tell her the truth?

(man) Student: That's what I'm thinking. Maybe say, "I have no excuse for having overslept. But can I take a make-up exam?"

(woman) Student: I dunno. Every professor has a different personality. But she might not have any respect for someone who sleeps through an exam.

模擬試題① 🎧 *Track 126*

(man) Student: Sarah, hi! Did you get moved out of your apartment OK?

(woman) Student: Not exactly. I mean, I cleaned up the place yesterday, and everything seemed spotless to me.

(man) Student: So what's the problem?

(woman) Student: At inspection, my landlord pulled out a black light and it showed all sorts of stains on the carpet. He's saying my cat must have made the stains and he wants me to replace all the carpeting.

(man) Student: Wait, I'm confused: You couldn't see the stains with the naked eye?

(woman) Student: No. Just with the black light. And I don't even know if it really was my cat that had the accident. The previous tenant had cats, too. Or they could be some other stains, like food stains.

(man) Student: Gosh. What are you going to do now?

(woman) Student: Well, I paid a four-hundred-dollar deposit. So I might just ask the landlord to use that money for carpet cleaning services. That would be the easiest way to deal with this.

(man) Student: Will he be willing to do that?

(woman) Student: I'm not sure. So I may have to come up with another plan of action...

(man) Student: Which is?

(woman) Student: Well, my other option is to threaten to take him to court. First ask him to show me the inspection report from the last tenant. To prove to me that there weren't any stains there.

(man) Student: And...

(woman) Student: And then ask him to show me the dates that the original carpet was installed. If the carpet is four years old, for example, he has to charge me a lot less for replacement costs. The expected life of a carpet is only about five years.

(man) Student: Hey, maybe you should be studying law instead of biology!

模擬試題② 🎧 *Track 129*

(woman) Student: Rob, you're on crutches! What happened to you?

(man) Student: It's my ankle. I sprained it while I was working out yesterday. I shouldn't even be walking around now, actually. It's pretty swollen.

(woman) Student: Oh no! And right before midterm exams. What are you going to do about getting to class? The engineering building is, like, a mile away!

(man) Student: Good question. I was thinking about trying to borrow one of those little motorized carts. You know, that you can put your crutches in and drive around on campus.

(woman) Student: There's a lot of snow and ice outside now. Do you think you could maneuver one of those in this weather?

(man) Student: Maybe. And I don't even know for a fact if the university has any available right now.

(woman) Student: Hey, I have an idea! What about moving? I mean, Miller Dorm is right next to the engineering building. If you moved in there, you'd be really close.

(man) Student: I hadn't thought of that. [pause] Hmm. It's convenient, if they have any empty rooms. If the university would even let me do it.

(woman) Student: Well, it's a thought.

(man) Student: And the other thing about that option is having to actually move all my junk—my books, my clothes... Just thinking about it gives me a headache.

(woman) Student: Hmm. I guess it'll depend a lot on your recovery time. But one thing's for sure, midterms start on Monday.

23 Financial and Other Resource Shortages 資金與其他資源的短缺

舉例試題　🎧 *Track 131*

(man) Student: Hey Tara. What's up?

(woman) Student: I just got out of a staff meeting for the University Daily News. Our school newspaper is in big trouble financially.

(man) Student: Really? So many students and townspeople read the paper, I'd think you'd be in great shape.

(woman) Student: We just can't afford to buy paper—newsprint. Apparently there's a paper shortage in the market.

(man) Student: How about adding a classified advertisement section? You could sell ads and the money coming in from the ads might help cover the cost of newsprint.

(woman) Student: I don't know if businesses around here would advertise in a university newspaper. But it's definitely a possibility.

(man) Student: Or, you could do something more radical. [pause] What if you published an online edition of the paper?

(woman) Student: You mean, instead of the print version we do now?

(man) Student: Well, you could do online papers Monday through Friday, and maybe one print edition a week—on the weekend.

(woman) Student: Students all have computers, but I don't know if our entire readership would feel comfortable reading the news online.

(man) Student: You could do market research, see what people think. It would be cheaper than buying all that paper.

模擬試題① 🎧 *Track 133*

(woman) Professor: So, Jack, what are we going to do about the summer field camp? The costs have skyrocketed!

(man) Professor: I know. Four weeks of marine biology field camp is now going to cost a student over fifteen hundred dollars. And that doesn't include insurance!

(woman) Professor: That's a lot more than we paid last time. This trip is required, and some of the kids just won't be able to afford these fees.

(man) Professor: There are a couple things we might do. We could, for example, shorten the camp to three weeks, instead of the usual four. That would help some.

(woman) Professor: Yeah. But don't forget a lot of the experiments take a while to set up. We don't always find the marine specimens we need right away.

(man) Professor: Right. So if we did three weeks, we might have to stop working with hard-to-catch fish. We'd have to focus on more common marine life.

(woman) Professor: Hmm... Any other ideas of ways to cut costs?

(man) Professor: Just one. A big chunk of the cost of field camp is the rental of research boats. They're expensive, 'cause they've been fitted with labs and fancy equipment.

(woman) Professor: But don't we need those research boats for our deep water studies?

(man) Professor: Well, if we limited our activities to the marine life in shallow waters, we wouldn't need those big vessels. That way, maybe we could keep the camp at four weeks.

(woman) Professor: It would be such a shame not to go out into the deep water habitats. But it's definitely one other option.

模擬試題② 🎧 *Track 136*

(man) Student: Yo, Sarah! What's up? You seem kind of anxious...

(woman) Student: I just found out I was accepted at two engineering schools.

(man) Student: That's a good thing, isn't it?

(woman) Student: The problem is, I don't have enough money. I can't afford to pay for tuition.

(man) Student: Did you get any financial aid?

(woman) Student: That's just it. I got a full scholarship from City College, but as you know, it's not very prestigious. The other school that accepted me is a top-tier university. But they didn't offer me any money.

(man) Student: I see what you mean. So if you decide to go to the high-ranking school, you'll have to take out a student loan?

(woman) Student: Yeah. For all four years. That's a lot of money.

(man) Student: But if you go there, your engineering degree will be more prestigious when it's time to get a job. Worth more in the marketplace.

(woman) Student: Yeah, theoretically. But no guarantee. And I'll have a lot of pressure to pay back the loan.

(man) Student: And if you go to City College to get the full-ride scholarship, your education might not be as good... But you'll be going to college for free.

(woman) Student: Yup. That's the trade-off.

24 People Problems 人際關係問題

舉例試題 🎧 *Track 138*

(man) Student: [in a low voice] That guy sitting over there is so obnoxious, the way he keeps talking and laughing so loudly. I can't get any work done.

(woman) Student: I know. At this hour, the dorm computer lab is usually pretty deserted, but tonight's a nightmare.

(man) Student: Seriously, at this pace I don't know how I'm ever going to get this English paper finished. Of course, my laptop would break today of all days!

(woman) Student: Why don't you go find your Resident Assistant? She can tell him to quiet down.

(man) Student: It's almost two in the morning! She's probably sound asleep.

(woman) Student: I guess it is kind of late. But this seems pretty important...

(man) Student: Yeah. This paper is one-third of my grade. And I have to turn it in tomorrow morning at nine.

(woman) Student: Yikes.

(man) Student: Plus, if I go wake up the Resident Assistant, the guy is going to hate me. I don't want to get him into trouble. I just want him quiet.

(woman) Student: Well, to state the obvious—have you considered going back upstairs? Maybe your roommate would loan you his laptop.

(man) Student: Maybe. He was using it when I came down here. I don't know what he's doing now. If he's even awake any more...

(woman) Student: Well, if you want to have a decent paper written by morning, you'd better come up with a solution pretty fast.

模擬試題① *Track 140*

(man) Student: Hey Lisa. I haven't seen you around.

(woman) Student: I've been locked in my room doing research for my master's thesis. And the worst of it is, my advisor is leaving for Hong Kong for a whole year.

(man) Student: Oh, no! Doctor Anderson's going away? What are you gonna do?

(woman) Student: Well, I spoke with her this morning, and she recommended a colleague to me. She said this professor would have time to advise one more graduate student.

(man) Student: So that's cool.

(woman) Student: [not convinced] It should be OK...

(man) Student: You sound hesitant.

(woman) Student: It's just that this guy's research specialty is computer networking. And as you know, my thesis is on computer translation. They're pretty different fields.

(man) Student: I see what you mean. Did you voice your concern to Doctor Anderson?

(woman) Student: I did. She said the only other possibility would be for her to advise me over the Internet, through e-mail and stuff.

(man) Student: From Hong Kong? [pause] Well, you're both computer experts, so I guess communicating that way shouldn't be too difficult.

(woman) Student: E-mail is OK for some conversations. But I wonder if the Internet can replace working face to face in the lab. We're used to trying out ideas on super-fast computers and writing down our ideas on the white board.

模擬試題②  *Track 143*

(woman) Student: Larry, hello there!

(man) Student: Did you hear what happened? You know my play?

(woman) Student: Yeah, the one you wrote as part of your senior thesis.

(man) Student: Well, yesterday, John, the director of the play, walked out of the rehearsal, saying he was gonna quit.

(woman) Student: What? John's such a good student director.

(man) Student: OK, here's what he said. He loves the play but he's tired of working with actors who keep fooling around. He says they're not serious about their acting.

(woman) Student: Oh my. [pause] So now what? Maybe you can step in and direct the play yourself. You wrote it. You could certainly direct it.

(man) Student: I'd enjoy that, actually. But I've got to write fifty pages about the playwriting process in the next couple weeks. I'm a tad nervous about taking on too much work.

(woman) Student: You'd be busy, that's for sure.

(man) Student: And part of me still thinks John is the best candidate for director. OK, he's got a temper, but he's brilliant.

(woman) Student: So why don't you try to persuade him to come back? He's probably calmed down by now. You said yourself—he loves your play.

(man) Student: I'll have to think about it. Who knows if his temper will flare up again?

25 Physical Sciences 物理科學

舉例試題　 *Track 145*

(man) Professor: Now bats are not blind—that's a myth! But they don't use their eyes as much as they use echolocation. Many bats eat a lot of little insects, like mosquitoes. When they hunt, they send out pulses of high-frequency sounds through their noses. The waves that are reflected—the echoes—get picked up by the bats' sensitive ears, sent to their brains and analyzed. So that's the system. Now because of their diet, bats spend a lot of time in areas with vegetation—forests, dense bushes, fields. Certain insects are found on certain plants, and bats need to find the right ones. We know that—somehow—bats can recognize specific kinds of plants. This is remarkable, because the acoustical echoes reflected off plants are particularly complex. There are numerous reflections from leaves and branches, especially if you approach the plant from different angles. So a group of scientists designed an experiment to understand how bats can do this—recognize individual plant species. The scientists selected five different plants. Then, they used a machine to produce sound waves that imitated the bat's high-pitched frequency. A computer system was used to send bat-like waves to each of the five different plants, and record the echoes that came back and store them in a database. The researchers found that, although each plant's echo was complex, an echo clearly indicated each plant species. The computer was able to identify each plant's echo "signature." For a bat, that means even if it only hears the echo with one ear, it can accurately classify a plant without having to gather additional information.

模擬試題① 🎧 *Track 147*

(woman) Professor: Now, we've seen how irrigation has developed in many parts of the world, beginning in Egypt and China. The earliest challenges of irrigation systems had mostly to do with the mechanics of moving water to where it was most needed. People had to first find sources of water, then they had to find ways to make water move from low ground to higher elevations. Of course, with the advancement of science and engineering, there are now many sophisticated systems available, although many are expensive. But nowadays, one of the biggest problems associated with irrigation is environmental impact. Farmers must ask themselves, how will their irrigation system affect—not just the crops that are being planted, but their soil and water. Different methods of irrigation pose different problems. Let's take, for example, flood irrigation. In one form of flood irrigation, farmers use water to quickly create "ponds" on level basin areas—an irrigation method used, for example, for wheat. In arid climates, one problem with flood irrigation is that most of the water is lost, either by evaporation or by seeping into the soil outside the intended area of irrigation. Drip irrigation involves slowly dripping water to the plant, oftentimes directly to each plant's root. One problem with this subsurface drip method is the accumulation of salts in the soil. In dry areas, which have high evaporation rates, drip irrigation can make the problem even worse, because the salts in the irrigation water build up in the root zone of the plant.

模擬試題② 🎧 *Track 150*

(man) Professor: So, we've been looking at the two properties of sound waves. One property of sound waves is their loudness. And the second property of sound waves is their frequency—how quickly the waves move in time. By using both these properties, we can cause a wine glass to break. We need to match the frequency of the sound wave to the natural frequency of the glass and make sure it is loud enough. For your lab assignment, you worked in groups to manipulate the sound waves of a recorded human voice and see if you could make the wine glass break. I've read the lab reports of the two groups, and I'd like to summarize the results. First, Group One. Group One successfully shattered a wine glass during the experiment. You accurately measured the natural frequency of the crystal glass and adjusted the audio recording so the pitch of the singer's voice was exactly the same wave frequency. By playing that tone very loudly on the speaker, you caused the glass to vibrate violently enough to break. However, Group Two, you were unable to make the wine glass break, even though you played the singer's voice very loudly. In your report, you hypothesized that you failed because the wine glass was too thick for the air molecules to influence. [short pause] That's possible. But it's also possible that you didn't adjust the singer's pitch to the correct wave frequency.

26 Humanities and the Arts　人文藝術

舉例試題　　*Track 152*

(woman) Professor: We've talked about the ways in which an actor can approach a role, hoping to flesh it out. Let's look at some specific examples. Take the movie *Jaws*, the epic film about hunting down a great white shark. There's one excellent scene which was a product of classic method acting. I'm talking about the dramatic scene in which the old shark fisherman—played by Robert Shaw—is in the fishing boat with the other two men, telling them about the famous sinking of a U.S. ship in World War II. The fisherman tells of how he and other sailors swam helplessly in the water as sharks attacked them. Even though this British actor was classically trained, he used method-acting techniques in this scene. He was introduced to a real-life fisherman—an old, working-class fisherman native to Long Island. The actor spoke with this fisherman for weeks, studying the rhythm of his language, his choice of words and the way he walked. Shaw himself created the famed monologue about the ship sinking in shark-filled waters. Another example of method acting in this scene is the subtle tension the audience sees between the old fisherman and the young marine biologist. The actors who played these roles did not get along in real life. During filming, both men consciously drew on this underlying hostility, making the performance very real.

模擬試題①　*Track 154*

(man) Professor: Medieval romances were extremely popular from the eleventh to the fifteenth centuries. And while they began in France, they soon spread elsewhere. In England, for example, writers borrowed the stories and themes of the French romances. We see this happening with the tales of King Arthur and his Knights of the Round Table. Romances based on the legends of King Arthur were so popular, that writers everywhere wanted to tell their own versions. The tale of the knight known called Sir Gareth is a classic example of a medieval romance written in English. The full story of Sir Gareth is long and complicated, but I'll tell you a short version: Gareth was born a nobleman but he's on a mysterious quest. He comes to King Arthur's court—but he's disguised as a beggar. He works in the kitchen, and the knights treat him badly. But Gareth works hard and shows good manners. He pretends to be weak. Gradually, the knights see his true ability. Gareth defeats many knights in battle, but he's always fair to them. Finally, Gareth asks to become a knight himself, and he's allowed to—but only after he reveals his true identity. So, in this tale of Sir Gareth we can see how the hero conceals his identity at the beginning, acts very courteously but is nevertheless very strong and very brave in battle, as he pursues his quest.

模擬試題②　*Track 157*

(woman) Professor: One of my favorite installation artists is Will Ryman. Ryman wrote plays for twelve years before he started doing art full-time—and so it's no surprise he thinks uniquely about how viewers will interact with sculpture. One of his exhibits was called "A New Beginning," in a New York gallery. The installation was a city garden filled with one hundred roses made of industrial materials. These roses were big roses—two feet to seven feet tall! So, they seemed unusual—the scale wasn't normal. And when visitors walked through the exhibit, they saw giant bugs and bees on the roses. They also saw over-sized cigarette butts, crumpled cans of famous-brand soda, half-eaten hot dogs and other litter, lying between the plants. It was disturbing, but also stimulating. In effect, they were looking at the garden from the perspective of a rat or a squirrel. Because Ryman had enlarged the scale of all these objects, viewers were confronted with the fact that humans are consumers who ignore—and interfere with—the beauty of nature. Oh, and one more thing: The materials used to make this urban garden also caused the visitor to stop and take notice. To make his objects, Ryman used industrial materials such as steel bars, wire mesh, plaster and house paint. And he left many of his roses only partly finished, showing raw materials sticking out. Ryman did this on purpose, to make us think. So, for example, we might start thinking about the big city and the unfinished skyscrapers that are going up all around.

27 Life Sciences 生命科學

舉例試題 🎧 *Track 159*

(man) Professor: Now we've seen one model of interactions between predators and prey. It makes sense: Fewer prey, fewer predators. And so forth. Based on our understanding of this predator-prey cycle, we can predict how the size of these populations will change over time. But this model works better in some situations than others. It tends to hold true for predators that feed on one species of prey, but not so much in cases where predators can eat different kinds of animals, or prey gets eaten by different animals. Interestingly, though, the simple model works well in the arctic zone communities. The North Pole supports relatively fewer species, so there are fewer relationships. A classic example of Arctic single predator-single prey interactions is the polar bear and the seal. Seals make up most of the polar bear's diet, and the populations of both polar bears and seals influence each other in predictable patterns. In contrast, the tropical zone supports many species of life. Tropical networks are complex. Predator-prey interactions in these hot, moist habitats are complex. And so a simple model just doesn't reflect everything that's going on. Tropical frogs, for example, have very diverse diets. They'll eat ants and a variety of flies. And other tropical predators, like lizards and small mammals, eat ants and flies as well. Thus, because the predator-prey relationship between frogs and insect species is not exclusive, the increase and decline in their populations are not as closely tied. If we see the numbers of frogs declining, then, we might have to look at other factors—such as climate change.

模擬試題① 🎧 *Track 161*

(woman) Professor: Not every seed needs to undergo a period of full-blown dormancy. But seeds of plants that grow in places with extreme variations in climate often do. For example, regions where there are hot summers and cold winters, or desert regions where there's rainfall just once a year. In situations like these, the dormancy protects the seed from germinating at a time where it won't germinate successfully, or it will germinate and then die. But dormancy alone isn't enough. Some plants require extra insurance to guarantee they won't be hurt by extreme temperatures or lack of water. Sometimes, seeds won't leave the dormant state unless they are exposed to both moisture and cold. In my garden, for example, I have an old dogwood tree which grows beautiful pink flowers. If I want to gather these seeds and grow baby dogwood trees in my greenhouse, I'll need to let them have a dormant period—but I'll also have to satisfy certain conditions. So, what I do is pick the ripe dogwood seeds and put them into a bag with moist sand. So now they have moisture! Then, I pop the bag into my refrigerator for three, maybe four months. And that's the cold! Now both conditions have been met, and the seeds will be able to grow indoors, in my greenhouse. Dogwood seeds need this special treatment of moisture and cold, to simulate the natural conditions of winter, as protection. When seeds are exposed in this way, the chemicals inside say, "OK, winter is over, it's safe to germinate now."

模擬試題② 🎧 *Track 164*

(man) Professor: In the rank order of wolves, each wolf has a set place. When two wolves from the same pack cross paths, one is always higher in status than the other. The lower-ranking wolf is said to be submissive to the higher-ranking, dominant wolf. However, it's important to remember that alpha wolves—the most dominant wolves—are not necessarily the strongest, the fastest or the smartest wolves. High rank has more to do with attitude than size or strength. And while a dominant alpha wolf generally acts more self-confidently than lower-ranking wolves, it adopts a neutral pose until it needs to confirm its status. And to make its status, uh, clear, the alpha wolf will stand up tall and look directly at the other wolf. A submissive wolf will then crouch down in response.

These subtle displays of dominance are enough to help the pack maintain social stability. But the alpha wolf isn't necessarily in charge of the pack at every moment. Alpha wolves sometimes are the ones to decide when to hunt, but not always. In other words, an alpha wolf is not always an active leader as much as it is the wolf which has the right to do whatever it wants, whenever it wants. Because alpha wolves have the freedom to do what they like, they have more opportunities to initiate hunting trips. The rest of the pack will then follow. But if the pack is in its home territory, a lot of times the younger wolves will be the ones to take the lead in hunting.

28 Social Sciences 社會科學

舉例試題　🎧 *Track 166*

(woman) Professor: What is important to remember is that, even though assimilation and accommodation are two different processes, the two processes serve to complement one another. And, well, as a part of assimilation, as soon as children discover that a new object they've recently categorized—or "labeled"—doesn't really fit into their existing internal framework, they've got to use accommodation, so they make sense of the external world. Take the case of a little girl Sally, who is three years old, who has a vocabulary of around three hundred words. She knows what a cow is and what a horse is. One day, her mother shows her a zebra in a picture book. Sally points to the picture and says, "Horse." Sally doesn't have a pre-existing category for "zebras," so she uses assimilation. She thinks it's a horse, with stripes. But if Sally's mother tells her all about zebras and then takes Sally to the zoo, Sally will create a new knowledge category to go with the label "zebra." She'll associate the horse-like thing labeled "zebra" with black and white stripes. This, of course, is accommodation. Then later, Sally may see butterflies flying around that have black and white stripes. Because she understands both the "zebra" concept and the "butterfly" concept, she can accurately link these two in an act of assimilation. This is called a zebra butterfly!

模擬試題①　🎧 *Track 168*

(man) Professor: Nowadays, a lot of people think that any way to grab attention is good. You know, that old saying, "No press is bad press." And in fact live buzz marketing can be very powerful and generate a lot of PR. If it's done correctly and the message is clear, the impact will last for years. But one has to be very careful.

Let me give you an example of an effective buzz marketing campaign. In its early stages, an ice cream company generated a huge reaction when it sponsored a free ice cream day. All day long the store gave away free ice cream cones, as many as you could eat. People on the street got excited—who doesn't like ice cream? The media got excited. One person told the next, and before you know it, everyone was talking about this company's ice cream and the brand. The ripple effect affected both brand awareness and sales.

Now, let me tell you about a buzz marketing campaign that failed. This particular case involved social media. On the Internet, a blogger was talking about family problems. Another man then posted a response to this blogger, and the two individuals compared experiences drawn from their personal lives. But it turned out that the man who sent in his response was not even a real person! A company that sold cleaning products had created a fake online identity—to push its cleaning products. Buzz marketing, right? But when the public found out that the company had created a false identity and false posts, they became extremely angry. Needless to say, the impact on the company's brand and sales was very negative.

模擬試題②　🎧 *Track 171*

(woman) Professor: People have always been aware that animals can manipulate objects to accomplish tasks. Primates, such as apes, have been the most obvious instance. But for a long time, scientists assumed that human beings were the only ones who had the cognitive ability to plan ahead and make tools. That belief has fallen by the wayside. Today many research projects involving cognition in animals show that animals can indeed create tools. One interesting set of studies involves crows. On several islands in the South Pacific Ocean, a unique species of crow has demonstrated the ability to use tools, modify them and even pass on tool-making techniques to their young. These crows use their beaks to manipulate tools so they can retrieve insects in dead wood.

Initially, researchers studied how the New Caledonian crows used tools. In the lab, they observed how the crows were able to choose tools—for example, sticks of wood—of the correct width and length. The crows almost always selected sticks that were long enough to reach inside the container and get to the food. Now, in subsequent experiments, researchers observed crows repeatedly demonstrating the ability to create tools. They've been given a variety of materials, including natural materials, like leaves and wood, and man-made materials, like wire and aluminum. They've made different tools for different settings. In one experiment, a crow used her beak to create a hook out of a straight wire so she could pick up a little bucket containing meat. Time after time she was able to get the bucket of meat, using different techniques. So it was clear that she was able to modify the tool to fit her task.

29 Physical Sciences 物理科學

舉例試題   🎧 *Track 173*

(man) Professor: When we look at the weathering of rocks, it's not always easy to know exactly what force caused the rocks to break down. There are so many types of weathering. So, to simplify things, scientists usually divide these processes into two categories: Physical and chemical. In physical weathering, rock is broken down mechanically into smaller pieces. The physical forces might be cold, heat, water or pressure—or a combination of these. One common example of physical weathering is frost action. We see frost action in very cold climates where temperatures fluctuate. For example, during the day, melting snow may trickle down into cracks in the rocks. Then, at nighttime, that water freezes. When frozen, water expands by more than ten percent, so the crack gets bigger. And, more water drips in when the temperature rises. Not surprisingly, this freezing and thawing process can repeat itself many times over the course of a winter.

Now in chemical weathering, various substances cause the rock to actually change its chemical composition. There's breakdown at the molecular level. The agents causing the change might be— um, oxygen or carbon dioxide. Chemical weathering can even occur through the actions of simple plants. You know—plants like moss and lichen—which live on the surface of many rocks. These plants only grow when the rock is wet. And as they grow, they release a small amount of acid which dissolves the nutrients in the rock and loosens its particles. The loose particles are then easily moved by physical forces. Keep in mind that water is also an agent of chemical weathering, especially when it reacts chemically with other substances. In other words, water is responsible for both physical and chemical weathering.

模擬試題①   🎧 *Track 175*

(woman) Professor: So, do winds have patterns? Well, people who live near the ocean are well aware of one wind phenomenon. Coastal winds blow from different directions at different times of the day—in a predictable fashion, especially during spring and summer. During the day, winds tend to come from the ocean—in what we call sea breezes. Then at night, the air flows in the reverse direction. It moves from land to sea, creating land breezes. To explain why this happens, we need to understand two concepts. The first is heat capacity. Some materials—like iron and other metals— heat up quickly. You've watched your iron frying pan get hot fast, then cool down fast. It takes much longer to heat up water, a substance with a high heat capacity. That's why, under the hot, shining sun, the soil and the rocks get much hotter than the ocean water does. As a result, the air above the ocean stays relatively cool, but the air above the land's surface gets warm.

But heat capacity isn't the only thing influencing wind patterns. Another factor is related to temperature and air pressure. Think, for example, of a hot air balloon rising in the sky. These balloons rise because hot air will rise in cool air. Hot air is less dense and gets pushed up. We see the same thing with coastal winds. During the day, the air mass on land gets heated quickly. It becomes less dense and begins to rise, leaving behind an area with low pressure. That pulls in the ocean's cooler air onto land to take its place. This movement is a sea breeze. Then, when the Sun goes down, the land loses heat at a rate much faster than the water. The air on land is now much cooler than the ocean air. So, in a reverse process, the warm air above the ocean rises, leaving a space beneath it for the land air to move into. And that's where we get land breezes, breezes moving from land to sea.

模擬試題② 🎧 *Track 178*

(man) Professor: We think of bodies of water as being permanent fixtures on the landscape. But compared to oceans and rivers, lakes have relatively short lives. This is especially true when we look at them over the extended period that has passed since the formation of the Earth. Why is this? For one thing, lakes are typically quite shallow—they can be as shallow as six feet. Of course, lakes that formed as a result of glaciers are quite deep. But even deep lakes come and go on the Earth's surface, due to a natural aging process. What often happens is that the lake gradually fills with organic matter. What was once a lake becomes a swamp or another form of wetland. Sometimes, all the surface water disappears, and the land becomes a meadow. Let's take a look at exactly how plant matter chokes a lake. In general, when a lake is first formed, the water is clear, devoid of nutrients. Gradually, though, algae and bacteria start to grow—concentrating along the lakeshore, where the water is especially shallow and warm. When the algae die, they decompose. Bacteria absolutely thrive on dead organic matter! The problem is, when the bacteria take over, all the oxygen gets used up—by the bacteria! And so, well, there's not enough oxygen for all the plant matter. That means the dead organic matter never fully decays and just sinks to the bottom. And this half-decomposed material lying at the bottom provides nutrients—it's perfect fertilizer for other plants. Soon, lots of new species start to grow on the shore. And when they die, the same thing happens. Another layer of sediment is added to the lake bed. More and more nutrients in the form of dead organic matter are added, and more and more plants grow in it until the lake becomes a wetland—or even a dry meadow. This natural process can take hundreds or thousands of years. Unfortunately, though, human activity often hastens the aging process by polluting lakes with chemical fertilizers.

30 Humanities and the Arts 人文藝術

舉例試題 🎧 *Track 180*

(man) Professor: The next principle we're going to work with is movement. How can we suggest movement—not in a movie or video—but in a two-dimensional work? Of course a flat piece of paper doesn't really move. When we say "movement," what we really mean is that the path our eyes follow when we look at a composition. We call this compositional movement.

We can guide the movement of the viewer's eyes by arranging a composition's elements in a certain way. The viewer's eyes will then follow a path around the composition. But how does an artist accomplish this? Before I go into the specific methods, we need to understand the two basic types of compositional movement: Static movement and dynamic movement. You may think that "static"—a word meaning "stationary"—is an odd way to describe "movement." "Static" seems to be the opposite of movement! But in the design world, static movement is when our eyes jump around between isolated parts of a composition—like a frog in a pond jumping from one rock to another. On the other hand, dynamic movement is when our eyes move smoothly and in a linear fashion from one part of the composition to another.

A composition with static movement is...well, let's say we have a painting showing a group of white balls lying all over the floor. Almost all the balls are white, but a few of them are black. When you look at a composition like this, the principle of static movement will make your eyes go to the dark balls first, and only later go to the white balls. This happens because the white objects are visually equal in importance but the value of the black is different. The obvious contrast makes static movement possible. Now, compositions with dynamic movement are quite different. They often have continuous lines; for example, a drawing of a long road winding up into the mountains. If the edges of the road are drawn with strong, flowing lines, our eyes will follow them upward. And the curve of a line often conveys energy. This is dynamic movement.

模擬試題① 🎧 *Track 182*

(woman) Professor: One reason that cities develop along rivers is that rivers are natural transportation routes. People tend to concentrate where goods have to be transferred from one mode of transportation to another, places where goods, uh, which have been shipped across the ocean, get loaded onto small boats or land vehicles. Similarly, cities develop where bridges can be built. Bridges facilitate land travel! Well, because cities are located at transportation hubs, they become perfect marketplaces. So that's the first geographic factor I want to point out to you. Rivers, throughout history, have created economic marketplaces where trading and commerce flourish. Yet precisely because of this economic advantage, outside forces have historically attacked these cities—to destroy them or to take them over for their own use. So, people who built cities next to rivers needed to think of rivers strategically—as boundaries. And this is the second important factor influencing how cities develop: Rivers as defensive barriers. City residents had to find ways to keep intruders from crossing the river. Any structures they built within the city—such as walls or bridges— had to withstand the attack of invaders.

In England, the River Thames is a classic example of how a river influenced the development of a major city—London! Though the Thames is not a particularly long river, it benefits by ocean tides and is very navigable. Throughout history, the Thames has supported a thriving economic marketplace and served as a defensive barrier, shaping the formation of London. When the Roman troops invaded England two thousand years ago, they had to build a bridge to gain access into the city. This bridge led to a new network of roads, and London became an important Roman trading center. The Romans built forts and protective walls, along the river and inland. Within these walls, the early city took shape. Later, every subsequent group that occupied London built on this area and used the Thames as a major trading base.

模擬試題② 🎧 *Track 185*

(man) Professor: Clay, you will discover, has remarkable characteristics. Before we begin to make pottery, however, I want to compare two very old methods of making pots: Coiling, which is a type of hand-building, and wheel work, using a potter's wheel to "throw" a pot. One of the oldest methods of making pottery is coiling. In this method, artists create many long rings, or coils, of clay. Coil pots are formed by stacking the coils on top of one another and then blending the coils together with one's hands or with a tool. Now the potter's wheel was developed much later. In this method— throwing pots on a potter's wheel—a ball of clay is placed in the center of a turntable that can be turned manually or by electricity. As the wheel rotates, the ball of clay is squeezed and pulled upwards into a hollow shape. Both of these methods produce beautiful pots that can be fired in a kiln. So what are the basic differences between coiling and the potter's wheel processes? Well, using coils is much slower than wheel-throwing. However, coiling offers several advantages over the wheel method. For one thing, artists can take their time and exercise a lot of control over each pot.

In addition, studio potters who use the coiling method pride themselves that each work is unique. They can advertise that each work is "one of a kind." In contrast, one advantage of using a potter's wheel is the relative speed of the method. It's efficient, especially in a business setting. But there are artistic reasons why many potters like the wheel method. Throwing pots on a wheel allows an artist to consistently repeat a style again and again. This is important, for example, to artists who create sets of tableware—matching plates, bowls and cups that will be used every day in homes. Here, the potter's wheel is preferable because the spinning force of the wheel helps create uniform-looking pieces.

31 Life Sciences 生命科學

舉例試題 🎧 *Track 187*

(woman) Professor: Everyone knows that the tears in our eyes are salty. They have water and salt—just like our sweat does. But not everyone knows that there are different kinds of tears, which flow from different biological processes and produce solutions with different compositions. One kind of tears—the most common kind—is made continuously. These are often called "constant tears" because the fluid is always flowing from the tear glands. Every time we blink, no matter whether we are awake or asleep, our eyelids spread the protective film of constant tears over the surface of our eyes. Why? Constant tears keep eyes lubricated. So what's special about the chemical composition of constant tears? For one thing, there's an oily layer on top. This oily layer helps keep the film on our eyes from evaporating too quickly. Just imagine what your eyes would feel like if they dried up! But constant tears also contain antibodies and enzymes that help prevent disease.

Now for the other type of tears—reflex tears. Reflex tears are produced by a separate gland. Our bodies produce these tears as a reflex; we're reacting to some external stimulus—an irritant or a foreign body. For example, we shed tears when we chop up onions for our dinner. Or, if we're frying red hot peppers—our eyes start watering. The oils from these foods can irritate our nose and eyes, causing us to produce extra tears—reflex tears. Our bodies are trying to "wash away" the problem. Reflex tears have salt in them, but they don't contain the oily layer that constant tears do. In fact, reflex tears are very watery. And the volume of tears produced in reflex tears is larger. The unusually large amount of tears serves to cleanse the eyes quickly, before any damage can be done.

模擬試題① 🎧 *Track 189*

(man) Professor: OK, seahorses are pretty interesting marine creatures. They swim upright, and their heads actually do look like little horse heads. So how did seahorses evolve into this type of body shape? There's no fossil record of these guys, because their bones have long since disintegrated. Still, in recent years scientists have developed new theories about what kind of evolutionary forces were at play. Seahorses appeared in our oceans about 25 million years ago. What was happening then? Well, land masses in Eurasia and what's now Australia collided into one another. And when they did, the floor of the ocean was pushed upwards—which created vast expanses of shallow water. This warm, shallow water was a perfect place for seagrass to grow. Large, dense clumps of it grew in the sandy mud. Seahorses—their body shape and what they could do—evolved in response to this new environment. Based on studies with DNA, we think that seahorses—which swim with their heads up—evolved from a fish called a "pipefish." Now in some ways, pipefish look like seahorses, but their bodies are—well, they look like a little piece of pipe! Pipefish swim horizontally, like regular fish. So how did the seahorse become a vertical swimmer? Well, for one thing, it evolved a tail that could grab onto the seagrass. That means it could attach itself to the seagrass, floating and hiding, waiting for little shrimp to swim by. In time the seahorse started swimming upright.

In addition to these useful tails, seahorses have another adaptation: Their bodies are in the shape of an "S." Now pipefish and seahorses have similar mouths, which look like tubes. But only the seahorse body has an S-shaped curve, which allows it to physically extend its neck thirty-percent farther than the pipefish. That means that seahorses can be sneakier hunters. They can hide and then strike out at distant prey.

模擬試題② 🎧 *Track 192*

(woman) Professor: Although wildfires can be destructive forces, they can also play a constructive role in nature. In fact, many habitats are actually dependent on fire. Periodic fires serve different purposes. First, they open up space where light can shine in and eliminate competitive vegetation. And another benefit is that fires can improve the area's soil by heating it and making it more nutrient-rich. Let's take a look at how fires affect the ecology of the Northern Forests which cover Alaska in the United States, most of Canada and much of Russia. These great forests lie just below the artic tundra and make up almost one third of the world's forests.

Now in a mature Northern Forest, fires can be very intense. But fires burn unevenly and leave behind different levels of damage. So we get some sections of the forest that are totally burned, some sections left untouched, and some sections only partially burned. The result is a "mosaic" or patchwork of habitats, and vegetation grows back differently in each of these. In the new sunlit areas, where burning was most intense, plant species that can't grow in shade can suddenly sprout and thrive. The Jack pine is one of these sunloving species. The seeds of Jack pines are normally tightly contained within pine cones: These seeds will only be released if a really hot fire occurs. Once the flames burn down, the seeds come popping out. In effect, the tree's reproductive cycle is triggered by fire.

The other way that fire can benefit the Northern Forest ecosystem is through the soil. Soils in these regions are cold and lack nutrients. When a fire removes surface-level and overhead vegetation, the Sun can shine directly on the ground. Now there's a lot more warming by day. More rain penetrates the soil 'cause there are fewer leaves. And the minerals in the ash are chock-full of nutrients, which when warm and moist, promote growth of all sorts of plant life.

32 Social Sciences 社會科學

舉例試題 🎧 *Track 194*

(man) Professor: In economics, "utility" is a term used to describe how useful or satisfying something is to a consumer. Products and services that have utility for one person may not have utility for another person. And something that has utility for a person when they are young may not be of interest to them when they are married and have children. Regardless of our circumstances, we'll look at all the options and choose the product—or service—that gives us the most utility. Of course, certain aspects of a product are more important to us than others—more valuable. Take, for example, the location where the product or service is offered. This component of economic utility is called "place utility." Look at the changes the banking industry keeps making. Nowadays, many banks rent space within large supermarkets. So, when I go to buy groceries, I can also do a little banking—cash and deposit checks. Behind the counter, tellers provide me additional banking services. Because I'm already at this location buying food, it's very convenient. This service has place utility, especially for really busy people who don't have time to make another stop. And some customers may eventually decide to switch banks to take better advantage of this satisfactory location.

Another way that some banking companies might decide to offer additional choices to customers is by increasing the hours that they're open for business. When a product or service is made available at the time when the customer wants it, this is called "time utility." So, in the case of the banking industry, a bank might stay open late on Friday nights, when people need money to get ready for the weekend. Or the branch might install twenty-four-hour ATMs in a separate lobby, to be flexible for customers who work at night. Both of these services illustrate ways of providing time utility.

模擬試題① 🎧*Track 196*

(woman) Professor: The word "culture" has many meanings, but within the field of sociology, culture refers to the thoughts and behaviors we have. Moreover, people learn culture. What we learn shapes our consciousness and our behavior. Culture can only be passed down from one generation to the next because we humans have the ability to think symbolically. We use symbols to classify and represent our ideas and experiences. If we didn't share this symbolic system with others, we couldn't communicate. Now it goes without saying that people living in different parts of the world have distinct cultures, even though all humans share certain experiences—like getting married and having children. But each culture classifies and represents experiences in different ways, using different symbols. So what are our symbol systems? The most important type of symbol in a culture is language. Language, whether it is spoken or written, is a symbolic form of communication. The English word "chair," for example, is a symbol for the actual object—the piece of furniture you can sit on. In other cultures, other symbols represent that object.

In addition to language, we have symbols communicated through material objects. Clothing, for example, is a powerful symbolic system. Members of a culture all recognize the meanings of the clothes they wear—the style and colors. For example, in many industrialized cultures, wearing a white button-up shirt, a dark suit and a tie communicates that the man is a mainstream professional who is willing to conform. This particular dress code is symbolic; it has meaning for both the wearer and the people around him. Dark colors take on symbolic meaning, as do bright ones. So a solid red necktie is seen as a "power tie," conveying dominance, whereas a dark blue necktie is seen as less threatening, sending the message that the wearer has seriousness of purpose but is not openly aggressive.

模擬試題② 🎧*Track 199*

(man) Professor: Advertisers like to make use of the public's fascination with celebrities. Every day we see entertainers and athletes employed as spokespersons for a wide range of products and services. Subconsciously, we consumers want the things that these VIPs endorse—even though, logically, we know that these celebrities are paid to say what they say. Still, there's something inside us that makes us want that product. So what are some of the factors that influence consumers when they're confronted with celebrity advertisements? In my mind, trust is the most important factor. Now when we talk about a celebrity's "trustworthiness," we mean the degree of confidence that potential customers place in that VIP. When viewers sit in front of the TV, they are asking themselves, consciously or subconsciously, "How much do I trust this guy?" Researchers have found that a highly opinionated message from a very trustworthy communicator will cause viewers of the advertisement to change their minds favorably; in other words, persuade them of the benefits or superiority of the brand. In fact, celebrities who are considered trustworthy can change customers' opinions to a much greater extent than celebrities who are perceived to be knowledgeable experts. Trust is more important than expertise!

Another factor influencing celebrity advertising is the attractiveness of the spokesperson. Not surprisingly, researchers have found that an attractive man or woman has a more positive effect on viewers than a less attractive spokesperson. Viewers will feel good about an attractive celebrity who's making an endorsement. And viewers will feel good about the product and the brand. However—and this is interesting—research has shown that, although attractiveness is effective in causing these positive associations, it is not effective in producing stronger purchase intentions. That is to say, even though the consumer likes the spokesperson and the brand, he or she is not likely to go out and actually spend money on that product or service.

原來如此 系列 E108

托福命題總監教你征服新托福口語

托福總監親自出馬！真的不是權威不出書！

作　　　者	秦蘇珊
顧　　　問	曾文旭
總 編 輯	王毓芳
編 輯 統籌	耿文國、黃璽宇
主　　　編	吳靜宜
執 行 主編	姜怡安
執 行 編輯	李念茨、林妍珺
美 術 編輯	王桂芳、張嘉容
封 面 設計	阿作
法 律 顧問	北辰著作權事務所　蕭雄淋律師、幸秋妙律師

初　　　版	2014年12月初版一刷 2019年再版六刷
出　　　版	捷徑文化出版事業有限公司
電　　　話	（02）2752-5618
傳　　　真	（02）2752-5619
地　　　址	106 台北市大安區忠孝東路四段250號11樓之1

定　　　價	新台幣349元／港幣116元
產 品 內容	1書

總 經 銷	采舍國際有限公司
地　　　址	235 新北市中和區中山路二段366巷10號3樓
電　　　話	（02）8245-8786
傳　　　真	（02）8245-8718

港澳地區總經銷	和平圖書有限公司
地　　　址	香港柴灣嘉業街12號百樂門大廈17樓
電　　　話	（852）2804-6687
傳　　　真	（852）2804-6409

本書由外語教學與研究出版社有限責任公司以書名《托福命題總監教你征服新托福口語》首次出版。此中文繁體字版由外語教學與研究出版社有限責任公司授權捷徑文化出版事業有限公司在台灣、香港和澳門地區獨家出版發行。僅供上述地區銷售。

捷徑 Book 站

現在就上臉書（FACEBOOK）「捷徑BOOK站」並按讚加入粉絲團，
就可每月不定期新書資訊和粉絲專享小禮物喔！
http://www.facebook.com/royalroadbooks
讀者來函：royalroadbooks@gmail.com

國家圖書館出版品預行編目資料

托福命題總監教你征服新托福口語 / 秦蘇珊著.
-- 初版. -- 臺北市：捷徑文化, 2014.12
　面；　公分（原來如此：E108）
ISBN 978-986-5698-28-7(平裝)

1. 托福考試　2. 口語　3. 考試指南
805.1894　　　　　　　　103021301

TOEFL
iBT SPEAKING

不是權威不出書！練托福，
當然就讓最專業的托福總監帶你練！

捷徑文化
Royal Road Publishing Group